TIME IN CARNBEG

Time in Carnbeg

Short Stories by

Ronald Frame

Polygon

First published in 2004 by Polygon,
an imprint of Birlinn Ltd, West Newington House,
10 Newington Road, Edinburgh EH9 1QS

www.birlinn.co.uk

ISBN 0 9544075 5 5

British Library Cataloguing-in-Publication Data
A catalogue record for this book is available
from the British Library

Typeset in Great Britain by Antony Gray
Printed and bound by Creative Print and Design,
Ebbw Vale, Wales

For my parents,
who took me there

Contents

'The Chimes', 'The Trinket Box', The Doocot',
'Away From It All', 'The Fitting', 'Bonfires' and
'The New' were broadcast on BBC Radio 4,
and 'Sugar Candy' on BBC Radio Scotland.
'The Doocot' was published in the *Mail on Sunday*.

Carnbeg Hairst*

Ceud Mìle Failte.

One Hundred Thousand Welcomes.

You are in Carnbeg. A resort town in the wooded Grampian foothills, surrounded by moorland and lochs.

Population 6,827.†

The Victorians popularised the spot, developing and demolishing much of the old town. Thy appreciated the mineral waters, and built big hotels for the city visitors who came to take the cures and breathe Highland air.

Some families put up for weeks on end.

People moved to the town after retirement age, and mixed – or didn't mix, as they chose – with 'them', the locals, who were the children of the children of those who farmed, laboured, kept shops. Another stratum of society occupied the big old houses roundabout, tucked away behind the town, situated up glens or by lochsides, and more in number than any casual visitor suspected.

You won't find those dark, lawless vennels from a time when feuds and vendettas split the town, three or four hundred years ago. Long before electric light, braziers burned on street corners, and pigeons flew with messages; water was carried from wells, and slop was pitched from upstairs windows into runnels. The high life of the glassy Kursaal has been and gone, killed off by the First World War. Even the prefabs, thrown up after the Second, are no more; Tintown has vanished.

All is change. Time is a river, and the Tirran (with its tributary, Vrackie Water) is the silvery thread that stitches year

* Hairst: Harvest
† Population (2003) 7,614

to year and century to century. A toiler in the fields looks up and sees a white vapour trail scoring the sky, and the salmon jump the falls against the current to spawn, and the Tollbooth clock is chiming the hour when a TV game show airs and a couple in cloaks elope and, in the longest long ago, a witch burns in the Geldie Field.

Baedeker mentions the 'healthful location'. Fresh breezes blow up from the Tay plain, but the southerly orientation and the protective shoulder of the hills make Carnbeg a sun-trap. The heat favours the more robust specimens of palm, and rhododendrons and azaleas blaze in their season; in echt-conservatories you can eavesdrop on the tail-ends of Edwardian conversations, describing how those plants made their way here from the Himalayas. In winter, the snow lies on chalet-drop roofs, icicles hang from the eaves, and the alpine effect is decorative; listen to the winds blow, though, and you'll hear the scream of Carnbeg's banshee, who – Baedeker recounts – took to hiding when the first trains came through, whistles shrieking and sounding like a fierce rival.

What to see?

High Street. Mercat Street. The Falls of Dreish. The Jubilee Theatre, rebuilt 1977, originally a sprawl of marquees in a walled garden, calling itself the Theatre in the Strath, now a construction in the outside-in Pompidou Centre style. Half a dozen large hotels, the largest in an estate of five hundred acres, and its arch-competitor, resembling a McDisney fantasy castle. A whisky distillery. Mill shops, a famous tweed-and-kilt outfitters.

Ospreys fly, and salmon leap, and you'll find a hundred thousand welcomes – in Gaelic, if you're lucky – should you turn off the main motorway north, take the sliproad and drive on up and through. It may seem to you a place to visit once, layer after layer of time weighing on you. Alternatively you may like it so much that you find you never want to leave; or simply, Carnbeg might choose to not let *you* go.

Industry is very light. It consists of that whisky distillery and a springwater bottling plant.

The local population provides work for shopkeepers, tradesmen and sundry professionals. The tourist season is theoretically year-round now, but some giftshops and tearooms close in late November and reopen the following March. All except a couple of hotels stay open, playing host to conferences. (There's a contest to provide the 'most inclusive', if not lowest, rate for delegates.)

The theatre operates for four months, across the summer period.

A weekly farmers' market is a recent innovation.

Carnbeg began as three modest hamlets. In the most westerly village there was an inn and a whisky still. A meal mill was the chief feature of the next hamlet. The third, on the east side of the river, contained the school.

Time drew the communities together. By the 1780s Carnbeg was recognisably a small town, with a High Street and Tollbooth and Square, and connecting wynds.

> The hills grew higher and higher, and Albert said it was very Swiss-looking in some parts. High, ribbed mountains appeared in the distance, higher than any we have yet seen. This was near Carnbeag (nine miles), which is charmingly situated and the mountains very lofty. [Queen Victoria, 1842: *Leaves from the Journal of our Life in the Highlands*, published 1868]

Water was the making of Carnbeg

In the mid-nineteenth century it was discovered that the water from the local springs had high levels of fortifying minerals: calcium, magnesium, and sulphates. The water was bottled by an early entrepreneur, and sold as far away as London and Bristol. But the temptation to take the water at source brought increasing numbers to the town. Hotels and boarding-houses were built to accommodate them.

On a later visit, in 1861, the widowed Queen noted the not altogether welcome arrival of the 'railroad', intruding into familiar views. But nothing could diminish her enthusiasm for the area.

> We came back by the Carn-mohr road, over that wild moor, reminding me very much of Aberarder (near Balmoral). The hills behind were different shades of blue. How Albert would have loved all this! We met a drove of cattle on the road, as it was the day for the tryst.
>
> All about here the people speak Gaelic, and there are a few who do not speak a word of English.
>
> Then we drove through Carnbeag (the people had been so discreet and quiet in recent times, I said I would do this) . . . [Queen Victoria, 1864: *More Leaves from the Journal of a Life in the Highlands*, published 1884]

It was quite a different town from the one the Queen had seen twenty-two years before.

Her personal physician had been instrumental in establishing Carnbeg (as it was now spelt) as a resort, one which sold itself on its fresh unpolluted air. The town, building on the promotional worth of the Queen's Highland holidays, didn't look back from this point.

> The woods surrounding Carnbeg (as I must write it) are in great beauty from the change of the leaf.
>
> The distance was enveloped in mist, which was quite like a thick Windsor fog, but perfectly dry.
>
> Carnbeg glories in its newly found success. We passed through the town, where this time people appeared at their doors, cheering, and the children made a great noise.
>
> I was reminded of our pleasant visits and excursions here. In future, even if I should never be able to return, I

shall remember this splendid evening, the sky yellow and pink, and the hills coming out soft and blue [Queen Victoria: 1866: ibid]

There's something of the feel of Czech spa resorts about Carnbeg still: the rolling hills covered in fir and pine, the transparent air, the echoes of bygone formality.

The High Street developed into a promenade, with visitors walking along one side and then the other, and carriages slowing, and hats and parasols being raised in salutation.

The original Kursaal premises have been considerably modified, but the proportions are the same and remain impressive; imagination can supply the ferns and reed palms and ornamental fountains in rockeries, and also the chiming of glasses at the drinking wells, and the voices rising fifty feet to the cupola of stained glass.

The thriving social life attracted the well-to-do to retire there, particularly those from the colonies and protectorates of Britain's empire.

Two miles to the north of Carnbeg is Carnmòr, originally (1924–8) a private development of individually commissioned villas with loch frontages, by architects of the calibre of Lorimer and Baillie Scott. In succeeding decades the number of houses multiplied several times, but the community has preserved its tag of exclusivity.

Carnbeg and its satellite Carnmòr are surrounded by some notable country houses and estates. Among them is the Place of Machers (sixteenth century and later), which has played host to Defoe and Chopin and Empress Eugénie. The sprawling Killiedrumquhan's most famous owner was the third baronet, the self-styled 'K'quhan Don', married to a San Franciscan heiress.

In 1954 the Alfresco Theatre Company launched its first summer season in a walled garden just outside Carnbeg. Performances continued under canvas, until new premises were converted from a former curling rink. Purpose-built quarters were opened by HM The Queen in 1977; the Jubilee

Theatre has since been enlarged, but a mood of intimacy prevails, in the spirit of the original 'theatre-in-the-strath'.

Other Carnbegs

In the 1750s Carnbeg lent its name to the property of a Scottish tobacco merchant who made his fortune in Viriginia. Carnbeg Place, as it is still known today, lies in northern Virginia's Fairfax County.

Ninety years later a party of Scottish adventurers found an area of the Colorado Rockies which reminded them of home. They established a small mining village and called it Carnbeg. About the same time as the original Perthshire Carnbeg was developing into a watering spa, an equivalent process was taking place in its American namesake. A German settler, Dr Karl Zander, embarked on the construction of a Utopian town in the vicinity, but died before his scheme could be completed. Since the 1920s Carnbeg Springs has steadily grown into a smart year-round resort, extending towards the mountains and Glacier Lake; it now includes some of America's finest intermediate ski runs.

A transatlantic exchange programme operates, linking the two towns and fostering community relations.

APPENDIX A

We reached Carnbeag as night fell, & the welcome was frugal, in keeping with the inclement weather. The houses are squalid, and ramshackle how they are set upon the street. It is no surprise that they burn so few candles, & of such inferior quality. The mind so longs to leave that the parish (as it dignifies itself) makes little impression, excepting the frankly disagreeable. I have been assured that the landed properties in the vicinity, as I saw for myself when I travelled (at the first occasion) north and away, having decided better of my intention to spend the night there. I had no letter of introduction on my person – which I now had cause to regret – and so I could do no more than view those distant comforts through drizzle and dusk from the filthy inadequate road. [Daniel Defoe, *Tour through the Whole Island of Great Britain*, 1727]

APPENDIX B

Killydrumquan [*sic*]
Carnbeg
Scotland
August 26th

. . . Here we are spending a few days on the moors.

The house is very grand, and once the owner called himself the Don, because he had some Irish blood.

They held a dance last night, not at all sophisticated – with fiddles and an accordion – but very enjoyable.

The big old room (it's hung with antlers) grew very warm, and I feel several pounds lighter today!

For us they played the Virginia Reel, which made me think of Carnbeg Place, out nr Mount Vernon. (They have a hunt, the Standfields took me, it's supposed to be one of the oldest inhabited houses in North Virginia.)

Someone showed me how, the steps, and that someone turned out to be a Duke. A brand new Duke with a very old title, which he has inherited from an uncle. 30 or so, a solid man, but such supple ankles, with the turn of speed you need for reels.

I was intrigued – and I could tell he was intrigued by me, he bent his ear to hear.

Ooh la la!

He has a little Yankee blood too, and it turns out we either know or know of some of the same people, in Loudoun County and Fauquier.

Our supper finished with a dessert called Athol Brose. My Duke explained to me, they make it with oatmeal and honey

[7]

and lots of whisky, whipped together. You can imagine how mellow I felt! In the moonlight afterwards I could picture them celebrating a holiday at Miss Porter's to celebrate: an Old Girl has just become a very nouvelle Duchesse. (Better *that*, girls, if you can!) [Jacqueline Bouvier, unpublished letter to Margot Buckley, August 1950]

APPENDIX C

These Carnbegg grandees have lived too long in isolation, with only their own company. They labour, and LABOUR their guests, with the delusion that they are supreme wits, and laugh loudest at their own remarks. They spend so long talking, and asking others for their opinions, it must be a means to disguise the paucity of the fare of table, and the inferiority of what there is. Thus as frequent hosts they suffer from a regular lack of healthy sustenance – and inflict it on their innocent guests. Thin and pinched, they become more so, dwarfed by the height and ridiculous majesty of their chairs, believing themselves potentates of all they survey. While this may or may not be so, it is surely the case that, other than their personal seating arrangements, they give little enough evidence of wealth. Notwithstanding all the thrawn throats and talon-hands on display, they yet have no lack of airs and graces: indeed, they demonstrate a plenitude of *noblesse*, with at the same time a miserly modicum of *oblige*. [Tobias Smollett, unpublished manuscript, *c.* 1766]

APPENDIX D

OK if your idea of holiday fun is bracing hikes or killing things with a rod and line or through a viewfinder.

3 types of shop: old-fashioned bespoke (a couple of appointments to HRHs) and you pay for delivery; or veggie-wholemeal/

it's-only-rock'n'roll; or touristy tat (has so much rubbish ever been crammed under one roof as in Button Ben's?).

NO NIGHT LIFE worth talking about, although the Rod & Line bar in the Errol House Hotel (lots of stuffed fish in cases, and stuffed shirts on the bar stools) gets lively enough in a yah-yah way. So it's an early to bed kind of place.

We're not saying give it a miss. Your granny will love it – she probably broke her heart here many years ago, which is why so many of them keep coming back, year after year after year after . . . [UK Unplugged: OnlineGuides].

APPENDIX E

high road low road I'll be in Scotland before you
like as if I never left, only **disembodied** from
    the spirit in this place, legendsurfeited
doppelganger country, they talk of the walker beside you,
    a companion,
    and if you speak to him first he will haunt you to death
so
be careful
and don't speak to the poet who lies by the river
thistlestalk in mouth, olé, in slippered grace
    or he'll rob you (charmingly) of your soul
    (in floating free-verse time)
by the swirling brackenbrown water (water=<u>burn</u>?)
Time is a river without banks, merci M. Chagall, let's
    raise a glass of Highland firewater (with Signor Ovid)
    in recollection of
    lost selves and
    might-have-beens and
    maybe-still-is's
Isis Moon Lady Saraswati & Kali-Matoo
    (doubles all round, lassies!)
Hebraic elegy, in tartan and dun
poet reclining, dreaming of

Allen Ginsberg, unpublished poem delivered at Jack Kerouac School of Diesembodied Poetics, Naropa Institute, York Harbor, Maine, 4 May 1976.

Useful web sites, providing information for visitors and some historical background:

www.visitcarnbeg.org.
www.carnbegleisure.co.uk
www.carnbeg-hydro.co.uk
www.sgianpalace.co.uk
www.errolhouse.co.uk
www.theatre-in-the-strath.org
www.killiedrumquhan.co.uk
www.castle-oshnie.co.uk
www.carnbegdistillery.com

The Doocot

Every summer, before the last war, the artists used to come.

They arrived on the train, or in loaded cars. The men wore linen suits and the women loose skirts and gypsy blouses.

Here and there about Carnbeg you saw them with their easels, painting views of vennels and picturesque corners and – pitched further out in the fields – the heathery straths and wide Perthshire skies.

The shops stocked up on white spirit and turpentine, and the pub-owners knew to buy in a few bottles of French absinthe and ruby port, even an occasional fancy fresh lemon.

'She'. 'He'.

She was the wife of a man who delivered post in the mornings and did odd-job gardening about the town in the afternoons.

He was one of the summer visitors, wearing a baggy linen suit and suede shoes.

The suede brogues fascinated her the first couple of times she passed him in the street. They were of a piece with the easy, self-assured air of the man, his imposing height and straight back, his open features, a fair-haired unScottishness about him, even though his accent was genteel Glasgow.

Apologising to her when they collided outside a shop. Recognising her another day on the High Street, and asking her – seeming to make the question up on the spot – were the midges any better or worse this summer?

They spoke about midges, until she couldn't think what else to say.

'I'll keep down by the river for a while,' he said. 'Insects notwithstanding. There's enough for me to paint by the river.'

She heard herself agreeing with him.

When she encountered him by the river, not near a path but in a field, she pretended it was a surprise, coming across him like this.

'You've come at just the right moment,' he said. 'I need a figure.'

He told her where to stand, and he arranged her – with the slow-flowing, reedy river in the background – and she stood.

When he'd finished he set out tea for them both, 'back at base' (as he called it), meaning the round stone dovecote – former dovecote – which he told her he'd rented for a few weeks.

'Doocot,' she said.

'Doocot?' he repeated.

'Don't you call them that in Glasgow?'

'My wife is English. And sometimes I forget. "Doocot", you're quite correct.' He bowed. 'I do apologise,' he said.

She smiled. He smiled to see her smiling, and she didn't know where to look.

'I've done the place out myself,' he told her proudly. 'Here, let me show you.'

She followed him inside. She smelled the whitewash and white paint. There was some furniture: a bed, a table, an armchair.

'My bolthole,' he said.

'It's very nice.'

He told her where he was staying, one of the hilly back roads up in the town. A house he was sharing with a few artist friends.

'This is for when the mood takes me.'

'The mood?' she repeated.

'Well, if I have to go to ground for a while. If inspiration sweeps me away!'

He laughed, and she laughed too, because she was thinking how strange it was that she was talking to an artist, and he to her.

Why should she *not* have gone back there, to the field, to the doocot?

Anyway, he seemed to be expecting her.

She had brought him some jam for the loaf she'd noticed last time. Damson jam in a glass jar. He kept asking her about it; it fascinated him. She had to describe to him how she'd made it, every stage of the process. She told him where the damsons had come from, one of the gardens where her husband laboured; but she neglected to say that they'd been windfall, taken from the long grass without asking, gardener's perks.

(Did his own wife make jam? it occurred to her. No, in cities they probably didn't, women – ladies – of a certain station in life.)

So together they ate sweet damson jam spread on thick slices of bread – the same loaf, a little too hard. He savoured the jam's taste, praised the texture, as if it were a rarity being served to them in an expensive restaurant.

And once they'd eaten their fill, when he asked her if she wanted to rest, perhaps sleep for a wee while on the divan . . . Ought she to have anticipated that?

Or even what happened afterwards?

Oh . . . Oh . . .

When she reached home, unable to think straight, she took off her clothes – the clothes he had helped to remove a couple of hours earlier – and she threw a pail of cold water over herself. She dressed in a different frock, tidied herself, powdered over the flush on her neck; she acted out normality for her family, and thought that if she could have had her life over again she might have trained to be an actress with this newfound talent for it.

Actresses had lovers.

But not women like her, with a husband and children, all of them living on top of one another in a cramped house without an unclaimed inch of space, where the walls seemed to be moving in on you.

She went back. Back to the doocot.

She had known that she would.

And *he* had known, too.

Was it love, what was to happen to her that summer?

For her it was to prove an exhilaration, a dependence, a freedom. She didn't weigh herself down with thoughts, with anticipations, or even with guilt.

She couldn't undo the first afternoon with him, and by the fifth or sixth she believed that there was an inevitability to what was taking place.

In the converted doocot. In this place apart.

To begin with she didn't like the thought of it: not the passion, but all those birds, doos, once filling this same space as themselves. Birds alarmed her with their sudden unpredictable motions, their sharp beaks, their claws, their panic much worse than hers. Their moulted feathers, their droppings.

He asked her one day to tell him what she was thinking about.

'Och, it's daft,' she said.

'No, it's not. Not if you're thinking it.'

So she told him. He looked up from where his head rested, on the pillow next to hers: up into the high cone of ceiling, with its criss-crossing wooden rafters where doves and pigeons had once roosted.

'It's odd how few dead birds you see, isn't it?' he said. 'How discreetly they go about dying, I mean. Out of sight.'

In grass verges, under hedges, at the bottom of ditches.

But he could tell she didn't want to talk about it, such a gloomy subject.

'You're right,' he said. 'Are you always right?'

Sometimes, just like this, she felt he must be secretly making fun of her: even though his face showed nothing more than a smile, and those admiring eyes. Oh yes, she saw how his eyes roamed over her, feasted on her. She wanted to ask him about this annual arrangement, he in Carnbeg for the summer and his wife – where? It seemed not quite proper to enquire, and she thought maybe it would be unlucky to speak of his wife at all, so she didn't.

She didn't want to think about the birds, either, and yet she sensed that they had left something of their presence behind, really the best part, the upwardness, the instinct for flight, rising up into the air: up and off and soaring free.

Because whenever she was with him her spirits were always gloriously light like this, gravity couldn't hold her, she cast off. A soul in free ascent, filled with grace.

There was always the return to ground, of course, with a bump. Her rude awakening as soon as she reached the end of Pends Loan.

The children rampaging, quarrelling about something, and John coming in and hearing them and the look on his face, always blaming her for keeping an unruly house. But they were as much his children as hers, and she wondered if it augured badly, the mother's dissatisfaction with things as they were crossed with the father's urge to flare up and hit out.

She'd had the rough end of John's tongue often enough, and sometimes he also took his hand to her, just as he took his belt to skelp the weans. She knew all about the need to close the door, to accept what comes, to suffer the pain of it and say nothing.

The days were running down, there was bound to be an end to it, and yet she wasn't prepared for the afternoon when she saw the car standing in front of the doocot and his canvases outside, propped against the curving wall.

Even the bed had been stripped.

'I've been summoned back,' he said.

'You *were* going to tell me, weren't you?'

'I was waiting for you.'

'What if I hadn't come today?'

'You always come.'

'Oh my God!' She had tears in her eyes.

'It's best like this,' he assured her.

'Like what?'

'A *fait accompli*. Something that's already been done.'

'I know what "*fait accompli*" means,' she said, angling away from him.

'Look, I'm sorry. Really I am.'

She turned back to him, in her own time.

'The summer comes round again,' he said.

'Anything could happen,' she told him.

'That's true. Because *this* happened, didn't it?'

He didn't specify what. But she allowed herself to nod.

'I don't suppose we need sheets and blankets, do we?' he said.

He took her arm. She didn't intend to be led, though. She walked on a little ahead of him, into the doocot. This final afternoon she would offer herself grandly, like . . . oh, like an ancient queen, laying down the royal person, sacrificing to the seasons.

He didn't write to her from Glasgow. She saw the sense of that: of course they must be careful.

She listened to the Carnbeg gossip, about the past summer's visitors. She guessed that he must be quite well known, since they said his name cropped up in the newspapers. Someone mentioned they had seen him in a group photograph, taken at some social function, but a few months ago; by now it was too late to track it down, or so it seemed to her, at Carnbeg's distance from civilisation.

Sometimes she made her way down to the doocot, and walked circles round it. Shutters had been fixed over the two windows, and the door was padlocked. She remembered their afternoons – really one long composite afternoon – and she liked to think she was the guardian spirit of the place. A couple of white doves flew on to the roof one day, out of nowhere, but the roosts had been blocked up and so they left their perches and, while she watched, they winged it into the blue beyond.

Once she must have loved her husband.

Perhaps.

But that wasn't yesterday, and she didn't imagine that she would get the feeling back again. What was left of her life was tomorrows: and hoping for better than she had.

Next summer the artists didn't return, or only a few.

Everyone knew a war was coming, and suddenly farther-off places – Iona, Skye, Lewis – must have threatened to become inaccessible. Carnbeg was already lodged in the artists' minds, and now most of them were off north to stock up on white beaches and outlandishly shaped mountains.

She scanned the incomers, but he wasn't among them.

She eavesdropped on the town's gossip, but his name wasn't ever mentioned.

She knew she had to get away for a while.

She told John that her invalid great-aunt in Glasgow was asking for her; she'd invited her to stay. He demanded to know why the old woman was more important than him and the bairns, and he made a show of being inconvenienced. But he must have realised that none of them would be the worse for a break; it might help the air to clear.

She found his house, on a leafy cul-de-sac in Glasgow's West End.

She only meant to look at it, imagining that it would be empty. But that evening the windows were open, figures moved about inside.

What possessed her to walk up the gravel driveway to the front steps, swept so clean and with two boot-scrapers?

A maid answered the door. The girl looked her up and down before instructing her to go round to the back premises to discuss her business there.

'This *is* the painter's house?'

'And what is it to you?'

At that moment some figures emerged from a room. Laughter, party voices.

'Dinner, everyone!'

Her heart jumped up into her throat. It was *his* voice speaking – she was quite certain of that.

Then another voice.

'Who is it, Ellen?'

A tall woman was looking over. 'We're all present and accounted for, aren't we?' Her voice was cultivated, confident, South of England.

'It's nobody, ma'am,' the maid said, and started to close the door.

The view of the hall narrowed to a diminishing wedge.

The visitor stepped back, to prevent the toes of her shoes being caught under the door's heavy brass runner.

In that interim the maid pushed hard, the door shut, and the lock bit.

Dejected, she decided to return to Carnbeg the next day. Her aunt, whose illness had become no more than a habit – neither improving nor worsening – would be able to manage well enough without her, only lacking now an audience.

The tram along Sauchiehall Street was passing the Art Galleries when something made her get up from her seat and go lurching towards the boarding platform at the back.

Standing in front of the mass of red sandstone, turreted and domed, she almost felt defeated again. Almost. But she persevered, drawn by the swelling sounds of organ music, up the front steps and inside. The instrument's pyramid of was curiously uplifting, and briefly – why? – she imagined a flight of fluttering birds set off inside her head.

On the upper floor she found the galleries where the Scottish artists were hung.

Was he famous enough to be among them? she wondered.

She examined the nameplates on the frames. She quickly passed along the walls, scarcely noticing the subjects of the pictures, reading the frames instead.

In the glass of one frame she caught sight of an attendant watching her, and herself in the opposite corner watching the two of them.

She went into another room, and was aware of the attendant's haunting presence.

More pictures, more frames – the names meant nothing to her, some of the print was too small to bother deciphering – and she couldn't recall why she had wanted to be here at all.

She was turning to leave when she saw herself again. Not a reflection this time. Herself, covering one of the canvases.

Definitely herself. Lying on the divan in the sunny white-washed doocot.

She stood staring, shocked by what was there in front of her.

Shocked not by her nakedness – a deft shadow rolling over her groin – but by the happy smile on her face as she slept, abandoned to the world and quite unsuspecting, the lazy and luxurious contentment of her.

She had thought it was *her* secret, not even his. He had always been so brisk at his lovemaking, if apologetic. While she had wanted the afternoon in the doocot to go on and on, to be never-ending. He brisk but somehow gentle at the same time, and she for that precious time imagining she was at the centre of his life.

She would doze off afterwards, aware that he was sitting sketching, drawing this or that in the room or the view from the window. Somewhere out there in the town her husband was toiling, and scrounging windfall; the children were playing, bawling their heads off probably. What a relief to her to have experienced this contrast, his gentleness, to be hearing nothing except her lover's pencil scratchings and his even breathing and birdsong through the open door.

Life back in Carnbeg had never seemed so confining or so dull.

And yet she didn't shrink to the smallness of its size and ambitions, not just yet.

She settled back into the routine of Pends Loan, after a

fashion. She went about her chores, and might have appeared to be much the same person: the woman she had been before the summer before last.

She would go on accepting what happened to her in this house as her fate, she would suffer the pain of it and say nothing. She knew to close the door and not be heard.

But in her mind . . .

That was different.

In her mind she continued to see the interior of the doocot, the doocot *then*: a round white turret at ground level, warmed by the sun, with its door left open. She had the spirit of the displaced birds inside her, she gave them a soul when some said birds had none.

She remembered the painting hanging in Glasgow, on the gallery wall. She thought of it briefly impressing the browsers, those who stopped to look. She thought how strange it was that they – who had luckier lives than she did – should see her there, dissolute in sleep and perfectly contented, and that for those moments of looking they might be envying her.

Away From It All

Blue wistaria, they dreamed of. And a rainbarrel.

The cottage they eventually found didn't have wistaria, or a rainbarrel. But a visit to a garden centre would help to put that right. The structure was in reasonable nick, and they'd gut the interior, get things just how they wanted them.

They packed the 4 × 4 and fled Edinburgh late every Friday afternoon, speeding up the motorway. Their Carnbeg weekends were all given over to the cottage, but their exhaustion on Sunday nights was the best sort, sweet and happy, as they drove south again, with some reluctance, kept awake by their Rai tapes.

This was what the past few years of 9-to-6 (and longer) had been for, slaving in the financial bear-pit that Edinburgh had become. A city-centre apartment for Monday to Thursday, and a rural bolt-hole for their precious leisure time.

Carnbeg was just the spot.

Close to a fast road. Good food shops ('suppliers' and 'purveyors') which stocked organic Scottish cheeses and plump pheasant breasts. Lots of fresh, invigorating Highland air, blown off the heather hills. Log-burning open fires. Leisure to experiment with food, that recipe for venison casseroled in 'oak-spiced' red wine, they'd have it bubbling away on the Rayburn. Time to read some of those Booker books, and to discover composers – Piazzolla, Janáček, the ones on that mental check-list. Maybe an opportunity to paint the scenery in water-colours or (literally) pick up the reins again at the Hydro's riding centre. Or try hiking up the south side of Cnoc na Mèilich.

They went through the 'Happy, darling?' routine, very Celia and Trevor. It was nice get back to 'making do', as if they were playing at house. Gingerbread-cottage stuff.

Flat-packs that were still in their packaging. A space for a chair here, and a table there, which they were going to buy from an antiques shop when they were ready. And wouldn't one of those simplified half-fat Scandinavian chandeliers (in the-spirit-of-Gustavson style) set up the sitting-room very nicely?

The pleasure was planning, what-iffing, and all the better when they thought they could afford it, just about.

They preferred their venison in milder pâté form. The wine from the High Street off-licence was a little rough, not 'oak-spiced', but rough was more okay drunk on a cottage floor than in a New Town upper conversion.

While the house was being worked on, they used a portable gas-cylinder fire, and fell asleep in each other's arms, in the glow of its efficient heat. Never mind that they woke up with pins and needles, and cricks in their necks, and a bad dose of fireside tartan reddening their skin down one side. All it did was help to make the experience more real, and forget the gingerbread doo-dah, blah-blah.

Work on the cottage took longer than planned. A hired hand's pickaxe severed a waterpipe, and in the panic to repair the damage too many bricks were dislodged, which weakened one of the interior walls. The floor didn't sand up to the required standard and had to be relaid from scratch, which was an extra expense. The double-glazing company went into receivership before the windows were delivered, and lawyers' letters had to be despatched before the company that had taken them over would observe the terms of the original agreement in full. The tiles on the roof had to be repegged, once it was discovered that a north-blowing gale would lift them high and bring them clattering down again. A crooked secondary flue made the living flames in the bedroom grate a bit too lively, flaring up alarmingly; being several miles short of a gas pipe they put in a big iron stove, which lessened the room's romantic appeal but certainly kept them warm – at tropical heat, it sometimes felt.

The cottage was peaceful. Yes. An *echoing* kind of stillness, which had them clinging to one another in bed. But if you listened hard, *through* that silence . . . You could hear nocturnal sounds, rustlings and scrapings behind the walls and up in the roof, and from outside muffled cries and bellows and yelps which must have been foxes or deer or wild mountain cats or God knew what.

Here they were, though. Living the dream, pretty much.

The air in the town was fragrant with woodsmoke from old-fashioned fires. The locals said, 'Good morning' to you, 'Nice day', and you replied in kind. The man in the By Royal Appointment fruiterers recalled from last time that they liked Falstaff apples, and the poulterer offered to skin a rabbit for them. (And how could they politely refuse him? Phone call to a friend in Edinburgh, asking for a do-able recipe involving fresh rabbit.) They picked late wildflowers, and collected pine cones to burn, and gathered holly for the festive season.

Calum's family took precedence over Ro's this Christmas, and they had three weeks away, visiting his parents and younger sister in Canada. Scotland meantime was blessed: the weather stayed mild, no pipes in the cottage froze so none burst; the plants were spared a cold snap with snow or frost.

They were back in Carnbeg in time to buy the last of the Christmas chestnuts, and roasted them on the fire. They invited some friends up to stay, on the weekend when a stag got into the garden and threw a wobbly, before a wall of their (cautiously) advancing bodies directed it back towards the break in the hedge it had caused in the first place.

So much for the winter.

They were glad they had made Carnbeg their second home, more or less, and they felt their friends at heart envied them. All that New Yeary, turning-over-a-new-leaf kind of thing – although in the end none of the other couples decided to follow their example. Perhaps their friends felt that their double life, the luxury of an alternative existence up here in the pine hills – and the glossy lifestyle magazine ambience – was just too hard an act to follow, to get as right as Calum and Ro had done.

Or as they *appeared* to have done.

Because, of course, stories and presentations invariably have two sides to them, at least.

And, because nature is only too predictably unpredictable, a false and treacherous sum of conditions, constant in its inconstancy.

Et cetera.

They walked, they strode out across the springy heather – and returned a couple of hours later, with a shade less enthusiasm. Three times they reported to the stables, saddled up, and did the forest trail from the map. But the horses they'd been given seemed to be confederates in mischief, and afterwards their arms and legs ached from coaxing Bissum and Rocky back to the straight and narrow; unfortunately, there wasn't enough hot water in the cottage's small tank for a steaming bath each, and the tub was a tight fit and a distinctly unerotic experience. Riding was off the agenda for the immediate future, and they pondered idly the mental benefits of fishing the shallow silvery river – but let's leave it awhile, they decided

It turned into a wet spring, and it felt like forty days and forty nights of rain. But they reached the summer, when the heat seemed to get trapped between the high hills. They also discovered midges and tested the sprays and roll-ons and creams available in the chemist's (and a better selection than in Edinburgh), and they even invested in a couple of beekeeper's veils for lying out in the garden. (They thought a mosquito net for the bedroom was going a bit too far, although it put them in mind of sexy eastern harems. But this *was* (very) rural Perthshire.)

And then, in rustic terms, the two worms turned.

They got homesick.

They realised, guiltily at first, that they missed some of Edinburgh's weekend attractions: the West End bistros, the lazy Saturday drift from shop to shop, a play or a film in the evening. Although they got Sunday newspapers in Carnbeg, it wasn't the same as reading them in a café, to a soundtrack of Gainsbourg

or Gréco or Jobim, and there were no galleries open if they felt
they needed an infusion of culture. Walking the early-dusk
streets looking into shop windows held fewer surprises here in
Carnbeg than it did in the New Town. They brought their his
and hers phones with them, but the computer and fax stayed
in Edinburgh, and they found themselves wondering what
messages might have come through. There were no late-opening
shops in Carnbeg, and only the touristy ones on a Sunday, so all
their stocking-up had to be done on a Saturday, and as you
queued you were left with the impression that the made-to-
order deliveries in boxes received the best produce, and wasn't it
perhaps simpler in the end just to get their favourite cheese or
pasta or ham from that new genius place in Dean Village?

Where in Carnbeg could you lay your hands on okra to serve
with lamb, or those tree-tomatoes in the cookery columns, the
savoury-tasting 'tamarillos', and not a honey-sweet sapodilla
fruit to be found in the town even if your life depended on it.

There was no particular moment when The Decision was taken.
Rather, it was an instinct with them both, that Carnbeg wasn't
to be an ongoing arrangement.

They missed a couple of Saturdays, which meant driving up
on a Sunday and an unearthly early start on Monday morning
to get back. Then they missed a couple of weekends altogether.

A damp mark reappeared on an outside gable. In their absence
a bird fell down the open chimney in the sitting-room and must
have sootily flapped about before expiring. The brackeny water
turned mysteriously darker, which meant boiling all the water
for drinking and cooking.

It was just too much trouble and effort all round, wasn't it?

They each surprised the other, standing reflecting at a window
or outside in the garden, as if remembering all they'd put into
this venture and what they might be going to regret if they
weren't here. What they would lose was the myth of escape, of
becoming different people when they got to Carnbeg – improved
versions of themselves. But escape was only ever temporary, and

what was so wrong about the lives they had in Edinburgh? If the impulse overcame them, they could hie off to a hotel for a night or two, or take a week's rental on a serviced cottage from a brochure.

It had *cost* them, but life is a learning-curve, with steeper gradients to keep you alert. Better to sell up now and cut their losses.

Which was just what they did.

No more preparing the fire and putting it out again, no more throwing everything back into the car and debating if this or that would last the week in the fridge. No more joining the tailback of traffic at the Forth Bridge or anywhere between Carnbeg and there. No more wondering why on earth they bothered as they climbed upstairs to the flat, to the creature comforts they had worked so hard to acquire. No more Sunday-night flaking out and not having the presence of mind even to turn off the TV set. No more waking up late on Monday morning, and feeling godawful.

No, none of that, not any more. Three cheers, hip hip.

They continued reading the Sunday property supplements in their favourite West End trattoria, drinking lattes and sharing a slice of indecently rich marble cake.

The country cottages continued to look beguiling, photographed against an idyllic blue summer sky; but now they believed they knew better.

You don't train a wistaria vine in a year. And that rainbarrel: God, do you remember that? they ask each other. The garden centre in Perth did one, but they'd decided no. Made in Poland, six-month guarantee, and a small-print proviso about no liability against acid-rain contamination. Plastic with a wood-effect finish and fake hoops, which made them think of Snow White on speed, and has them laughing now at their café table. They lift the colour supps to smother the sound, laughing with sheer relief until the tears run.

The Fitting

There is to be a wedding at Schiehallion.

A marquee on the lawn. A string trio, and a ceilidh band for the dancing. The whole bang shoot.

Geraldine's mother is determined that they'll do things by the book, even though money is tight. Angus's family is going to provide this and that, and *they* can certainly afford it, with all their Edinburgh business connections. But it's up to the bride's family to make a show of it, and that's as true now in 1968 as it ever was.

Geraldine, up in her bedroom, flicks through recent isssues of *Queen* while she waits for the water to heat up adequately for a bath. She's off to be fitted this afternoon, and a bath seems *de rigueur*. In London they're getting married in registry offices, or in hot-air balloons, matching white outfits from King's Road and doves released with the exchange of vows.

Here in Carnbeg it's different.

She sighs, and hears herself. She closes the magazines.

For the wedding she'll be wearing her mother's dress. Which was her mother's sister's dress, and – originally, to begin with – their mother's, Geraldine's grandmother's. Every time it gets subtly altered, and the veil is shortened, and there's a new head-dress. Her grandmother's white dress was cream a generation later, and now it's an ivory shade. Probably, since Geraldine's one female cousin doesn't believe in marriage, this will be the last wearing it gets.

It will need to be adjusted. They have arranged to call on Miss Melhuish, who made her dress for the Aeolians' ball in Edinburgh four years ago, when she was twenty-one. Customers go to Miss Melhuish, she doesn't go to them. Her mother says they're very lucky to have this opportunity, their second, and that one day she will appreciate the gift of Miss Melhuish's time.

Geraldine's mother, driving them into Carnbeg, remembers the days when her parents used to be driven in by Mr Johnstone, whom they called their 'driver' not 'chauffeur', supposing that word had pretensions. Then the war came, and Mr Johnstone was sent off, and there was much less driving about because petrol was in short supply. Her own wedding managed to be a proper Schiehallion wedding in spite of the restrictions: a marquee on the lawn, a string quartet, a soprano to sing 'This is My Lovely Day', a fiddle band for the reels and strathspeys.

A new dress for their daughter would have been the best option, but needs must, and conveniently Geraldine's mother can shelter behind the word 'tradition'.

'It's a tradition in our family . . . '

'You know what they say, "tradition dictates" . . . '

The dress was made to last. The style was already a little nostalgic for its first wearer, and now the summer-of-1913 look is quite fashionable again: *plus ça change*. Miss Melhuish will know what to do, how to make it fit as it should but also how to revive it, freshen it up for this latest outing.

They turn into an unmade road.

The houses are substantial sandstone bungalows with chalet-style overhanging eaves. Miss Melhuish has gateposts and a monkey-puzzle tree.

'It's quite big, isn't it?' Geraldine says. 'Considering.'

'Considering what?' her mother asks.

That she's really a seamstress, Geraldine means.

'Considering she lives by herself.'

'I remember when she moved here,' her mother says. 'She needed more space.'

'Did she inherit it?' Geraldine asks.

'Inherit it? Why?'

'It must've cost a lot.' Geraldine has been aware of prices and costs all her life.

'But she's the best at what she does,' her mother says.

Geraldine doesn't speak.

'The name Melhuish is a byword,' her mother tells her, speaking proudly on the woman's behalf.

For years she's been said to be the best seamstress in Perthshire – in the north – in Scotland.

For years Jean Melhuish has received clients in the front room, with a full fall of netting at the windows to ensure discretion. Material is laid out, the client's requests are discussed and measurements taken. Or work is returned, admired, complimented upon. (Surely there is never any need to inspect and scrutinise there and then, not when her skills are considered impeccable. Afterwards, though, the customer – at her leisure – will peer at the delicacy and precision of the stitching, as if it's been worked by charmed fingers, and she will be astonished and amazed.)

The two women are admitted, and shown into the front room.

It's big enough to accommodate a long worktable as well as a sofa and a couple of *bergère* chairs.

'May I offer you both a cup of tea, ladies?'

'That's very kind of you, but we had something before we set out, thank you.'

Geraldine, not expecting the untruth to sound so pat, looks at her mother. Her mother quickly smiles in her direction, wanting to be excused for a little white lie.

'In that case,' Miss Melhuish says, 'I suggest we turn our thoughts to the business in hand, shall we?'

Geraldine's mother laughs, and starts to remove the wedding-dress from its box of tissue paper.

Miss Melhuish takes off her spectacles and lifts a magnifying-glass in front of her face. While Geraldine studies the cobweb of lines beside one screwed-up eye, enlarged by the glass, Miss Melhuish examines the fine work she applied herself to the bodice and the sleeves nearly thirty years ago.

'Isn't it remarkable?' Geraldine's mother says.

'No more than the job I was given to do, madam.'

Geraldine's mother smiles, over the woman's stooped head of permed grey curls, as if she is reminding her daughter: how often do you hear that said *these* days?

Only – so it's claimed, far and wide – only in a famous Parisian atelier, or in the fabled workrooms of the Forbidden City in Peking, would one find work to equal Jean Melhuish's. In the past, couturiers from London have 'made representation', travelled up on the night sleeper and beaten a path to her door and been offered not a cup of tea but a polite and firm refusal. They were unused to such eccentric behaviour, and to being told that really there was plenty of work to be getting on with at the moment, thank you very much for enquiring.

Here in Carnbeg she wasn't able to be anonymous, she didn't go unnoticed as she would have done if she'd been employed by a West End modiste. Not that she sought the vanity of recognition: but she took pride in her handiwork, and was prepared that it should be a matter of personal honour. She preferred to see and speak to those who hired her expertise and labour. Her name was immediately recognisable to the *cognoscenti*, but that was almost accidental. Jean Melhuish had been brought up to believe that it was a sin before God to do any less than your best.

Geraldine's mother points to the magnifying glass, at the opposite end of the long table from where she's sitting.

'Is that what you're looking for, Miss Melhuish?' she calls across.

'What's that, madam?'

'The magnifying glass?'

'You've found it?'

'It's just next to you.'

'Oh. So it is.' Miss Melhuish turns round on her stool, but she doesn't pick up the magnifying glass. 'I'll be forgetting my own name next.'

'Not much chance of that!' Geraldine's mother laughs.

Meanwhile Miss Melhuish turns back the hem on the bell of the dress and reaches up inside, examining the lining by touch.

Geraldine's mother looks on with admiration. The customer it is who's the privileged party, she's thinking, not Miss Melhuish, who might have gone on to ply her trade with royalty and aristocrats, and even with them named any price she liked.

This way, that way. Geraldine complies, and watches herself and her mother and Miss Melhuish in the mirror.

She always complies, she thinks. To a fault. But, never a rebel, she has always supposed that everyone older must know better than her. Angus is older, by five years, and five years is really an age.

Miss Melhuish on her knees fumbles with the tin of pins and they spill. She passes the flat of her palm across the carpet to find them.

Her mother comes over to help. Geraldine wonders if Miss Melhuish has the shakes: maybe she's already taken a snifter or two this afternoon. But she hasn't smelled any drink.

Geraldine offers to bend down to help find pins, but her mother tells her not to ruin the profile. So she continues to stand, tall and straight, and – only because it's been asked of her – inflexible and aloof.

Afterwards, the fitting over, Geraldine and her mother get back into the car and drive off.

'The poor woman,' Geraldine says, sighing.

(Angus tells her that he finds her sighs quite sexy: or 'becoming', as she reported to her mother.)

'The poor woman,' Geraldine repeats, thinking that her mother mightn't have heard.

'Yes, we just got there in time,' her mother says, wrestling with the gear stick, which is becoming a problem in this fifteen-year-old car.

'How do you mean?' Geraldine asks.

Her mother replies, 'How do I mean what?'

'About being just in time.'

'Well,' her mother says, 'she's not going to have her sight much longer, is she?'

Geraldine looks at her mother. 'How do you know that?'

'They *go* blind,' her mother says.

'Who?' Geraldine asks. 'Her family do or something?'

'No, seamstresses. The best ones.'

Geraldine stares at her mother.

'It's all the tiny stitches,' her mother says. 'What we go to them for. In China they're revered. Because everyone knows there.'

'Knows what?' Geraldine asks.

'What we're talking about,' Geraldine's mother calls out over the revving engine.

The car gets into its stride. The leaping chrome jaguar mounted on the bonnet devours the road in front.

'That's why *we* respect the Miss Melhuishes,' her mother says. 'We pay what they're worth. Or your father does. Because we know they've only got so many years. Before . . . ' Her voice trails away.

'Before they can't see?' Geraldine says, unable to keep her dismay out of her voice.

'That's just the way of it,' her mother says.

Geraldine is shocked by her mother's matter-of-factness, the cool dry way she's expressed such a horrible truth.

Geraldine looks away again, through the windscreen in front of her, at the road.

Now when she wears the dress she will be thinking only of Miss Melhuish, losing more of what little precious eyesight she has – *had* – labouring over her dress.

'We'll have to invite her to the wedding,' Geraldine's mother says.

Geraldine stares at her again.

'Of course, she probably won't come. The getting there and walking about. Probably better off at home. With her comforts.'

What do 'comforts' matter – Geraldine can't fathom it at all –

when you don't have your eyesight?

'Oh well,' her mother says, checking her hair in the rear-view mirror.

But the 'Oh well' doesn't sound very sorrowful to Geraldine.

What is this terrible hardness, coldness, which has appeared and ruined today for her? But it isn't so new, when she thinks about it, and she thinks about it during the next few miles when her mother doesn't speak, presumably totting up wedding costs in her head.

That's what it's about, Geraldine tells herself. About facts and figures and doing what's expected of you. Mummy and Daddy will make sure the big day passes off well, and I'll say and do the right things – most of all 'I do', and signing the register – and I'll let everyone admire the dress, and laugh at the cleaned-up jokes Angus's friends will be on their best behaviour to regale us with. We're like the warlord rievers here, centuries ago, cattle-barons making their politic contracts. *They* needed more land; my parents need Angus's money just to hold on to ours.

So, what does the eyesight of one well-paid seamstress with her best years behind her matter? Of course, I *shall* be able to say, 'Miss Melhuish worked on my dress. You've heard of her, haven't you? Completely blind at sixty years old.'

Geraldine feels sick. It has nothing to do with the motion of the car, the speed her mother is getting out of it, this gas-guzzler, the same marque *her* father used to have. She can mention the horror to Angus, but she suspects that the morality of his Edinburgh banking set – asset-strippers to a man – won't stand up to much moral scrutiny, either.

She's thinking of her wedding-dress – not blessed but cursed, surely, even while the others are busy admiring it – and she's thinking of Miss Melhuish's clotted, suppurating, nearly sightless eyeballs crawling up over the silk.

Geraldine sits stuck to the cracked leather of the passenger seat. She stares past the devouring jaguar on the bonnet, stares wide-eyed ahead at the approaching distance of red road, and she sees nothing of it.

The New

In our teens we used to play tennis at the New Club in Carnbeg, on summer passes.

Nothing about it seemed very *new* to us.

Then, farther down the hill, we discovered a dilapidated wooden pavilion in a tangled beech copse. The windows were broken. Angry thistles and stinging nettles grew up through the verandah.

Over the once-elegant double doors, in faded – nearly invisible – lettering, the initials CLTC.

Carnbeg Lawn Tennis Club. So there must have been another, earlier one.

We peered inside. Pale shadows were mapped on the timber walls, where plaques had hung. The lost roll-calls of players' champions and club secretaries and tournament fixtures. Empty shelves in a cabinet, for showing cups and shields. All gone.

The original Carnbeg Lawn Tennis Club was founded in the early 1900s.

Anyone who was anyone was a member.

When the holidaymakers started to come regularly to the resort, suburban families from Glasgow and Edinburgh who spent several weeks of the summer at the big hotels, they tried to befriend members so that they might have an opportunity to play as their guests. Although the hotels had their own courts, also grass, there was an arcane air of exclusivity about the CLTC which put it in a different league.

Here was an entrée to Old Carnbeg, to those charmed circles inside circles. Once admitted, you *belonged*.

Fast-forward.

1955.

The name Kerrigan was entered on the register of those seeking membership of the venerable Carnbeg Lawn Tennis Club.

Joseph Kerrigan owned property to let, mostly residential, in a number of towns in this corner of Perthshire, including Carnbeg. Other professional landlords had been members of the CLTC in the past, but were less blatant about their occupation. Mr Kerrigan drove a Bentley (purchased new), he wore cashmere sports jackets, also brightly coloured slacks which he bought on continental holidays. Whenever he went to London he put up at the Grosvenor House Hotel on Park Lane; his fifth wedding anniversary had been celebrated with a party on a pleasure steamer on the River Thames.

One of his proposers was Mrs Chavasse, sister of the owner of the Hydro Hotel, an (unhappily) married woman who had a habit of showing up to play on her favourite court with anonymous sleepy-looking young men whom she referred to in company only by their Christian names.

'Kerrigan? Kerrigan?'

Memories were jogged at the CLTC.

There had once been a caretaker called that over at the Hydro, before the war. He'd been a sort of janitor. Worked nights. With a frumpy wife, and a difficult son who'd had a guid conceit of himself.

'Left-footers,' someone recalled.

The members got talking, remembering, speculating.

The night janitor's son had disappeared suddenly, following several incidents of jewellery gone missing from guests' bedrooms. (There might or might not have been a connection; perhaps it was enough that fingers of suspicion were pointed in young Kerrigan's direction.) He vanished for a few years. Into the war. Then, after his demob, he travelled several times round the world in the merchant navy, seizing his opportunities in the new peace. (So many places, so many scattered clues, so many covered tracks.)

Now here he was, back in the locale. A landlord no less; but – it was discovered – of not very salubrious properties. Whole tenement blocks in Perth, rows of labourers' damp cottages round about. And a dispenser of high-interest short-term loans, to boot.

Here he was, darkening the CLTC pavilion's hallowed portals.

Vivien Chavasse was heard saying that the place needed a good shaking-up anyway, and Joe Kerrigan would be a boon for them.

At the same time a few rumours started up concerning her past relationship with the said Kerrigan, in the days when his father was a humble employee in her brother's hotel.

So, what did *that* tell them all about the fellow?

The committee turned down his application.

'Not quite the calibre we're looking for,' the club secretary said, strictly off the record. The ladies' representative nodded conspiratorially.

There *were* some words of support, from just a handful of members. Their thinking went: couldn't they have tried to persuade this Kerrigan chap to spend a bit of money on the courts, help with refurbishing the pavilion? If you disregarded the background stuff . . . don't look a gift horse, all that sort of thing . . .

But the general talk reverted to 'standards'.

'We have ladies here.'

'It wouldn't be fair. On *him*, either. Not being able to join in the jaw-jaw.'

'People need to think they're talking about the same things, the values they share.'

'Give a chap like that an inch – '

'And he'll bring his pals. Flash Harries, I'll bet, the lot of them.'

Kerrigan was reported to be livid.

He was persuaded by his proposer, Mrs Chavasse, against his will, to submit another application. This second one wasn't even put before the committee.

The man vowed revenge.

He bought the donkey field farther up the hill, on Letham Brae. It wasn't a flat piece of ground when he acquired it, but it was once he'd finished constructing his sextet of tennis courts.

There were no problems with planning permits. Unlike his CLTC humiliation, it all went through on the nod.

The enterprise took two years from start to finish. The greater part of that time was needed to raise the capital. The contractors completed their work well within the stipulated schedule, under threat of penalties.

The clubhouse was the *pièce de résistance*. Outside, pebbledash and timber-crossed solid walls, rustic rainbarrels. Indoors, Oregon pine panelling and floors, a fitted kitchen with a refrigerator, a proper Ladies' room and a sanitary Gents'. Brand-new Lloyd Loom wicker furniture, and sets of stags' antlers in the vestibule, as if you were walking into a country house. Here and there an arrangement of flowers, provided by the socially practised Mrs Kerrigan, born a Marjoribanks.

The defections started from the CLTC to the New.

At first only a few. Then, once the waters had been tested, so to speak, more followed.

The high heid yins at the CLTC held out: remember where your allegiance lies, stay loyal, keep the faith.

They wondered how Kerrigan had wangled an unrestricted drinks licence from the powers-that-be – through friends of friends, no doubt, with the help of a backhander. They pooh-poohed the decision to hold a series of social evenings in the New's fancy clubhouse: a dance (with small orchestra) for the more mature members, and a hoolie (with ceilidh band) for the younger crowd.

The members of the CLTC felt beleaguered, imperilled, they were an endangered species – fuddy-duddies. For most of them, that was not how they wanted to project themselves. They also didn't much appreciate being told what to think by those who ran the works. They had minds of their own, and terms like 'loyalty' are – well, to be frank, they're relative, comparative, *flexible*.

Yet more defections followed. Why should politics get in the way of friendships? Anyway, once you were invited over to the New to sample it for yourself you couldn't really go back. (Have you seen how close a cut that mower gets on the courts? Like velvet.)

That left the hardliners behind, those who wouldn't switch clubhouses on principle; or who, because they felt they had held out *this* long, couldn't allow themselves to be seen to be caving in now.

They stuck together: after a fashion. Someone on the committee called the once genteel CLTC 'a midden of bad feelings', someone else 'a dunghill of antipathy'. The remarks had to be entered in the club minutes, copied out in accountant's best copperplate hand: they stood there, not for eternity, but for as long as the CLTC was left in operation.

That was to be only another twenty months.

An unsolicited offer was made for the CLTC's land. Then another development company from up north put in a second, higher bid. There was a possibility that houses might be built, but the depleted committee decided on a quorum that the ground should be handed over *as a gift* to the council. They insisted the function be changed, that the tennis courts must be decommissioned. At their specific behest, the CLTC's concluding riposte was to furnish Carnbeg with the site of . . .

A municipal car park and public toilets.

This gesture seemed satisfyingly final, to have their field of dreams overlaid by – worse than red asphalt – one and a half acres of tarmacadam.

The site would now never revert.

In a manner of speaking, it was to be perfectly preserved. Home to rows of neatly parked cars, the CLTC would be safe and sound in the perpetually sunny afternoons of these last members' distant memories.

Another couple of years on, Mr Kerrigan sold his healthily solvent venture – lock, stock and rainbarrels – to the New Lawn

Tennis Club of Carnbeg Ltd. He retained no financial interest himself.

It was naturally expected that he would continue to visit, but before long he had a grass court laid in the garden of his house and played there instead. Some years later he acquired an American machine which automatically served tennis balls, hurling them across court for a return.

By then Kerrigan had become embittered by several more experiences like the Carnbeg one. The wealthier he got, the less acceptable he seemed to be, which he couldn't understand. In every fairytale the ambitious poor man will be transformed into a rich man, or a prince, and live happily ever after. In this new world of the 1960s, money was supposed to open any door, take you anywhere.

Was supposed to.

Not here in Perthshire, though.

But maybe in London.

Kerrigan sold the lochside house and three acres with private tennis court. He bought a flat in Mayfair, and his wife went on ahead with the removal vans.

On his last day in Carnbeg Kerrigan was seen stopping the car on Letham Brae. He looked over at the New, where every court of the six was occupied and the next players due on stood waiting their turn.

He drove off, and turned into the municipal car park. Searched for a space big enough to take a Bentley coupé. Parked, locked up, left the car. Set off along one of the trodden paths through the long grass, into the beech copse behind the big villas where some of the Old Carnbeg families who had settled here two or three generations ago still lived.

He was looking for something – and found it. The timber pavilion that had once been so desirable as a focus for his social ambitions. A local had bought it, out of pity or offended pride, and re-erected it at the bottom of his garden – but then forgotten about it.

After only five, six years the structure was semi-derelict, it had started falling to pieces. The rotten steps, broken windows, a sodden curtain, dirt. Leaves everywhere, in drifts. Cigarette stubs, spent matches. A light-blue ankle sock. A rubber johnny, used and withered.

Kerrigan must have realised as he stood on the verandah, peering inside, that his triumph had been hollow.

Yes, the plaques of honour had been unscrewed from the walls and carried off: the trophy shelves were empty.

But the victory he'd won was Pyrrhic.

The lettering was still just visible on the lintel, CLTC. The once-elegant double doors, on rusty hinges, were still closed to him, and no key in the lock.

Apricot Jam

My Uncle Jim and Aunt Jean lived at Home Farm, on the west side of Carnbeg, three miles away from the town.

The farm was where Uncle Jim grew up. Aunt Jean came from Oban, and although she accepted her lot as a farmer's wife she missed the sea and the life of a port.

After fifteen years she felt that she and Uncle Jim had paid their dues to the land. She worked hard on her huband, trying to convince him there were easier ways to make a living than this. Her plans didn't seem any clearer than to sell the land and invest the sum they got for it. Her brother had a car franchise in Fort William, and said it was money for old rope – why not try operating one up Oban way?

Their neighbours got to hear. They didn't see Jim Menzies standing on a forecourt, but they also knew that his wife, once just about the best looker in these parts, could be very persuasive with her feminine charms.

A close acquaintance of the couple, but not a neighbour, was Mrs Tinning.

She was always spoken about as an unmarried woman, because her marriage had been long ago and for a very short time. She had been brought up on a small farm next to the Menzies', which was how she had a claim on their friendship. She lost out to Jean Menzies in looks, and she didn't share all her enthusiasms; my aunt had discovered oven-to-table pre-cooked meals, she read *Hello!*, watched Richard and Judy, she did the lottery and had highlights put in her hair. Iris Tinning made a show of being interested, at least, which other farm types didn't do, and she laughed at all Jim's well-worn jokes and liked to talk about Old Carnbeg, but not in a way that excluded Jean.

Mrs Tinning, too, had heard – although not at first-hand – about the plans to sell the farm, to up sticks and move.

Once when I was visiting, doubling as nephew and as Oban estate agent, I heard her say to her old friends, 'I really don't think you will, you know.'

'Oh no?' Aunt Jean said. 'And why not?'

' Because' – Mrs Tinning timed her smile carefully – 'because who else can I invite for afternoon tea?'

'Is that an offer?' Uncle Jim asked.

Afternoon tea wasn't her usual manner of entertainment. Picnic fare or sherry and biscuits was her speciality, but this time she was clear, she would be held to an afternoon tea.

'Certainly it's an offer,' Mrs Tinning said.

She told them which day to come, if they could.

Aunt Jean replied for them both.

'Of course we can, Iris.'

'For our oldest friend,' Uncle Jim added.

'Not *so* old, if you don't mind,' Iris Tinning corrected him, and amiable laughter rang round the room.

The afternoon went very pleasantly, even though Aunt Jean took along some brochures I had provided her with, for new-build bungalows in the Oban area.

Mrs Tinning, so Uncle Jim told me later, scarcely looked at them, as if she thought they only fuelled folks' daydreams.

'I want you to enjoy this tea I've made you. Sandwiches. Fruit cake. Scones, fresh butter. And my apricot jam. But that'll be too sweet for you, Jim.' (My uncle had mild diabetes.) 'So *you* get a savoury instead.'

'It's not sweet at all,' Aunt Jean said of the apricot jam with her scone. 'Quite . . . tart in fact.'

'*Too* tart?' Mrs Tinning asked.

Aunt Jean shook her head, diplomatic guest that she was being. 'It's rather interesting. How did you do it, Iris? You just cut down on the sugar, did you?'

'Yes and no.'

Aunt Jean laughed. 'You're not going to tell me?'

'I'll keep you guessing.'

'And if I don't guess?'

'You can ring me from Oban,' Iris Tinning said. 'When you . . . *if* you . . . ' She didn't complete the remark.

'You put something *with* the apricot?' Aunt Jean persisted. 'Another fruit?'

'Oh, it's all apricot,' their friend said. 'Every bit of it.'

A happy afternoon.

Which was to be Jean Menzies' last.

She had an accident that evening, when she was alone in the farmhouse. She was up on a stepladder in the kitchen and lost her balance and fell off it, landing head first on the floor.

She wasn't found for another hour or so, when Uncle Jim came in from completing his evening rounds.

He called an ambulance at once.

His wife didn't survive the night.

He returned to the farm next morning, heartbroken. He saw Aunt Jean's blood on the kitchen floor.

She'd never had a head for heights, she must have had a dizzy turn, reached out, grabbed for some support, and been left flailing at empty air . . .

Beside the stepladder, open with covers splayed, was one of the cookery books she kept at the back of the top cupboard.

She had been talking about the apricot jam on the way home in the car. It *was* very unusual, and bitter: she shouldn't have taken so much. She would dig out that old book with jam recipes and give it to Iris, a farewell present ('D'you think she'd mind?'). In those days they'd liked their jam sweeter and maybe Iris would take the hint.

'A good idea,' Uncle Jim had said, little suspecting, and the pair of them laughed.

After the funeral I delivered the recipe book myself.

Mrs Tinning obviously wasn't expecting company. She asked

me to come in, sounding awkward about it. I stepped inside the kitchen. She stared at the book's cover as I explained my aunt's wish was that she should have it.

'Apricot jam,' I said.

She straightened. 'What about it?'

'My aunt – she was talking about your jam.'

'Saying what, might I ask?'

'If you're keen on apricots,' I stumbled on, 'you might . . . find . . . something here.'

Mrs Tinning accepted the book without looking at it, and without thanking me.

I glanced around. The kitchen was spotlessly clean, meticulously tidy: to the point of neurosis, I felt.

'A mortar and pestle?' I said, for something to say, nodding at the objects.

Not a word from Iris Tinning.

'The old ways are the best,' I continued, 'aren't they?'

The woman didn't smile. I thought, the death of her friend must have hit her very hard.

'I really should be going,' I said, taking a last look round.

'How is he?' she suddenly asked.

'My uncle? Oh, he's coping.'

She smiled now, for the first time. But she was smiling to herself, not to me. It was a private gesture, made out of long ago's and all a younger woman's wiles.

My uncle seemed to think that now wasn't the time to talk about Iris Tinning, and an instinct warned me not to ask him why not.

I got neighbours to tell me what I wanted to know. They dipped into their wells of memory.

Iris Mackie as a girl, dancing with Jim Menzies at the farmers' hops. The two of them riding on the red tractor along the lane. Mr Mackie losing his tenancy, and the family moving across Carnbeg, and Iris walking all the way over some days to be able to chat awhile to Jim. Soon there was news of an engagement, but it was to a girl from the west, and it was as much as Iris could do to get a sight of him, now that Jim Menzies was keeping to himself rather more.

It's an old story, I was told. People usually get over it, that sort of thing.

'And if they don't?' I asked.

The answer came back: 'Then beware.'

I returned to Home Farm for a few days, to see how my uncle was settling down.

Two or three times the phone rang, and when I picked it up and gave the number I heard the line go dead in my ear. It struck me, maybe my presence was starting to become an intrusion?

Uncle Jim had looked out some books my aunt had been lent. Two came from Iris Tinning.

'Would you mind?' he asked me.

Aunt Jean, he explained, hadn't been the quickest reader in the world.

'Don't you want to give them back to her yourself?' I asked.

'No.' He shook his head. 'No, not at the moment.'

He wasn't ready for other people? I wondered. Or he wasn't ready to face a woman he had known for longer than his wife, in that time before?

I phoned Mrs Tinning. 'Could I pop in on my way home?'

I thought I heard a hesitation.

'Yes. Yes, if you like.'

I looked towards the window. Uncle Jim was outside in the yard.

'Maybe we could discuss my uncle,' I heard myself say.

'What . . . ' That hesitation again. 'What is there to discuss?'

'Maybe Aunt Jean was right. It *is* time for him to stop.'

'Stop?'

'Call it quits here,' I said. 'With the farm.'

'That's what *you* think, is it, Mr Spence?'

'I'm trying to work out if it's what my uncle thinks.'

'Have you asked him?'

'Not yet.

'Will you?'

'At some point.'

'I would leave it for now. I really would.'

'Perhaps you're right.'

'Oh, I *am*, Mr Spence.' She sounded in no doubt. 'Now, when will you be dropping by?'

I gave her a time.

'I shall be expecting you.'

I was about to put the phone down when she reminded me, 'I'd just hold your wheesht about the other matter a wee bit longer. That's my advice.'

I thanked her.

'Thank *you*, Mr Spence,' she said with perfect affability, sounding like a different person now.

This time she had a smile already in place to welcome me.

I gave her the books.

Would I join her for tea? she asked.

'I'm very sorry. I have to head off now. It'll be dark in a couple of hours.'

'I quite understand,' she said, not at all surprised or put out. 'Don't you worry, your uncle will be in *our* good hands now.'

I smiled, a little tepidly.

'Oh,' she said as I was at the door. 'Since you've got a long journey, I thought you might like . . . ' She gave me a soft parcel wrapped in tinfoil. ' . . . here.'

'Sandwiches?' I said.

'Yes.'

I told her I was very grateful.

'Well, you might not be if you don't like them,' she laughed.

'Of course I shall,' I said.

I forgot about them, then remembered, and started to eat them on the final stretch of road home. The filling was salmon, the tinned sort, with cucumber slices.

If I'd thought about them sooner, I might have eaten them all.

And then what?

I was rushed to hospital.

Salmonella, I learned afterwards. If I had been less robust, and not so young, if I had polished off all the sandwiches in the package, I might not have survived.

It was a particularly violent strain, and after intensive care, having been in such a bad state – touch-and-go, they said – I knew just how lucky I was.

I continued my recovery at home. My appetite came back only slowly. I found I had an aversion now to fish, and – inconveniently – to bread.

Those bloody sandwiches.

I called my uncle. He picked up the phone. I heard the tail-end of a woman's laughter in the background.

'I've got company in,' he said. 'I'm trying to get back into the swing of things.'

'I'm very glad to hear it,' I said, but not at all sure that I was.

I was listening to the car radio as I made my evaluation rounds. A celebrity chef was talking about apricots.

'Remember now, avoid the stones at all costs, they're poisonous. They've got cyanide in them.'

I nearly drove my car into the nearside sheuch at that.

The next weekend I paid another visit to Carnbeg.

I thought my uncle was going to throw me out of the house once I'd told him of my suspicions.

'You don't know what you're talking about.'

'Please calm down, Uncle Jim.'

'Do something useful, will you?' he snapped at me. 'Pour me a whisky.'

I went into the kitchen. I was taken aback by the tidiness. This wasn't how Aunt Jean, God bless her, had kept it.

I couldn't find the whisky. I opened the flaps of a deep cardboard box. It contained kitchen utensils wrapped in newspaper. They were arranged very neatly. I slipped my hand down. At the bottom, because it was heaviest, was the weight of a mortar and – separately wrapped inside – its pestle.

On the drive back I looked out for Mrs Tinning's cottage. There in the front garden, shameless to the world, was a FOR SALE sign.

I got neighbours to keep me posted.

Which they duly did.

Mrs Tinning's cottage was sold, and she moved out.

She didn't go to claim Home Farm, though. She left Carnbeg, left the area; after all these years, it was as if she'd just vanished into thin air.

Uncle Jim stayed on in the farmhouse. A year ago the local talk had been of the Menzies' moving. But death disposes matters differently.

I went to visit him. The kitchen, I was glad to see, was in disarray. No sign of a mortar and pestle anywhere.

'Have you got over your illness?' he asked.

'I have now.'

'I expect it knocks you out mentally for a while. Makes you see everything from funny angles.'

(That, I realised, was going to be his take on our last conversation: what I had suggested to him, my suspicions, might only have been the after-effects of my illness, and fancy after all.)

I made us both tea. I cut some bread for him, took a couple of cracker biscuits for myself, and fetched the butter from the fridge. In a cupboard I found a new jar of diabetic strawberry jam.

'Open it,' he said.

It tasted awful. But the jar came with a tamperproof seal, and wheezed expressively when I opened it, and I knew that we weren't going to suffer on that score.

We sat at the window, with a view uphill of fields. My uncle seemed withdrawn, but I realised he was watching the sheep.

'No money in that lot,' he sighed.

He didn't say he was going to give up, though.

The acres of land were his recompense, in every sense. Aunt Jean had based her hopes on that. So, too, had Iris Tinning, although for her the farm was undetachable from its owner, the man who strode about it in all weathers.

Why, I wondered, why hadn't he insisted on a police enquiry? Even an exhumation and post-mortem?

Because, in all those country towns, there's always a past which an outsider like you isn't privy to. You surmise it in someone's furrowed brow, the remote look that comes into their eyes.

Another brow was being furrowed, in some town fifty or five hundred miles from here. The eyes had got into the way of narrowing, the mouth was set straighter. It had become the cast of that woman's features, even though she still imagined herself young and loose-limbed, fresh-faced and better than plain for looks, and for ever in love with a farmer's son who only half knew it.

Sugar Candy

It was the last day of their summer holiday.

She was in the hiking-shop on the High Street when she heard the name being taken over the phone.

'Alistair Napier.'

She froze in front of the rack of yellow cagoules.

Alistair Napier. Could it be the same one?

She listened as the shop owner repeated the address.

How long ago was it? Twenty-five years. They'd both been in their late teens.

It must be the same Alistair Napier. After all, it was the same location: this resort town nestling in the hills, a patchwork of grey slate roofs and red rosemary tiles, where families descended for their vigorous summer vacations. A cocktail-partyish sort of place, too, which she and David had resisted returning to as adults until the children clamoured to come, to be with their friends from school. All these Edinburgh and Glasgow lawyers and doctors, and David – being a suburban vet – not properly admitted to the charmed circles.

She walked back from Hi-Trek, along the sober, scrubbed High Street, feeling oddly disturbed. She remembered how, at sixteen or seventeen, she would set off – along the very same High Street – for another of those socials which spinster matchmakers used to organise, where she knew Alistair Napier would be, her heart beating a little faster. They had met at the tennis courts; not really *met* until the third or fourth occasion, until they were formally introduced, after much furtive eyeing one another up and down.

As she remembered now, twenty-five years later, she found she was shaking her head. She stopped herself, then she turned away from some people – a posse of golfers – walking along the pavement towards her. She took refuge in a shady cobbled lane. There, right in front of her, buddleia tumbled voluptuously over a garden wall, and butterflies hovered about the long blue flowerheads, flashing their riotously coloured wings. It was a beautiful omen, she felt.

Back at the house, she couldn't settle.

The others' conversation glanced off her. David's. The children's.

Something about this evening's dress-down party at the New ('Life's a Beach'). And Rhona asking , could *she* go too? And Lorna cutting in, no, she could *not*, you had to be fifteen. (Which was rubbish, and only said to put Rhona in her place.) Rhona looked tearful.

'It doesn't matter, Rhona. Your turn will come.'

'Next summer, Mummy?' Rhona asked.

'Well . . . we'll see, darling.'

Nothing had been decided about next summer. House-lets were very hard to come by in Carnbeg, and jealously protected. As it was, for this summer they'd only got a last-minute cancellation.

'Let's just wait and see, Rhona, shall we?'

When supper had been cleared away, when she could already see the bonfire alight on the playing field for the tennis crowd's barbecue, her thoughts continued to niggle and fret.

Over the years her memory had intermittently drifted back to 'then'. She had wondered What If?, but only vaguely, believing she was stealing precious time from her family.

This evening, though, she couldn't help herself.

She recalled the name of the house that had gone down into Hi-Trek's order-book, and the address. She kept turning them over in her mind.

Over and over.

David announced that he was going to watch football highlights on television.

'I'll take the dog out, then,' she said.

David nodded.

'Yes, all right,' he said back, topping up his glass tankard of lager from the can. (She insisted on glasses to drink from in the house.)

She went to pick up Laddie's lead from the hall table. She halted in front of the wall mirror, pulling at her hair, teasing it back into shape. The sun had bleached it to a lighter shade than usual, so the contrast she was used to between the brown and creeping grey was less obvious. Her skin felt tight and chafed from the long hours of sunshine, but at least she looked . . . well, healthy.

She turned up the collar of her shirt, which the other wives did too. She wondered if she should change out of her madras-check golfing-shorts, but in a fortnight she hadn't even unpacked her skirts.

She found the house where they were staying. The Napiers'.

A converted coach-house, built for one of the spruce greystone Victorian villas.

Twilight was coming on, but she could see quite well.

Swimsuits drying on a rope hung between two apple trees. Bicycles thrown down on to the grass. Discarded tennis rackets. A collapsed deckchair. Empty wine and whisky bottles lined up by the dustbin.

At sixteen, seventeen years old, a gang of them used to haunt the network of wynds and alleyways that connected the houses, the grand and the so-so semi-posh and the upgraded, low-slung former cottars' homes. More and more she had found herself included in Alistair Napier's set.

The second year a Scottish country-dance group was got up. (The spinsters' doing again.) Country-dancing was one of her accomplishments. Strathspeys, reels, jigs. Those funny names they had: 'The Machine without Horses', 'Maxwell's Rant', 'Miss Nancy Frowns', 'Rakes of Glasgow', 'Madge Wildfire', 'Deil amang the Tailors'.

She and Alistair Napier were the best dancers there. Alistair, who played rugby for his school and used weights, but so light and precise on tidy feet on the American pine floor. She knew they danced well together, but that only made her more anxious not to disappoint Alistair: it knotted her stomach every time and squeezed her heart inside her chest, hot-flushed her cheeks. In the overheated hall her nostrils could distinguish the traces of his perspiration from everyone else's, a sweetness combined with an animal (wolfish?) darkness . . .

Her favourite dance was a strathspey, 'Sugar Candy'. She and Alistair were always put first couple. Setting and casting off one place. Passing each other on the left shoulder, then round first corners on the right. Three hands round. Alistair facing up, she facing down. Setting to one another, link hands, a three-quarters turn to face first corners. Right-hand turn, left-hand; right, then left. Threesome reels. Left shoulder, right hand, cross. One place down.

That was 'Sugar Candy'.

She couldn't see anyone in the house. The Napiers' house.

Daylight was starting to fade, there were no lights on indoors. Were they over at the playing-field by any chance?

The car parked outside had a hook for a boat trailer. A DOCTOR ON CALL card was relegated – temporarily – to the shelf under the back window.

Dusk was collecting in the dense trees. The air was cooler, but not chilly. She whistled for Laddie to come, and turned for the town. Sand on the potholed tarmacadam, put down by the Hydro's stables to slow the horses on the hill, crunched under her plimsolls.

All the time she was thinking back, remembering . . .

'Sugar Candy'. The steps of the strathspey, the sensation of movement, she and Alistair Napier . . .

It had gone a little further than dancing. A few kisses, wet kisses. Alistair's tongue prising her teeth apart, flicking into her mouth. A fumble or two, below the belt.

How far *was* it going to go? When the summer was over, she

[53]

wrote to Alistair from Glasgow, and he wrote – shorter letters, and fewer of them – from Edinburgh.

And then the third summer an English family came, all the way from Surrey. There were three daughters, and she lost Alistair – not gradually, but quite suddenly, with no apology offered – she lost him to the middle daughter, who was called Annabel. Annabel with her saw-edged voice and those angular, planed Southern English features.

Annabel couldn't reel or jig, couldn't even do the elementary skip-step, but none of that mattered to Alistair. Annabel was rather uninteresting to her eyes, and predictable, but she had a certain manner about her, a vexing air of self-confidence. She also had the peerless gift of knowing, here in Perthshire just as in Surrey, all the Right People.

Alistair was hooked, hooked good and proper. And all Annabel had to do – a different sort of reeling – was draw in the tasty catch at the end of her line.

She was lost in the recollection of it, her humiliation. She was still hurting a little, feeling ripples and echoes of that original pain.

And so she didn't hear, at first, the footfalls in the dusk. Then – time-travelling twenty-five years in a second or two, zapped back to now, present time – she did hear. At first, ridiculously, she thought it must be Laddie, bounding out of the hedgerow vegetation. (Behind that sound, voices – shouts and laughter – seeped across from the playing-field. The smell of bonfire smoke; barbecue meat grilling, charring.)

No. No, it wasn't a retriever. It was a man. Thick-set, in T-shirt and shorts. Approaching her. He had a moustache.

One of the tennis crowd organisers?

He smiled nicely at her as he ran past in the gentle gloaming, he smiled maybe with embarrassment. She caught an after-whiff of (very) male perspiration. The soles of his sandals slapped on the road.

A few yards farther on, at the corner, some people stood

about in a garden, ready to set off somewhere. Suddenly a voice was pitched over the hedge. It yelled uphill. A woman's voice, with the volume turned up to full.

'Alistair! Don't forget more kebab sticks, will you?'

The accent was Home Counties. Lady of the Manor stuff, 2003-style.

Meanwhile the man went running on up the lane's steep gradient, obedient as a dog. A bald patch shone on the crown of his head. He had a Saturday rugger-player's build, but still – amazingly – he kept light, agile, on those neat dancing feet.

By comparison she felt leaden, dragging herself back home in Laddie's wake.

She saw from the garden that David had dropped off in front of the television. He would wake up when he heard the front door close (he always did), he would deny having slept at all. And if she denied his denial (as she sometimes did), she would hear herself sounding shrewish, suspicious.

She closed the front door behind her, loudly, so that this time David would have the opportunity to compose himself.

(It was the last day of their holiday, she ought to be charitable.)

She unhitched Laddie's lead from his collar.

The football commentators droned on in the sitting-room.

She looked at herself in the wall mirror above the hall table. She was surprised, briefly, not to see a seventeen-year-old girl looking back at her.

She reviewed herself critically.

She didn't much care for what was there.

A 42-year-old vet's wife, dutiful daughter to a difficult mother, mother herself of three wilful children.

The grey in her hair was still quite obvious after all. The Highland tan on her skin made her face look rounder, fuller, and – frankly – not very intelligent.

Still keeping watch on the mirror she stepped back, to the staircase, climbing backwards up the first three, four treads, so that she could get the whole picture.

The racy madras-check golfing-shorts didn't flatter her. The hips. That bottom. Her legs went down straight, the wrong kind of straightness, creases of skin gave her podgy knees. Her ankles were too thick.

She sat down on the staircase, on the runner of carpet, so that she didn't have to see herself any longer. She leaned against the banister posts, closed her eyes, ignored the television voices.

In her mind's eye Alistair Napier with his moustache was still running up the lane in T-shirt and shorts, thickset and so agile on his feet, doing that woman's bidding, running on and on into the dusk. (And not a flicker of recognition for *her*.)

She found herself humming a snatch of the tune they'd done that strathspey to. 'Sugar Candy'. Fancy remembering. She hadn't country-danced for years. But she still knew all the steps, all the turns, in her head.

'Sugar Candy'. Something sweet. An instant energy-boost, they would call it now.

'Su–gar Can–dy'. Enticement and temptation.

But even sweetness, too much of it, palls.

(Oh, how despondent she felt with her middle-aged sensibleness. She knew the truth of it, though.)

She opened her eyes. Heard the television football pundits again. Slowly, knees cracking, she pulled herself to her feet. She straightened up. Fidgeted with the string of little pearls circling her throat, Granny's pearls, the garnerings of long-dead South Sea divers.

She had another load of washing to go in. And some ironing from yesterday still to finish, her blouses, which she didn't trust to David, who set the temperature on the iron too high.

(Who ironed Alistair Napier's T-shirts and shorts? Here in Carnbeg Annabel would send out, she guessed, using the silver-and-blue van that did a door-to-door service, and – another old Surrey habit – charging to account.)

Tonight, like any of those occasional memory jolts over the years, had been a blip. These were the final hours of their summer holiday, so there wouldn't be another chance.

She reminded herself, candy is for just once in a while. It's duller fare which nourishes us, gives us our protein, vitamins, minerals.

Real-life living.

Husband, children, dog, the mortgage or the rent, the routine. From day to day, that's how we survive.

And she started to climb the stairs.

A View of the River

The Shepherds had always said they would retire to Carnbeg.

The town was filled with retired folk, but there were good reasons for that: the mildness of the spot, the unpolluted air, the fact that people were still courteous to one another, proper shops on the High Street instead of supermarkets and out-of-town warehouses in vast car parks.

All Elaine and Colin had to do was find a house. It took them several years, because a fair number of properties changed hands without being advertised. They had first thought of somewhere at the back of the town, up on the wooded roads behind the High Street, but it occurred to them that the climbs up and down the gradients wouldn't become any easier, and so they turned their thoughts to the other end of Carnbeg, down by the river.

Yes, they increasingly liked the notion of the river, running past the end of the garden.

Eventually a house did come up for sale. They were on to it at once. A bungalow, in a small development. South-facing public rooms away from the cul-de-sac road; a decent-sized but manageable garden, which went down to the river-bank.

It turned out the owner had died, and died on the premises, which Elaine would have preferred hadn't been the case; but Colin shrugged; it was a plus to him, because it meant they could make their inspections this time without having to exchange small talk with the vendor.

There was the usual risk in submitting an offer, not knowing if they were bidding too high. But when their offer was accepted they decided against trying to find out how many other bids had gone in, and how much above the asking price they had been.

Instead they celebrated their good luck, splashing out on a bottle
of champagne.

The bungalow – called Carn-How – was fifteen years old, which
meant neither new nor old. A halfway house, so to speak. It was
in quite good condition: serviceable. They redecorated it, however, so that it would seem more theirs than the previous
owner's.

Sunlight filled the back rooms, yet there was always a slight
chill on the other side, which faced north, even with the central
heating turned up. From the sitting-room at the rear, and the
connecting dining-room, and from one of the kitchen windows,
they looked down the sloping garden towards the river. Thank-
fully they still had open fields on the other side, and a further
view to hills and sunsets.

Elaine had envisaged a new Perthshire life of gardening, and
walks, and matinées at the theatre during the season, and an
occasional round on the public golf course. Maybe they would
join a few of the town's societies. She had supposed their days
would be very full.

There was *some* of that. But two years on in Carn-How she
felt that Colin's idea of retirement wasn't chiming with her own.
He seemed to do a lot of sitting down, at the sunny back
windows or out on the garden bench: just sitting and looking at
the river. She knew she had to be careful what she said, because
retirement is a sore issue with many men. It comes as a blow to
them, to their self-esteem, and it flags the loss of some physical
vigour. She realised that Colin already wasn't so comfortable
with the short walks into and out of town, and that he was
taking the car for the quarter-mile to the newsagent's. Even the
newspapers didn't get read so thoroughly; he seemed to lose
interest, and put them down in order to watch the river instead.

When she asked him, he told her, for every second of looking
at it the river is different. Yes and no, she thought: because
really it's the effect which counts, and that was usually the

same, except when the water was high and loud or when it was briefly darkened by a fall of soil or mud farther up.

But Colin's fascination never wavered.

'What are you looking at, Colin?' she would ask him, following the track of his eyes.

'Nothing much,' he might say.

But he continued to watch, just as keenly as the herons that sometimes flew past to fish the higher reaches. Could he see something she couldn't?

'Nothing much?' she would repeat.

'Just the view,' he would say, as if that accounted for everything.

Where the bungalows were, the river moved quickly, the current was agitated as it turned the corner and passed over big stones; a mile or so farther upstream the river was slower, more spacious, it calmed and soothed. Which would have suited Elaine, but not Colin, who liked the continual hurry of water and the sounds of slapping on stone.

She was forever trying to rouse him, to enthuse him about going out and doing something different.

'Doing what?'

'Whatever you like, Colin.'

'Whatever *you* like, you mean.'

'Well, I'm giving you the chance to say.'

'You're interrupting.'

'Interrupting what, for God's sake?'

'Never mind. I'm fine, Elaine.'

But I'm not, she wanted to shout at him.

She didn't care for the way he was growing more irritable with her; it crossed her mind that this was him starting to ignore her altogether. I must be cautious what I do, she thought, but I've got to break the spell of whatever has got hold of him.

She came home from the shops one day, let herself into the house, and when she walked into the sitting-room Colin was sitting upright in his armchair, looking out at the river, and quite dead.

Heart disease took him off, the hospital told her. Somehow it had gone undiagnosed. It wasn't surprising, perhaps, that no one should have seen, given Colin had a man's pride in not going to see a doctor. She had been wondering over the past few weeks, watching him yet again looking out of the window or across the garden from their crazy-paving terrace, just how much was repressed, bottled up inside him.

The same question. 'What are you looking at, Colin?'

The same reply. 'Nothing much. Just the view.'

One time time she noticed that he lifted his hand, as if he was about to wave to someone. Then he realised she was there, and dropped his hand to the chair arm. It happened another day, as she was looking out of the garage window and he was slowly, tiredly, hoeing a border; Colin looked up, half straightened, and raised his arm. But she saw no one to wave *to*. None of their neighbours was gardening; across the river some sheep grazed, and that was all.

Midges, she supposed. It was an instinct to raise your hand and flap them away. The only real drawback to Carnbeg living, which of course they never told you about in the estate agents' brochures.

Carnbeg living, and now Carnbeg death.

Elaine Shepherd was having to adjust to widowhood.

The practicalities occupied her in the short term. Her neighbours, who had tended to keep their distance from Colin, were well-meaning and kind. But after a while she felt they were becoming a little too obtrusive, and she began to understand why Colin hadn't encouraged them.

Sometimes she didn't answer the phone or go to see who was at the door. In the garden she used a night of high winds and the damage it did as an excuse to get new fences; she couldn't really afford them, but what price could she put on her privacy? So the fences were sunk, sturdier than before and higher, and she planted quick-growing greenery as an additional excluding screen.

She would sit where Colin used to sit, on the crazy-paving terrace, looking down at the river. It was true, something about that view – the timelessness of it – your present-moment concerns fell away. You became less inclined to get up and do. It was as if there were two realities: the world's hurly-burly in the newspapers, and this slow-motion one spread around you in one small corner of Carnbeg. You focused on the flowers, the profusion of greenery that hid the fences, the mossy lawn, the trees, the sheep grazing, the heather-clad hills, the paint-box sunsets: all this contained placidity. The speed of the river smoothed out to a silver sheen. It even got to the point that when her niece phoned and started talking about internet shopping she found herself agreeing to let Hazel put in a weekly order for her with a supermarket down in Perth, and have it delivered.

That wasn't what Elaine had once thought of as 'retirement', but back at that time she'd had a husband and they'd considered themselves hilltop people, not riverside. *Tempora mutantur.*

And then one day she saw him. A man in a boat. A flat-bottomed black slipper-shaped boat, between a punt and a gondola without the prow.

The man was using a long pole to make his way downstream. She couldn't tell how old he was. He was dressed neatly in shirt and trousers, and wearing a straw hat; as he passed he looked up at the terrace and lifted his hand, tipped the hat's brim.

Elaine started to raise her hand. The stranger waited to see her response before turning back to what he was doing, pushing on the pole and steering himself away.

It happened another three times.

She mentioned to Mr McKenzie, in the house next door, she'd seen a man going past. A man in shirt and trousers, who wore a straw hat. It was the first boat she'd seen.

'A fisherman?' she wondered aloud.

'I've never seen them this side of the bridge,' her neighbour, an occasional fisherman himself, said. 'Did he have a rod with him?'

Elaine shook her head.

'A net?'

'Not that I could see,' she replied.

'Maybe it was a kayak or something?'

'Oh no.'

'It's fast water, that,' Mr McKenzie said. 'And the stones. You couldn't even if you wanted to.'

He looked at her sympathetically, as if he thought she might have dreamed of the boatman, and forgotten she'd been dozing, catnapping, at the time.

'Well, it doesn't matter,' she smiled back falsely at Mr McKenzie.

Hazel came to visit.

When they were both in the kitchen, the boat passed again.

'Who is it?' Hazel called across from the cooker.

'What?'

'I thought you were waving.'

'There's a man in a boat, a sort of punt.'

'Where?'

Maybe Hazel didn't realise where she was pointing, because as she stood in front of the window she said she couldn't see anyone.

'A punt?'

'Something like that.'

'But it's not that kind of river, sweetie,' Hazel laughed, treating it in her bright and breezy worldly way as her aunt's wee joke.

Elaine saw him again, as she anticipated she would.

She knew she had to warn him that the river was too fast for him.

She called out from the back door. He heard her, and looked up towards the house. She ran outside, ran down across the lawn, over the springy, neglected turf. She thought, oh my God, he's bound to have got away by the time I reach him. Her

[63]

heart was ready to burst inside her chest. (It did occur to her, let him go, watch him from the garden seat, there'll be another chance . . .) She was winded by the effort of running all that way to the water's edge, she was left struggling for breath. For a few moments white flares fell in front of her eyes, her head reeled.

He was standing somewhere in front of her, in his boat. She struggled to get her focus.

She couldn't see his face because of the straw hat's brim. Also, he had the setting sun behind him. She could tell he was a man in his prime, tall and broad-shouldered, with the strength in his arms to steer himself along the river.

But now, instead of exchanging words, he was holding out his hand to her. He meant to show her the boat, she supposed. She was in half a mind to stay where she was, on dry land, but she suddenly wanted to talk to him about Colin: did he remember seeing her late husband? She missed having Colin here so much, he used to be forever watching the river view from . . .

She stepped, a little unsteadily, into the boat. There was a seat in the middle, and she lowered herself on to it, facing forward.

The pole dropped into the water. The boat inched away from the bank. It felt colder on the water, she realised she needed an extra woollen.

But it was too late to go and fetch one.

She looked back at the garden, and noticed someone sitting on the bench, a woman, of her own age. She was motionless: no, not quite, she was tipping slowly sideways.

She turned round to ask the man, it's the oddest thing, if you look up at the terrace there – But in the split second before the hat brim's shadow fell and shaded his face, she saw the shocking and unspeakable truth: the yellow flesh rotting on the man's skull and the hollowed-out eye sockets.

Terror completely froze her.

She had ice in her veins. She couldn't reach out to save herself, to grab at the trailing tree branches.

She couldn't even feel her own heartbeat.

The pole dropped again, steering the boat out into rocky midstream. Silently the river roared beneath them, carrying all away.

Oats and Beans and Barley-O

We very nearly had a brush with the revolution.

Or, should I say, if the revolution had ever rolled north, as far as Perthshire, Carnbeg would have been one of the hot spots. Not that any of the rest of us were particularly caring, but we had the Ingrams in our midst – briefly, for those two or three years – ready to pledge themselves as martyrs to the cause.

I'm talking about the first half of the 1970s, which is like prehistory now. And I'm talking only about a shop, not a political upheaval of the sort happening fitfully elsewhere in Europe. But it was a shop in a small country town, and not like any other shop there, in that conservative backwater in the lush Grampian foothills where we suburbanite adolescents came with our parents to spend our long summers.

The new owners supervised the structural alterations of the Misses Wylie's old-fashioned haberdashery into a retro-mode provisioner of health foods. The wooden floors and panelling were retained, but sanded back so that the final effect as we snooped through the window was – how can I put it? – of an overexposed photograph after years of knowing only the negative.

On Glebe Street the name went up on the signboard in fashionable Gaelic script: The Girnel. A consultation with a Scots dictionary in the local library told us that a girnel was a storage bin for flour or meal. Bins of the same duly appeared in the shop, and sacks of oats and barley and lentils, pulses galore, and more sacks of nuts and dried fruits. 'And now,' we joked, 'the winds of change are going to blow through Carnbeg, too!'

The owners were a couple without wedding-rings but who shared a surname – Ingram – for convenience's sake.

They were in their mid-thirties or thereabouts when they arrived, but acted younger. Quite well-spoken, products of private schools (hers a boarding-school), which satisfied the more snobbish among our parents. He had a trimmed beard, and wore Moroccan or Cossack-style shirts with blue jeans, and sturdy pale pig-leather zipped boots concealed beneath the flares. She, a little plumper, favoured long, woven skirts and cheesecloth tops, and heavy clogs. They were suddenly the most up-to-date people in Carnbeg, and we wondered how on earth Inverness had produced them and not Glasgow or Edinburgh, where novelty counts for more.

It wasn't exactly a matter of 'image', though, as smart Glaswegians would have called it. The Ingrams gave every indication of genuinely believing in this alternative life-style of theirs.

'Hi, I'm Robbie,' Mr Ingram introduced himself to us over the sack of buckwheat groats. 'And this is Alice.'

His wife with her voluminous perm beamed at us. 'Hi!'

A mite surprisingly to us, she shook our hands; hers had a strong grip. We might have been guests socialising at a cocktail party, and Robbie felt constrained to shake hands likewise.

'Remember,' he said, 'remember, Euan, Lorna, Scott – *we're* Robbie and Alice. See you at the revolution.'

What revolution? We didn't ask, but it didn't matter; we just felt honoured to have been acknowledged, and to be treated by the pair like adults.

In the shop Joni Mitchell played on the tape machine, which was a step beyond Carole King at the Pine 'n' Art gallery and even Carly Simon at Perth's new boutique, the Raspberry Happening.

In those initial days we were welcome browsers, when the Ingrams were fresh to homespun Carnbeg and when their way of life seemed to be fulfilling their hopes. We were innocents, all of us: well, not quite innocents but almost.

[67]

The Ingrams set up home in a cottage of a traditional sort on the edge of the town. In the bay window they placed a rattan peacock-chair with a fan back, which obscured the view of the interior from the road. The back and side gardens had been turned over to vegetables and were set out with canes and wigwams of netting. (We presumed they must be vegetables, of an unknown sort.) A collection of Tibetan wind bells chimed from the eaves. The original stained-glass front door, recessed in the vestibule, was covered on sunny days, not by a striped canvas screen as was the custom but by strings of threaded beads.

We repeatedly walked past the house, not at all by chance. We observed the new name being painted on the latch gate, Karma Cottage. We heard music wafting through the open windows: a more extreme choice than was played in the shop, Janis Joplin and (so I was told) the Grateful Dead. Over the hedge we saw their friends, men with Zappa–Zapata moustaches and women with Medusa ringlet manes, sitting cross-legged on the lawn or on the slats of two swings hung on ropes from the pear tree.

Sometimes in the shop Robbie was forgetful, sometimes Alice couldn't stop laughing and struggled to keep her balance on her clogs. Robbie would slur his words, Alice would seem to have difficulty reading what was in front of her. It was hard for them both some days distinguishing between the types of bean, aduki or mung or foule, and even telling nuts from dried apricots or prunes. One afternoon Robbie asked a succession of his middle-aged customers who were coming round to this healthy-eating idea, 'What am I doing here, d'you know?' before blithely walking off into the back room and leaving them unattended.

'Trouble Child', 'Kosmic Blues', 'Ball and Chain', 'For the Roses', 'Cryptical Envelopment', 'A Woman Left Lonely', 'Quadlibet for Tender Feet', 'A Lesson in Survival' . . .

'You've got a very productive garden, haven't you?' an elderly resident remarked to the Ingrams in the shop one day.

'Oh, we don't grow all this,' Robbie replied, waving at the sacks.

'No, I mean what grows up your canes. Fairly sprints up, doesn't it?'

Alice laughed. Robbie stared at her, then turned to stare at the man.

'It's your compost, I expect. You feed your stuff well?'

'Oh yes, we do,' Robbie said, scratching his close beard. Alice laughed again, not seeing or failing to heed her husband's warning shake of the head.

'Good advertisement for the shop, young man.'

'Yes?'

'Green fingers. You two knowing what's good for us.'

Alice spluttered laughter into the floury sleeve of her smock. Robbie leaned over, grabbed her other arm, and pushed her behind the Welsh dresser, into the nook where they kept the book of accounts they had been obliged to start for all the customers who wouldn't pay cash. She wasn't silenced, but Robbie was able to contain the damage at that, and when the man went off and promptly spilled the beans – so to speak – to his friends, he recounted the wife's queer behaviour and the young fellow's gentlemanly courtesy to him.

It was known that there was a list of customers who had 'special orders'. It was only a small number, but social stratification didn't have much to do with their esoteric tastes. When they came into the shop they were ushered past the run-of-the-mill customers, past the stripped-pine dresser and into the back room.

There was a young farmer's wife out of a beat-up Mini-Moke; a Monet-lookalike artist up from London; a schoolmaster from a prep school; a widow with her own printing-press; a garage mechanic; a local landowner's son and heir.

For the rest of us it was oats and beans and barley, bulgar wheat and millet, (bought-in) granary and wholemeal and rye loaves, nuts shelled and otherwise, black Barbados molasses and agar-agar, a culinary voyage of discovery which was really just a return to the cannier diet of our ancestors.

'In the Forest of the Highland Kings.'

I was sure that was what Robbie was saying. He repeated it over and over to himself as he put my mother's order together one day, while I stood by the counter waiting, pretending to be distracted by the posters for meditation and self-awareness programmes.

Robbie smiled at me as he totted up, then he tried adding up again, subtracted a little. At last he seemed just to pluck a round figure out of the air, in my favour. As I was leaving the shop his parting salvo to me was, 'Don't forget now, my friend. Get your preparations made, the revolution's on its way!'

They took on an assistant for the shop, and subsequently things went less well for the Ingrams.

When she came to work there, the girl could have passed for Carnbeg normal. After several weeks she had acquired frizzy orange hair, and purple fingernails, and stick-on silver paper stars on her brow and cheeks and neck. The stars had a habit of falling off whenever she was called on to do any stretching and bending down; nothing flustered her, though, as befitted someone who had re-christened herself Heaven.

And then we noticed that the cottage's cultivated side garden – and probably the back one also – had been dug up overnight. What was the point of that? All the stakes and climbing-frames had come down, the plants were uprooted and nowhere to be seen.

Also, not overnight but in a matter of a week or ten days, Alice assumed more external gravitas in her manner. She no longer laughed so readily in the shop, but watched us carefully with her eyes narrowed; now quite steady on her clogs, she was keeping all her wits about her.

The business of staff – viz. Heaven, aka Morag McBain – became a bone of contention between the Ingrams.

Alice patently wasn't happy, and would enquire of customers whether they had found recent service 'disappointing' for any reason, meaning Heaven in particular. People often heard the pair having words about how much or how little the girl was doing; and several times the door into the back room was firmly closed, when their conversation took a more personal turn.

Heaven, who had developed Robbie Ingram's habit of vagueness, managed to be rather more vigilant whenever any of the select customers came in for their special orders. She mentioned those visits to her pals in the town, with a reasonable degree of detail. When Alice Ingram discovered this, Heaven was there and then given her cards.

Three days later, an extremely awkward scene took place. The girl sat out on the kerb in front of the shop for most of the morning and half the afternoon, crying her eyes out. This very public spectacle didn't convince the couple they'd been correct in doing what they had done; quite the opposite, in fact; they decided they'd been over-hasty in getting rid of her. Net result: Heaven was reinstated.

To the ordinary customers it was noticeable that the girl who attended to them (if that was the term) was considerably vaguer than before. She was more cheerful, however, and there were gummy silver stars in plenty, like an infestation which had reached the tops of her bare thin arms.

The Ingrams' accounting system appeared to be quite haphazard. No more credit was being given to the no-cash brigade, although they sometimes accepted payment in kind – firewood or peat or paraffin, DIY materials, ducks' feathers to stuff cushions and pillows, kiln-thrown pots, or wool newly carded and slubbed off the sheep's back.

The couple freely helped themselves to whatever they needed out of the till, taking care since Heaven's re-employment that they used the key to unlock it and then lock it up again.

Their arithmetic was still approximate. Customers invariably disputed the sums, at any rate when they exceeded expectations – which, to be fair to the Ingrams, happened no more often than under-charging.

Presumably suppliers received *their* payments, although

when the phone rang in the back room a code of nods, shakes, twitches and tics exchanged over customers' heads between the Ingrams and Heaven communicated just what she should say to whoever was calling.

'Och, we get by,' Robbie replied to those tedious husbands sent shopping by their wives, whose only small talk was about business, turnover, profit.

The revolution, when it came, was clearly going to be financial chaos: but who cared? The world would still keep turning on its axis.

Heaven swapped dungarees for looser trousers, then for a still looser shift, and it was evident to all that she was pregnant. She was getting very muddled indeed with orders; her bloodless pallor suggested she would have benefited from a hearty meal of butcher's meat, or at least from the application of more sticky-backed silver stars. But she was starting to forget about the stars, too, and her fingernails were chipped and less purple, the frizzy orange hair was straightening and darkening from its roots.

Curiouser and curiouser – simultaneously Alice had discovered orthodox dressing. The clogs vanished, and were replaced by espadrilles, and even by a pair of black court shoes and a pair of buckled navy kid loafers, worn with tights over shaved legs. She'd had her hair cut very short gamine-style at a salon in Perth, and had bought some stylish knee-length dresses and a trouser suit which flattered her slimmer figure. It was in Perth that she was spotted with one of the select customers, the landowner's son and heir, Lachlan Bonnar, walking along John Street with her arm linked through his for all to see.

And it was to Perth that Alice Ingram went later, to make the physical break with Robbie which formally initiated The End.

She spent a week in a hotel, sharing a room with Bonnar, who was paying their bill.

At the week's end the infatuated scion drove her back to his father's estate outside Carnbeg, and by then the relationship was official.

Some afternoons The Girnel was closed, when Robbie Ingram's rage got the better of him, or when he was too depressed to face any more of those middle-class shopping-lists.

He accused several customers to their faces of holding up the revolution, of using people like him to unblock their constipation and clear their bowels, and he told them he was tired, heartsick, of being shat upon.

The cuckolded Robbie must have realised that he couldn't object too strongly about what had happened. The estranged Alice knew things: they all knew things about one another. He, Robbie; she, Alice; her lover, Bonnar; mother-to-be Heaven. A circle which had well and truly squared itself.

One Sunday morning Robbie threw Alice's things out of the cottage.

Word reached her and she appeared at lunchtime, driving Lachlan Bonnar's open-topped MG. Robbie caught sight of her arriving; he untied the bead curtain in the vestibule, and then locked and bolted the front door. He preferred to communicate with her from the moral high ground of an upstairs dormer window. Worshippers on their way back from the town's kirks were able to hear them, every word.

He rained down his taunts on her. She didn't respond at first, but picked up her belongings from the grass verges where drivers and pedestrians had been laying them all morning. She extracted clothes, her former style of dressing, from the top of the yellow privet hedge. Eventually she did find her voice, and she gave full vent to it.

'But there isn't going to *be* a sodding revolution,' she shouted up.

'How do *you* know?'

'I just know.'

'Like hell you do.'

'And *you* wouldn't know it if you fell over it, Robbie Ingram.'

'What does that mean?'

'You want me to tell you in front of everyone?'

With a titan's strength he flung some wooden coathangers from the window. They cleared the hedge and clattered on to the road, narrowly missing her.

'As if they don't know already,' she called up to him.

'You've got a tiny mind. Just like them.'

'And *you're* out of yours.'

'Ha bloody ha.'

'So that'll make two of you, Robbie. Or three. You, her and the wee sprog.'

'I *knew* you'd say that.'

'How's she going to run the shop? Have you thought of that?'

'And how're you going to get anywhere with his lordship? Have you thought of *that*?'

Robbie had started to believe that the town was ganging up on him. He told his regular customers that *they* were the ones who were trying to put him out of business. Even the friends, 'guys' with walrus moustaches and 'chicks' with Afros, had vamoosed. He saw spies out there on Glebe Street, snitches and finks, skulking past his front window several times in an hour.

Then the true enemy revealed himself.

He was called Erskine, from Perth, and he represented the bank that had given the Ingrams a loan to help finance setting up the shop. He was also in contact with the landlord, who was owed five months' rent.

Mr Erskine was politeness personified, but his client told him to go and fuck himself, which assisted affairs not a whit.

'And when the revolution comes, amigo, you'll be the first to know it. Just mark my words.'

Something about being strung up from a lamppost, some-thing else about eternal bog-cleaning duty, but Mr Erskine didn't dally long enough to hear any more.

The whole population was ranged against him, Robbie Ingram was quite certain of that.

Before the shop was repossessed, he exacted his revenge. Not that any of us appreciated the situation until later.

Dotted about Carnbeg in respectable households where sensible eating-habits were encouraged, strange effects were experienced. Light-headedness, a feeling of contentment and tranquillity but also of vast personal potential, a conviction that anything was within your grasp and accomplishment. Standing on your head, getting the hang of advanced calculus, singing louder than Tom Jones, bursting the atom apart, juggling with three eggs, levitation, scoring for Scotland against England at Murrayfield, walking on water.

Why so?

Into a batch of wholemeal loaves (baked 'exclusively' in the next strath) The Girnel's nominal proprietor had tipped several scoops of an additional ingredient, the best quality his 'speciality' suppliers could provide. Rather a waste, of course; but his privileged customers – the A-list – were keeping their distance; alerted to renewed police interest, and with the net tightening around him, what did he have to lose? Let Carnbeg wake up to what it had been missing out on.

Alice tired of waiting for the brave new world.

Against the odds she married the landowner's son.

A happy ending? Perhaps.

Afterwards her life was to be quite different. She had one, two, three children, the couple employed a nanny and a housekeeper. She attended stock shows and cattle auctions in Perth. She filled out, and was rarely seen without a silk square on her head, and she looked very much of a muchness with the other landowners' wives. Her husband was due to inherit the estate in time, so everyone was respectful to her; if anybody recalled who she used to be, it didn't signify now.

Meanwhile . . .

Robbie ran away, he absconded.

No one from the town set eyes on him again, although reports did filter back that he had joined a first and then a second commune up north, the sort of alternative society where the paid-up members share everything and venerate the mushroom.

But I *should* prefer to regard him more heroically, and give him his due. And so, for me, sometimes he still flies Chagall-like over Carnbeg, not a day older than he was, and looking down on us as he inclines a little awkwardly with flares flapping and Cossack shirt ballooning. The revolution has yet to take place, but never mind; to its *aficionados* a certain species of forest mushroom when eaten raw confers the quality of infinite patience. Overhead Robbie Ingram flies his patient aerial loops, imagining that he knows so much more than we do or ever shall, although for the moment he forgets just what about.

The Chimes

It was a dark and stormy night.

The radio in the dashboard crackled with interference. As she drove she tried to reset the buttons, but they wouldn't obey her. Her hand felt oddly heavy and inert. She looked at it, as if she couldn't be certain that it really was hers. An old woman's hand, with those brown marks on the back. The 'flowers of death', they were sometimes called.

She shifted her eyes back to the road, tried to concentrate. Leaves swirled in the track of her headlights; leaves, twigs, a branch or two. Through the radio sizzle she heard the wind roaring.

Ye gods, she caught herself thinking, and wondered when she'd stopped using that expression of her girlhood, her schooldays, so long ago. It was a night for the gods to be angry.

She had been in two minds whether or not to set out, and then she had. She wasn't sure why it had been so important that it should be now, on such a wild night.

The interference on the radio cleared for a while, just long enough for her to hear the newsreader's voice. Local news: about an accident on the road. A tree had been uprooted, and had toppled over, falling on to a moving car and crushing it.

Ye gods, the expression came back to her again, unbidden. It seemed to be the only reaction that she *could* have. Why were such horrors allowed? A tree torn out of the ground and flattening a car? Ah, but it was done to test our faith, to mock our expectations of God. Or something like that.

The clarity on the radio, that little patch of respite, vanished, the sizzle washed over it, and she lost contact with the voice again.

Through the windscreen she recognised the old landmarks from years ago, from so many years ago that it might have been another woman's life and not her own. It was – what? – two decades since she had been back to Carnbeg, but there they were. The four-ways sign at the crossroads. The mounting-stone, where riders used to get up on to their horses. The dip in the red road, which always used to fill with water like a ford. The doocot. She thought she saw the flutter of white doves' wings. Were they back, too? When she was a girl there had been doves, but then for some reason they'd gone, and the roosting-boxes had stayed empty, and the structure had fallen into disrepair. Years ago, so long ago. And now, was it possible that, with white wings flashing, they were back?

She was, very nearly, back herself. Back home.

The woman in the estate agents' had said, 'Certainly you should go and see the house, there's no one staying there, they've moved out.' The woman, with her frosted hair and chilly smile, had said she would make an exception and give her the keys. Character references weren't necessary in *her* case, a famous novelist and so forth. (As if she had ever read a single word she'd written!) But her supposed 'fame' had done the trick. It opened the door, so to speak. And the keys, with a tag and the name of the house, were handed to her.

'But you may have to wait a while, madam. It looks like a rough night to come.'

Her own family home, up for sale again. After all these years. Maybe the opportunity had come too late, though. What she would have given when she was younger, in her literary prime, to have been able to make a bid for the place, to prove that sometimes black sheep can make good. She'd had the money, she'd made discreet enquiries but the owners weren't selling. And now they were, and she knew this was meant to happen. Standing in the estate agents' office in Perth she had understood perfectly well that – blustery weather or not – she would be making the journey down in the car this same evening, not just to inspect the unoccupied house but to claim it back for herself.

At any rate, she had been expecting to find the house empty. But when she turned into the driveway, several lights were on, and the rooms – she saw through the windows – were still furnished.

She parked the car. The same gravel driveway. Although the wind blew, nipping at her ankles, and leaves crackled as they spun, she found she was advancing effortlessly towards the front door, with all her limbs in coordination. She was surprised, very briefly, because this was the season when her arthritis was always dependably bad. But of course her mind was focused on this and nothing else, on reaching the door, and putting the key into the lock: it's about mind over matter, isn't it?

The door opened easily. The same door, the same old lock.

For a moment she found she was thinking – why? – of the news item, when the radio in the dashboard had temporarily cleared. About the car crushed beneath the weight of the uprooted tree. About a journey someone hadn't been able to complete.

She walked in.

The door banged shut behind her in the wind, and she jumped.

She needed a few moments to settle again.

She walked forward, into the middle of the hall.

'Hello?'

She called towards the downstairs rooms that were lit.

'Hello?'

Her voice sounded peculiarly light. Not timid or nervous, not at all. But somehow weightless, as if she wasn't this person who had always had a rather grave manner older than her years and who had gone on to confound everyone by earning herself a little fame.

Nobody replied.

Hmmm.

Was someone else in the building?

Foolish for a woman alone, of course. But where should she feel safer than in the house where she'd grown up?

She looked into one lit room, which used to be their sitting-room.

The furnishings were the ones she had grown up with, too. Plus a few things which her parents had bought later, once she had left home – so eager to get away. To make a life for herself, to think her own thoughts. The furniture might have been bought along with the house, and yet – surely that sideboard and that wing-chair had found their way into the flat her parents moved to: the shrinking, cramped flat. And the painting of the cornfield, the field in late summer just after harvesting, that had also gone with them. Yes, she was sure, quite sure. But the painting was back on the wall; and the sideboard and chair were back in place on the old threadbare Turkey carpet.

She retreated to the hall.

Hmmm.

She ran her hand over the carved serpent's head at the end of the staircase banister. It had taken her half her childhood to cure herself of her terror of the thing. Now she started following its long, smooth, trailing back. Up one half-flight of stairs, then another.

Her parents' bedroom. Her sister Marion's. Her brother Andrew's. And her own.

She pushed on the door, that one certain door, and it opened, it pulled back. In the semi-dark she smelled the room, the past, and that's how she knew it was true.

Why do the British mistrust smell so much, she wondered, even more than the other senses? A smell, an aroma, a fragrance will ambush you, shanghai you all that long way back to somewhere and sometime. It won't be denied.

A smell of – what? – the old leather rocking-horse, whose outline she could just make out. And the bag of pot pourri, which had been a present from a great-aunt she hadn't wanted to offend, so the pot pourri had always hung there behind the door, sickly sweet – and the dusty non-smell of the embarrassingly pink bedspread . . .

And there was the spindly-legged chair with the cushion, the same ripped gingham cushion placed on the cane seat. This was where whoever had come to see her to bed would sit, by the bedside, trying to cure her fear of the dark by confronting it in a story.

'It was a dark and stormy night . . . '

All her life since then had been given over to making stories. Why? Perhaps because, as a girl growing up, she saw too much: saw the minutiae that others overlooked, the insignificances that weren't. Because she glimpsed into rooms before the doors quite closed, she picked up bits of conversations not intended for her to hear. Always it was her mother and father to whom these stories came back: two people who had begun their married life happily enough, but who had ended up thinking they were caged together in this house.

Up another floor.

She stepped into the loft. Found the light cord, just where it always used to be, pulled it. There in front of her was her brother's model-railway layout.

She walked round the big trestle table. Papier-mâché hills and tunnels, little villages, farms. She leaned forward at one point, examining some activity on a road. A wirework-and-foam tree lay on top of a car. A green car, much the same colour as hers. She stared at the model accident, perturbed for some reason. For a few seconds she was gripped by a feeling of cold; she shivered, into her heavy camel coat, into the depths of her turtle-neck.

Nearby, a small church made out of balsawood. She screwed up her eyes, noticing the tiny foil-covered bells set inside the belfry, positioned as if they were ringing. She had never been religious, but she had always felt the loss of it in her life. Peeling bells/tolling bells, what was the difference? She couldn't tell.

Bells . . . She straightened up, listened, listened very carefully. Up here the wind crawled over the roof like a clumsy lion, rattling the tiles; it rumbled its roar down the chimney flue. But through the loud effects she could hear – yes, she *could* make out the sound of bells.

Wind-chimes.

No, it couldn't be. Her mother had had the chimes pulled down when her father was away on another of his business trips. The chimes had been a present from two of their friends: the Rennies, he so solid and decent and she such a live-wire. The chimes were thrown into the dustbin. Her father wanted to know why.

'You can ask me that?' her mother snapped back. 'And I suppose every time you hear them,' she accused him, 'you can think of — '

The door had been shut at that point. But the scene was branded on her mind. The world was revealed to her, at sixteen years old, in all its fickle complexity. And all her life since she had been recovering from the incident, as she tried to refashion that past.

Downstairs again.

She made a mental note. The keys. I must hold on to those damn keys and not mislay them.

But then it was as if she had interference in her head, and a memory, so close to her that it might have been happening now, at this precise moment. The shrieking of roots as a tree was wrenched out of the ground by the wind. Flailing branches. The mass of the tree already crashing down a split second ahead of her. The car's windscreen smashing, blurring to white. The roof of the cabin cracking. And then . . .

But how *could* she remember, when that was the moment at which she'd lost her life, *that* life, the experience which belonged to the topmost surface of time?

There was another life, though, at least another one life: which endured, and was constant. It had its own logic. Its own weather, maybe. Night-wind which felled trees. But which mysteriously blew out again, because she couldn't hear it now: the wind, the invisible lion clambering over the roof. The silvery chimes were silenced.

The sitting-room where she was was reflected in the lit windows, a duplicate of this duplicate room, which seemed to go on and on and to last for ever. Outside, night, but one which offered no fears, no terrors. Gentle and forgiving.

She turned round. Her parents stood out in the hall, smiling at her. They were – oh, absurdly young. In their late thirties, which was the age she most often thought of them as being. Her mother didn't have that martyred look she was to acquire, her father didn't seem inward and furtive as he later did. They smiled openly, restored to something like their best.

She smiled back at them, their daughter in her sere and yellow.

She loosened her camel coat, then she sat down in the wing-chair, her hands placed in her lap. She sat still, waiting patiently.

On the other side of the window was the infinite night: out of which we come, and which claims us back.

She focused her mind down and down, until she was thinking only of the darkness out there.

Time in Carnbeg

The coach will stop at the Coronation Gardens car park at approx. 12.45 p.m, and depart at 4.00 p.m.

In Carnbeg your time is your own!

A chance to stroll about, to browse in the shops, to go back to that tea-room which caught your eye and sample the edible goodies on offer.

'A cop-out, that is,' Nell said, scrunching the piece of paper into a ball. ' "Your time is your own." Bugger off and don't bother us.'

'Are you looking for somewhere to put that?' Vera asked.

'I'm very inclined . . . ' Nell said, eyeing the tall drink of water of a driver – 'Lofty', she'd christened him – who made you think he was doing this job on sufferance.

'Here, give it to me,' Vera said, and dropped it into her hold-all. Nell was being difficult, and sometimes Vera had to be firm with her friend. But it had been a warm journey up in the coach from Stirling, and no blinds to pull down at the windows, like on some.

They both stood in the municipal car park while their fellow passengers fanned out. They both stood squinting into the sun, unsure what to do.

'We ought to get going if we're going,' Vera said.

Or what? Nell's silence seemed to reprimand her.

'What d'you fancy, Nell?'

'Nothing hilly, anyway. Nice and flat.'

'It's been ages,' Vera said, setting off at a sedate pace. 'I wonder what's changed?'

'Preserved in . . . '

[84]

Aspirin was the only word Nell could think of, but that wasn't right.

'I know what you mean,' Vera said, only able to think of Aspen at first, because they had a feature on it in a lifestyle-of-the-rich-and-famous programme she'd watched in their hotel bedroom last night, while Nell was washing out her smalls in the en suite.

'It's on the tip of my – '

'Apsic,' Vera said. 'No, aspic.'

'That's the one.'

'Like a jelly.'

Which set Nell thinking of food again. Food was never very far from her mind; it strayed off for a little while, then came moseying back.

'We'll need to keep up our energy levels,' Nell said.

Vera looked at her friend a little warily. It wasn't just the travelling; they'd spent rather a lot of time on this holiday, sitting on their beam ends, eating and drinking.

'I'll need to find a girls' room,' Nell said, and Vera mentally spoke the next words an instant before Nell did.

'Give us a shout if you see one, won't you?'

It was amazing to Vera how Nell could keep going even when she said she needed the Ladies, if a Ladies didn't present itself. Mind over matter.

'It's not *pressing*,' Nell said, in a way that made Vera think of internal organs pushing on one another.

Everything comes back to our bodies, Vera was telling herself. Better safe than sorry, Nell was thinking, but aware that she was picking up cooking-smells from somewhere.

'Along this way looks the best bet,' Vera said.

'You lead, I'll follow,' Nell responded.

Which, they both knew, was how it often *looked*, but wasn't necessarily so.

Nell was in her 'late sixties', as she told people. Vera was sixty-three, a fact she usually kept to herself. Nell seemed a few years younger than her age, while Vera's habitual sobriety added a few. So really they met somewhere in the middle.

To strangers they might have seemed unlikely friends. Nell: outward-going, plump, sedentary. Vera: reflective, a size 10, with the sort of quick and jerky movements which unsettled people.

Here was scientific proof of the attraction of opposites.

Nell and Vera had met when they both went to work serving in the same Glasgow dairy. When dairies bit the dust, so to speak, they found other jobs: Nell in a baker's shop, and Vera in a newsagent's. They were both married, both childless. Later they were widowed within a couple of years of one another. To them, whatever others might think of their dissimilarities, they felt as if they were *destined* to be friends.

Both Nell and Vera had been to Carnbeg before, but long ago and alone and in quite different circumstances.

Nell had been evacuated here for some of the war, until she begged to be sent back to Glasgow. Vera had come here on holiday sometime in the early 1970s; she mentioned the Sgian Palace Hotel.

'Divvy come up?' Nell asked.

'No.'

'Win the pools?'

'It was just a treat, you know?'

At that time Nell was coaxing her husband into package holidays in Torremolinos and Benidorm. But they had never stayed anywhere as posh as the Sgian Palace, if you will.

'Was it for something special?' Nell persisted, stopping in her tracks on the pretext that she was looking across town to identify the hotel's towers and turrets and battlements through the summer trees.

'That depends.'

'Depends on what?'

'Depends on what you mean by "special".'

'An anniversary? Or a birthday, a celebration?'

Vera shrugged. Nell smelled a rat, but let sleeping dogs lie, she had other things on her mind this afternoon.

Nell wanted to find An-Cala Brae, where she had gone as a wee girl to stay.

'I want to find the way by myself.'

In the end though, she had to ask someone, because the roads were confusing her.

The house was smaller than she remembered, and closer to the pavement, but it was just as unattractive, even with its double-glazed replacement windows and the plastic weather-sealing on the gable end.

'*I* don't think it's unattractive,' Vera said.

Or perhaps the ugliness chiefly lay in its associations? Nell didn't tell Vera about those. She had never told anyone properly.

The Jarvies weren't physically cruel: not like the cases that kept getting into the newspapers these days. No, the Jarvies' crime was to be utterly – unremittingly and unforgivingly – *joyless*. That was mental abuse, which can last just as long as or longer than bodily weals and fractures. The Jarvies, husband and wife, also tortured themselves, living (if living it was) with terrors in every corner. The terror of doing wrong, or doing less well than your best, of being judged severely by your neighbours, of not giving a good impression. Town clothes had to be spotless, you never said anything that might be misconstrued or thought impolite, you had to remember to talk in your better 'outside' voice. You should never *ever* let the side down.

What a hard education it had been for an eight-year-old. It was to affect her for life. She made it her mission once she was back in Glasgow to break all those rigid rules the Jarvies had dinned into her, to break them as often in the day as she could.

Rule Number One was to defend yourself against committing any pleasurable act.

Although she never saw the Jarvies again, the recollection of their dour unsmiling faces haunted Nell's teens. She hadn't forgotten any of the talkings-to, when she'd got the sharp end of the couple's tongues. She remembered not having any free time, and constantly having to justify herself.

'Time comes to us just once, Nell Skinner.'

Employ it usefully. Make the most of it.

(Could that not mean, by enjoying it, by making your enjoyment last, by forgetting all about time for a little while?)

Once, when a little depleted wartime circus pitched camp in Carnbeg, the Jarvies had locked the doors and snibbed the windows so that she couldn't get out of the house, so that temptation wouldn't get at her. From her bedroom she had seen the pennants fluttering on top of the tent, and the crowd of people milling about. Never mind that she'd heard the circus didn't amount to much, she felt she had lost out on something others considered no more than their due. It should have been her reward for doing the tasks she did about the house and garden, but to the Jarvies it was all the Devil's work. Off to Sunday School the next day, reciting the names of as many books of the Old and New Testaments as she could remember, and in strict sequence; accompanying the Jarvies on their Sunday afternoon walk (steering clear of the park and band-stand), and being on her best behaviour when the Jarvies' joyless friends called round, and then being excused in order to double-check her weekend homework.

Nell hadn't spoken of these things since, even with her husband when he was alive. She smiled as she shook her head at Vera, she even smiled, as if her memories were happy and not doom-laden and bitter. They were memories of the *old* Scotland, which she had spent the rest of her life trying to get out of her system, which she continued to see all around her but which she never again allowed to come so close to her, which she tried to defeat by laughter and shrugs, rolling eyes and flippancy. She had gone to war on the past by living out every minute of her existence, by indulging several senses simultaneously – not least her tastebuds, and eating so often just a little over. (The Jarvies must have been the only people in Carnbeg not to use up their full household rations, giving them away rather than indulging *her*.)

They returned by a crooked back street, once considered disreputable but now so tarted up that Nell thought she must have got her bearings wrong.

Carefully matched cobbles, bollards with lights inside them, a smell of coffee grounds and fresh baking – the sort of spray-on ambience she'd learned from working in a succession of bakers' shops.

'This is more like it!' Nell said.

They went into a woollen-mill shop. The assistants seemed to recognise that they'd been in the same line themselves, and respectfully left them to browse.

Vera looked at her watch.

'We must have hours left,' Nell said.

'Not as long as you think.'

'Don't spoil my fun!'

'Fun?' Vera asked.

'Somewhere in Carnbeg, there must be.'

'Well, we haven't it found it *yet*.'

'I'm always hopeful.'

'If anyone can find it,' Vera sighed, 'you will.'

'Of course I will. I'm on my hols.'

Vera nodded.

'You haven't told me about *your* holiday here,' Nell said.

Vera referred again to her watch. 'We don't want to miss the bus.'

'They'll wait for us.'

'It'll be black looks,' Vera said. 'From that lot up at the front, behind Lofty.'

'D'you think *they*'re having much fun?'

Vera smiled and shook her head.

'So, tell me about your holiday here.'

'I don't think there's much to tell,' Vera replied simply. 'It's not very interesting.'

'So *you* think.'

'No, really.'

'How many people have ever asked about it, then?' Nell asked.

'Not many.'

'Then tell *me*. And I'll be the judge of that.'

Nell imitated Vera's jaw hanging open, and Vera was lured into another smile.

But Vera didn't supply what she knew Nell wanted. The truth was, it hadn't been a holiday at all.

Half the townsfolk of then must be dead by now, Nell thought. It wasn't a melancholy thought: time passes, and we have to make the most of it, seize the day and let tomorrow look after itself.

She lifted her face to the sun, alert to every break in the clouds.

Vera preferred to take care of her skin, and thought she should steer them towards the shop awnings across the way.

Nell was aware of the drag leftwards, and resisted. One of her favourite songs was 'The Sunny Side of the Street'. The Nat King Cole version, which always cheered her up. Some summery days, when she was still working, she used to leave the house in the morning humming it. 'Redirect your feet . . . '

'An arcade with a glass roof,' Vera said with relief, spotting the walkway ahead, just round the corner on High Street. 'That's new.'

Nell viewed the sky. More clouds. Suddenly the sunshine was fading on the cobbles and walls, as if it was on a dimmer switch. You had to be quick to catch it, you had to live in hope.

They did some more shops. Nell's ankles were giving her problems these days, so she didn't linger (it was worse when she stood still); back to clouds and silver linings, at least it meant that they didn't spend what they couldn't afford. They looked at the goods, and that was enough, first in an out-of-the-Ark chemist's with an apothecary's cabinet and coloured glass jars for display – Nell availed herself of a bentwood chair thoughtfully supplied beside a counter – and then in the country outfitters along the road, which was also made for another age, bales of tartan and estate tweeds and stags' antlers up on the walls.

'Just having a wee look,' they said when asked, and nobody

serving in the shops seemed surprised or bothered, which was all very civilised, wasn't it?

Vera looked at her watch.

'Is it time for tea yet?' Nell asked.

'We passed a place,' Vera said.

They returned to it, The Shieling. Nell was glad to take the weight off her feet and rest her ankles, and Vera was pleased to have the distraction of other people, given that Nell wasn't quite her usual talkative self.

They read the menu, and the girl told them which cakes they had. They gave her their orders.

'This is the life,' Nell said, settling back.

Vera didn't reply. She was trying to remember if the tea-room had been here in 1973, that fateful year.

Coming to Carnbeg had been a terrible mistake. How could she even have considered it?

Because he had persuaded her to come, that's why. Such was the guile of the man, she'd told herself afterwards. But a part of her could never admit that Jimmy McCance *had* been duplicitous at all.

He worked for the company that bought over the newsagent's where she worked. The shop got a new name, well known in the West of Scotland, and a logo, and a layout. He told her in a chaffing kind of way, the first time he called by in his Vauxhall Victor, that she, too, would be given a new look. A uniform, he meant. 'Not that *you* need improving.'

He delivered the skirt and blouse in person, and asked her if she'd like to go and slip them on for him. She hesitated, but reminded herself he *was* management. That gave him an excuse to study her, although he told her he was there to monitor customer reactions, which he did for half an hour or so, from the other end of the shop.

'That seemed to go all right,' she told him, innocuously enough.

'*Very* all right,' he said, with a gleam in his eye which no man, not even her husband, had given her before.

His visits became more frequent. He was photographed

standing beside her when her branch won the company's Outstanding Achievement award. She got talked into staying on for stocktaking every few weeks, and they would go for a drink afterwards. When she got home she told Eric that the other girls in the shop had been helping her.

Jimmy McCance wasn't really her type, but she was flattered by his attention. Now she was manageress, and he implied that her promotion had been on his say-so. When she asked him about a desk job at the company offices, he didn't seem so keen on that.

'You get along so well with your customers, Mrs Wallace. I'm thinking here of the general public, you see.'

One evening, following another out-of-hours stocktaking with Jimmy McCance and another trip to the Pewter Pot, Eric told her that he'd been speaking to Marie at the bus stop, and she hadn't said anything about any bloody stocktaking.

'I let her off.'

Eric didn't look as if he believed her.

And then it came, out of the blue. An invitation from Jimmy McCance to Carnbeg.

'I'd like to show you the place, Vera.'

She wondered long and hard. There had been some kisses and some fumbles after hours, but nothing more. At home Eric wasn't being very affectionate, and he'd started to find fault with her housekeeping.

'Maybe I'll come with you, maybe not.'

Why on earth *did* she take the train north?

(Apart from telling Jimmy she definitely wouldn't be going anywhere in his two-tone Vauxhall.)

She suffered agonies during the journey. She wanted to get off the train, first at Stirling and then at Auchterarder. Both times she left her seat and stood by the door case in hand; and yet, when the train came to a halt, she didn't open the door.

She knew where they were to meet from a postcard he'd given her. A big fancy hotel like a castle, with turrets and towers and (for all she knew) a drawbridge as well. She walked uphill from the station, with her limbs like sandbags, weighing her down and down.

She stopped on the first corner of the steep driveway. Dusk was falling. (She'd had to work a half-day, making her excuses to Eric, a get-to-know-the-senior-staff social and overnight.) The spot felt dank and gloomy, the trees were too tall, they dripped and were starting to take outlandish shapes. She could believe in wolves and ghouls in a spot like this.

No, she couldn't do it, walk the hundred yards left. If he'd happened to come sweeping past in his car at that moment, he might just have managed to get her to change her mind . . . But he didn't; no Vauxhall Victor turned the corner.

She was suddenly terrified, of everything she didn't know and understand about the world. She longed for safety and security. That meant Eric, and home, and their neighbours and friends, and closing the door and pulling the curtains shut.

She turned on her heel and ran downhill, down the chicane of driveway. She carried on running, all the way back to the railway station. Her legs sped her there, no trouble at all, because she had rediscovered virtue. At the fifty-ninth minute of the eleventh hour, only in the very nick of time. She ran past a church, and thought that God must have been watching over her.

She was reliving it now in The Shieling, that return to sanity.

Others might think her life since then had been dull and predictable, but it was either that way or the other. Dullness and predictablity in fact meant continually having to be on your guard, not letting down your defences. True drawbridge stuff. Anyway, that castle of a hotel was just an architect's fantasy, a – what was the word? – a *folly*. She had read somewhere it was a bit run down these days, because it had been built for another age and its needs.

Running away, she had been excused from – the waiting ogre, of course, but just as much she had been saved from herself.

'Your tea, ladies,' the waitress said.

' "Ladies" is what I like to hear!' Nell laughed, in the girl's hearing.

[93]

'That reminds me.' Vera looked round, to see where the facilities were.

All that pent-up nervousness, and now the relief of knowing there wasn't time to look for the hotel, that it was all in the past, storybook fiction, in the setting of a fairytale forest she sometimes still had disturbing dreams about. Eric was no longer alive, to wake up beside in the middle of the night. So she depended on her friends instead, on Nell in particular: dizzy, over-the-top Nell who usually didn't give you a moment to think about yourself.

Nell cocked her head on one side.

'What's up, Nell?'

'It's my fun detector.'

She nodded downhill towards a screen of trees. Vera couldn't see anything, but she caught the sound of music; snatches were wafting up on currents of air. Fairground music.

Nell led the way, which was in the opposite direction from the bus park. The music grew steadier, louder.

'Look!' Nell pointed, with the expert instinct of a fun snuffler.

They saw the flashing lights of a carousel. Clattery bells rang.

'Look at the horses,' Nell said.

Jumping as if hags were after them, Vera thought. Jumping for pure joy, Nell thought.

Vera was apprehensive, but Nell walked steadily on, sore ankles forgotten.

She was eight years old, and carrying her gas-mask case. She thought that everybody must be like the folk who lived cheek-by-jowl in their tenement block beside the Clyde – cheerfully enough, with now and then an impromptu ceilidh on the patch of green behind. Here in Carnbeg the buildings still stood, and the houses had their own gardens, and vegetables grew in neat rows, and the air felt fresher, and you could see for miles without any pall of smoke, and not a plane or a drone in the blue sky: it should have been perfect.

It might have been, except for the Jarvies.

Don't. Mustn't.

Don't touch, don't fidget, don't mumble, don't talk with your mouth full, don't ask for what you can't have, don't just stand there doing nothing. You mustn't stare, you mustn't lie in bed late, mustn't leave any food on your plate, mustn't send letters home without letting us read them first, mustn't dally down in the town, mustn't put off your homework. Have you memorised your books of the Bible?

No time was to be unaccounted for. No slacking. There's a war on. And she wondered if in the whole of Germany there was any girl sent to be safe in a little country town who was as miserable as herself.

' . . . Deuteronomy, Joshua, Judges, Ruth, 1st and 2nd Samuel, 1st and 2nd Kings . . . '

Vera looked at her watch.

'Is there time?' Nell asked, already walking past her friend.

'Some.'

'Then that's enough.'

'What're you going to do?'

'Get on a ride, of course!'

Vera followed in the wake of the laughing Nell. 'You're not serious?'

'Watch me.'

Nell stopped at a carousel and paid a man from her purse.

'Surprise yourself, Vera.'

'Someone around here needs to keep a level head.'

'No, they don't.'

'Oh, Nell!'

Vera and Nell both knew that only one of them would risk the indignity of getting on to a painted horse.

Next thing, Vera saw the flesh at the top of Nell's thigh. She wore old-fashioned stockings, although on Nell they ended up looking more sleazy than anything else. Clearly Nell didn't care, and Vera envied her a little, but not too much.

Vera held up her wrist, tapping the face of her watch.

'Just for old times' sake,' Nell called to her, bubbly-voiced and sounding years younger than herself.

Nell didn't want to come off the horses. She didn't want them to stop. Everything felt perfect, just like this. There was Vera looking up at her and seeming a little anxious, which was Vera's way and which somehow added to the pleasure.

Round and round. The rising and falling motion was gentle, and her stomach was hardly complaining at all. Round and round, and up and down.

From her high mount she could see almost as far as An-Cala Brae. Wouldn't *they* be spinning, too, in their narrow cold graves?

On the ground Vera stood watching. She felt like a big sister to Nell, even though she was three years younger. She liked having this responsibility of keeping an eye on her, because as the youngest of three daughters (and less an afterthought of her parents, she suspected, than an accident), she'd had everyone at home nagging away at her, telling her what was good for her.

Nell felt like a child, the one who'd had to grow up too quickly during the war. The horses plunged on, reckless and proud, and she could feel her pleasure spurting up into her throat, she had oxygen in her blood.

It was rising again, Vera noticed, the skirt. An amplitude of white flesh wobbled on Nell's upper thigh; she was blithely disregarding as Vera tried to signal, look out, any second you're about to show your knickers.

The music was starting to fade, and the horses on their stripy poles were slowing. It was only now that Nell felt a little queasy, as normality took over again.

The man helped Nell off. On the grass she was shaky, and Vera had to support her.

'Time to go,' Vera said.

'*That* bucked me up, anyhow.'

'Did you need it?' Vera asked.

'*I'll* say.'

They walked back. Or, rather, they ambled. Vera had to slow

for Nell. She wondered how Nell could have demeaned herself like that. She looked round and saw Nell watching her, as if she'd been trying to read the thoughts in her head.

'Some actress,' Nell said, 'American she was, on yon break-fast programme on telly, was talking about a film she was in.'

'Was she really?' said Vera ominously.

'And her favourite line was about grabbing hold of life and *riding* it. Or something. Like a horse, I mean.'

'I see.'

But Vera wasn't convinced. She hadn't foreseen when they set out on the bus yesterday that Nell was going to turn all literary on her, if that's what it was. She wasn't friends with Nell so that Nell would confide her inner reflections to her. That wasn't what the relationship was supposed to be about, not at all.

The coach was waiting for them with its engine running.

The troutmouths in the front seats glared at them as they got on, and Lofty didn't waste any time in closing the door and getting going. The sudden forward motion propelled the two women down the aisle. They crawled into their seats.

Carnbeg sped past on the other side of the windows. One hilly street toppled into another, and nobody on the bus was bothering to distinguish as – *en masse* – they looked into carrier bags and compared purchases.

Only Nell and Vera had come back empty-handed.

'You two got off lightly,' the English woman behind leaned forward to say, smirking at them. ' "Scot-free", don't they say?'

Vera pursed her lips and didn't deign to reply. What was the woman suggesting? That they couldn't afford to shop, or that they were too tight-fisted?

Nell couldn't think of anything to say in response, but she smiled back at their neighbour, over her shoulder. She was still thinking of the carousel ride, her thighs were still straddling a painted horse and she was rising, falling by turns but always rising again.

A sign as they were leaving the town urged, HASTE YE BACK. Nell nudged Vera to take a look.

'Well, we've been,' Vera said.

Nell nodded her agreement.

Neither woman realised just how much nerve her friend had needed.

Vera opened her bag.

'Here, Nell.'

She shook out a couple of sweeties, pandrops, one each to suck.

They were on dual carriageway now. Lofty came on to the intercom and said they were making good time.

The road opened up in front of them. There was a clear view as far as they could see, reaching to northerly blue mountains and tasting of crackly peppermint.

The Trinket Box

When I and my friends were young, in our early teens, we weren't cruel, but we were thoughtless. We thought less charitably than we should have done.

Youth very seldom has the range to see beyond itself. Most of our opinions we shared – all for one and one for all – and if we all agreed about something, then it must be right. We didn't suppose that we caused offence. Our consensus life inured us to criticism, except when it came from our parents.

But in the course of our thoughtlessness we did some terrible things.

The couple were English, and had come to Carnbeg, here in the Perthshire forest hills, to make a new life for themselves.

They had included the small spa town on their honeymoon itinerary sixteen years before, and possibly they imagined that by returning they could rediscover earlier selves they had somehow lost sight of since.

It was evident to customers in the small gift shop they'd opened that the husband was the keener. Mr Bradley bought the goods from reps and local suppliers, wrote the newspaper adverts; it was he who had come up with the name for the business, the Trinket Box.

Their stock-in-trade was knick-knacks.

They also showed in selected hotels about the town; the Sgian Palace even had a Trinket Box display-case in its foyer. The Bradleys must have considered that their wares would appeal to our solid middle-class tastes, failing to understand that to people like my parents – so cautious with their money, not caring to spend too brazenly on themselves – the objects were largely superfluous, much of the taste highly dubious. The shop carried the sort of merchandise which – quite frankly – *arrivistes* and aspirants thought was middle-class but which amounted to a travesty: glass bon-bon dishes, gilt musical boxes, porcelain thimbles and ring-trees, onyx hand-coolers, crystal paper-weights, After Eight dispensers in very meagre silverplate, factory-produced tapestry views of uncredited Scottish scenes which might as well have been fictional or perhaps were.

Mr Bradley had been in the Navy during the war and acquitted himself well. He had stayed on, because that was the only occupation he'd known. (And thereby he deftly relegated his humble social origins to the convenient mists of time.)

He came out after fifteen years, back on to civvy street. He may have wondered what other talents he had, or perhaps he wanted to get his wife away from that hearty services milieu. The base, on the south coast of England, was famed for testosterone over-capacity and the bored wives' fondness for gin.

Mr Bradley had found work in an estate agent's, then in a hotel, then with a firm of printers and then in a chandler's office. Nothing seemed to suit him, however. His shoulders had started to droop, and the skin was hanging a little slacker on his bones than of yore. He appeared even more anxious to please people, to be agreeable to them.

Next, courtesy of cooperative-minded bank managers impressed by his naval credentials, he set himself up in a succession of small shops. A tobacconist's. An antiques shop. Finally, in the fancy-goods line.

The last uprooting from north Yorkshire to Perthshire was unexplained. His first job had been down in Devon, in Dartmouth – umbilically tied to the Royal Naval College there – and every subsequent move had taken the couple east and north. Neither claimed that Carnbeg was the end of the road; rather, it happened to be as far as they had yet reached.

In the local shops the indigenous wives of Carnbeg were

politely formal with Mrs Bradley, but no more than that. Irene Bradley wasn't – yet – one of them, and their circumspection had to do with more than her Englishness or her living above commercial premises. Maybe it was a natural defence of the species, to react so tentatively, sceptically, concerning anyone who dared to look different from the norm.

Mrs Bradley had chosen to have the appearance at forty-five years old that she did: the brass-coloured hair, the meticulously made-up face – eyebrows plucked to regal arcs, blue eyeshadow, blusher on her cheeks, fresh magenta lipstick – and her up-to-the-minute clothes à la mode de Bournemouth: pastel woollens which hugged her uptilted breasts, cardigan sleeves pulled back on her sunned forearms, jangly charm bracelets, narrow skirts tight on her hips, feet arched on high pencil heels. This was the woman the wife of modest Leonard Bradley had elected to make of herself, so her neighbours were surely entitled to declare (mostly out of her hearing) a response.

We weren't Carnbeg natives but annual summer holidaymakers. The Trinket Box was somewhere new for us to go on wet days, when we had nothing better to do.

We would lift up the goods, examine them, and – gently enough – put them down again, without any intention of making a purchase. We'd keep looking out of the window, to see if the rain was easing, trying to judge from the state of the drips on the tasselled fringe of the floral awning. It was a Home Counties awning, a Thames Valley awning, transferred north to a douce no-nonsense Scottish street where it patently didn't belong.

We were embarrassed to be there in the shop, but it was done as a kind of dare to ourselves.

Slope-shouldered Mr Bradley worried about the wet footprints tracked over the carpet-tiles by our shoes and sandals, and about the damp trails smeared by our cagoule sleeves. He was also afraid to lose a hypothetical customer; for all he could tell, one of us might have a birthday present to buy for a member of the family, and a bad critique might persuade our parents or their friends that they ought not to come in. His wife didn't have the same qualms, and she watched us closely without bothering to disguise her suspiciousness, as if she was quite aware what our opinion of the twee merchandise was.

Reps visited the shop. (They parked outside if they drove a car to be proud of; round the corner in Glebe Street if they didn't.) Some had pot bellies, some reeked of perspiration and tobacco, but among this class of automotive manhood were other younger and more preposessing specimens. For them Mrs Bradley always had a coyly welcoming smile and some playful banter before she summoned her husband through from the back.

'Leonard, have you got a moment?'

When there was a lull in activity in the shop, Mrs Bradley boiled water on the downstairs gas ring and made coffee or tea. She would return with perfume dabbed behind her ears, her lips repainted and face newly powdered, her feet fitted into shoes with even higher heels.

Once the got-lucky visitor had gone, the shop would be filled – crowded – with that sweet fragrance, and the day marked out to any of us habitual browsers as special.

The reps developed a rota, so Mrs Bradley learned to prepare herself for their arrivals: whom to try to avoid, whom to stay around for, whose footsteps and stride along Mercat Street she should keep her hearing tuned for.

Maybe it was no accident that an undue number of salesmen called in at the Trinket Box, attempting to hawk their latest lines. The majority still smelled of sweat and cigarettes, wore nylon shirts that wouldn't stay tucked inside the dipping waistbands of their trousers. Which was why the exceptions continued to receive that smile of false bashfulness when Mrs Bradley seemed merely to chance to materialise from behind the curtain, emerging like a (mature) mannequin from the back quarters into the shop. Then that husky round-midnight Londonish voice, with the commonness – old vowel-slides – very nearly eradicated from it. 'Oh, *hello*, stranger! I didn't see you there.'

Some of the reps hung on in the town for an hour or so afterwards, taking a breather if the weather was fine or sitting down to another coffee or tea in the Shieling and going through their paperwork, before heading off to wherever they were expected next, or back to base, Aberdeen or Edinburgh or Glasgow.

One afternoon we caught sight of Mrs Bradley entering the tea-room, too, so it must have been on her own Carnbeg circuit, but the windows were steamed up and we were already on the trail of someone else. To us the reps fell into two categories – the favoured and the unfavoured – and we didn't distinguish any more closely. Mrs Bradley, however, had the time and leisure to classify them, to sort and sift, to identify exactly who was who among her preferred callers and in which order of preference she currently rated them.

Another rep in the shop. Switch again to that posher front-of-shop voice.

'Oh, *hello*, stranger! I didn't see you there.'

Mr Bradley, on his summons, would appear from the back room. His shoulders immediately fell and his forehead crumpled, as if he had a pebble set deeply into the central portion of his brow. In a couple of seconds his expression changed from bland charm, that tradesman's blatant yen to please, to something much darker: to what I know now was distrust and misapprehension, a grim foreboding he was helpless to do anything about.

We witnessed this several times. Mrs Bradley must have realised we were there in the shop to spy, but she let us watch anyway.

At heart – so I can understand in retrospect – Irene Bradley didn't believe in the middle-class world, in our hackneyed prejudices, our narrow-mindedness. Disregard that put-on accent which imitated ours. She had seen a hell of a lot of life, enough to educate her that snobbery is moral cowardice and complacency is the condition of sots. Now from the vantage-point of her high stilettos, overly fragrant and protected by her rattly charm bracelets, she felt that *she* was in a position to pity *us*.

But very soon it would be a silly bourgeois custom, one she should have known not to have any truck with, which succeeded in bringing the Trinket Box existence that was her cover crashing down around her.

In the town to buy postcards in Malloch's the Stationer's, we came across a Valentine card which hadn't been removed from the display racks on the walls. Outside again we debated who in Carnbeg deserved to receive it. Walking back along Mercat Street and past the Trinket Box, it crossed several of our minds at the same moment.

At the back of the showroom, just visible, Mrs Bradley was perched on one leg with one foot out of her shoe, caressing her stocking at the ankle where it had rippled, and smoothing out any creases higher up, on her calf. She lifted her head, noticed us lagging boys, but didn't stop what she was doing.

We went back the next day and bought the Valentine card.

We wrote nothing on it, but drew a big heart pierced by an arrow. Sealed the envelope. Printed IN CAPS Mrs Irene Bradley's name and address, placed a stamp very neatly in the top right-hand corner.

We gave the card to Iain Benzie to post; he was returning home to Glasgow, and we thought that that must excuse *us*; such a slick alibi would get us off the hook.

The card was intended ironically, wasn't it? Well, only partially so. Mrs Bradley looked to us precisely the sort of woman who ought to receive such a token of fond devotion. From somebody or other. We doubted very much if her soft-spoken and rather hangdog husband was the man for it. And if the card was six months late, so what?

Our motives were as haphazardly casual as that. The possible consequences simply didn't occur to us.

It was an early-closing day when the second post, a little later than usual, delivered the card. Straining to see through the window into the shop, we could just make it out, the envelope with its RECIPIENT'S NAME AND ADDRESS IN CAPS, lying on the mat behind the locked door.

We reported back, laughing at what we'd seen. The others in our Hydro gang looked less sure that it was such an amusing turn of events; some weren't smiling at all. 'A bunch of soppy little schoolboys', Fiona Telfer called us, and we played up to that all afternoon, still untroubled by our consciences.

The next day Mrs Bradley had gone.

She had been spotted setting out very early that morning – walking as quickly as she could in her sling-backs, high heels scraping – across the empty cobbled square on a diagonal and downhill, a suitcase weighing down each arm. Her mackintosh kept flapping open to impede her progress. She wasn't looking to left or right but had her gaze concentrated straight ahead, towards the roofs of the railway station and freight yard.

The first stopping service to Perth came through at half past five, and she was on the platform with just a few minutes to spare: presumably out of breath and already warmer than she wanted to be. Someone on the train who recognised her kept tabs, and in time word got passed round the grapevine that she didn't leave the station in Perth, not even to go into the hotel, but changed to another train waiting there, one which must have been south-bound, for Edinburgh or – more likely – Glasgow.

And that was the last that anyone in Carnbeg ever saw of Irene Bradley . . .

Stories shouldn't peter out in a trail of conjectures, in suspension dot-dot-dots . . . But that is the habit of life.

Her Lochinvar was waiting for her, or so Mrs Bradley assumed. An examination of the postmark on her summer's Valentine card had told her who he was: someone she didn't have any doubts must have sent it, who had given her the signal she was waiting for.

Her one hurried concession to etiquette was to scribble a note to her husband, but it proved too cryptic for him to make any sense of.

Whatever she might find in Glasgow would be worth leaving this dump of a town for.

The train approaching, belching diesel fumes, round the wide curve of track from the river on to the final stretch leading to Carnbeg station. Mrs Bradley found herself a seat in the corner of the carriage, on the off side, farther from the streets and houses. Once she'd reached her destination, a commercial traveller in fancy goods had one hell of a surprise awaiting him.

The final door banged shut, whistles blew, the carriage chassis shuddered, there was another updraught of diesel exhaust – and she was away.

Everything in the shop that Mr Bradley could break he broke. Shelf after shelf of the stuff. Whatever they had sold him, or provided sale-or-return, on those nifty rates of commission they worked to, 'Very nice to deal with you again, Leonard, you're a proper gent, and thanks for the coffee, Mrs B., just how I like it.' The bastards. Gents don't notice, of course, don't have eyes in their head; they don't get angry, don't lash out, because they don't count.

He smashed everything, crunched it all underfoot – porcelain, pottery, crystal, lightweight silver plate – ground it into the soiled carpet-tiles with the heel of his shoe, every last reminder of the runaways in the goddam bloody place.

And still, somehow – until we learned more – we didn't see ourselves as implicated in this domestic drama being played out simultaneously in the shop behind lowered window-blinds and eighty-odd miles away to the south, in Glasgow.

When Mrs Bradley had tracked down whoever she imagined had sent her the card, he would have denied it, but the sender of a Valentine always does. Maybe she laughed off the denial; or maybe it struck to the very quick, and she had to admit there was nothing she could do to persuade the man, no matter how huskily and Londonish she sweet-talked away at him.

Either way, she couldn't go back now, to that little backwater, to hicksville stuck up there in the lee of the hills. It was where they'd gone on honeymoon but where, on an early-closing day, for the very lack of romance, that same marriage had stuttered to its dead end.

The shop was unoccupied the next year. Mr Bradley had disappeared.

The girls preferred at first to hurry past the spot, then later to cross to the opposite pavement. We boys wouldn't be put out of *our* steady gait, that semi-swagger, and yet for us, too, there was something unsettling about the sight of the premises. Another twelve months on, and we were gradually becoming conscious that this minor local legend referred not only to the Bradleys but to ourselves as well.

A silence grew around the shop. No one else took it on.

Over the raised awning the signboard stayed in place, with its inappropriately jaunty-sounding name writ large above our heads.

Old dames and housewives didn't linger by the shop even to chat, as if they were afraid of its reputation for unhappiness. It was true that, because of the various steep roofs across the way, less sunshine fell on its frontage than on its neighbours'. If that reach of Mercat Street had been sunnier, some folk said, with more brightness in the showroom and the upstairs living-rooms, maybe Mr Bradley (now they seemed to be blaming *him*) would have kept in a safer, saner frame of mind.

Perhaps so.

But as it was . . . The shop remained empty. The windows became grimy, the property had an unlucky look which no amount of estate agent's hyperbole could compensate for.

To us the Trinket Box was already like a monument, of ourselves, of the gauche adolescents we formerly were. At that juncture in space and time we would always be fourteen, fifteen, sixteen years old, caught fast in that difficult interlude between boyhood with its cohesive certainties and the irrational adult realm of passion and dream and the reckless actions which men and women are sometimes driven to.

Lives of the Saints

The weather forecast for Thursday was for an improvement, and when Thursday came – once Moira McKean got up out of bed, after a sleepless night – the sky was grey, but clear and dry.

A decent day always brings out a good-sized crowd for a funeral. Too fine, of course, and people will find other things to do. But a town doctor, as Kenneth himself always used to say, is a bigger draw than most.

She forced herself to eat a slice of toast. It still felt odd not to be making breakast for Kenneth and herself, keeping an eye on the porridge pot as she infused the tea. And now here she was, only hours from burying her brother.

About a hundred, she guessed.

Their parents had been church-goers, and so it was cut and dried to him: *he* was meant to be also. A doctor should show an example to those who didn't know better. To those who, unlike him, had to struggle with their demons – with laziness or with the mental torpor of the times or, worse, with red-dyed and clapped-out bolshiness.

Would Kenneth have approved of her outfit? ('Rig-out' was the term he preferred.)

She turned in front of the wardrobe mirror in her bedroom; the mirror in his room was better, but she couldn't bring herself to go in there, not on this of all mornings. It was her customary funeral wear, although she wasn't in the habit of taking her best black lizard handbag with her. Today, because this was a funeral like no other, it hung from her arm.

It weighed a little heavily, she realised, as she walked up the gravel path, taking care not to scuff her shoes and at the same time returning others' little bows of condolence with a quiet and dignified smile. Kenneth wasn't one for smiling at funerals, even so tactfully as she was doing, but now she was having to make such decisions for herself: the sole McKean left in Carnbeg, alone in that big house on Gil Brae.

All that would have to be thought about. How she was going to live, how she was going to cope. (As a sister she wasn't even allowed a widow's prerogative, to be the hapless recipient of others' advice.) She was conscious of a flood of decisions being dammed up in the meantime, and she was almost glad to have this practical business of the funeral. Especially when she was being guided through it, by the undertakers (Kenneth wouldn't have approved of the hand hold on her arm) every now and then, and by the minister in his black crow gown and university colours (worn for the important funerals in the town, as Kenneth would have been the first to appreciate).

The service proceeded, and Moira McKean remained – somehow or other – dry-eyed, in possession of herself. None of this felt as if it was happening, she might as well have been watching it on television. This was the saving grace – the unreality of the day – and it spared her having to confront her true feelings and responses.

Even standing on the hillside in full view, spotlit by sunshine that came flickering through the trees, she kept her self-control.

Kenneth would have been proud of her, although (inevitably) he would have let her see he had some misgivings. All her life, child and adult, she had been trying to prove herself worthy, despite those doubts of his.

Occasionally she caught their acquaintances' eyes moving off her, and she wondered what it was she was seeing on their faces. Sorrow, yes, in that decorous way of funerals; pity, for her, watching her standing *sola* and unprotected by her brother. But wasn't there something else stirred in with that pity, which was the real reason for the evasive eye movements? She felt they were *dismissing* her, which was the polite form that ridicule took.

*Look what that woman's had to put up with. And who's she
had to blame for that but herself? You don't have someone
keep you under his thumb unless he knows he can get away
with it . . .*

They couldn't think anything she hadn't thought herself. But
while Kenneth was alive, no one would have dared to let her see
what might be in their minds.

For the first time she started to feel a rush of emotion. But it
was indignation which was making her eyes smart. She looked
off into the distance, trying to regain her composure, trying to
clear her eyes of the tears threatening in the ducts: hot and, she
sensed, bitter tears.

She blinked, several times, and the hazard passed. She found
she was looking at a woman she didn't recognise. She was
young, and wearing a long, fitted black coat and an elegant
high-brimmed hat which would have been old-fashioned in her
mother's time, pre-1920s, with a feather and a fine veil. Like a
film costume. She was standing a little apart, not included in the
Carnbeg community. What also distinguished her was the
crumpled white handkerchief she held in her black gloved hand.
Her shoulders were hunched – broad shoulders which looked
set to take her share of burdens, but which now seemed to be
raised defensively.

'Miss McKean.' The undertaker's hand touched her arm.

She snapped out of her reverie. 'I'm sorry?'

She was being motioned forward.

Another man held a trowel of earth for her to drop on to the
coffin in its lair.

What?

She stared between the two of them.

This was what they did in American films, those made-for-
TV movies she watched whenever Kenneth was out on evening
calls and she had the house to herself. It wasn't what they did at
Carnbeg funerals.

How could she refuse? Kenneth would hate this. But he was
dead, and she needed to take a decision herself.

She looked at the mourners. Which had the effect of making them stop watching *her*. Time was held in suspense. Slow motion, slowing right down to nothing at all.

Now someone was standing in front of her. A black hat with a greeny-blue feather and a veil. *That* hat.

The woman put a posy of flowers into her hand. Lily-of-the valley, with a pungent perfume. The stranger turned and looked across at the grave for an instant.

' "I am the rose of Sharon",' the minister murmured close by, ' "and the lily of the valleys." ' He beamed appreciation of the gesture. ' "Come the Advent of Our Lord." '

The unidentified woman had walked off, melting into the crowd of people behind her, she'd disappeared.

'Miss McKean?'

The undertaker stepped forward, meaning her to follow. She followed. Now the deed seemed sanctified, by the intervention of the unknown woman.

At the graveside she dropped the posy; the twist of flowers somersaulted on to the coffin lid, skittering inaudibly across the polished wood. Maybe Kenneth wouldn't mind so much, it was a more discreet ceremony than the thud of earth from a trowel, it was a feminine touch. Surely he could excuse them this?

Afterwards there were hands to shake. A file of faces moved past her, and her hand and wrist operated separately, on the programmed arm of a robot. All the time she was thinking about that enigmatic woman in the veil who'd given her the fragrant little spray, simple spring flowers, as if she had a perfect right to do so – and who had then walked off and away and no one able to tell her who she was?

At the Glendall House Hotel, where a light buffet was laid on in a private room, Moira McKean looked around for the woman.

It was disappointing that she wasn't there. And that set her wondering, why *hadn't* she come?

She felt perplexed, disorientated – and hugely curious. She needed something new to concentrate on, and this was – .

The door opened, and she spun round. No, no, it was one of Kenneth's former partners at the surgery, who had been glad enough to quit, here probably under some duress from his incorrigibly pushy wife at his side.

Damn, *damn*!

Moira McKean returned to the big house, which had been their parents' house, and she returned to silence.

She lacked the energy to change out of her black clothes just yet.

The phone rang several times, but she didn't pick up the receiver. She listened to the messages on the answerphone, well-meaning encouragement from their friends.

All she could think about was the young woman in the blackest black coat, who'd been able to keep everyone's mind in that churchyard full of distractions (the sky, birdsong, the hooter of a train) focused on the sadness of the day. Who was she? How did she fit into Kenneth's life?

A patient? It was the obvious possibility. Not a local: perhaps a holidaymaker in the past? (But how had she got to hear of the death?)

Somebody who was ready to stand with shoulders hunched, in full view of the rest of them, attempting to control her grief: while the rest of them held back tears, being commendably stoical, or perhaps just in two minds about Kenneth Alexander Fiddes McKean.

Eventually she did get changed, not into her pastels but into more sedate duns and mosses. Sometimes she longed to throw out all her sensible clothes and start again, but only sometimes, because Kenneth was a stickler for the known and tried. (Past tense. Kenneth *had been* a stickler . . .)

The silence in the house reminded her that she didn't need to bother considering Kenneth's responses now, she could decide such matters for herself.

Having so much freedom suddenly, it terrified her.

There was no one at the end of a phone line to call, to ask, how do I cope with this? All her adult life she had relied chiefly on Kenneth for advice, for the simple reason that Kenneth had wanted it so. And now he wasn't here, and she didn't know if it was a burden or a release.

Had he had such a hold on her that she ended up like this, not able to think for herself?

Briefly she felt that old anger welling up, which she had always tried to keep a lid on. Now she didn't need to. On television one evening, when Kenneth was late home from another of his Glasgow conferences, she had watched a programme about scream therapy, fascinated and repelled by the patients wailing a storm of devils out of themselves. If only, if only, she'd thought, knowing at the same time that a genteel upbringing like hers in mid-century Scotland made such behaviour inconceivable.

They came back to mind now, those caterwauling hysterics. She opened her mouth, opened it wide, and let out one long, rusty-sounding scream. It expanded, gathering pace and soaring, a shriek of complaint pent up for six decades, which had nothing to do with grief for the deceased but everything to do with sorrow for herself.

She hadn't breath for any more, and the scream was left to fade, trickling into every last corner of the house. She found she was shaking from head to foot. She had carved a great swathe out of herself, pitched it anywhere she could, just to try to be rid of it. She could almost believe she was physically lighter; she experienced an uplift, a surging liberation.

She looked outside at a noise, up into the sky.

Geese.

Flying in V-formation.

From the window she followed their raucous progress, and for those moments she was airborne, flying with them in the pure ether, into the blue yonder. She had watched them before, but she had never felt this elation to be flying with them – what was that song about, the sort of Radio 2 music Kenneth had no time for? – soaring high, with the wind beneath my wings.

Some fortunate people had easy parents, who either died young or lived long and healthy lives. The low-maintenance sort, one way or the other.

Theirs had grown ill, first one and then the other, and the illnesses of each had become protracted and humiliating. Their father had turned crotchety after his second stroke, and their mother had succumbed to Parkinson's. It didn't help that Kenneth could diagnose their problems a little ahead of time; in the end both parents were left feeling just as vulnerable and as cheated of luck as anyone else in the same position.

When their mother died, it was difficult to accept that her life was only over at that point; but Moira hadn't foreseen how much relief she'd feel, and joy, to be sharing the house with just Kenneth.

She suggested to her brother that she might do a refresher course and return to teaching at the primary school. He didn't say she shouldn't, but she could tell that he wasn't enthusiastic.

Once she'd completed the course, she applied for jobs. One was nine miles away, and they offered it to her; Kenneth said, a class of mixed eleven-year-olds would be cussed, just plain awful. At that point she realised he would prefer her to be at Windy Knowe, organising his life for him.

She did turn down the job. But five months later, when another position came up here in Carnbeg, they settled on a compromise: she would ask to share the job with a young mother she'd met at the college, who had a toddler of her own. The school agreed, ready to experiment with this mix of youth and experience.

In effect it *was* a full-time job she found herself with, teaching the eight-year-olds she shared *and* being Dr McKean's sister/housekeeper/secretary/factotum. (At the surgery they had trouble keeping their receptionists, and if nothing else she had a lifetime's familiarity with Kenneth's handwriting, so that she could read his scribbled memos and prescriptions.)

Kenneth passed on to her a certain amount of money every week, while never asking that she should contribute anything of her own salary: that was his 'hush' money, she realised, to keep her sweet – not payment as such, but household expenses plus whatever she felt inclined to divert to herself.

It was *more* than a nine-till-five-thirty, since she had to answer phone calls some evenings, and on others – when Kenneth wasn't on call – she stayed up late working on classroom projects or setting tests or writing the assessments with which the headmistress was so keen to establish her authority.

Kenneth came first. To himself he came first. To their parents he had come first. She had always felt guilty whenever she railed against that orthodoxy – inside her head, of course, not within anyone's hearing. She would tell herself that she was being very ungrateful, and even more selfish than she imagined Kenneth was being.

She was aware that Carnbeg saw her as a dependant, the McKeans' daughter and the sister of Dr McKean. But it was a conservative place – and anyway (her counter-argument against herself went), didn't she encourage them to believe that, because here she still was, living in the family home?

Perhaps they all pitied her behind her back. But more than that she pitied herself.

Two days after the funeral she found a pocket diary in one of Kenneth's jackets.

It was smaller than the diary she gave him every Christmas as a stocking-filler. For a few moments she was irritated by the discovery. Why did he go buying a diary unless he didn't care for the one she always gave him?

She looked through it.

She saw her own name marked beside her birthday, and the date recorded when she'd gone off with Joan for their tour of the Hebrides. She recognised the names of his golfing friends, the fishing group, some of the Church elders.

Other names puzzled her. Who was Mark, for instance?

She consulted her own diary. Mark appeared on a day when Kenneth had gone to Glasgow. He next appeared on another Glasgow day.

Was Mark one of his medical colleagues? A student?

Then Mark disappeared.

She found another mention of Glasgow in her own diary, and double-checked with his. No Mark. Instead, he'd written '*Return to Eden*'.

Again, on his next visit. '*Return to Eden*'.

She picked up the phone and called directory enquiries. The girl gave her a number, and she dialled. A man answered. Behind him she heard loud music.

'Return to Eden. How can I help you?'

'You – you're open?'

'Would you like to book a table?'

'I don't . . . '

'They've put you through to the brasserie.'

The next Glasgow entry contracted the rendezvous to '*RtE*'. And beside it another name. *Lindy*! With an exclamation mark.

Three weeks later. It was now a matter of a question mark. *L?*

She'd been aware of Kenneth's popularity with the women.

They complimented her on her brother's 'charm', as if it might have something to do with *her*. But she was quite glad to acquire that aura of approval for herself, however it came.

She had heard him talking about some of those same beguiled women behind their backs. She sometimes wondered if that might not be Kenneth's attempt at a double bluff: to put her off the scent.

The years passed, and Kenneth didn't become linked romantically with any of them. There were no strong rumours of an engagement pending – and so she learned to become easier in her mind, that their domestic arrangement at Windy Knowe wasn't going to alter unless *she* chose.

But men are men, she knew. She'd had a couple of boyfriends long ago, and they had shown her that romance isn't enough for a man, he has urgent drives. What did Kenneth do about *his* urgent drives?

At least he kept that side of his life under wraps, out of sight. He didn't do anything to offend Carnbeg propriety. She didn't discuss his amorous adventures (or the lack of same) with him; but isn't it a woman's way to be inquisitive . . . ?

Into their forties, then fifties, they remained single – so she felt – for each other's sake.

Well, I'm in Glasgow anyway, she told herself, but already heading up St Vincent Street, as she had known she would.

Return to Eden was beneath street level. Squiggly metal chairs and tables, a '*hommage*' – wasn't that the word? – to Gaudí. Barcelona in Glasgow.

'I'm looking for Lindy,' she said to the young man serving at the bar.

'Lindy?' he repeated.

'You've heard of her?'

'Yes, I've heard of her.'

'D'you know how I can speak to her?'

'That's a bit difficult.'

'Does she work here?'

'Not Lindy. No.'

'She's a customer?'

'Not a customer either.'

'I really don't . . . ' Understand. Anything.

'Can I ask you what it is you want to see her about?'

She wasn't sure what the answer to that question was.

'We – we both know someone,' she said.

'Is this about Carn – '

They said 'Carnbeg' together.

'Yes, it is,' she told him.

'There's another bar,' the man said. 'It's easier to talk in there. I'll get her to meet you there, if that's okay.'

'When would that be, do you know?'

'Say, six?'

She looked at her watch.

'Well,' the man said, 'she could make it a bit sooner, I expect.'

'Are you sure?'

'Half five.'

'Yes,' she said. 'All right. Thank you.'

She spent the next three hours walking about in mental neutral, as Kenneth used to describe the condition. She looked into shop windows, she had a cappuccino at a table outside a trattoria, just as she might have done in Italy. She tried to take in the classical grandeur of the buildings, the Courts and the old banks' headquarters and the former stock exchange, which her Glaswegian father would have been familiar with.

And all the time she was wondering how Kenneth had fitted into this cityscape.

She had to adjust her eyes to the low light.

Spotlights and table lamps.

The decor here was brown and fawn and taupe, all those 1970s colours which were back in fashion. Very now.

One of the wall tables was occupied. By a single woman. She wasn't wearing black, no stylish hat with a veil, but it must be her. The stranger at the funeral.

The woman stood up and was going to hold out her hand, then seemed to think she shouldn't, maybe she took fright.

'Hi,' she said in a husky voice.

'Hello.'

They both sat down.

'I was talking to a young man. At the other bar. He said he'd get in touch with you.'

'As good as his word. I'm Lindy.'

'And – and I'm Moira.'

'Is this table okay?'

'It's fine.'

'What'll you drink, Moira?'

'I'll have . . . ' What? 'A g and t, please.'

The young woman stopped a waiter and gave their order.

'They're really models, the staff here. Pretty, but not very good.'

Her voice was low, confidential, and purposeful. The spot-lights somehow invited intimacy.

'You didn't mind?' she asked.

'Didn't mind?'

'That I came to the funeral?'

'No.'

'You're not here to tear me off a strip?'

'You were the one person I didn't know. I was curious. You didn't seem . . . '

'I didn't seem what?'

'A Carnbeg type.'

Was *this* Kenneth's sort of woman? The sultry cocktail-bar siren type? How had it come about? He'd been introduced to her? Or he had chanced to go into that other bar, and there she'd been, and his eye was caught by her? Not a Carnbeg type. But that was exactly the point.

Moira realised how closely the young woman was looking back at her. She felt flustered suddenly, and self-conscious. A fish out of water, in the sort of two-piece – a long, pleated checked skirt, harmonising jacket – that she took herself into Country Casuals every second year to buy, for parents' evenings and Carnbeg socials.

It didn't compare to what her companion was wearing: loose black trousers and a red bolero jacket, and a brightly white shirt with the collar pulled up.

'You're wondering about me, Moira.'

'I am?' Moira felt her face reddening.

'I can tell.'

'I'm sorry. I wasn't meaning . . . '

'I don't mind. Your brother was giving me medical advice.'

'You were a patient?'

'I . . . '

'You went to see him?'

'We sort of met. And got talking. About my medical history.'

That was the explanation – of course there had to be one – thank God, it was all accounted for – she should have known, shouldn't she? Kenneth must have charmed her, as he had charmed women for years. This one might have her own ploys, but Kenneth had the experience to deal with patients who played for some more personal attention.

Moira smiled charitably at her new acquaintance. Her brother had done a lot of good, and he might not have appreciated how much. Even such a thoroughly practical and – yes – worldly man might have had a quality of naivety as well: after all, we *are* those contradictions in our natures, aren't we?

She talked about Carnbeg, because Lindy wanted to know. She told her a little about their home life, but only a little.

Lindy said she did 'this and that' to pick up a wage, and was tantalisingly vague. Bars and eateries appeared to be her haunts.

'How old are you?' Lindy asked.

It was a blunt question, but she felt ready to answer it. 'Fifty-six,' Moira said with a sigh.

'That's nothing.'

'I feel older sometimes.'

'You only *think* you do.'

Moira smiled bravely. She wished it could be true.

What was she doing sitting in this low-lit cellar with its teak tables and taupe-carpeted walls, its squeaky burnt-orange banquettes, its slimline bar with backlit bottles, almost puritan in its simplicity, all this retro-newness? This morning she'd been in the house on Gil Brae, with her shell firmly in place on her back; and now here she was, winkled out of that shell and fighting for life in another element, and yet coping. She hadn't keeled over, she was sitting on the banquette feeling pretty placid, she was looking at the passing life – up at street level, the leathers and flares and goatskins (all back in style again) – looking at it with, yes, equanimity.

'What're you thinking?' the woman asked her.

'I'm thinking – what on earth would Kenneth have thought about this?'

'Maybe not what you imagine.'

'What d'you mean?'

'He might've surprised you.'

'My brother?'

'Why not?'

'You don't know Kenneth.'

'No?'

'Didn't know, I mean. I get all confused with my tenses.'

'And you're not confused about him?'

'I – I've had a long time to form my opinions.'

Lindy nodded, then said 'I *didn't* have.'

'That's the difference between us, I suppose.'

'But I think we have a lot in common probably,' Lindy said.

'Have we?' The question came out sounding rather sharp. 'Well, we're two women,' Moira added quickly, to compensate. 'We've got that in common, so it's a start.'

Lindy smiled back at her, more broadly than the original remark justified.

'Look, Lindy, I should go home now.'

'Why?'

'Because – ' Moira smiled again, at Lindy's Glasgow naivety – 'because I've got a long journey. Eighty miles.'

'The trains run late, though.'

'I'll get tired.'

'Don't go yet,' Lindy said.

'But . . . '

'Stay, will you?'

In the end Moira gave in. They went to see a film, at an arthouse cinema. The six-thirty showing. *Place Vendôme.*

Catherine Deneuve's face filled the screen. These days it was as indecipherable, as mask-like, as Garbo's.

She was the alcoholic widow of a bankrupt jeweller, who agrees to a diamond scam organised by an old flame.

'I saw Deneuve in the Proust film,' Lindy said afterwards in the foyer. 'Odette goes to – I forget whose funeral it is. Her hat's got this high brim and a big feather and a veil you can see through, she's got jet drop earrings – '

'Like at Kenneth's funeral?'

'Ken took me to see the film.'

'He *what*?'

Lindy's hand fastened on her arm with surprising vigour, and she walked them both towards the front doors.

'No, Lindy. Tell me about Kenneth.'

'Tell you what? You've known him all your life, you said, remember?'

'*Ken*? You've got to explain all this to me.'

'This isn't the place.'

'What are you doing?'

'It's all right, Moira.'

'Where are you taking me?'

'I think Ken asked me the same thing.'

'Tell me. Please. I'm his sister. *Was*. That's different from – '

She stopped herself.

'From?'

He couldn't choose *me*, she meant. Me apart, he was able to pick whom he'd give his time to.

'Oh, I think I had to take my turn,' Lindy said. 'He was shared many ways.'

'He was?' Moira asked, surprised.

The pressure of bodies was directing them towards some spotlights. Lindy seemed bothered, blinking up at them. Did she have a problem with her eyes?

'Let's go.'

'I'll need to get my train.'

'Don't go, Moira.'

'But I must.'

'*Please*.'

Moira heard the crack in Lindy's voice. Clearly it meant a great deal that she should wait a while longer.

For the sake of emphasis Moira tipped back her cuff and consulted her watch.

'You can stay over with me,' Lindy said.

'Oh no.'

'Or I'll pay for a hotel. There's a Travel Something – '

'I couldn't let you do that.'

'I can afford it.'

'I didn't mean . . . '

'Let's just go, Moira.'

Was this safe? Over her shoulder Deneuve looked out of a poster for another film in her short season. Somehow her presence was soothing, reassuring: as if she was in on the conversation, and heard nothing to widen her eyes or tense her mouth with apprehension or alarm. Her expression was inscrutable but placid, almost serene.

'All right,' Moira heard herself saying.

'What?'

'If you want me to stay.'

Lindy stared back at her.

'I thought that was what your plan was?'

'Ken was always off for the ten o'clock.'

'But I'm not my brother.'

Lindy squeezed her arm.

The two of them smiled conspiratorially.

Lindy phoned, and booked a room at a chain hotel.

'My place is a tip, I'm afraid. I couldn't inflict it on you.'

'Did – did Kenneth think it was a tip?'

'If that's what he thought,' Lindy replied, 'the man – bless him – was too polite to say so.'

They ended up in an Italian restaurant. There were candles on the table, and Neapolitan songs on the sound system.

'Did you come here with Kenneth?'

'Yes, I think we did once.'

They talked a little about the film, about Deneuve, but wasn't there another topic they should be discussing?

'I realise now I didn't know an awful lot about my brother.'

'Do we ever know? Family least of all.'

'Do you see much of yours?'

'No,' Lindy said. 'No, I don't.'

'Is that intentional?'

'On their part it is.'

'I'm sorry.'

Lindy shook her head, as if it was water under the bridge, under several bridges by now.

'My brother, he did concern himself about his patients. Some doctors don't.'

'No. Ken was different. A one-off.'

'I never asked him what he did in Glasgow.'

'No?'

'When you live with someone, you have to – to respect their privacy. Both sides, I mean. Or it becomes claustrophobic.'

(Was she giving too much away? So be it.)

'Did you ever try to puzzle it out?' Lindy asked.

'Oh . . .'

(Well, I certainly couldn't have guessed *this*.)

Lindy put her elbows on the table and leaned forward, as if she was going to say something more confidential. The candle illuminated her face. She was wearing a lot of make-up. 'Slap', as Kenneth liked to call it. Perhaps she wasn't as young as first appearances suggested?

The McKean women were fortunate. 'Good bones' was one of Kenneth's yardsticks: whether or not you had them, and what they could do for you. In Moira's own choice of clothes, yes, she piled on the years. But facially she was spared. She had a younger woman's skin, thank God, and she didn't – yet – need to worry about her hair thinning.

Suddenly she felt sorry for Lindy. Having to keep up appearances. Putting on a front. Hair brushed forward, magenta lips, a silvery-blue sheen to her nails.

Everything a Carnbeg type wasn't.

The candle's flame wavered as Lindy sat back again, sliding her elbows off the table. The moment for disclosure had passed. Had the close scrutiny put her off her stroke?

'This is unusual for me, Lindy.'

'You can do what you like now, I guess. Live differently.'

'I – I haven't thought about that.' Moira fidgeted with the sachet of matches in the empty ashtray. 'How – how differently?'

'Do your own thing.'

'If I know what that is.'

'Your brother had quite a personality, didn't he? It's not easy, I s'pose, if you've to live with *that*.'

'No. No, it's not.'

'It's sad and everything, of course. Him getting ill and – But Ken wasn't a down-in-the-mouth sort of guy, was he?'

'No, he wasn't.'

(Funny to hear Kenneth called a 'guy'. But why should anything surprise her now?)

'Not one for the doldrums, my brother,' Moira said.

'No.'

They exchanged smiles.

'So, you've got to be yourself. How Ken was.'

'Do you think I'm *not* myself, Lindy?'

'What do *you* think?'

Wasn't the idea of 'being yourself' one of the world's big cons? Moira had grown up with a quite different ethos. You didn't declare everything, you kept certain things in reserve, secret if need be; you didn't inflict yourself on others, just as you expected a similar courtesy from them.

(All these thoughts whirling away in her head, after the long day, and now confronting a lit candle.)

'I think you're perfectly entitled,' Lindy was telling her. 'You've earned it, I say. No one's going to begrudge you it, honestly.'

'But I live in Carnbeg.'

'Carnbeg isn't going to tell you who Moira McKean is. It doesn't have the right.'

When Lindy spoke, Moira listened. To that soft, low, breathy, *sexy* voice, which always seemed to have something valuable it wanted to say to you. The timbre gave her a curious thrill, as it must have done to Kenneth also. Can voices and presences hypnotise? Lindy's silvery-blue eyes, to match those manicured nails, had an intensity and a force shining out of them. Even by candlelight, especially by a candle's flame, Moira could see that.

'I know you mean well, Lindy.'

'But?'

'No "but". I'll think about what you've said.'

'You're tired now?'

'Yes.'

Was Lindy tired, too? A few bloodshot traces had appeared in the whites of her eyes.

'I'll grab us a taxi,' Lindy said.

Taxis had always been a last resort for the McKeans, guilt-inducing, and only to be taken *in extremis*.

'Your brother always said, just get a cab.'

'*Kenneth* did?'

'Yes.' Lindy laughed. 'You haven't any more lovely brothers hidden away, have you?'

(Kenneth connects the two of us, for better or worse. The same Kenneth and a different Kenneth, and we shall always agree and never agree. He'll keep us guessing, an enigma to the last.)

'Can I ask you a question you might not want to answer?'

Lindy straightened in her chair. 'You can try, Moira.'

'You said you were a patient?'

'Yes.'

'You went – for advice?'

'Yes.'

'He gave you that advice?'

'He explained things to me. Very . . . sympathetically.'

'A woman's matter?'

Lindy nodded. 'I wanted to know about surgery. Certain adjustments. So we talked about that. Nothing embarrassed him.'

Lindy looked up at a young couple walking past. It was the man, not the woman, who held her attention.

(Was it possible . . . ? Moira wasn't aware that she had ever met a prostitute before. There was a thin dividing-line between what was and what wasn't selling yourself. Lindy had the look of a professional about her: God forgive her for thinking so, but that hair, those lips, the voice, the appraising eyes which expressed a different kind of interest for the man than for herself . . .)

'Quite a man of the world, Dr McKean.'

'Did you go to him in Carnbeg?'

There was a split-second's hesitation.

'No. No, it was here.'

'Because I thought maybe I'd have seen you around.'

'He *told* me about Carnbeg.'

'That sounds ominous.'

'No. Nothing like that.'

'I just wondered.'

'Shall we go now?'

Out on the street Lindy hailed a cab with the assurance of someone who was very practised at it. One arm shot up. 'Taxi!' she bellowed. Had she learned that lesson from the masterful Kenneth, who didn't have the opportunity in Carnbeg where taxis didn't tout for their business?

They drove off. On a corner Lindy rolled against her. The contact was – briefly – thrilling and threatening. The weight of her was greater than Moira might have imagined.

She was sitting here in the taxi in Kenneth's place, she felt. For those several seconds she and he had been sharing the experience of Lindy. Fragrant, unsubtle, feral and (frankly) mesmerising. Lindy who didn't have a surname, who frequented bars and restaurants and hadn't mentioned what she did for a living. Lindy, who had wanted Kenneth's help. Lindy, who had opened Moira's eyes to Glasgow and who might open her eyes to Kenneth also, if she was to allow her.

Moira couldn't get to sleep in her strange bed. She kept thinking of Windy Knowe in darkness.

She lay awake thinking of Kenneth, as she remembered him in the different rooms of the house, or out in the garden.

Kenneth going off to the surgery or returning home. Kenneth and herself with their friends, with their parents.

It was odd, but the harder she tried the more difficult it became to get his face into focus. He was there (or so she thought), and the next instant he was gone again.

It was easier to see Lindy, who was almost larger than life. She came into her line of vision, even showing up at Windy Knowe, unbidden. The features were all slightly too big, like a caricature.

She must have drifted off to sleep about four o'clock. She was woken by dustcarts in the street just after six, but managed to doze for a while longer.

When she got up she didn't feel much rested or refreshed.

Perhaps the bed was too new? Comfort wasn't everything. Familiarity counted for more. But maybe things could get *too* familiar and routine?

She tried switching on the TV, and discovered it was on red-eyed STAND BY. Noisy studio chatter about nothing very much. When she came out of the bathroom after her shower, they were discussing the coming season's colours. Normally that wouldn't have kept her in the room, but today was different. She stood watching and filing away the information, to have another topic for discussion with Lindy later.

Moira sat at a table in the coffee shop. She was hungry, and glad of the food placed in front of her, convenience-fare as it was.

She felt overdressed in her two-piece. She wondered why she had bought it. Just because she had always bought nice, safe two-pieces? Did she ever think whether or not it suited her? Kenneth would say nothing, supposing that it must be her taste. It had struck her in the mirrored lift coming down, the long skirt and crisp pleats made her look dumpy. The colour-matching was the equivalent of toning decor. For the first time she felt apologetic about clothes she had always thought almost-for-best.

Time for a rethink.

She looked across to the foyer for a first sight of Lindy.

Guests were paying their bills and departing. A new group arrived and deposited their luggage.

One younger man appeared, and stood looking in her direction. She realised that he wanted to speak to her.

Don't let him tell her Lindy couldn't come, and that the morning in Glasgow would have to be scuppered.

He came over. He pulled out a chair and, without speaking, sat down at her table.

Who was he? Lindy's boyfriend? The man she lived off, or did he live off her?

He leaned over and helped himself to a corner of croissant from the basket between them. What on earth would Kenneth have had to say about such behaviour?

'Your brother liked croissants, too. Big fan.'

Moira stared at him. Then she recognised him. He was the man she'd spoken to yesterday at the Return to Eden.

'Is Lindy not able to come?'

'Would that disappoint you?'

'Yes.' She nodded for emphasis. 'Yes, it would.'

The man unfolded a napkin and wiped his fingers.

'Quite a good film at the Film Theatre, so they say.'

'Did Lindy tell you?'

'No.'

'Then how do you know?'

Suddenly Moira was uneasy. She knew nothing really about the world Lindy inhabited. Everything and everyone round about her in the hotel was untested; she felt she was in hostile territory.

Now the young man was smiling at her. He couldn't stop himself smiling. Was he making fun of her?

'You don't see, do you?'

'See what?'

'I'm sorry,' he said.

Sorry?

'I am, Moira. Really.'

She wondered if she should call someone. Better just get up and walk across to the reception desk.

She pushed back her chair.

'Please don't go.' He had his hand on her wrist. The pressure hurt her.

'Please take your – '

'Ken wouldn't want you to go.' The tone of his voice was different. It was Lindy's voice talking to her. 'You mustn't go, all right?'

'I don't understand.'

'Ken really *didn't* tell you?'

'Tell me what?'

It wasn't clear to her, even at the end of their conversation, how Kenneth and he, Mark, had met. She glossed over that troublesome aspect of the past.

A smear of silver mascara on his right eyelid was the proof of what he'd been telling her, his fabulous tale.

Mark was sometimes Mark and sometimes Lindy.

At some point in the future Mark might be Lindy all the time.

Kenneth would have advised him about that, the surgical options, but now Kenneth wasn't here to do that, and all their lives were poorer.

'It's a long process, you see. And there's the whole legal side of it.'

Moira didn't know what to say in response, so she just let Mark talk. Earlier on it had occurred to her, perhaps he's mad, or bad, but suspicion evaporated.

This was Lindy's story, and Lindy she *could* believe: Lindy fighting to be Lindy, and let the world go hang.

She agreed to go outside with Mark, they'd head for the city centre.

As she came back down in the lift Moira thought, there is fortitude to be found in small corners, in unexpected places: acts of heroism taking place at any moment, unbeknown to you.

'Not every day,' Mark explained after he'd settled the bill and they'd stepped out on to the street. 'I was Lindy just at the weekends.'

'No luggage?' the porter called after them both.

Moira shook her head, and the porter gave her a knowing look.

'Come on,' Mark said, taking her arm.

'The weekends?' she persisted. 'You were telling me . . . '

He/she would spend Friday evening to Sunday evening in women's clothes. He/she put Lindy to the test: travelling in trains, standing in supermarket queues, visiting a coffee shop, slowly perusing the shelves in the local library, striding purposefully into the Ladies and – afterwards – walking unconcernedly out again.

'I don't know what to say,' Moira told him. 'I really don't.'

'You don't approve?'

'Why do you think that?'

Mark shrugged.

'You couldn't be more wrong about me,' she said.

'Good. Good, I'm glad.'

'I'm not the person I seem to be, you know.'

'Then that makes two of us.'

She needed the fresh air, and gulped it down. She was glad for the walk, for the simple motion.

Mark showed her where he bought Lindy's clothes. They slowly made their way round the counters of a cosmetics department, and the assistants exchanged cheerful greetings with her companion.

He told her which creams and foundations he liked best, and had she tried this one or that one? No, she hadn't, but she let him persuade her. She jotted down some names, and then decided, why not splash out on that Colors Number Three they had, which he assured her – very politely – was what was required.

'Just what the doctor ordered,' he quipped.

Moira admitted that she didn't give her appearance much thought.

'Some folk prefer that,' he said.

'I'm not sure *I* do,' she said.

'Is it from, well, laziness or something?'

'I was never much encouraged.'

'If you'd got married . . . '

'If I'd been married, yes, it might have been different.'

Over coffee Moira told him about herself and Gordon Ritchie. Her second boyfriend, a fling which got serious. Getting engaged, and then both of them having second thoughts, and calling it off. She had never told anyone out of the family before. And she hadn't said to her family, no, he *wasn't* suitable, not at all, which is why I wish we'd run off and had a silly, frivolous, dangerous life together and been happy for a while. She didn't censor some of the details but Mark didn't bat a silvery eyelid.

She was seeing him both as Mark and, from little giveaways (hand movements mostly, also that sideways tilt of the head), as Lindy. They discussed Lindy not as someone else but as a briefly absent presence from the room. Mark referred to her affectionately, although it was clear that Lindy had caused him many problems.

'It was more difficult than I thought. Getting her right. But you have to start somewhere.'

Moira sat shaking her head. She couldn't begin to comprehend the enormity of the task. And for every minute of being Lindy in public, he'd been there in the firing line – sometimes literally, when missiles flew.

Kenneth floated in and out of the conversation, a little elusively. He'd been in this place, in that place, at such and such a time. (She could check up later, but maybe Kenneth deserved his privacy on the matter. Mark was disclosing as much or as little as he meant her to know. Fine. Kenneth as his friend, his mentor, perhaps as his lover.)

They saw a girl not unlike Lindy walking along the street, and they both stopped to turn and look back at her, lost in admiration.

On the train back she recognised one of Kenneth's patients, a Mrs Frew. They stood talking for a few moments.

Mrs Frew offered her condolences. 'He was a fine man.'

[133]

'Yes. Yes, he was.'

'I wish there were more like him about, Miss McKean, so I do.'

'I'm sure he'd have been glad to hear you say that.'

'It's a fine thing to do good, I mean. And leave good thoughts behind you.'

The words stuck in Moira's head for the rest of the journey; and, yes, they did give her comfort.

She felt better for Glasgow, she decided. She felt *lightened* by it.

She sat looking at her reflection in the carriage window as the train passed through a long tunnel by the Tay. Funny, she thought, how being a woman – doing unthinking feminine things with your hands, your feet – should be so awkward and so desirable for someone like Mark to do, starting from scratch.

Everywhere around you, nothing was quite as it appeared. Could people guess what a turmoil of thoughts she was trying to order in her head, torn between grieving and rejoicing?

And with that the train roared out of the tunnel into daylight and, unexpectedly, into scatterfire afternoon sunshine.

When she reached Carnbeg, obliging gusts blew Moira uphill.

At Windy Knowe everything was just the same. Except, of course, that there was no Kenneth.

Although, in another sense, Kenneth was everywhere. He haunted the house, just as – she supposed – he had haunted her life.

She defied him. 'Poor Kenneth!' she said aloud. But she wasn't in a mood to feel angry with him.

She picked up the little pocket diary from a table top. One thing leads to another, she thought, and the route is erratic, wayward, leading you don't know where. It was exciting, and daunting, and she felt exhilarated by the past couple of days. Somewhere in her bag was Mark's/Lindy's telephone number and the address of the 'tip' where he/she lived.

She dropped, flopped, down into an armchair.

'The case is not hopeless,' she heard herself saying, in a voice which came out sounding oddly like a feminised version of Kenneth's. On the journey she had studied the shiny pages of her magazine with an unusual degree of attention, reading the cosmetics round-up and fashion tips, comparing the clothes in different 'promotional features'.

She pulled herself forward in the snug chair and got to her feet. She felt restless. She pulled up the bottom sash of the window. The old wood rasped. She needed air to breathe.

She could hear the hurried, urgent bell of St Aloysius's sounding for mass. It had always had a neurotic, defensive ring to her ear, as if it realised it might be swamped by the big bells of the Presbyterian churches on either side.

She had problems with RC aesthetics: the green and gold, the candlelight, the vestments, the craven assault on the nostrils. But as she listened, she heard . . .

What?

Something she hadn't been aware of before.

The persistence of dogged faith. Madcap heroism.

She thought of the martyrs who had gone down, only to rise again. She pictured the blessed saints in their stained-glass glory.

Kenneth was under turf, and Mark was between two lives. And she was here.

Standing at her open window, feeling the fresh breeze come in over her arms, she listened to that tinny bell. It had been chiming past her for centuries, singing of souls redeemed by suffering, but singing out.

She stared at her wrist. There, like tribal marks, were the lines of foundation Mark had traced on her skin. She held her wrist to the light. He'd been right. The middle tone, that was the choice for *her*: Number Three, no doubt about it.

Kimono

Many years ago.

The window of a dress shop in Edinburgh.

A man stands outside on the pavement admiring the silk of the garment, its hang, its colours. The mannequin's elegant pose reminds him of someone who is anything but frozen, who is intensely alive when she's with him.

He pushes on the door. A bell rings. The assistants hear and stand to attention behind their glass display-cases. The owner, wearing a fur tippet, takes a few steps forward.

'Good afternoon, sir,' she says in her refined diction for refined callers. 'In what way may we be of assistance to you?'

Many years later.

An elderly lady, living out her days in a Scottish inland resort town, takes up the story.

Imagine her standing at a window at the back of her house, looking out on to her washing green.

Her neighbours saw it drying in her garden on wash-days and called it a 'kimono'.

The silk was Japanese, patterned with gold chrysanthemums on a rich blue ground. Really, though, it was a peignoir, a morning-gown. Parisian, reaching to her ankles, almost weightless.

The silk followed all the curves of her body. When she was younger, much younger, the garment had flattered her, and shamelessly so.

Archie always used to find it hard to take his eyes off her when she was wearing it. Perhaps their neighbours had supposed he must have bought it for her, never mind that he was a kirk elder and on this and that Carnbeg committee.

She'd had it for their honeymoon, producing it from her suitcase. 'Just part of my trousseau,' she quipped to Archie. And then, seeing his confusion, she diverted responsibility for it to (nameless) friends of her mother. That was an outright invention, a lie, but she couldn't admit the truth. Archie was troubled enough by the heat of Sintra, by the heavy Portuguese cuisine and the water, by her keeping their bedroom in darkness at night, by his finding her rather more knowing in conjugal matters than he had expected.

The peignoir had been a gift to her from her lover.

She had known David wasn't the sort ever to marry and settle down. But it was her fate to cross paths with him at twenty years old, to experience his passion – and simultaneously to alight on her own.

Somehow she kept the relationship a secret from her widowed mother. Her mother, meanwhile, searching round, found Archie for her. Girls from genteel backgrounds like hers didn't accuse their mothers of being mercenary, and nor did she. In the far-off 1930s, in hidebound rural Perthshire, marriages were complex social and financial arrangements. Girls of her upbringing weren't meant to have affairs before they became engaged: in her case, an affair with a different man. But for her it made marriage an easier prospect. Archie liked her well enough, but he was affectionate rather than loving.

David started hanging back. But every so often during Archie's protracted old-fashioned wooing she persuaded David to meet her incognito, to sustain her – physically, emotionally, against all received Calvinist wisdom – sustain her for what she foresaw would be her inevitable return to the fold of middle-class morality.

She had been a good wife to Archie. Everyone in Carnbeg agreed about that, even though the union was childless.

Archie had been faithful to her, she didn't doubt, for all those years. And, miraculously, she had been faithful to him. From their wedding-day in that draughty old church – all through the war – to his dying day, and ever since.

A cardboard box with the name of a swanky Edinburgh modiste. Candy stripes, a line illustration of a willowy young woman in hat and gloves and smart town tweeds.

'It'll last you a lifetime,' David had told her when she unwrapped his present from its nest of white tissue paper. Adding cryptically, 'If you're careful, Elspet.'

She had wondered during her first year of marriage, and then the second, when would she see David again? He had understood the advantages to her of becoming Archie's wife: Archie would give her a comfortable home, he would look after her mother, too, he would allow her to discover new virtues in herself.

Did David mean those to include fidelity?

However it happened, she had lost contact with David after the war. Canada, someone said; another had heard New Zealand.

She was left with her memories. Those might have dimmed more with time if she hadn't had her silk wrap to help.

The profusion of gold blooms against dark navy, flecks of silver on the chrysanthemum petals. A haiku mood, a melancholy kind of joy. The kimono transported her back . . .

Walking through the rooms of their gaunt sandstone villa in its pine garden, in her mind she was wearing it that first time for David, in a Perth hotel room she could no longer recall the details of. David was telling her she was beautiful, that she should always remain beautiful, please, just for him.

She had washed the kimono very carefully whenever she needed to, then laid it over a winterdykes on the green behind the house. In the old days she was more cavalier, used hotter and soapier water, and then let it hang up on the line to blow, to turn somersaults in the wind.

Now she was terribly afraid of doing it any damage. They were old companions, and they knew too much about each other. Without it, she wasn't sure that her memories could find their way back unaided to then. To that mad, rapturous interlude of only eighteen months in her young life.

DV, she would go first, before the kimono. Please God. (The same God Archie used to hold out a collection plate for, every Sunday without fail.) Then, after she'd gone, everything in the house would be sold or, like the clothes in the wardrobe, given away.

She feared for the kimono.

Dry-cleaning wasn't going to save it from a careless owner, if anyone should take an interest in the contents of its box. (There was no shop of that name now in the Edinburgh street, it was all building societies and estate agents and soulless watering-holes.)

In the middle of the long, dark night, when she couldn't sleep, she ached for the kimono and its fate as if it was her own.

The first tiny hole would appear. Then a second. The silk immediately round about would begin to corrode.

More and more holes, more and more vanishings – faster and faster – across the shrinking surface of the silk until the chrysanthemum garden had gone, and no one to know it had ever been there.

It was the last thing of her aunt's that Mrs Monteith came to as she was clearing out the big bedroom.

The cardboard box on top of the wardrobe.

She stood on the stool and reached up, got dust on her sleeve, and wanted to scream. She screamed inside her head.

Bad enough having to deal with your parents' effects.

She had never been able to work out her aunt. Her late Aunt Elspet. Something about her manner, behind the politeness. As if she had you sized up, as if she could read you like a book.

Living as she'd done in a backwater like this. What was her experience of the world?

Mrs Monteith stepped off the stool. She dropped the box, and the lid fell off.

Damn it!

Tissue paper. And what else?

She was too tired by her day's labours to be interested.

For the 'save' or 'bin' category?

She looked at her watch. She was late. The house oppressed her, with its atmosphere of an unfulfilled life. She'd be glad to get away. She was someone who liked to be kept busy.

The phone was ringing in her bag, and she went to answer it.

When the man from the charity shop came back upstairs he thought the box had been placed among the 'save' items, and took it out to his car.

When Mrs Monteith returned from speaking to her family at home, she had forgotten all about the box. Other matters preoccupied her now. How to cope with life and all its chaos threatening to break out on you . . .

Well, you never know, Mel says, what might show up in a thrift shop.

She goes in, and at first she thinks Jim isn't going to follow her inside. But, a few moments later, she hears the door opening behind her, as she trawls the rack of second-hand clothes.

Even when she was a little girl, people told her she had an eye for colour. Colour and form.

She likes to mix 'n' match.

She used to think that when she grew up she would become a designer. But when she left home early, money was tight; she needed to get a job, and serving in a shop was the easiest option. And then Jim came along, and her head got turned, and what with one thing and another . . .

But. But it's been four years now, and her twenties are starting to go in, and in four years you can learn a lot about someone: even if it's realising there's just as much you *don't* know about them.

'Look at this!'

She opens the old box, with its shop name she's never heard of and a line illustration of a woman in hat and gloves and tweeds. She pulls out what's inside, with a sixth sense to handle it carefully.

'What is it?' Jim asks, with little interest.

'Silk. Something to wear. It's one of those . . . What're they called? The Japanese wear them.'

'Search me,' he says.

She remembers. 'A kimono.'

'Oh, put it away, Mel.'

'What?' she says.

'You're not thinking of giving *that* thing house-room, are you?'

'Why not? Why shouldn't – '

He interrupts her. 'What would you do with it? Not *wear* it?'

'Look at the colours,' she says. 'And the stitching. It's exquisite.'

'Some old woman's, probably. Dead and gone.'

'So?' she says. She is on the point of telling him, it's how we all end up, eventually.

'It's probably spooked,' he tells her. He laughs, without any fun in his voice.

'You watch too many videos,' she says.

'What's wrong with that?'

'Ssh, Jim! People'll hear us.'

'Deaf as posts, this lot, I'll bet.'

She sighs. It's heartfelt.

'What's the big sigh for?' he asks.

'It doesn't matter,' she says.

But she knows that it does. Oh yes.

She stands there with the box open, holding in her hands – hands which are shaking slightly – the delicate silk and its blazing garden. This moment, she feels, this moment has enormous significance. For her. For them both.

What does she do after she's put the kimono back into its box? Does she turn her back on it, and let Jim suppose she's heeded him? Or does she buy it? And if she buys it, what is Jim going to say?

She returns the kimono to its box, the box of faded candy-stripes, and then she takes the box across to the counter.

'I'll have this, thanks,' she says, before she can stop herself. She smiles at the woman, knowing how a customer's smile can lift you.

Jim has seen and left the shop.

Outside she looks for him. He's walked off, spinning his car keys on an index finger. She stands watching him. He doesn't look round.

She spots a sign to the railway station, across the street.

She waits for a break in the traffic and crosses, holding the box close to her. She can feel her heart beating faster against the cardboard. This is ridiculous, this is mad, but she isn't giving herself time to change her mind. She's following her instincts. In her imagination she's crossing a Japanese garden, a glorious chrysanthemum field.

On this side of the street, somewhere, is the station. And a train back from Carnbeg to Glasgow.

She already knows that it's over with Jim. Two or three years down the line she will be a designer, making rooms for her customers – no, for her clients. They will be spare interiors with an oriental bias, and clean space in which to think straight. People will pay her so that they can find themselves; and finding who they are, perhaps with luck they will hit on happiness too.

End of story. But this one, Mel tells herself, it's only beginning.

OTTAKAR'S

a love for books

The Edinburgh Bookshop
57 George Street
Edinburgh, EH2 2JQ
0131 225 4495
george.street@ottakars.co.uk

SALE

27   2 64291   22 Aug 2004 12:46

CASHIER: AURELIE

9780954407551 Carnbeg		9.99
BOOKS		6.95
9780948877575		

TOTAL	ITEMS	2	16.94

CASH		17.00
CHANGE CASH		0.06-

Head Office: St John's House,
72 St John's Road, London, SW11 1PT

Vat No: 561997200
Company Reg No: 2133199

All of It

A garden in Highgate, one summer's night in 1975.

A young couple in evening dress lie back in a vast saggy sofa which has been mysteriously spirited out on to the garden terrace.

Bill Evans's trio at Montreux trails out of the open window of the drawing-room.

Richard puts his arm round Joanna's shoulder. It's a good strong shoulder, just what she's going to need as a GP: and there for him to cry on, if things don't work out when he starts his job at the hospital. He tells her this, and she loves him enough to think it's about the funniest thing she's heard all night.

Of course they're slightly drunk. But this is the proper graduation party for them both, although it's their friend Miles's as well, which (being best friends) is why they're here, at Antonia's parents' house, but they feel they have all the generosity in the world, so why not share the occasion?

And in three months they'll be married. Dr and Dr Ebdon.

They both know they're clever, in their physical prime, they have other talents (sporting, cultural), and this is a perfect time for ambitious bright sparks. Why deny the obvious? Medics have to be practical above all else, don't they?

They both lie looking up at the stars.

'I'll always remember this night,' Joanna says.

She laughs again, the low laugh from deep inside her that Richard fell for the first time he heard it.

'Always,' she says.

'Yes?'

Richard runs his hand slowly down the brocade of her dress, on the thigh, fingers spreading to the inner thigh.

'Oh, doctor!' she says.

'No, *I*'m the one with the problem, doctor,' he says.

'What problem is that, doctor?'

'I keep getting this fantasy.'

'A fantasy?'

'Yes. I fantasise my doctor's the one doing the undressing.'

'Really?'

'And I don't know what to do.'

She turns and stares into his eyes, fairly seriously although she's holding in her laughter.

'What do the textbooks say about it?' she asks.

'They're no help.'

'So what *would* help?'

'I think I need some revision of anatomy.'

He takes her hand and pulls her to her feet.

In the summer-house they make love in the shadows, half naked, on a moonlit divan of old cushions and rolls of canvas, with a tennis net for a bolster. It's the first time they've had sex somewhere that the coitus might be interrupted, and he comes almost before he's inside her and as she's still positioning to receive him.

The jazz gets a little louder, and Richard slithers off, pulls up his trousers. There's seepage on to the cushions, a trail of dampness. Nothing should surprise her now, a freshly qualified doctor, but she's still puzzled about exactly where with Richard the emotions come in.

'Come on, darling,' he urges her, buttoning up. 'Folks on the prowl, from the sound of things.'

He helps her back into her dress, does up her zip. He finds her shoes for her.

'Christ, that was exciting, Jo,' he whispers loudly.

'Well,' she says, 'it was certainly different.'

He kisses her neck, that good strong shoulder. She stands and lets him, because he is her fiancé. And because she's still shaken by the speed and fervour of it, unlike their long sweaty rituals in bed followed by morning lie-ins.

They could have alighted on somewhere else to live, but scanning the house adverts in a solicitor's window in Perth – when Richard had finished work at the hospital for the day – they noticed two cottages for sale in Carnbeg. They remembered driving through the town three years ago, and the recollection wasn't displeasing for either of them.

They made an appointment to view both properties.

They arrived early intentionally, wanting to put off time and reacquaint themselves. Carnbeg had possibilities, they agreed. It felt a little unreal after London: no crowds, no build-up of petrol fumes, polite 'Good afternoons' from passers-by.

They could have settled anywhere perhaps, but there always has to be a somewhere.

Joanna spent a year in the cottage, their new home, bringing up Charlotte. Then she heard that one of the local Carnbeg doctors was moving on, and she made enquiries.

Dr McKean ran the smaller of the town's two practices, and he decided, with some encouragement from his sister, that it was time to have a woman on board. He would have preferred it to be full-time, but they came to a compromise.

Richard was agreeable to the notion of paid help in the house, perhaps because their old friends were going down the same path (London being London, that meant Scandinavian au pairs). For themselves, they found a local girl, one of a big farm family with plans on doing paediatric nursing and the reddest country cheeks outside a children's picture book; she proved very reliable, and just a little dull, and adjusted so easily to the job that she was still around when, secondly, Emily was born and, thirdly, Imogen.

Miles and Antonia down in London were into kindergartens and Montessori, and so Richard wanted nothing less for their own. Later, they would have ballet lessons and pony classes and – give Richard his due – no expense was spared. Their daughters deserved only the best that Carnbeg and their corner of Perthshire could offer.

Dear Antonia and Miles,

Come and see us if you do come up, won't you? Remember, August 12th is the big day round abouts – bang, bang! We'd both *love* to see you.

Richard is kept very busy at Perth, I feel so sorry for him. I can't compare the practice here with anything – I suppose they all even out for bizz. Altho' it's the regulars who bother me, the hypochondriacs I mean, I feel I should be more sympathetic with them but, oh they do waffle on. One of the Carnbeg chemists told me even *he* couldn't read my hand-writing, and I said, oh they teach it now, and ne'er a twitch of amusement on his granite visage.

You've got to come and make us laugh. We'll take you Highland dancing, which is a huge hoot for us, but how v. solemn and po-faced everyone else is about it!

Richard was all for trying new positions.

The Missionary is for the world and his wife, he said.

Joanna was persuaded to experiment. Side-on, legs going this way or that way, or her perched at the end of the bed facing forward and with her feet and ankles over his shoulders. From behind doggy-style was last of all, and her least favourite, but Richard said it was especially arousing for him.

'I can't see you, though,' she told him.

'You see me for the other twenty-three hours and fifty-five minutes of the day.'

'Fifty-nine, don't you mean?'

'Sorry . . . ?'

'It doesn't matter,' Joanna mumbled, aware that the remark – the barb – was lost on him. 'Can I turn round now?'

'You *are* funny, darling. My funny Valentine.'

She gave the rearguard approach lowest marks as they lay debating which was best.

'We should try the stirrups in the hospital sometimes,' Richard said.

She presumed he was joking.

'No, really,' he persisted.

Weird and semi-public, and nothing left to the imagination.

'Well, *you* only have to lie there, Jo.'

'Yes. Yes, that's true,' she said, deadpan.

The cottage was what was wrong. It wasn't 'them'.

A semi-detached villa came up for sale, high ceilings and bay windows. They bid, more than they could truly afford; but it was only because Richard launched a charm offensive on the owner, 'Old Ma Mauchlin' as he called her in private, that the woman agreed to let them buy Nithsdale, notwithstanding that another sealed bid had trumped theirs.

They didn't have enough furniture to fill it. But what did that matter? It would be fun deciding what to get next and then scrimping and saving.

They did lay a terrace at the back, which was south-facing. It meant they could sit out on summer evenings: if they had an evening free together, that was, when Richard didn't have any rota duties and Joanna wasn't on call. It wasn't so easy. They planned parties and, forty-eight hours before, there would be a hitch, which meant re-scheduling, and finding replacements for any fellow medics who now couldn't come.

Joanna thought that Richard – no, 'Rick' she had to remember to call him, since he had recently decided he wasn't a 'Richard' after all – Rick was putting on some weight. But he denied it.

'Well, maybe a couple of pounds or so,' he conceded.

More than that, she thought treacherously.

'I can still get into the clothes I wore before we got married.'

Well, not everything from those days was still wearable in fashion terms, so she didn't know where that sort of reasoning took them.

She was trying to keep them on a healthy diet, and now tried even harder. She expected it was the canteen fare at the hospital, and the pint of Tennent's – maybe two pints – Richard/Rick usually ended up downing after he came off duty. She suspected he drove with too much drink inside him, but so far so good, or so lucky.

Which could be the motto of their marriage, really.

London was beckoning, Richard felt.

He would phone Miles, or Miles would phone him, discussing this and that career option.

He mentioned them to Jo, trying to sound casual. Perhaps that made her think he was only half-hearted about it, but he sensed that she was a lot less keen on the idea of moving south.

'It's not as if we'd be going *back*,' she said. 'These are the only jobs we've known.'

First jobs, yes. The jobs you have before you get other, better jobs.

'But what about the girls?' she asked him, as if that was an insoluble dilemma.

London, he persisted, would provide all the mental stimulation they needed.

(She *was* pulling his leg, wasn't she?)

Somehow the parade of bodies which passed in front of Joanna daily, so many of them malfunctioning and in various states of decline, didn't diminish her sense of the erotic. She longed to have her sense of *normality* confirmed as well. She needed to feel her body working, as it wouldn't always be able to go on working for her. But she also needed to be taken to a plane beyond and above, call it the spiritual or whatever.

Come and see us if you're down, Miles had PS'd on their Christmas card.

It was Antonia who answered the phone when he rang.

'Richard? Are you in London? Whereabouts?'

Close enough for dinner. Antonia came to the restaurant on her own, because Miles was away with a delegation to Canada.

'He's trying to get himself a profile,' Antonia explained.

'It's all right for some, isn't it?' Richard ventured.

'You were very welcome to have supper at the house.'

Richard tapped his inside pocket, where he kept his wallet. 'It's not lovely Canadian dollars, but I get expenses, too.'

'I'm not medical,' she said.

'*They* don't know that.'

'Won't you get caught?'

'Only if I'm stupid enough.'

It was an enjoyable evening for them both. Neither wanted dinner to end.

'They've got a piano bar at my hotel,' Richard said. 'You've got to see that.'

They sat in the plush and gilt piano bar, drinking brandy coffees, laughing at the ribbed velvet wallpaper.

'They don't know when to stop, those designers,' Richard said.

'It's Arab taste, I expect.'

'*They* don't have much to teach us, do they?'

'They bring in the money, though. Miles gets some of them.'

'But his place isn't decked out like a tart's boudoir, is it?'

They were each conscious that they had drunk quite a lot. The mood was mellow and forgiving.

Richard said to her, come and see the view from the twelfth floor. Upstairs in his room, standing at the window and rubbing her sore foot, Antonia pointed with the shoe in her hand to where Barnes must be, and then in a different direction to where her parents lived, up in Highgate.

'I'm just wasting my life,' she said suddenly.

Richard laughed.

'I mean it, Rick. Who needs art dealers?'

'You can't possibly – '

'I'm wasting it compared to you.'

'I'm only doing what Miles does.'

'No, he does it in Wigmore Street. You're in a hospital, with *people*.'

'His patients are people, too. They're just as real.'

'Are they?' she said.

'Well, aren't they?'

'God, like the type who come swanning into the gallery. Looking at you as if you're a bad smell.'

'Aren't you awfully brisk and businesslike with them?'

'Is that how you think of me?'

'Able to look after yourself, I mean – and put *them* in their place. '

'Cold?'

'Did I say that?'

'No. But maybe you don't need to say – '

'Cold is the last word I'd use for you, Antonia.'

'That bloody awful name!'

'What name?'

'Antonia.'

'Is something wrong?'

'My God. *Everything*'s wrong!'

'So, what would help to make it right?'

She closed her eyes as Richard pulled her hair back from her face. She dropped her head on to his shoulder. The shoe fell from her hand.

Richard went with her to Barnes, and he waited outside in the cab until she'd opened her front door and was safely in the hall. She was holding the morning's delivery of mail, ready to embark on another day, as she waved out to him.

He told the driver to let him off in West Brompton. From there he walked into town.

This wasn't an entirely new experience for him. Since moving north there had been a young nurse in the cardiovascular unit; and then a temp they got in to the X-ray department, Janice, who'd gone off afterwards to this job and that locally, which involved him in tracking her down but – usefully – they had his car for their extramural activities. Once Janice had left her folding umbrella behind, under the front seat, and he'd told Joanna it was his vinegary superior Dr Waddell's, giving her a lift to the station one day.

Neither of them was in competition with Joanna. Janice had auburn hair, and Keltie was a bottle-blonde. Both girls had the sort of body no red-blooded male was capable of walking past, sniffing those pheromones. Everything was out on display, temptingly on offer, and it was yours if you knew how to ask nicely. You weren't *meant* to resist, for God's sake.

It was harmless enough, it was froth, looked at like that. The two girls didn't want more than a good time, Richard was sure. They'd had other boyfriends, and knew their stuff, and even managed to slow him down a little at his all-or-nothing Big Moment. Both parties (he, she) had got what they needed, hadn't they. It was just a kind of basic accounting, without surplus or deficit.

Doctors were pragmatists, and perhaps that was part of the attraction they offered.

They worked hard, and they also played (pun intended) hard.

The devil will be in the details, and Joanna sometimes felt Richard lost the minutiae, he was so intent on the bigger picture. She had married a man with ambitions for himself, and she was glad that his abilities were being recognised – his consultancy work, standing in for more senior external examiners (as *he* would be one day) – but he was happy to leave others to deal with the business he hadn't time to finish.

Rick planned their family holidays and away days, he motivated and organised; the mundane aspects of preparation didn't interest him, however, and she and the girls were delegated to deal with the clearing up and tidying away. Rick's justification would have been that he took the responsibilities, and was on the receiving end of any brickbats. The glory also came to him, Joanna sussed, and her husband knew from his work to milk the recognition factor for all it was worth.

Antonia and Miles had moved into her parents' house in Highgate. 'Come on in, Jo,' Antonia said, leading her into a conservatory which she called 'the orangery'.

'You used to have a terrace out here.'

'That's right. But we thought this was a better use of space.'

'You had a sofa out on it. That night of the party.'

'Did we?'

'Don't you remember?'

'God, I needed to be everywhere at once, that night. Making sure nothing was getting damaged.'

'A long squashy sofa.'

'Must've been the old Liberty one. Sounds like Miles's mad idea.'

'And Rick and I watched the stars.'

Antonia pointed up at the raked double-glazed panels on the roof.

'Well . . . ?'

'I can't see any,' Joanna said.

'We don't get them now like we used to. I don't know why not. There's no smoke, I mean.'

'We don't know everything about everything,' Joanna said. 'Not yet.'

'Like what?'

'Abouts stars and space. About lots of things. Which is quite consoling, I suppose.'

Antonia smiled brightly.

The wattage of that smile came back to trouble Joanna a few weeks after she'd tackled Richard and opened a few doors, figuratively, into previously closed and darkened rooms.

Antonia's smile in the orangery lured Joanna to talk.

No, Carnbeg wasn't really her kind of place. No, the worst of general practice was thinking 'this is it', it was always going to be like this, a straight run to the grave. Your patients turned out to be the second generation of a family you'd treated, or a third. The genes of the fathers, etc. Funny, too, how motherhood wasn't quite the great panacea, seeing how much else acts as an influence on your children. And no, Rick wasn't going to change the world, and he knew it, and it made him grumpy some days.

Antonia said to her, wasn't it better to try, at least, than not to make the effort at all?

'It depends what life's like for everyone else. Others are involved, too.'

That was more than Joanna had meant to say, but she couldn't help herself, it tumbled out. Antonia looked so receptive and understanding, and anyway they'd been friends ever since Miles introduced them (the same day he'd introduced her to Richard).

'I don't know what the answer is,' Antonia said simply.

'Your painters and writers must know.'

Antonia looked puzzled by that. Joanna didn't see why; she had always been a little in awe of Antonia's High Art credentials. If Antonia didn't have a clue from her reading and from dinner-party talk with artists and gallery colleagues, then who among her acquaintances *did* have the grey matter to cope?

Dear Dr Ebdon,
We still await . . .
Richard had put in for a job in London.

He had asked Miles if he would write him one of the references he needed, but the hospital informed him they hadn't received it, not even the copy Miles said he'd sent to replace it, which (he claimed) must have gone missing in the labyrinth of its bureaucracy.

In any event the job-chase didn't come to anything. Richard had second thoughts once he was there for the interview (that one unsupplied reference notwithstanding). He had a presentiment about it, streamers of doubt in his water.

The atmosphere was cut-throat, and on the return journey north – he'd told Jo he was at another of his conferences – he wondered if she wasn't correct after all about London. At home he was on the receiving end of some awkward questions from Jo, who had clearly wised up in the interim, guessing that he hadn't been where he said he'd been.

A stilted couple of days resulted, but they got through them. He brightened up, his spirits lifted, and somehow he won Jo round. He could just about believe – after some alfresco malarky in a castle ruin and a quick screw in a turret, after recouping their energy on piled bowls of mussels at The Smokehouse – he could just about believe that *this* was the good life here in Carnberg, and the best option.

Almost.

A car was parked by the roadside, awkwardly slewed into the verge, with its outward indicator light flashing a warning.

Joanna was driving back into Carnbeg from a house call when she saw the man waving to her. She recognised him as an occasional patient, and drew alongside.

'My car went into a spin,' he said. 'Something's failed, and I can't tell what.'

'Can I help?' Call in at a garage for you, she meant.

He asked if he could come with her.

'Yes, of course,' she said, scarcely thinking about it.

She drove them along the Carnmòr road. He relaxed in the passenger seat, spreading his legs. She thought, I suppose that *was* the real reason?

She found herself stumbling about for things to say. Usually it was the patients who were tongue-tied.

He sat slumped, with his elbow up on the sill, hand to the side of his head: as if he wasn't wanting to be recognised if anyone saw him.

He had a wife, a family, she remembered. A self-employed plumber – no, a joiner.

Twice it happened. Her hand, changing gear, brushed against his thigh. She wasn't used to a big leg sprawled there beside her; usually Rick drove when they were together, unless he was one over the eight.

She felt self-conscious after that. She kept watching herself in the windscreen mirror, to check how red her face was. At one point he turned his head to look out of the side window, and she glanced over at him. He was quite good-looking, in a rough and ready way: not *her* way at all, of course.

She had to concentrate on the concealed corner on the steep turn up on to Achistiel Road, and it was there that he put his hand on her breast. She stalled the car, and they started to run back downhill.

Afterwards, what seemed the most curious aspect of it all was that she didn't tell him to stop, she didn't shout at him, what the hell d'you think you're doing?

She continued driving, up to the junction. She crossed straight over on to the opposite side of the main road, without being in any fit state to judge if there was traffic coming or not.

She was lucky, they both were. The engine revved, she crashed through the gears. She still hadn't spoken, and neither had he.

She realised that she was on the route back to the surgery. What she should have done was turn left to reach the first garage, Bannerman's.

'I'm up here,' he said.

He nodded in the direction of Knockie Brae.

'I – I'm going the wrong way.'

'I wouldn't say that.'

It wasn't road directions he was meaning, was it?

She knew he was going to ask her inside when she stopped outside his house. And at the instant when he did ask – in a gentle, deep voice which she found thrilling her to the quick, as if she was some silly little girl – she listened, she let his words wrap round her, and she couldn't honestly think of a single reason, here and now, why not to do as he was inviting her to do.

The way in off the back road was private. She could claim she was paying a house call, if anyone enquired.

She understood as he unlocked the door from the yard and led the way inside that he was double-checking no one was at home. He quickly picked up a pencilled note from the kitchen unit and tucked it into his trouser back pocket.

'I always report back,' she said, 'to the surgery.'

'But today you're on a mercy mission.'

'Is that what it is?' she asked him.

He smiled.

'Well, I suppose,' he said, 'we've got to figure out who's rescuing who here.'

How perceptive of him, she thought.

For the first time she allowed herself to smile. She felt her whole being lightening. Smiles and laughter. It's what she should have been recommending to her problem patients, the ones who didn't respond to pills and medicines. Open up to experience – try something new and the opposite of what you expect – astonish yourself!

He had strong, capable hands. A craftsman's rather than a workman's. They passed over her body appreciatively, as if he was approving some planed piece of wood before he got to work on it. That didn't trouble her, somehow it helped to make the business less personal.

Afterwards, though, she saw it as a sign of his consideration for her. It was as if he'd been, yes, *revering* her. Even his silences had been – what? – they'd had a kind of eloquent solemnity, as he transported her, as he raptured her.

(Rick by contrast kept up a running commentary; he expressed every gradation of pleasure, excitement, attainment, diminuendo.)

Alec Mooney. Her carpenter-redeemer.

That little blasphemy appealed to her.

In his silences she imagined all sorts of courtesies and kindnesses. He respected her enough to leave her with her own silences, not to pillage and plunder like Rick.

The longueurs helped to relax her. At home Rick's climaxes came suddenly, and she never knew just when; she had to hang on to the headboard of the bed, to keep from being flung to and fro like a rag doll. This way was quite different: this way she felt floaty, serene, almost disembodied, the whole ethereal thing. It was a means of communication which surpassed words. If they'd tried to talk about their different lives, his at Knockie Brae and hers at Nithsdale, where would that have got them? Saying nothing was just as informative as any form of speech.

There were two or three wine-bars in Perth for Richard to choose from, depending on his mood and how discreet he felt he wanted to be.

Gail liked bright lights and noise. Lorraine was a different proposition: dimmer switches and shadowy nooks and crannies.

Which of them he took out depended less on his mood than on their availability, and if he could prise either of them away from colleagues. He had a way of wearing down their resistance, so that they gave in to him. It didn't occur to him that, once he'd pied-pipered Gail or Lorraine towards his parked car, they failed to get other than exactly what they wanted from him.

Rick was late again.

From the window Joanna checked the road before closing the curtains. The girls were upstairs, probably asleep by now. When he got home, Rick would look in; but he would have lost them for that day, another day of everyone's lives was over and gone.

She switched on the TV. No, that was like running time down a plughole, and she switched it off again.

Where was the *BMJ*?

She opened a newspaper. She closed it and picked up a book instead. Schnitzler, a second-hand Penguin, out of print. *Vienna 1900: Games of Love and Death*. Four novellas. Cool, analytical stuff, which still had the power to shock. That was a truer source of knowledge, she felt: the stories of people who had never actually existed but who were somehow in essence everyone she knew.

Through his windscreen in winter Richard would see white-coated stoats scurrying about in the fields, or along the roadsides. Perfect disguise for snow.

Take the colour of your ground. Carry on as per usual, and you'll just blend into normality.

He didn't think of Perth once he was in Carnbeg. He saw only what was in front of him. That simplified matters greatly.

He had a hearty appetite. He slept at night. He woke gently, refreshed, to each new day.

Joanna was having to deal with some of the surgery overspill.

A name leaped out of the patient's files.

MOONEY, Alexander.

He had come into the surgery with conjunctivitis in both eyes.

They hadn't had contact for nearly three months, and it was now he told her that he was leaving Carnbeg, moving down to one of the new towns near Glasgow. He'd got a job with a company which installed fitted bedrooms. (Well, what else? she thought.)

She examined his eyes, with only a slight tremor in her hand. The last time they'd spoken had been on Glebe Street. She wished she could ask him why it hadn't continued between them, but she was afraid to.

His real medical problem might have been amnesia, she felt.

She was writing the prescription when she looked up and saw him staring at her. Her eyes fixed and she couldn't look away, the pen stopped writing.

'How have you been?' he asked.

That would have been the sensible moment to close down, to kill the matter dead.

But she seized on the question.

'I've been okay,' she said.

'I've had work and everything. Sandra, she's been a bit poorly.'

'Yes, I know.'

His wife was one of Dr Trotter's. She had a blood disease; it would clear, but that took time and a course of hospital examinations.

'I felt she needed me.'

'That's very commendable.'

She saw the uncomfortable grimace on his ruggedly handsome face. He deserved better than that from her, she realised.

'I've just . . . got on with things,' she said, wanting to make the truth sound flimsy and unreliable.

'I sometimes see you both.'

'Do you?' She didn't ever see *him*.

'Where?' she asked, knowing she was betraying too much interest.

'The shops and that. You're always kind of busy.'

She had a way of not looking too closely at people's faces in the street, otherwise she would get nowhere for having to give the time of day to her patients. She wondered if she passed him, or if he knew to keep watch from his car, or from behind shop windows, not drawing attention to himself.

All this godawful small-town prissy etiquette: learning to play by the Carnbeg rules.

'I hope Glasgow works out well,' she said.

'It'll be a change of scene for Sandra.'

Lucky them.

'We've got our memories,' he said. 'You and me.'

Simply enough said. But it had a little touch of poetry, too, which she didn't know if she would have received from Rick.

She and Alec had tested one another with words. Silence had told them more than speech, though. And that was how to leave it, she felt.

She held out the prescription form. He took it.

He had used those hands to explore her whole body. Everywhere he went with them on her had proved to be an erogenous zone. Rick, with all his First Class credits, wouldn't have understood his method, that slow-burning approach; for him it would have been too approximate, too off the point of the exercise. She'd had to go to Knockie Brae (what else would it have been called?) to get some idea of what she was missing for all the rest of the time at home.

Now no contrived accident occurred. There was no fumbling or dropping the note and bending down for it. They said nothing, and so they could *imagine* all that was being left undeclared by each of them.

[159]

This was how true adults behaved. They also got anxious and guilty, but that happened once they were alone.

An urgent rap sounded on the door. That busybody of a receptionist. The surgery, on Dr Trotter's recommendation, had implemented a policy of checking up whenever certain 'high-risk' patients (the men virile, the women flighty) overstayed on an appointment.

Miss Marshall's grey pageboy appeared round the corner of the door.

'I'll be done in a moment,' Joanna snapped, testily enough to send the woman off in a huff.

Alec took his leave at the door, as they stood a couple of feet apart. The next thing she was watching him walk away down the hall, past the front desk. They were both relieved, Joanna sensed.

Unexpectedly, though, he turned at the front door and looked back. Her responses were delayed by a couple of seconds. When her eyes fully connected with her brain, she felt gawky and gangly, she dropped her gaze and looked away, she fussed with a sheaf of papers pinned to the wall.

The front door swung shut behind him, and she couldn't see for tears.

Paperwork mounted on Richard's desk. *For the attention of Dr R. L. Ebdon.* Admin bumf. He bought a new briefcase to put it all into, and took it back to the house as 'homework' for the weekends.

He felt exasperated. He was a doctor, not a sodding accountant. He envied Jo, just getting on with the job she was qualified to do.

At the same time he realised his staff called him a tyrant behind his back. But he was terrified of losing his grip on the place. He'd built up his department to be one of the best urology centres in Scotland, but a couple of serious misdiagnoses by him or his colleagues was all it would take to undo the good work.

As time went on, an increasing amount was at stake. He had to keep everyone on their toes. He needed to keep abreast of the latest medical developments. He liked to be a visible presence to the patients. He was asked to deliver papers at conferences, which meant more outside attention for the job he was doing while taking him away from his base of operations (pun permissible). He needed to know that those he worked with, in his young team, weren't falling beneath the standards he expected of them, and that entailed subterfuge in his methods of assessment. Sometimes word got round that he was 'spying', and he sensed an atmosphere of suspicion and mistrust. But if this was to be the price of a successful medical outfit – 'outpost', in what struck him at less optimistic moments as a provincial hinterland – then, shit, so be it.

She had a husband who could still, just about, fit into his dinner jacket.

Men got lucky, Joanna thought. Women's evening dresses changed with fashion, particular colours evoked an era. But black was black in any age, and for men the matter of shawl collars and shoulder padding and vents was insignificant. A suit with some history to it was a talking point in itself.

In his pomp and circumstance Rick might have been presiding at a college dinner, while alongside she dispensed a hostess's efficient politesse. Seeing him as the man he was meant to be, she felt she could have forgiven him nearly anything.

It was funny, Richard thought, funny peculiar anyway, how Jo could be a bit of a sobersides these days.

He remembered that night in Highgate, and sometimes wondered if *she* did, when they'd sat out on that sofa in the garden, and what he was recalling was the sound of their laughter, all the different permutations from stifled giggles and splutters to full-throttled and riproaring, braying too for all he knew, while they made light of the world and all its ridiculousness.

She seemed to have become more – what? – more theoretical;

he sometimes felt she didn't read or watch films to *enjoy* any more. For him leisure time was limited, and you needed your reading and watching as a release valve, to free yourself for another bout of down-to-earth pennyplain *living*.

Rick read detective fiction on holiday, and seemed content to explore no further. At one time he had tried books on her recommendation, *Perfume* and *Love in the Time of Cholera*, and then William Trevor and Narayan when she discovered their short stories. (Women authors, like Alice Munro and Ellen Gilchrist, she kept to herself.) But now he made straight for the CRIME section in a bookshop, to the moody covers with a bloody handprint or a killer's shadow on a wall, and that was enough for him.

By comparison, she felt increasingly drawn to those women writers, to their inwardness, their reserves of courage, to the language of the senses which the best of them could put down on to the page. They made her think, yes, that's exactly how *I* feel, only I couldn't have expressed it in words like that. She wanted to be moved, and enlightened, every bit as much as entertained; a plot, with thrills, she could get from television or a film.

Books were a private refuge, a fastness, with windows on all sides looking out on the world.

When Joanna's sister visited, she suggested the two of them go to church on Sunday morning.

'The Piscy?'

Episcopal, yes. What else?

'You can show me how you do it here, can't you?'

She didn't like to tell Jen that she'd never set foot inside the place. She had driven past the building how many hundreds of times. She had only thought how incongruous it looked. Mock timbering, a red roof, mullion-windows, a flint finish to the walls. Sussex, she always thought, that's where it belongs.

The interior smelt of old Bibles, of course, and pollen, and wax polish. The musty fragrance reminded her of childhood, and she felt an odd sense of peace, sitting there that Sunday and on future Sundays when she was tempted back. Rick wouldn't come with her, but the girls did, ready to trade glances with boys of their own age, and then to get bolder a little later.

The congregation included patients from Torrie Wynd, and they seemed glad to see their doctor there. Inevitably she was sucked into the social activities; it felt churlish to refuse the small demands those made on her time.

Rick went off with his golf clubs, and Charlotte sang in the choir, and they all got together again for a late lunch, and thus out of five individuals a family made itself.

They were talking one day in the house, and somehow the conversation turned into an argument.

Rick said you made your own destiny, even though he didn't like that term. Really you just swooped on whatever chances put themselves in your way, you grabbed them and ran with them.

Nothing was ordained, there were no unearned rights and privileges.

Joanna preferred to believe there were patterns and processes. Otherwise everything ended up as a free-for-all. A discerning mind looked for connections, it needed to refer. How else to get your bearings?

She wondered how they could disagree about something so vital.

It amused Rick, to think Jo couldn't see his point of view at all.

Grey Cowan was the up-and-coming gynaecologist, and she felt lucky to get hold of him.

'In all probability,' he told her, 'you've become desensitised, Dr Ebdon. Have you been aware of this?'

In retrospect, perhaps. Rick had made such a fuss about finding her 'secret spot' (aka her 'red button', her 'nuclear trigger') that she'd had to simulate the joy of discovery in order to persuade him that they had actually got there and not to worry about it any more. Rick seemed to think that they might come upon the elusive 'hot point' by surprise, and the best way was bound to be – wham, bam – the quickest.

If she had felt more friction, hurt, if he'd had her crying out into his ear, that might have dissuaded him. And so it was that they had grown into their habits, making love together at cross purposes.

20, 13, 11, 9.

His golf handicap went down and down.

Sandy Tait had put his name on the Muirfield applications list.

'Forget the Royal and Ancient,' Sandy told him. 'Muirfield's the only place to play.'

Sandy said that was where they picked the next judges for the courts, and who ran which august institutions; they settled it out on the links. That's how the big medical consultants' posts got filled, too, and well before the nineteenth.

'Look after number one, Rick. Into Muirfield, and you're set up for life.'

Small is Beautiful.

Joanna read the book in bed, wanting to make it last and at the same time eager to understand it all and apply its philosophy in her own life.

Rick thought it was narrowing your range of options. But then, Rick never read a local newspaper, while she loved now to get the Carnbeg angle; she enjoyed the local radio programmes, which Rick would have turned off if she hadn't protested.

Little things. Which added up to quite a lot.

God, it was complicated.

Richard didn't get into Muirfield.

Someone blackballed him. He didn't discover who, although he strongly suspected a creep who'd gone after the same job as him at Perth, been rejected, then leapfrogged over him by stepping into dead men's shoes at a couple of Edinburgh hospitals in succession.

The fucker.

Sandy Tait thought he should wait a bit and try again, in a few years' time. He might do. But his instinct was against it.

Don't revisit the scenes of past disappointment.

Move on.

Onwards and up.

Bugger Muirfield. Two fingers, and create your own good fortune.

As the years had passed, Joanna felt it all came down to the matter of Mrs Brown.

A fictional, emblematic figure.

But she saw Mrs Browns all the time. She had become more and more interested in the details of those individuals, each of them very different.

To Richard, the Mrs Browns *he* saw were cases. They were first and foremost bodies. To him they were, if not interchangeable, certainly anonymous. They responded to treatment or they didn't. He wasn't engaged by them any more than that.

Rick called her too emotional. He said it was bound to prejudice her, because it didn't allow her to make rational and clear-cut decisions.

Joanna hinted to him how fearful his patients must be, coming to their appointments with him: because of their illness, and because of the one-to-one.

'I'm never rude to them or anything.'

'I know that,' she said.

'Well, then?'

'They need to feel they're someone, an individual.'

'Aren't they?'

'But they've forgotten. They're sick, and all they can think of is the illness – it's taken them over. This *thing* – which has no respect for them.'

'I'm trying to cure the illness.'

'And that's all, Rick?'

'All?' He laughed, shaking his head at her. 'Isn't that bloody enough to be doing?' his expression said.

The taxi dropped Richard off in Wigmore Street.

The receptionist was on her way out, but she told him Dr Perry was expecting him.

From the green plush waiting-room he heard Miles's voice. He was on the phone, and sounding angry about something.

'Look, Antonia, don't you start telling me what – '

What he could or couldn't do.

Later, over a drink before Richard headed for his BA shuttle flight north, Miles was unforthcoming about life at home. Jo had asked him to fish about, because the last Christmas card (written as ever by Antonia) had been strangely terse; even the children's achievements were toned down, which wasn't Antonia's way at all.

Richard had always envied Miles his poise, his savvy, his unapologetically eyeing the main chance. Looking at him covertly over the upraised rim of his whisky tumbler, he noticed Miles was putting on weight; his face was puffier. Too much of the good life? Or maybe it wasn't so good after all?

Back at the hotel, he called Jo. He could hear the McKeans in the background, brother and sister, playfully disputing one another as they repeated an oft-told tale. Jo was simultaneously listening to him and laughing along, because she liked the McKeans.

He decided not to tell her what he'd heard from the waiting-room. He wasn't sure why he didn't want to. Perhaps he was trying to be loyal to Miles, and to Antonia, to them both, and to Jo and to himself, since they had shared the Perrys' life in a small but vital way.

So he left it at that, and felt he was restoring something to Miles and Antonia which they deserved: if not their innocence (no, far from it), the potential still to be their *best* selves.

Joanna knew that Rick's colleagues looked down their noses at her. They were gods as they strode the hospital wards, white coats flapping busily; in their hushed consulting-rooms they became arbiters of life and death.

She was just a dogsbody to them, shop-floor stuff; at the community's beck and call.

At dinner parties Richard liked to cue her up, ready to deliver another of her well-rehearsed stories about the Torrie Wynd surgery: imagined symptoms or misheard diagnoses, malapropisms, fainting-fits and panic attacks. Her tales never failed to raise a merry laugh.

But it was country town stuff to them, small beer indeed, something to prop up the conversation in the gaps between their supper courses.

They wouldn't have wanted to know that she enjoyed and valued her inclusion in her patients' lives. She saw them usually when they were at their most vulnerable, anxious and prey to their fears. She regarded them as syntheses of body and mind, with the two often at loggerheads.

In time she became, for most of them, a figure of trust. And knowing one generation helped her to understand the next rather better.

But her patients taught *her* that she didn't know as much about medicine's byways as she liked to think she did. As a consequence she was continually having to keep on her toes, consulting colleagues and brushing up from journals.

Mutual reliance could only come from working at the proverbial coalface day after day. No day didn't offer its successes as well as its disappointments. As a GP she was spared making the cruellest diagnoses: when these had to be attended to elsewhere, she offered all the moral support she could, without fudging or soft-soaping or lending hope which she knew to be false (and insulting).

She gave her patients every encouragement she could deep-mine out of herself.

Richard didn't see the need to bother Joanna with mentioning it.

An anaesthetist colleague had told him about a friend's daughter who was up the spout. Major stooshie with the parents, who thought it was the end of the world. They were terrified someone was going to find out. They had plenty of money, but they needed to buy *discretion*.

Richard got the message, and he obliged. At university he'd done six months as an obstetrics and gynaecology SHO before switching to urology, so by and large he was prepared. The operation took place one Sunday at a private surgery in Glasgow, and he included payment for use of 'prestige' premises in his account for services rendered.

A colleague of that first colleague heard of the matter, in a hush-hush roundabout way, of course. He asked if there was any possibility of a similar arrangement for a young cousin of his.

And so an alternative career began for Richard Ebdon, which brought profits a-plenty: he was able to set his own rate for the job, and his clients were at liberty to accept or not. The owner of the clinic in Glasgow's West End was happy with the extra income, as were the nurses fixed up in a rota.

Richard merely told Joanna that he was seeing patients down in Glasgow. He gave her the clinic's phone number, without explaining. He realised that, being brighter and sharper than he was, she might well twig to the situation one day. If she did and wanted to make something of it, so be it. But he guessed that was quite a long way off.

He didn't stint with accommodation for himself: a superior hotel room, a dinner at the Rogano afterwards with whoever he could round up. But even the expense of that didn't make much of a dent in the profits. The money was very welcome. It paid for some domestic 'upgrading' – nice pieces of furniture from house auctions – and for holidays, and for a new car for Jo, and two ponies and their upkeep (later, horses instead of ponies), and paintings and books and records and all the civilising details of a comfortable life.

He had worked hard, as Miles did, and he was determined to enjoy the fruits of those labours.

In the airport bookstalls he saw a novel on the racks, *Having It All*. Which was just what he intended for the Ebdon family.

Joanna was at a supermarket in Perth, loading up her big barrow at the check-out, when her eye was caught by the cover of a paperback.

Having It All.

Did anyone actually believe that? 'All' would mean you knew everything there was to have which was worth having.

She didn't imagine that she did know, or *wanted* to know.

It was the feeling she got in some patients' homes. They lacked for nothing. The thingyness of those rooms with their colour-coordinated decor (always a flowery dado on the wall) was overwhelming, the spaces packed with furniture and the shelves and laying-surfaces crowded with knick-knacks, the heat at the top setting. She couldn't turn, couldn't breathe, couldn't think.

As she watched, a woman lifted a copy of the paperback from the rack and dropped it into her trolley, ready to buy the dream.

Oh yes, just sometimes, standing at the basin in the bathroom or at the kitchen sink, watching water eddy down the plughole, it occurred to Richard, what I do in Glasgow may be no easy disregardable thing –

But life at that age isn't sacrosanct. No rights exist in the world, least of all to be born. You just have to choose which is the lesser of two evils.

He slept at night, quite soundly. (Except, naturally, when he had a raging hard-on, and he jabbed Joanna in the back until it was simpler for her to give in to him). They planned summer by a warm sea and a winter break in the Bernese Oberland, and the girls brought home their gymkhana rosettes, and Edinburgh's New Town galleries invited them both to their private views, and life (having it, why not make the most of it, all of it?) was peachy.

Shouts. Cries.

Joanna went to the window.

A figure was running up the road. About Charlotte's age. Richard stood at the gate, looking after her.

'What was that all about?' she asked him from the window.

'What was what all about?'

'The business with the girl.'

'Care-in-the-community sort.' Which was Richard's favourite put-down.

'She was shouting.'

'Exactly,' Richard said.

'So what *was* it?'

'You'd need to ask her.'

'I can't, Rick.'

'Yes. She's gone.'

Which was why she'd asked *him*.

'Don't bother about her,' he said.

She was only bothered because she didn't understand, and because she thought Richard wasn't telling her all he knew.

Silence.

No, she thought. No, I won't ask any more. She had a presentiment. Better a mystery, better that than knowing.

Referring to the house business, Joanna felt that a GP shouldn't be seen to be getting above her station.

'There's two of us in this equation,' he said.

'Actually there are five,' she reminded him, nodding outside at the girls.

In the end they did move: not to the house Richard had wanted, with its six and a half acres, but to a former shooting-lodge, which Joanna told him was grand enough.

'Well, it's out of the town,' Richard said. 'If it's going to embarrass you.'

'Doctors don't get embarrassed. As you know very well.'

But he sensed she wasn't quite comfortable about the arrangement.

'It's a ladder you climb,' he said.

'*We* climb,' she corrected him.

'Yes. Yes, I meant that.'

She wanted to call it The Lodge, and did so in her corre-
spondence. He preferred the name of the estate it had once
belonged to, Clashmeldrum. That was tonier, he said; The
Lodge could have applied to five or six other houses in the
general area. Joanna just shrugged, and continued to call it
The Lodge, or *in extremis* Clashmeldrum Lodge – which
Richard took as a concession of sorts, thankful for these
small mercies.

The new house had a different orientation from the old one.

The front caught the sun in the late afternoon and evening. At
weekends they missed out on sunny mornings indoors, but as if
to compensate the sun pulled out the stops for a technicolour
display from four o'clock onwards.

The rooms were gilded with light, the wood panelling ran like
liquid amber, the original chandelier, which Richard had insisted
be included in the sale, sent a spectrum of colours ricocheting
across the ceiling; the glass lozenges, every one a restless prism,
stained the dark-honey oak floorboards with ruby, amethyst,
emerald.

In other respects, so much light was a liability. It indicated
every repair which needed to be done, it showed each scuff and
score to the fabric of the place. Worse, it defined every crease
and furrow on a face, mercilessly insisting on the numerical
truth of your age.

'All things must pass', Joanna thought they could use as their
motto. Oh, come on, lighten up, Richard told her. He would
pretend the brilliant illumination was a stage spotlight, a
follow-spot, and he would give an impromptu dance, and when
she was in a receptive mood she laughed. Never mind that it
took an awful lot of laughter to fill the big spaces of those rooms
and also to sound convincing – laughed she had, and so Richard
would win that point.

'Our crepuscular irradiation,' he called it, as if – Joanna

thought – as if he meant this had been worthwhile uprooting themselves from their warm, cheerful old home to experience.

They used to walk along the streets of Oxford and London together, in perfect time, step for step. They would play that game where one did exactly what the other had done a split second before, as if you were closer than their shadow.

It was hard to believe now that they were still the same two people.

1993 was the year of the two Carnbegs: the Perthshire original twinning with its namesake in Colorado. (It turned out there was a third Carnbeg, in Virginia, but too small or snobbish to want to participate.)

A load of fuss about nothing, Richard had first thought, just an excuse for Rotarians to make exchange visits and local politicians to land themselves a freebie.

But in the event it changed his life.

A medical deputation from Carnbeg Springs appeared. They were also visiting Glasgow and Edinburgh, and participating in a conference at the Turnberry Hotel, but they dutifully called in at Carnbeg, where all that was on offer for their edification were the cottage hospital and a couple of general practices.

At the McKeans' house Richard got talking to two of the surgeon-administrators. They were both incomers to Carnbeg Springs, and all three hit it off. Out on the golf course with them next morning he discovered that a senior consultancy in urology was currently being advertised at a new $50 million private clinic.

He asked, not quite sure himself if he was being serious, did they think he should apply?

'Are you interested?'

'Yes. Yes, I am.'

'Then you should apply. With your qualifications. You bet.'

They said they'd put in a word for him as soon as they got

back. Meantime they'd phone and get the application forms sent to him.

'Someone may have got in before me, no?'

'We'll put their applications to the back of the file!' the American visitors laughed, and he really did believe that they would.

He flew to Chicago, then on to Colorado, for an interview, at the clinic's expense. He was careful about his Britishness: he played up the charm, enunciated c–l–e–a–r–l–y in RP, but chucked the dyed-in-the-wool cynicism of fellow medics and sounded gung-ho and super-positive and put an Anthony Robbins shine into his eyes.

He was given the job the next day.

Joanna had guessed that they wouldn't be flying Richard out for an interview if he didn't stand a very good chance of being offered the post.

So the news, when he rang her, came as no surprise.

Once he was back in Carnbeg, he said something in the first ten minutes that suggested she would be going with him.

'What makes you think that?' she asked.

'Well, I was just presuming—'

'Exactly!'

'Exactly what?'

'You *presumed*, Rick.'

They had been waiting for several years for this conversation.

'I thought you'd be pleased, Jo.'

'If *you*'ve got the job you want now—'

'And it'd be a fresh start for you, too.'

'It doesn't work like that for GPs. You establish relationships,' she heard herself saying. She opened the throttle, metaphorically, took her foot off the brakes. 'You get to deal with your patients on a basis of trust.'

'Yes, but—'

'And that takes a long time. A lot of building up.'

'It doesn't matter *where*, though, does it?'
'But that's the whole bloody point!' she screamed at him.
God Almighty, did he really not get it?

It was nothing like Carnbeg. Nor the more rarefied satellite of
Carnbeg, Carnmòr. It was like nothing Richard had known.

The Laurel Highlands Country Club had a school of black
Lincolns drawn up outside, engines idling. There were liveried
bellhops, and the golf caddies wore uniforms. Sprinklers
played on the crimped greens, and the bunkers were raked by
Vietnamese sandboys.

Local fraternities and charities met at the other hotels or
resorts, and you could have massaged your social conscience
every day of the week if you'd chosen to.

In the other Carnbeg he'd had a position in the community,
but also (by his own deciding so) a degree of privacy. Here he
had a sense of other people knowing much more about him,
not because he wanted or didn't want that, but because *they*
intended to know. He sometimes felt there were eyes everywhere, all of them trained on *him*.

Even with Richard not there, Joanna coped.

She managed much better than she'd thought she was going
to. The household finances were her responsibility now, and
calling in tradesmen for repairs; she also decided who got to be
entertained at the house, and whether she accepted or rejected
other people's invitations.

She missed Rick, of course, but she couldn't help thinking
that life like this was simplified, and streamlined, definitely low-
drag.

Black tie; or sometimes his Highland wear – (Ancient Suther-
land) kilt and plaid hose (bought from Kinloch Anderson in
Edinburgh, none of your dress-hire-shop vulgarity).

He was never placed at the end of a table, but always sat

where he could animate the conversation. He didn't run out of small talk; his laughter was easy, loud, infectious.

At the clinic – the three and a half days in toto per week he spent working for his salary – he could pick and choose who to let consult him, and who not. The wealth of his patients meant he could spend proportionally less time in his consulting-suite, and more out on the golf greens or gladhanding.

'Official' events shaded into the private. He accepted whatever hospitality he was offered. He didn't see who could be compromised by it. Self-made men were generous, usually because they wanted something; but, then, *he* wanted something too.

Touché. Checkmate.

In his absence, Joanna downloaded Carnbeg Springs from the internet.

The Rockies weren't Rick's sort of thing, were they? He had never been much of an Outward Bound man.

The pre-ski and après-ski routine, yes, she could see how he might get into all that.

Icicle-hung chalets – and downtown condominiums – and that tartan-upholstered lobby in the air-conditioned mock-baronial hotel: she didn't think any of that was *her* scene. He was welcome to it, and to those stick-thin women in big peroxided hair lunching on Caesar salad – the Joan Rivers lookalikes – who inhabited the public spaces illustrated in the advertising material.

The good life – having it all – fast track to happiness.

Rick couldn't have fallen for it, could he, not for that old snake-oil hooey?

It was if this was what the other Carnbeg, the old Carnbeg, was *meant* to be. Here it was in its ideal form.

Add American can-do, the entrepreneur culture. Some teutonic efficiency (the Austrian cakes, the Alpenhorn's beers, the ski stores). Some Hollywood pizazz, and lots of extravagance.

He should have come over here years ago, Richard felt. It wasn't Jo's bag, but maybe she would have gotten used to it. ('Past participle, please. *Got*, Richard. For God's sake.')

If the Springs folk thought he was actually Scottish, he didn't enlighten them, because it colourised – romanticised – him, and he wasn't averse.

Now and then he caught a glimpse of Scotland, or convinced himself that he did. It was a matter of how the light fell: with a certain purplish tinge, reminding him of cold autumn mornings or alternatively of spring evenings once the clocks were put forward. He used to catch the light just like this, slanting low on his windshield, as he drove to work first thing on frosty roads or headed north and home with his day's duties done.

The light found him, where he'd taken himself half a world away. It was like a searchlight, strafing into the corners of his mind where he meant to keep certain things hidden. He pulled down the windshield visors and drove faster to get away from it, to deflect that laser ray. It was the same sun, shining on him as it used to do in Clashmeldrum's garden, or up on the leads of the college roof in Oxford where they used to lie sunbathing between lectures, or against the creosote fence in his parents' strip of back garden in the purdah of lesser Croydon.

Foot hard down on the Z3's gas, Ebdon, you're *outta* here.

They had two years of the arrangement.

Rick to-ing and fro-ing, still taking time to do his private 'consultancy' work in Glasgow. And she going out to Colorado for two or three weeks at a time; her jet lag hardly had time to clear before she had another bout, only worse, from the return journey.

The Perthshire Carnbeg was *her* 'home' now, she felt, for good or bad. It was the start and end point of her thinking, to which everything got referred. She needed to be sitting inside the four walls of Clashmeldrum Lodge, or out working in the garden, to be able to get her hold on anything – and she had to be by herself. This was the only way for her to be able to think straight.

And from here it made less sense for them to be leading their separate lives as if they added up to one.

She was too tired to be sad about it. She had too much to do at home and at the surgery to be left despairing. She simply wasn't that sort of person, she reminded herself.

Richard felt Scotland had just been a phase of his life.

His Croydon boyhood was one; his teens – after his parents split up – was another. Then Oxford; followed by marriage. Just as he couldn't easily connect to the fresh student going to his first lectures, so his spell in Perth would come to seem of its time, a staging-post on the way to something else.

He wasn't a sentimentalist. In his line of work he couldn't afford to be: the stoic and engaging patient might die, while another – boorish and undeserving – lived.

He liked not knowing where he was bound on life's journey. He wouldn't see his boyhood friends again probably, but he was hanging in there (just) with Jo, because they were mature adults and because they shared friends and, thirdly, because each thought the other knew too many secrets about who Richard and Joanna Ebdon (née Harris) really were.

In Perth one day, walking down out of the multi-storey car park, Joanna met Alec Mooney on a corner of the concrete staircase.

In the bleak, unflattering light from the glass bricks, she couldn't hide her confusion.

He was with his son, and she was with Imogen.

Hadn't she seen the boy somewhere before?

Should she just walk on? The same thought seemed to be in both their minds.

It was he who spoke first. 'I've got a new car. No breakdowns now.'

'I – I'm glad to hear it.'

'Dr Ebdon gave me a lift once,' he explained to their children. 'Errand of mercy. Stuck out in the middle of nowhere, I was.'

She smiled emptily.

'You'd have done it for anyone, I'm sure,' he said.

She stood wondering what that might mean.

Then she was aware that he'd called the boy Kieran. Of course. She'd seen him at the stables, at the weekends.

'Small world, isn't it, Dr Ebdon?' Alec Mooney was saying to her.

'Yes.' She tried to make her smile brighter, but continued to be mystified. 'Yes, it is.'

Nobody spoke for several moments.

'And Glasgow is . . . ?'

'Oh, it's okay.'

'D'you miss Carnbeg?' (Wrong question.)

'I'd be lying if I told you I didn't.'

They all stood looking at one another.

'We mustn't keep you, Doctor.'

'You haven't.'

'Nice to speak to you.'

'And to you.'

She didn't want to concentrate on his appearance, but for the next few hours that was all she could think of. His face was moderately good-looking; no don't mark him down – seven and a half out of ten. She saw handsome men in the course of every day, but it was his unselfconsciousness about his looks, that and the matter-of-fact vigour of the rest of him, which she found so exciting, so completely disarming. She couldn't explain it to herself, but she felt her heart quickening, as if a hand in a steel gauntlet was held over it. She was perspiring, her skin was hot, and what she carried about – dragging it from shop to shop, to bank, to post office, to café, to food shop, to multi-storey – was some ridiculous, gaping want and emptiness inside herself.

And then –

A complication started to grow on top of that emptiness, filling the hollow space and starting to hurt, a continual downwards drag that became more and more painful.

She knew, an intuition, that she needed a hysterectomy. At

the same time she was trying to keep in a state of denial about it. (All these angles and trajectories and skewed perspectives.)

It was the symbolism of what was happening that distressed her. She felt she was bound to be a woman in one dimension less. Part of her purpose in nature was about to be sluiced out of her. All of which was nonsense, but the feelings struck home – as deeply as they did with patients of hers who had suffered the same.

Now she was required to be a patient herself. Mind over matter, she thought, opening her legs to their friend Grey Cowan for an examination. He was businesslike but sympathetic, he put his arm round her shoulder in an old-fashioned non-PC way he mightn't have risked on the litigious public, and she understood why he was so popular. (God bless and keep that man from harm, she found she was muttering to herself on the slow walk back to the car.)

Is this a punishment? she wondered, lying convalescing in a bed in the cottage hospital. She was angry for thirty seconds or so, and then she found meekness again, which accepts the world as being what it is.

To be uncritical would bring her quickest to the true state of things. Coincidentally, plumbing humility, she heard a peal of church bells, carried to her across the town on a breeze.

His copy of *Oxford Today*, the University magazine, got sent out to Carnbeg Springs every quarter.

Surprising himself, he grew almost nostalgic making his way through it, page by page, reading the articles and reviews and (because there was no one to see him) peering into the corners of the photographs.

At Oxford he'd been Richard Ebdon, a clean sheet of paper. He didn't talk about his home life, and was lucky enough that only two or three students in the entire place would have known who he was, and they were at other colleges and in other disciplines and he could avoid them.

You could become your own creation. The trick was knowing

how not to turn into a cliché, when there were so many of those already walking about the streets (usually in Arts). Better the spider stratagem: you spin your web from the inside out, and everything holds by dint of a triumphant, superhuman act of will.

Joanna now allowed herself to notice the faces on the Carnbeg streets. Patients smiled to her, or nodded a little apprehensively, they mouthed, 'Good morning, Dr Ebdon.'

Kenneth McKean went off on a six-month break he was due, and she took over some of his patients. A number asked to transfer to her, and although she didn't go out of her way to encourage them she was secretly flattered that they felt strongly enough to insist.

Every day there was a nearly full set of appointments for her, with just a little slack put in to deal with emergencies.

Patients in their teens were ones she'd kept a check on when they were in the womb. She saw miraculous recoveries, and also failures – the non-responders – who continued to baffle her.

When Kenneth came back he noticed the altered order at once, as she'd known he would.

'Fasten your seat belts,' he laughed, at an 'At Home' organised by him and his sister in their big house. 'It's gonna be a *bumpy* night.'

He had the Bette Davis delivery, pitch of voice and mannerisms, off to a tee.

'I don't know about this sabbatical of yours,' Joanna jibed back. 'You've been watching old films in the afternoons, haven't you?'

'Meanwhile you've been flyposting Carnbeg with your sweet smile and irresistible promises.'

Tit for tat!

At which moment Moira McKean decisively came between them with the tray of eats-on-sticks.

Richard was spoiled by those hostesses with their outside caterers. He could have survived from party to party, but sometimes he was obliged to do as Romans did, and in came the caterers (gay), and it was like *La Dolce Vita* at his apartment. A social life which began in student digs in Oxford, and had taken him to the rooftop duplex of a 'Swiss-style' condo block, the St Moritz, one of the best addresses in town. Just as his bedsit in Jericho used to be, this apartment was rented, but they were like lives connected by the insubstance of fantasy, at one end and the other of a rainbow.

Richard wasn't a letter-writer.

He did ring Carnbeg sometimes, but only when Joanna had left a voicemail message for him. If she'd left him to do it off his own bat, she wondered how often he would have picked up the phone.

The girls called him, and maybe they were just luckier than she was; they usually caught him before he went off somewhere, to another of his Colorado socials, to schmooze with his bankrollers.

Well, Richard was welcome to them. But he'd have to get his priorities sorted out. He had a family, even if his Carnbeg Springs friends didn't know, not the half of it.

He wasn't going to get away with this. No one could walk out of a marriage and think he was penalty-free.

Richard drives.

Steely Dan is his soundtrack. Twenty years on Fagen and Becker are still at it, maybe not at the peak of their game, but they're giants to everyone else's pygmies.

He drives to the gym, where he's had a fitness programme drawn up for him (moderate), and he drives to the country club where he plays tennis (a little) and swims (a little), and he drives to the parties he's invited to and drives back (mildly pissed) on a wing and a prayer.

He loves his new freedom. Even if he's by himself in the car he loves it, and hardly spares a thought for the Janices and Kelties.

And he never knows, loving almost everything about Carnbeg Springs, what's going to be round the next corner, the slalom twists of his *Kamakiriad* life.

'I'm Lester the night-fly. Hello, Baton Rouge . . . '

It's been so hard to write this. But I've felt I wanted to get my thoughts down, to see where we stand.

This is where the road forks, Rick.

She sent it as an e-mail. She heard nothing back. She wondered if he'd received it, or if he could have lost it. She worried that she'd been too blunt, too pessimistic. It was the peril of modern technology, you rushed into print and hey presto, the message was gone from you. Too little time to pick your words and weigh them.

She decided to ring Richard in Carnbeg Springs. Okay, so it was exposing herself, but she needed to know what his response was.

The phone was answered at the other end. Richard. Before he'd spoken a dozen words, a woman's voice was calling out in the background, from the next room.

'Rick, where d'you keep the . . . ?'

The voice trailed away, silenced by the look or the gesture Richard must be giving her.

There really wasn't any point in continuing, was there?

Joanna didn't have a soap-screenwriter to script her forward. 'It's over, Rick, we're quits. Now, just get out of my life.'

She put down the receiver.

Her phone rang a couple of minutes later, but she didn't answer it. She dialled services, and got the number of her last caller confirmed.

She went into the kitchen. She turned on the radio, found Radio 2. Just what was it about today – the timing of everything? The record that came on was Carmen McRae, 'How Long Has This Been Going On?'

At the sink she stood, oh my God, look at me, Hackneyed Moments No 44, *how long – has –* tears splashing on to the draining-board – *this been – going on –* crying my eyes, crying my heart out.

'Just to settle things,' Richard explained.

In Carnbeg Springs either you were married or you weren't. They didn't understand the indeterminate condition.

More than two years had passed.

'I don't know what the Church position is,' he said.

In the earpiece of the phone he heard Joanna's irritable intake of breath.

'They don't have any position,' she told him. 'They treat me as a mature thinking adult.'

'But we don't want any cloudiness.'

'*You* don't, you mean?'

'I don't have any plans,' he said.

'I'm not asking if you do.'

'It would make more sense, wouldn't it? To get things in black and white.'

'Do what you like,' she sighed.

'I'll speak to the lawyer Miles used for theirs.'

The best answer in the circumstances, she decided, was no answer at all.

'I have to go,' she said, pressing the OFF button, and closing down the conversation on him.

If it had happened suddenly, she might have felt the shock of separation.

But it was a gradual process, and she'd sensed the inevitable long before the end did come.

She was eased into singlehood, rather. Not that it properly was, with three daughters.

And with the separation permanent and the divorce pending, she told her friends she felt only relief. (Which was the case for most of the time, say, 90 per cent.)

[183]

They had the house to themselves, although things had been this way for a long while. How she thought of the situation was as if, four or five years ago, Richard had left the house one morning for Perth and he hadn't – mentally – returned.

It wasn't necessarily a case of one woman rather than another. She used to smell them on his clothes, but, as her mother would have said, that's men for you. The sexual shenanigans·didn't shock her; but his glibness, his lack of guilt, did. He didn't give away a single hint as he sat at the supper table, as he slumped in front of the TV set, as he snored contendedly in bed beside her.

Nothing.

Just as, she supposed, he thought so seldom – if ever – of the women, or even of herself.

Everything had been expected of Richard Ebdon.

He wasn't programmed for weakness and vulnerability.

He had higher expectations of others than *they* often had. He couldn't understand why they failed themselves.

Men are mostly men, but he knew that some – a very few – have the destiny of princes.

Now an attorney in Colorado was drawing up divorce papers, just to 'help tidy your desk'. Legal slang, Joanna supposed. Richard complimented her on her 'mature attitude', her 'graciousness' (*sic*, as if she were royalty), and she wished she knew how to be *im*mature, how to be disgraceful (up to a point).

She wondered if Richard had earmarked a replacement wife and if they needed to get a pre-nuptial contract agreed upon?

But, the oddest thing, what might be going on as of this moment in the Colorado Rockies mattered almost not a jot or tittle to her, as if it was the trash plotline of *Dynasty* or *Melrose Place* and disposably forgettable, happening to someone whom she didn't know and who in his reinvented form had no existence for her anyway.

The girls.

Charlotte, Emily, Imogen.

Would they see why it had come to this pass?

He was sitting out on the terrace of the old Balmoral Hotel. Before the war there had been an ice floor, and waiters sped past balanced on ice-skates holding their trays high. Now they'd tried to revive history, using waiters on roller-blades. But the wheels made too much noise, you heard them even over the music. Once upon a time they might have had a string trio; the purpose would have been to hear the music, not the hiss of the blades as they sliced the ice.

The girls, again.

Would they learn to forgive him?

It would be seen to be *his* fault. But he would explain to them, sometime, when he was over in Scotland or when they came here to visit.

A young woman had walked into his line of vision. She reminded him of Charlotte. Queer thing, the father–daughter relationship: it wasn't surprising she should remind you of her mother as she used to be. That was just nature rubbing your nose in it, because you're getting on, *tempus fugit*, the sands are running away, hee hee hee.

The woman looked across from her table, did a double-take, maybe she was going to smile. At that instant a couple of men appeared, ski-bums, they sat beside her, plus another woman. The beautiful moment was gone. All those ties and claims: just how it used to be in the puffball days of waiters elegantly skating by in black tails with trays raised.

She would be glad to leave The Lodge, Joanna decided. She could have put up a more spirited defence, and it would have been justified: but not for the house's sake.

The Lodge was symptomatic of the problems that had occurred between her and Richard. The Lodge marked the point where they exceeded themselves; they'd tempted fate, and then they'd been set on the process of their marriage's slow unravelling.

And now another significant point had been reached. She could get up and start a new life somewhere else, in theory. But now, more than ever, was when she needed her old assurances. The girls didn't want to leave their friends, and she saw the wisdom in that; *they* were cooler-headed and less partisan than either of their parents.

The Lodge came top of the list for junking.

A twelve-year-old bungalow on the other side of Carnbeg came on to the market: the sort of house Richard would have simply hated. Ornamental stonework outside and in; big single-pane, double-glazed picture windows; a conservatory with white plastic 'Victorian' detailing on top; an imitation-Georgian fireplace, gracing a coal-effect gas-fire.

Warm and cosy, and easily maintained. It was perfect, really.

Joanna bought it, in her own name.

In the conservatory she could put her head back at the day's end and, from the comfort of her creaky, cushioned rattan armchair, she looked up at the stars and thanked God things weren't any worse than they were. The same stars would be scattered over Colorado in seven or eight hours' time.

She wondered if Richard was ever tempted to view the sky in the same way: as a kind of super-mental map charted aeons ago by the ancients, transcending the humdrums of place and time.

No. No, she guessed not.

'This is Astrid.'

Astrid Someone. Richard missed the surname. But her Christian name stuck in his mind.

Astrid, stars, he thought of the vastness of space, and *film* stars, because this girl looked like a natural for Wilshire and Rodeo. She was intrigued by his accent, by his manners (standing up to shake hands, staying standing until she seated herself).

Was she an actress? She had a slightly studied self-assurance, which could mean she was a rich man's wife. She mentioned Belgium, and it flashed into his mind: she comes from a good family, solid Euro-stock.

She only said that she was searching around for opportunities, and Richard noticed their host's eyes moving off him from the other end of the room. He'd been leaning very close to hear her, and he now drew himself up in his chair, trying to give the impression he was merely being sociable.

Momentarily he caught an expression of anxiety in Astrid's eyes, panic even, as if she thought she was being abandoned. Under cover of an anecdote Richard reached out, lightly touched her arm, to put her at her ease. She smiled at him, in a grateful but unfocused way, as if she was snatching at a lifeline.

He felt, even as he was chatting to her, this is a warning, I have to be careful, here's a young woman who lives too intensely inside her head.

He was aware he was being flattered by that smile, by all Astrid's attention, even if it *was* partly a show.

Jesus Christ, all these Colorado complications. It was much simpler back in homespun Old Carnbeg. Here, where they spoke their own money-money form of English, all the stakes were ratcheted higher. Every remark and gesture seemed to acquire an exaggerated amount of significance, and he felt terribly unversed in the language.

But this man was no quitter.

ASSEMBLY INSTRUCTIONS.

If only.

If Richard had been here, he would have browbeaten the instructions sheet into surrendering its obtuse mysteries.

'Oh, I see, it means . . . Well, let's try *that*.' And then that would have been the matter solved, be it logic or luck or sheer bloody-mindedness, I'll beat those demons if it kills me.

A flatpack bookcase wouldn't have defeated Richard. She couldn't let the side down now. She would get this damned bookcase assembled, however long it took her.

About an hour and a quarter, which she could ill afford. But something like a principle was at stake: not to be cowed by a sheet of badly explained, typo-beset instructions on sub-joinery.

She kept hearing Richard's voice, and seeing him again make the coffee-table or the garden hut three-dimensional; that became her motivation, and maybe – she sadly recognised, sitting back on her heels on the rumpled rug – it was the only inspiration he'd left her from nineteen years of marriage.

All his life Richard had been used to women sending a glow of well-being through him. It had begun with his mother and grandmother, and by way of dozens – scores – of others the power of the glow had been passed to Astrid.

She was the last in a long and distinguished line.

Jo had been something else, a kind of supernova in their galaxy, the one he'd starsailed by.

Women inspired the best in him. He wanted to be the best for them. He didn't know the name for it (whatever it was), but a mystery – being exceptional – is never revealed in the shorthand of the ordinary.

It was her again. The girl who had come to the surgery asking for her, then disappeared.

She'd been hanging about the car park yesterday.

And now she was back.

'Can I help you?' Joanna called to her, but the girl turned her back and hurried off, towards the road.

She needed to go on the pill? Or she thought she was pregnant?

There was something about the girl's face which told Joanna no. There was a terrible fury there, and it puzzled, disturbed, alarmed her.

Then some Newell money came the clinic's way.

'Realty developer' was Hobart Newell's euphemistic occupation. It was true that he bought land and built on it. Planning permits were granted with astonishing ease: astonishing, that is, if you didn't know that the Newell Corporation's philanthropy touched every corner of the Colorado community. Not enough was ever constructed to explain the vast sums of money involved; but gift horses, etc.

It was Hobart Newell's son, Nathan, that Richard had got to know. Nathan's wife, Melissa, was treated in the clinic, and when she recovered (defying earlier prognoses from Denver and Chicago) the couple showed their appreciation.

There was more funding to be had where that came from, and so the clinic board persisted.

Nathan was the age his father had been – mid-forties – when he joined the $100 million club, circa 1950. He had never found any means of competing, so he didn't try, and enjoyed the Newell wealth instead. He was generous to his friends, and considered Richard Ebdon one.

Sometimes it bothered Richard that he was in a group which included other rich men's sons who merely lived fast and loose and didn't have Nathan's intelligence and charm to recommend them. But you didn't write anyone off when your own existence depended on largesse; you smiled, and laughed along with them, and tried to live just a little faster and looser yourself, as the rules of friendship decreed.

The front door bell rang.

Joanna recognised the girl standing there before she opened the door to her.

'I've seen you,' she told the girl straight off.

'I want to talk to your husband.'

'He isn't.'

'Isn't here?'

'He's not my husband. Not now.'

The girl looked shell-shocked. 'But – but I've got to find him.'

'Well, you won't find him here.'

'I have to talk to him.'

'He doesn't live in Carnbeg.'

'Where is he?'

'America.'

'What?'

'In Colorado.'

'But . . . he can't be.'

'I assure you he is.'

The girl reached out to the wall to support herself.

'Are you all right?' Joanna asked.

No reply.

'D'you want to see a doctor?'

She shook her head.

'I can make an appointment for you. That's no problem.'

'But it's *him* I want to . . . '

'Or one of his colleagues. They could help you.'

'No. No, they can't.'

The girl was quite definite about that. Her thin face was as sharp as a blade.

'I . . . I'd like to help you,' Joanna heard herself say

'It's no use.'

In the end the girl just walked off. No parting curse. No backward scowl.

Walked to the gate, and vanished on to the main road.

Should she have gone after her?

'Who was that?' Emily asked.

'I don't know.'

'What did she want?'

'Nothing *I* could do for her.'

'Is she a patient?'

'No. Just . . . an occupational hazard.'

'I'll close the door.'

'Let's forget about her,' she said to Emily, more in hope than certainty.

The girl didn't reappear.

Joanna hoped it wasn't merely a hiatus.

At the next Sunday service she kept her eyes closed in prayer a little longer than usual: to impress the point upon their model English gentleman of a God.

Keep her away from Carnbeg, please.

They met again at the Alpenhorn.

'Dr Ebdon.'

'Astrid.'

'Hi.'

'Hello there.'

Nathan Newell knew her, through his cousin (he said), and there was nothing so formal as an introduction. Just a shaking of hands, in slightly slowed-down motion: a certain pressure of the fingers.

Richard found it hard to take his eyes off her. Wherever he looked in the room, he came to collect her again in the sweep of his gaze.

'I'm off for lunch, Joanna!' Ali at the desk called over.

Joanna waved across to her.

She was in the waiting-room, about to drive the new locum to the house for something simple to eat: soup and ciabatta bread and cheese.

She picked up a magazine and leafed through it, saw the familiar faces. She recognised the tell-tale signs from the tales of her friend Rowena Fletcher, one of Richard's Perth colleagues (the few) who had stayed loyal to her. The evidence of surgical tampering on the faces of those women who appeared to have it all, posing in their immaculate, clutterless homes. The upward tilt of the chin, the hair brushed forward, the wide-awake eyes, those ineradicable smiles.

If you had the money, you could do it. If you were scrabbling by, working part-time with no one to help you and every minute of the day with some demand on it, then you couldn't. Not a bloody hope. And the gap between the two experiences just went on widening and widening.

'Pinko!' Richard used to tease her. The tincture had darkened since then, but politics was latterly a no-go area for them both.

Now Richard, among the mint facelifts, could be as Republican as he wished to be, and it didn't have to concern her at all, did it?

Not in the slightest.

She closed the magazine, dropped it on to the table. She must remember to drop by the little supermarket this evening, she was nearly out of milk and flour, and they were running low on loo rolls, maybe the offer on the twelve-pack was still on?

It was a slow dance, and Richard was caught out, expecting an up-tempo.

He had never been much of a dancer. But Joanna used to know the steps, and he would follow her.

Astrid had her hand on his shoulder. Was it so simple after all? You just dispensed with all the romancing, was that it? Cut to the chase.

Hey, if I'd only known this years ago . . . If I'd got on to that Carnbeg exchange scheme a whole lot earlier . . . If . . .

It took an age, and it took no time at all, just to get round the room. She was holding on to him, Richard felt, as if she meant not to let go. Once, long ago, it used to be like this, before Joanna started backing off from the smoochy ones.

Used to be. But this was here and now. A new country, and you can live too much with the past, with history, all that suffocating backstory. No thank you.

Give him a hand on his shoulder, and the sweetness of shampoo and perfume and youth, a strand of hair across his lips, the heat of her body in his arms. Her back was almost undressed already. He breathed very very lightly on to the top of her spine, and he felt the echo of her suppressed laughter. She moved closer, and it occurred to him he was being led he didn't know where, and didn't care.

Antonia sent her old friend an invitation to the opening of her new gallery.

I'm not expecting you'll be able to come, but drop in and see me sometime, won't you, if you're ever over in Normandy.

Honfleur is pretty, and some of the streets are pretty steep

*too, but it's good exercise. I'm loving <u>winding down</u>, altho'
the gallery is exciting, challenging, etc. Bright white rooms
and good floors, which have come up gleaming. <u>I must have</u>
LIGHT!*

*We sold Mummy and Daddy's house – lots of people after
it – and the spoils all got split up, but there was enough for me
to buy a big old house in the middle of the town. I'm living
above the shop. Low ceilings upstairs, so it feels intimate.
Thick walls, and I <u>do</u> feel protected; well, you need to, when
you're a divorcee on the loose! I'm the first in the family, ∴
much raising of eyebrows, but I'll show them it's for the best.*

Reading Antonia's declaration of intent, Joanna could just
about believe in the efficacy of happy endings.

Sometimes Astrid asked him about his patients.
'That's classified.'
'It's still classified, even like this? In bed?'
'I guess.' He surprised himself every so often, with another
Americanism.
'It wouldn't hurt to tell me.'
'Why d'you want to know?'
'I want to know everything about you.'
'About me or my patients?'
'Well, that's your profession. So, it's about *you*.'
'Oh yes?'
But he wasn't in a mood to disagree, and anyway they always
got to the subject in this fashion, kind of joshing their way there.
And so he ended up telling her, wanting to smooth away that
little pucker which formed on her brow, complicating the skin
there and making her look a little older than her twenty-four
years.
Jesus Christ, he reminded himself, but she's young, she's
young. She knows how to put it all together, though, she's
watched and studied, everything from Sinatra and Camelot DC
to Alannis and W.

He liked her with her hair swept back, and the ponytail, when she looked like herself and no one else. Ponytails were new to him, except on ponies, and Imogen didn't give him an update on goings-on at gymkhanas any more, because she couldn't remember what her father knew and what he didn't.

So he told Astrid about the patients at the clinic, because that was about NOW, and it helped to put his daughters to the back of his mind again. He told her who was on what medication, and whether they were wise to it or not.

'You mean, you don't tell them?'

'Helps to keep them sweet.'

'You've got them drugged?'

He laughed at that, but she wasn't far out. If she got much sharper about all this, she'd be getting herself Mickey Finned as well.

Astrid was discreet, he supposed, or something would have got back to him by now. He whispered into her ear, only a couple of inches away from his mouth on the pillow. French pillows, trimmed with convent lace. Or that's what Astrid was told in the Denver boutique. The thought of nuns at their stitching cramped his style a little, but only a little. It was never enough to make him lose his huff and puff. With Astrid he always got there – just before time was up on him, he hit the target, shot his load.

'I've had an idea, Joanna,' Dr McKean said, 'about what you should do.'

'Do I have to hold my breath for this?'

'Oh, I hope *not*.'

In the end she allowed Kenneth to talk her into going on a refresher course, which she suspected had been his sister's idea to begin with.

Off to Cambridge. Long days, and most of the doctors updating themselves turned out to be younger than her. She was determined to keep abreast of them, though, and not to get left behind.

She was aware of a pair of eyes trained on her during their lectures. She decided not to affect surprise when he introduced himself.

'I thought you must be confusing me for someone else,' she told him.

Frank Tresidder. From a long line of Tresidder doctors in Cornwall.

'I live in a little place there you'll never have heard of.'

'I don't expect you'll have heard of Carnbeg, either.'

They got talking, about how each of them had adjusted to small-town life, after London and Bath. They agreed that they had both made a deliberate choice, and that the compensations won out.

Something about her fellow medics on the course alarmed her. An earnest, stressful air of competitiveness and one-upmanship. It was a South-Eastern thing, which she had got out of kilter with. She took refuge in Frank Tresidder's Cornish burr, in his corduroy-suited unfashionableness, in his hand-painted silk bow ties. She liked how his hair flopped over his high brow. She liked the twinkle in his eye, and those laughter lines, how he didn't seem inclined to take anything *too* seriously.

They were the same age, which struck her as auspicious: as if she was meant to recognise the fateful significance of that fact. His wife had died of cancer four years before, but it hadn't been a happy marriage latterly. He had a son and a daughter, both doctors, one forensic and the other with a research fellowship at an American university.

A very high-powered family, Joanna told him.

Oh, his children left *him* standing, he said, with his smiling eyes which creased at the corners.

She explained as best she could about Richard. She fought to keep pain or disappointment out of her voice. Frank merely nodded, and looked kindly.

He suggested a concert on the second last evening. She took him up on it. They sat in a college chapel listening to Haydn trios. He was a Haydn fan, and Joanna thought, maybe *I* could become one as well? The music had charm, and melody, and wit, and *joie de vivre*.

'Nothing seems too great a problem when I listen to Haydn,' he said.

He told her about the wealth of music festivals in his part of the world. Would she consider coming to one as his guest?

She hesitated.

He asked her in the next breath, would she like to bring one of the girls? What about Emily, who was studying the clarinet and piano and played in a youth orchestra?

'We'd like that,' she said, speaking for Emily and admiring the man's tact.

Richard woke, and realised that his cellphone was ringing, he'd left it on, and that now was the middle of the night.

The phone was beside the bed. Could it be Scotland calling, an emergency? He picked up the phone.

The voice he heard, it took a few seconds for him to recognise. Ralph Leddy, a friend of Nathan Newell, who worked for the attorneys Hobart Newell used. (Some people said Newell Senior used them to make his affairs look more respectable than Newell and the lawyers knew them to be.)

Astrid Brier had had an accident. She was in her apartment at Greenglades.

'What kind of accident?'

'I don't know. But is there some way you could get up there?'

How did he explain to Leddy that he wasn't an on-call doctor?

'I guess it's what we all want, Doctor.'

We all?

Richard looked at his watch: 3.20. He wouldn't be able to get back to sleep now.

'Yes. Okay.' He let his voice sound a little grudging.

Leddy didn't sound surprised that he should be agreeing to go.

'You know how to get there, don't you?'

It was as if this was nothing more than they'd expected of him. Security wasn't big at Greenglades, unlike at some of the shore compounds, where you paid an arm and a leg to be protected round the clock.

A car passed him on the avenue, which struck him – momentarily – as unusual.

Yes, he knew his way, even in the dark. Especially in the dark, since he had only ever been here driving on mainbeam.

He wondered again why Astrid hadn't called him herself.

He saw a light on inside: discreet lamplight. He rang the door bell. Nobody answered. He rang again. He noticed the stars overhead: like shavings of glacier ice.

He turned the handle, and the door opened. Strange.

He stood on the threshold. He remembered the first time he'd smelt the interior. A little airless, sweet and spicy (candles), a trail of cheroot smoke (Astrid's only real vice).

He closed the door behind him. He called her name.

He walked from the hall into the living-room.

He had felt uneasy all the way up here. Now he was seriously apprehensive.

He walked into her bedroom. A lamp was lit by the bed, and in the bathroom a vanity striplight hummed.

He felt the heat of water from the bathroom. The steam had cleared.

It was in the bathroom that he found her.

His heart suddenly juddered in his chest.

Astrid was lying in the whirlpool tub, submerged beneath the still water and turned on her side. Her eyes were open, and seeing nothing.

He held on to the door jamb, staring at her. This was crazy. This couldn't be happening.

But he was here, at four in the morning, as wide awake as he'd ever been in his forty-nine years.

Another trip to the supermarket to stock up, Joanna was thinking at that moment. *Prioritise.* And she'd take one of the girls with her to help.

Hey, look! All done without a safety net, or a facelift either.

'Who's coming with me?' she called upstairs.

No reply. She was having to compete with Atomic Kitten.

'Emily! Imogen! Who wants to be the shopping fairy?'

He doubted very much if she had drowned in the jacuzzi.

It was *just* possible, but the chances were remote. He'd noticed the bourbon bottles, and the sleeping-tablets, and hell, yes, it *might have* happened like that: she'd blacked out, slipped beneath the water, maybe she'd twisted round on herself, she hadn't been able to get a grip on the plastic surfaces, which were slippery with oils.

Maybe.

He stared at her. Sometimes death struck home to him, if he happened to be looking at an attractive corpse. Such a bloody damn waste of life. He might get the sense of a quantity of energy left behind in the room, still crackling somehow. But he didn't get it in this instance.

He suspected that the dying had occurred longer ago than he was supposed to think. But the heat of water in the jacuzzi confused matters greatly. (That, too, might have been no accident.)

He sat on the lidded toilet. He thought of the rendezvous they'd had, and the brisk hygienic efficiency of those mixed with Astrid's old-fashioned weakness for flowers and candy boxes.

And now she was this vast and cumbersome and totally inert liability.

He felt he should be more shocked by her death. They had been intimate with one another many times. But he was also coping with the fact that Ralph Leddy had rung him in the middle of the night, clicked his fingers and – surefire thing – he'd jumped to it.

She still turned over in the morning, expecting to find Richard there, the weight of him in the bed beside her.

The shock of discovery had gone, and also the sorrow of it.

She would spread out her arms and legs, as if she was running across the flat of some imaginary field.

The silence in the bedroom was soothing to her now. It quietened her. More seemed possible in the day ahead, although she knew that the next twenty-four hours would be much as usual, because that was what kept her on an even keel.

Breakfast was less high-speed than formerly. Not *leisurely*, but she had taught the girls not to overtax their digestive systems.

They used to do a bit of performing for their father, bidding against each other in the affection stakes, but now they didn't need to, and *Morning Choice* on Radio 3 was the worst they had to put up with these days.

More a case of Colette – *My Mother's House* – than *The House of Bernarda Alba*, she hoped. And both authors well off Richard Ebdon's reading-list, not a homicide agent or police DI in the picture.

Acute pulmonary oedema.

Which, Richard realised, only meant that the lungs had filled with fluid.

But a pulmonary oedema can result from an overdose of barbiturates.

He searched the apartment. All he could find was a bottle of amphetamines: which wouldn't be the choice of an insomniac or a would-be suicide. No barbiturates.

She'd had some kind of accident in the tub? And by a tragic sequence of events she hadn't been able to hoist herself upright?

He heard footsteps and jerked his head round.

'Mr Leddy . . . '

'She's dead, isn't she?'

They went through and sat in the living-room.

'Godawful business, Doctor. Sorry to bring you out.'

Richard shrugged.

'I've got to reimburse you for your time.' Leddy pulled out a chequebook. 'Would twenty-five thousand dollars sound about right?'

The offer was absurd. So precise and absurd.

'Not a cheque,' Richard heard himself say.

'No?'

'Cash.'

Leddy hesitated. Then a faint smile appeared on his face.

'Just as you like.' He closed the chequebook. 'That's no problem. I need to go out to the car.'

Leddy left the room and went outside.

Richard didn't even turn round to look at him.

He was trying not to think.

He was staring at the pattern on the curtains, big exotic blooms. (Caribbean?)

'Doctor knows best,' Leddy said at his shoulder.

'Does he?'

'A distinguished one like yourself. Who wouldn't think *his* decision was final?'

A Neiman Marcus carrier was placed on the table in front of him.

'Care to count it, Dr Ebdon?'

'No. No, thanks. That won't be necessary.'

'I like your European approach. Very civilised.'

'I'll need to file a report, Mr Leddy.'

'Yes, of course.'

'For the investigators.'

'You'll have the chief evidence.'

'It's kind of negative.'

'It is?'

'Can't tell if there was an overdose.'

'I understand.'

'And I can't judge if . . . '

'If?' Leddy prompted.

' . . . if foul play was involved.'

'You can't?'

'So, the cause of death . . . '

The words were left to hang in the air, suggesting the impossibility of an answer.

'I think you'll find it adds to twenty-five thousand.'

'Thank you.'

'Just a token payment. I know Nathan would think it's the least we can do. After luring you out to the backwoods here.'

'Luring me out?' he repeated, uncomfortable with the term.

'Nathan, he just had a hunch about the girl.'

'He was right.'

'Only *you* could tell us, Doctor.'

Silence.

'I've got a Gap carrier if you'd prefer that?'

Frank Tresidder was in Scotland, visiting Edinburgh to attend the funeral of his erstwhile tutor, a professor who had enthused him for a life of medicine. He stayed on a short while to help the professor's widow settle what should happen to his books and papers. While he was in Edinburgh, he called Carnbeg and invited the two of them to a concert at the Usher Hall. *The Creation.*

Emily couldn't come, so Joanna went down by herself. In the programme she saw mention of Chopin's music, and she told Frank the tale of the composer's sojourn in Carnbeg, when he was fêted as the darling of the local châtelaines.

'You should come and see Carnbeg,' she told him. And added, 'Before you head back home.'

She drove him up, and she realised how comfortable she felt with him, and that she would miss him when he wasn't here. He had a very good memory for all the things she'd ever said to him, details which would have been lost to most people.

He didn't tell her that the bungalow was in bad taste. He waxed lyrical about the views from the windows, and didn't criticise the windows because they were the picture sort and sealed units of white plastic. He had no difficulty in talking away to the girls, and for once they were ready to listen to medical stories, because he had a silver tongue to tell them. Very Celtic that, and Joanna found herself as captivated as they were.

She took him back to Edinburgh for his flight to Newquay.

At the Departures gate he planted a kiss on either cheek, and kept his hand on her shoulder. How well their bodies fitted together, she noticed. She had found herself talking about her hysterectomy on the earlier drive from Edinburgh to Carnbeg, and it had brought out a physical protectiveness in him which both consoled and excited her.

A young woman gets off the coach from Denver.

She squinnies in the sunshine, much brighter than where she's from, four or five thousand miles away.

She waits for her backpack to be unloaded from the hold.

CARNBEG SPRINGS OFFERS YOU A ROCKIES-HIGH WELCOME!

I *don't* think, she says to herself. Can't fool me. They just want your money here like anywhere else.

She buys a newspaper at the kiosk, and tucks it under the flap of her knapsack.

She has breakfast in the coffee shop. She's hungry. She could eat for two. And as she's thinking it, she catches sight of a toddler and her mother. The sight of them disturbs her, badly, and ruins her appetite.

She nearly forgets to pay, and the man at the till has to call after her. Out of embarrassment the girl talks away, and he comments on her accent, which he calls 'Irish'. She's going to correct him, but then thinks better of it. So, in his estimation, Irish she remains: as he will tell the police later.

She finds, at long last, the motel she's booked into.

It's one of the cheapest in town, and far from the action, but it'll serve her quite well. She intends spending her time out and about; after all, she's here on a mission.

There was another side to Nathan Newell, Richard knew.

He'd heard about weekend parties at a lodge somewhere up beyond Glacier Lake, much fancier than any of the Greenglades properties. Some of Nathan's smarter friends were invited. There they mixed with a different set, his Denver circle, who wouldn't have made it to the pages of *Town & Country* or the *Colorado Days*. For forty-eight hours they all got druggy and hung-over, and sexually anything went.

An invitation would have had its compensations, but for Richard it would also have been playing Russian roulette with his professional reputation.

Astrid hadn't liked to talk about it. She told him she'd been once, but he imagined it must have happened several times.

'That's Nathan's place,' she said. 'His father knows most things, so I guess he knows about the lodge, too.'

But so long as Hobart Newell had Washington as an objective for himself, a seat in Congress, it was a case of out of sight and out of mind.

'Things aren't, like, pure and simple, not in Carnbeg Springs,' Astrid had told him. 'You *think* you know all you're going to need to know, but . . . '

Those final moments with Frank preoccupied Joanna during the following weeks. He told her in his e-mails that he'd been able to see her from his altered embarkation gate at Edinburgh Airport, standing watching, even though she probably hadn't been able to see him.

She scanned her screen several times a day for a message – anything – from him. The day was brightened whenever she found something from him. She liked the silly-girlishness of looking; it reminded her of the person she'd been all those years ago, her hand searching her college pigeonhole in the porter's lodge for any scrap of scribbled missive from Richard. (Their infrequency, she realised now, had made his notes (not letters) all the more desirable; and their brevity when they did come was forgiven.)

Totnes next, a chamber-music festival. Frank had Friends tickets which would allow them to pick and choose at the time. Then over to Wexford, if she wanted, although the standard was up and down.

Music was a metaphysical language. For the two of them, it

was a means of communication which perhaps allowed them to say more than they intended or quite understood. At home she now listened to Haydn, and Mozart, to cheerful Dvořák and quirky Poulenc. It was Frank, with his floppy hair and robust good health and disguised learning, who quoted George Eliot to her one day in an e-mail. 'It is never too late to become who you might have been.'

On the 7th line of longitude, 105 degrees west, Richard Ebdon of the Bon Secours-Barrington Kaye Clinic of Carnbeg Springs Inc. was seated in an outdoor tub at the Amira Country Club when he heard a name, two words, 'Ralph Leddy'. A couple of strangers were talking, not always clearly above the rush and tumble of water.

Leddy had been seen having dinner at an out-of-town hotel north of Denver. Dinner with Sanford Callan. And not for the first time.

(Hearing that, Richard's instinctive reaction was to sink into the water up to his neck.)

Callan, the gossip said, intended fighting Newell for congressional nomination. He hadn't expressed himself on the matter formally, but it could only be a matter of time.

Richard got up out of the tub, and returned indoors, behind the plate glass. Somehow, he felt, Leddy's doing business with Sanford Callan – at their out-of-the-way rendezvous – changed the nature of everything.

Everything.

He wasn't sure how, but the instinct that it did was like a knife blade turning in his gut.

How was this happening to *him*?

So much had been expected of him, since the time he was in short trousers. He had sailed through life with plaudits and straight As. And now . . .

Now he was at the mercy of these shysters with God knows what history of skulduggery – thuggery – behind them, who thought they had some right to his very existence. He wasn't

ever going to break away from them; there would always be a
threat of worse-to-come if and whenever *they* chose.

She'd had to wait to discover the pleasures of gardening.

After half an hour or so you got into the groove of it. It
quietened and calmed you. The tiredness you were left with
was the satisfying, enveloping sort, which consumed you and
sent you to sleep immediately you lay down on the bed or a
floor.

Now she couldn't keep away from garden centres. She looked
forward to her conversations with Sheena Grimble over at
Strome. Whereas everything had been lawn here originally, she
had planted rockeries and herbaceous borders, placed quick-
growing shrubs to provide maximum shelter, and (with
Sheena's help) had even dug a pond. She read the gardening
books Sheena recommended, which was like a crash course in
horticulture. She was going to visit Tresco in the Scilly Isles with
Frank, followed by Garsington and Glyndebourne, where the
gardens were part of the operatic experience.

Her life went on taking new turns, and – she knew quite
well – all the better for it, too.

'I'm sorry, Dr Ebdon, it's her again.'

His receptionist had told him that a woman kept calling, she
wouldn't give her name or say what it was about. She sounded
Irish.

It occurred to Richard that she might have some connection
with the Hennessys, an Irish clan from Boulder who mixed with
some of Nathan Newell's close friends. Some relation of theirs,
maybe, or a maid or live-in?

She wasn't Irish, as he realised straightaway. But Scottish can
sound very much like Irish.

She said she had gone to the other Carnbeg looking for him,
but his wife had told him he'd moved.

'What is it you want?' he asked into the receiver, already
uneasy.

She needed to see him, she said. Urgently. She had come all this way.

'Not to see *me*?' He simulated a laugh.

'Yes,' she answered him, perfectly seriously.

'D'you want to come here to the clinic?'

'I can't do that.'

'You want to meet?'

'Yes.'

'A bar? A coffeeshop?'

She didn't reply.

'A diner? A park? You just say.'

'Anywhere.'

He gave her the name of a bland chain-hotel, which had a Tahitian theme bar. As far away from associations with Scotland as he could think of on the spur of the moment.

'Okay.'

'What about a time?' he asked.

She changed her mind several times, and he wondered if he would even hear from her.

The morning of Kenneth McKean's funeral was bright and clear. The world felt washed clean.

And so it goes, Joanna thought, standing on the hillside. We come and we leave, and it's too soon done.

The great and the good of Carnbeg were here. She also recognised scores of other patients, who wanted to pay their respects.

Suddenly everyone was levelled.

Which had become the bias of her mind more and more, and no regrets from *her*.

Every morning she liked to get to the surgery early, so that she could have twenty minutes or half an hour to herself. She wasn't preparing her notes, but taking time to read: Virginia Woolf, or Lampedusa, or the two good doctors, Schnitzler from Vienna and Chekhov from Moscow, something European and serious enough and illuminating on the human condition.

Come ten past nine and she was ready to begin, but only after this infusion of inspiration from her favourite great minds, who viewed society in its complexity and human nature in its archetypal straightforwardness.

Carnbeg had turned out today for one man when it might not have come for any other. Kenneth McKean had seen through to the blood and the bone and the soft tissue, and nothing could have been hidden from him. He'd had most of his career already before the litigants, the ambulance-chasers, learned their rights and got in on the act. Lucky man.

Kenneth had given *her* a career, and a purpose to her life. As she was leaving the churchyard she pressed his sister's arm and kissed her cheek.

'Call me any time, Moira,' she said. One good turn in life.

'Yes. Yes, of course.'

'If there's anything at all I can do. Will you, please?'

'Thanks, Joanna, I shall.'

'No, no, I'm the one who should be thanking you.'

As she walked downhill the day's brightness hurt Joanna's eyes. A generosity of light, garnered from the four corners of the land, and funnelled through the valleys surrounding them. It made her long for transparency, for nothing to hide, for simple faith and the lodestar hope of salvation.

For all of it.

He was there in the Kon-Tiki bar, one vodka down and turning the empty tumbler on the table top, when – on the dot – in she walked.

He immediately recognised her as one of his Glasgow patients. Her family had brought her, much against her will. Light preparatory sedation, he remembered, just to stop her running away.

She didn't look as if she planned on running away today.

'You know who I am.' She didn't ask it as a question.

'Please sit down, won't you?'

She sat down, without taking her eyes from his face.

'I know about you,' she said.

'I don't go to Glasgow now.'

'No. About *this* place.'

He stared at her, and she stared back.

'D'you think I've been just pissing around doing nothing?'

'What d'you mean, you "know" about me?'

'And that girl who died. I *know*.'

That was all she said. But suddenly his life had changed, in an instant. He felt the blood icing in his veins.

He looked away, towards the window and daylight.

He was in a story. A movie plot. This wasn't him sitting here. It was an actor's job. Richard Ebdon was somewhere else, watching this.

'Who have you been talking to?'

'What?'

'Who else have you – '

'I don't . . . '

Have anyone to tell, she meant. She was the only person who understood. It hadn't gone any further than her. Yet. But how much longer would that state of affairs last?

He looked at the girl with her silly, unformed face. What did she want from him?

She was so much less sophisticated than anyone else in the room. She couldn't be as stupid as she seemed, threatening to bring down a man like himself.

She didn't take her eyes off him.

She had him in a cold sweat. It was ridiculous. But that didn't make events any less true.

How – how in *Christ's* name – ?

He felt frightened of her, because he truly didn't know what she might be capable of.

She had such a terrible air of sureness, rectitude, about her. As if she was on a mission.

And he was even more frightened of himself, not knowing the lengths she might drive him to.

Joanna took off her funeral clothes.

She put Haydn on the CD player. To lift her spirits, although she wasn't sure they needed lifting. She would miss Kenneth; but it would take a long time to lose his presence at the Torrie Wynd surgery, and that reassured her.

Frank had promised he would phone this evening.

All the girls were coming for the weekend, and Charlotte was bringing her boyfriend; perhaps Emma's best friend would be there as well. The house would be noisy, and she'd scarcely have time to draw breath. This was their normality, and she knew to savour every hard-won moment of it.

Richard sat turning the paper parasol in his hand, spinning it between his fingers.

Polynesian guitars played out of the speakers.

Five thousand dollars, he'd suggested, I'll give it to you in cash, and the girl had laughed in his face. She'd actually *laughed*. And then she'd got up and walked out.

Walked out on *him*.

He glanced over at the window. An empty, bleak Edward Hopper Street.

He had been sitting like this for half an hour.

He looked down at his hands, at the cocktail parasol he'd snapped into tiny pieces.

Bonfires

Alison could see the bonfire from the foot of the brae, as she turned the corner in the car. A plume of dark smoke through the trees. A flash of flame.

Yes, it was in her mother's garden.

Nearer the house she wound down the window and smelled smoke. Autumn was the usual season when fires were lit in gardens across the town, and the air was heavy with melancholy. Back in the city where she lived, one great smokeless zone now, your spirit wasn't worked on like this, filling your head with apprehensions and regrets.

'Hello, Mum!' Alison smiled across, but she heard her voice wound up tight in her throat.

Her mother took her time before offering a smile back. One of those yes-I-know-what-it-is-you're-thinking smiles.

God, Alison thought, is it going to be another of those days?

'You're early,' her mother said.

Was that a disapproving tone? Very probably.

'Yes,' Alison said. 'Well, I thought I'd try to get away before the traffic.

Her mother just shook her head. Meaning, I'm glad to be away from the city, from traffic, oh, to be here in Perthshire.

'What are you burning?' Alison asked. 'Old leaves?'

'I've nearly finished,' her mother said. 'I wasn't expecting you so soon.'

As so often, her mother had chosen not to answer a question.

She didn't see any piles of raked leaves: just a couple of cardboard boxes, and, sticking through the wire cage which contained the fire's embers, the white of unburned pieces of paper.

'What's in those?' Alison nodded at the boxes.

'Oh, just some odds and ends.'

'What kind of odds and ends?' Alison persisted.

'Personal things,' her mother said.

'Nothing you shouldn't be burning, I hope!' Alison tried to inject a little humour into her voice.

But she was bothered none the less. Her mother had always had an unsentimental approach to the past. Not, Alison knew, *not* a Scottish characteristic. Nostalgia is the Scots' undoing, and she was aware of such stirrings herself. But her mother curiously had the ability to resist.

'Shall I go and put the kettle on?' Alison asked, thinking that should have been her mother's cue.

'By all means,' her mother merely said.

'Right, then.'

Alison started walking towards the house. She felt her mother's eyes were trained on her. She would be wondering how much her clothes had cost her, why did she have to buy so many, was that how you lived in cities as a professional woman? But her mother wasn't an ingénue, far from it, *she* had been born in a city, grown up there, she'd had a job herself before she married.

All that was an act, the out-here-in the-sticks countrywoman pose. Her mother browsed through the shiny lifestyle magazines in the newsagent's on the High Street, she didn't say 'no' when old gossip rags were passed on to her. Alison wanted to say to her, 'Oh, Mum, come on, I wasn't born yesterday'; but of course she hadn't, not yet.

(She hoped her mother wasn't going to be the sort who regresses and becomes girlish in later years – thinks everyone is bound to be charmed by her vagueness. I shall see through all that, Alison thought – and so will everyone else with half a brain.)

She walked into the kitchen, and made straight for the kettle. She filled it at the sink. She could still smell the bonfire smoke. It got everywhere, even though you couldn't see it. That inopportune bonfire.

She stood at the window, watching her mother. Today she seemed a little stooped; Alison hadn't noticed that before, normally her mother was obstinately straight-backed. Maybe, too, she was a little slower, when she thought she wasn't being observed like this. In her slacks and big gent's jumper, which she preferred to the women's skimpier sort, in her clumpy walking-shoes, she had the maddeningly independent look she had taken on during her Perthshire years, once Dad had died and she'd sold the Glasgow house and moved up here. But today the independence seemed more careworn, weathered, more forced: like a defence, against giving too much of herself away. And suddenly Alison, in spite of herself, felt sorry for her mother: the outfit unbecoming, her movements slower, the job of fuelling the fire and poking air into it hard going.

She had surprised her mother, obviously. She wasn't supposed to see the bonfire, the task was to have been attended to before she got here. Hence her mother's irritability, and hence her own as well after the long drive up.

The water was boiling. Alison turned round and looked for the teapot, and the tea caddy.

What had her mother done with them? Why were things not where she expected to find them?

Alison caught sight of herself reflected in the cooker fascia. She looked hot and flustered, not how she liked to think of herself as seen by her clients. She was aware that city life got her worked up; on holiday it always took two or three days before she could even begin to relax. A few hours away like this wasn't going to be enough. And being with her mother was *not* the ideal circumstances: it wasn't now, and she had to confess to herself, it never had been.

Alison called her mother in for tea.

'I have to get this finished first,' her mother called back.

'Let me help.'

'No, thanks.'

'Why not?'

'I can manage a bonfire by myself.'

'As you like, Mum.'

Alison took out the tea, and went back inside for hers.

She walked through the house, from room to room, cradling the hot mug in her hands. A pottery mug, not new, but she didn't recognise it; she'd taken it from the back of a cupboard. She wouldn't have carried her tea about if her mother had been watching, but that was why she was looking round the house, downstairs and upstairs, because her mother was elsewhere.

She looked into her mother's bedroom. Before she could walk out of the frame, she caught a glimpse of herself in the wardrobe mirror. An impression. The same build as her mother, the same colouring. It was her she took after, not her father. But her father, when Alison thought about it, had belonged more and more to the periphery of their life. Sometimes she used to wonder about those secretaries he had at work, attractive in a samey cut-price filmstarlet-ish way.

Her mother, her father – and herself, an only child, stuck in the middle. Wanting to be like neither as she grew up. Going off to the new university her mother pretended not to have heard of, shinning up the promotion ropes with a speed and determination which her father thought not *comme il faut*. Having boyfriends she didn't talk about, because none of them came close to the mark, or were her hopes too high? Having an abortion along the way because that was par for the course, but the clinic had used unsterilised equipment. Throwing herself into her career because that was all she had left.

Hasn't your Alison done well?

God, if they only knew.

A photograph lay on the floor. It must have been dropped. An old holiday snap.

Alison picked it up.

Goat Fell on Arran, from – where? – Brodick?

In her mind Alison suddenly made the jump. From Goat Fell to Myra Graham.

A couple of months ago she had noticed an obituary in one of the Scottish newspapers. Myra Graham. One of her mother's friends, and a name from the past. It was a past which largely pre-dated Alison's life. Myra Graham had been a friend of her mother's in the days before she married. A few times in the early years, Alison recalled, Myra would mysteriously materialise – once on Arran, when they were on the island for a holiday – and then for some reason the appearances stopped.

Myra was a biologist. A keen mountaineer, Munro-bagger. She had a pottery wheel at home. Made her own clothes. She had never married. It would have been difficult to imagine Myra Graham married – even a small child realised she wouldn't have been happy having to defer as women were wont to do in those days. Myra Graham was a woman who knew her own mind.

But, to married couples, a woman who's unattached will always present an element of danger. Never mind that Myra Graham didn't resemble a film starlet.

Alison had phoned her mother that evening, after she'd read the obituary. Her mother had said very little, she'd hardly spoken at all, and Alison realised that she wasn't listening to anything. The fact of the death her mother already knew, she had understood about Myra's condition for the past months.

'Did you two keep up?' Alison asked. Perhaps the tone of the question was too hectoring, or too patronising. Or chafed at old marital wounds.

Answer came there none.

Was that a sob being swallowed, at the other end of the line?

Alison had never quite worked out where she was with her mother. She loved her, of course, but it wasn't unconditional. She was irritated by her mother, vexed, and also she pitied her, terribly sometimes.

She felt that, in the end, she had learned very little about who her mother was. Irritated by her, pitying her, loving her – while time and again her mother got the better of her, by keeping her secrets to herself.

An obituary like Myra Graham's only skimmed across the surface of a life. Politic words, but it was what fell into the spaces between, which didn't rise to the surface and the scrutinising light of day – it was that which told the true story.

It's later, after the visit.

Here I am, a grown woman, Alison thought, down on my hands and knees in the darkness, scrabbling through charred bits of paper, this is absurd, but somehow, too, this seems necessary, that I should *know*. Saying goodbye at nightfall to Mum, later than my usual, and then driving off but turning back when I got to the bottom of the brae, and making my way back uphill on foot, forgetting that of course the old gate still creaks, rasps like fury, and thinking it must give me away, lying low for a while, but here I am, in my mother's garden, and she hasn't come out, no nosey neighbour has appeared to look because they've been disturbed by a noise, here I am like an idiot on my hands and knees in the darkness scrabbling around, picking out any piece of paper that's paler than the rest, what have I come to, my mother's own daughter.

Another generation on, another woman with my secrets.

Alison took the scraps of paper back to the car. She saw that there was handwriting on them. Not her mother's, not her father's, either. A script which might have been a man's or a woman's. A little crabbed, certainly, handwriting which was making an effort to be legible. Only just legible, like a scientist on best behaviour. Here and there a higher letter than the others, an 'l' or the staves of a 'k' or a 'b', looking – oh, like a jagged mountain peak to scale, a Munro at least.

Some words caught her eye. *'Dearest'*. *'Affectionately'*. *'Your own'*.

But she didn't look any more. She didn't want to know.

She noticed a wastepaper bin on a lamppost, and got out of the car and walked across. In went the fragments of paper, she stood in the pool of light until she'd shaken every one from her fingers, into the bin.

The potter's wheel, she remembered. And that pottery mug in the kitchen cupboard.

Alison stepped back out of the light, into the shadows.

For a few moments she had a crazy picture in her head. A fantasy. This hillside of gardens behind hedges, and a bonfire in every one, dozens of bonfires, quietly but urgently burning away: kindling the evidence of hidden lives.

The smoky reek of charred letters and melted photographs.

The whole hillside ablaze in the dark.

Miss Connell Meets Her Match

A brief history lesson.

Between the wars and later, in the long sort of peace, the Carnbeg Hydro and the Sgian Palace Hotel were famous hunting-grounds for parents seeking future wives and husbands for their children.

They were aided by two other institutions of Carnbeg life, the matchmakers. In the 1950s those were Miss Connell at the Hydro and Miss Ralston, over at the Palace.

The two women would come up, one from the west coast and one from the east, for Easter; for the two autumn weekends which Glasgow and Edinburgh observed; and for the long weeks of summer when the schools took their break. They had long memories, which held the histories of the families who returned at the same time every year – the grandparents, their children and *their* children.

For its regular visitors the point about coming to Carnbeg time after time was to mix with those of their own kind. Families became friends, and it was quite cosy and comfortable, and perhaps everyone could have been paired off without any assistance. But there were always fresh arrivals on the scene, new blood, and the skill of the two women lay in calculating which elements of the traditional and the unassimilated might be compatible.

Neither woman was officially for hire. But everyone knew them for the sages they were, and found pretexts for making their acquaintance. The Carnbeg newcomers, little daunted, would realise this was the quickest way to get an entrée.

Each woman would tease out the details she needed to know, and file them away. (Miss Connell was a part-time bookkeeper back in Glasgow; Miss Ralston was a university librarian.) Then, for one at the Hydro and the other at the Palace, the mulling process would begin: two simultaneous mulling processes. Miss Connell or Miss Ralston had a conversation with fellow guests; she mentioned so-and-so – 'Have you ever met?' – and an invitation was contrived, and it was made to seem like the most casual thing in the world.

But not every Hydro or Palace candidate for marriage had qualities immediately appealing to the other candidates (and their parents) at the hotel. In which case either Glaswegian Miss Connell or Edinburgher Miss Ralston, following precedent, addressed a formal note to the other and the two women met for a consultation, usually on neutral ground, in a lounge of one of the town's lesser hotels. Sipping from their tea cups and sharing exactly equally the contents of the cake-stand, they set about pooling their resources and – so to speak – laying out their cards.

Both women wanted to claim equal credit for a successful matching-off. If the outcome was as hoped for, it was inevitable that the Hydro or Palace habituees would see their own – Miss Connell or Miss Ralston – as the principal instigator. Normally, though, it turned out to be a case of even Stevens.

Business was business. Otherwise Miss Connell and Miss Ralston didn't mix, in a town where – for the visitors – mixing and matching was the social be-all and end-all. Each had her secret sources and knew how much esteem the other was enjoying: depending on whether or not last year's friendships had blossomed into romance. Luck was certainly an issue, but in such a traditional – hidebound – society what counted was not the individual will but seeming not to fail or to be found wanting. People of the same background had values in common, and those were considered more important than private feelings. You didn't let the side down, you didn't distinguish between love and duty – how could you really love someone whose opinions and principles weren't much the same as your own?

A neat and tidy world, and self-ordering, although a little prompting was sometimes needed, to identify like with like.

That required an overview – from Miss Connell or Miss Ralston, ensconced in their corner chairs in lounges, at their corner tables in the dining-rooms.

The matchmaking didn't work out every time. Now and then the calculations went awry, and the women blamed not themselves but the fickleness of youth.

Their few detractors argued, how come the two women were still spinsters unless the system had gone wrong for them, too? Shouldn't they have been able to find husbands for themselves if they were such experts?

But mostly the business *did* work, the counter-argument went, and the failures were far and away the exception. Look at all the weddings and christenings the women got invited to (even if they seldom chose to go), the number of times they were *hello*'d and *how are you*'d in the hotel corridors. Some of us prefer to put others' welfare before our own, either because we're selfless or because having pride in our talent leaves us wishing (naturally) to perfect it – and how can we, with a husband demanding our time?

Which argument was stronger? Take your pick.

And then it happened that the two women had a dispute about something, and relations between them grew frosty.

They avoided one another on the High Street, darting into shop doorways or the nearest vennel to get away.

Neither dared venture on to the territory of the other, and surrogates were out of the question, because who had a surer knowledge of the business – who had better attuned social barometers? – than themselves.

So, even at second or third hand, there was no communication between the two.

For each, it was as if half of her antennae had been removed.

Before, they had been complements of each other, occasional colleagues by self-serving necessity. But now, thanks to this separation over a point which no one was ever clear about, they had become rivals.

The longer the situation went on, while neither felt able to approach a reconciliation, the deadlier the rivalry got.

Miss Connell resolved to work with the material at her disposal, namely the guests at the Hydro. She kept an ear closer to the Carnbeg ground, so that she might hear of any local parents in the marriage market. She also tried to catch any titbits of news from the Palace, without making her intentions too obvious. As far as she was aware, there was no poaching; to her knowledge, none of the current Hydro brood was being matchmade by Annette Ralston, which would have been inexcusable.

So why should Miss Connell have felt that this was a false calm?

When she had enough to concentrate on, how strange it was that Miss Connell should now find herself prone to distractions.

Not so much about Miss Ralston, although the woman did niggle away at her thoughts.

Rather – No, start again.

Miss Connell had just come out of the Hydro's table-tennis room. Inside were four tables, all in play this afternoon. Nobody had bothered about her as she slowly patrolled the room, eyeing the players and their friends, eavesdropping on their conversations, storing all the piecemeal information in her retrieval system, 'file under':

Newton Mearns/Broom Estate
Western Baths
Hutchie Boys'/Craigholme
Stirling County Show
RSAM/Athenaeum auditions
Arran cycle race (Lochranza)
Scripture Union

The man was turning the corner of the corridor, and they walked straight into each other.

He apologised. She also, but she allowed him to claim more of the blame, feeling irritated that she'd suffered a loss of dignity.

He was looking for a godchild who was downstairs, somewhere.

'Can I direct you?' she asked.

'I don't know my way around, I'm afraid.'

'It's confusing the first time you come.'

'I'm staying over at the Palace. But I heard he was here.'

'So, you're an interloper?'

'I'm sorry?' the man said.

Miss Connell smiled. 'You're either one or the other,' she told him. 'Hydro or Palace.'

The interloper raised his eyebrows. 'You are?'

'It's a tradition.'

'Not in this day and age, surely?'

It was his turn to smile, and again Miss Connell felt a little caught out.

The following evening she was in the dining-room when he appeared.

She did a double-take, recognising that upright deportment, the carefully brushed hair, his genial expression. Tidily turned out, with polished shoes.

A few years older than her; late forties?

He was shown to a table.

They were busy tonight. Half the dining-room was given over to a function starting later.

Soon there was a queue to get in.

Miss Connell averted her eyes, her famously bright violet eyes; she didn't want to be embarrassed by the stares of the queuers.

But she did she notice the man speaking to the head waiter, offering to share his table: even though there were no singles in the procession at the door.

He looked across at her, surprising her. Miss Connell glanced away, then back again. The man smiled, shrugged, conveying. *What else can I do?*

Miss Connell fidgeted with her beads. Da–di–da–di–dum.

What possessed her, though, that she should stop a waitress and ask her to go over to (was it?) table 11 and ask, *Would you care to join me, and then two can have your table?*

The man accepted, and Miss Connell had the waitress set a place for him.

'What brings you back among us infidels?' she asked.

'I was talking to someone. She said the Hydro is snobbier than the Palace, and not one good reason she could think of. Which struck me as a very snobby and self-important thing to say. But it whetted my appetite to up sticks.'

'You decided to move?'

'Yes.'

'And here you are?'

'And here I am.'

Miss Connell liked to have her time to herself, to observe and take mental notes. Parents approached her, as a rule, only when she signalled her accessibility, putting down her book or newspaper and sitting with her hands in her lap to consider the view through the windows. (Miss Ralston's technique was to pull out a piece of tackwork, which everyone could see never progressed much from one day to the next.)

Otherwise Miss Connell's use for people was as conduits of information.

She tried that method with Lawrence McFarlane. When she thought he would have had enough of being quizzed about the Edinburgh social scene, he didn't try to slope off.

He told her he enjoyed her irreverence, her caustic asides.

'That *is* me you're talking about?' she asked.

'Yes. You.'

'Then I think it's you who must have made me like that,' she said.

He laughed, which wasn't quite what she had intended. But something about such lighthearted laughter was infectious, and she couldn't keep her own smile from pushing up her mouth, into her cheeks.

He had to go back to Edinburgh, but he reappeared later in the summer.

'I have the cheapest room in the place,' Miss Connell told

him on his return. 'And I'm on half-board. If you're costing it up.'

'I wouldn't have dreamed of it.'

'I'm not an heiress.'

'And I'm not a bounty-hunter.'

'You're not offended that the thought crossed my mind?' Miss Connell asked.

'I think you know your own mind.'

'That's true.'

'I like that in a lady.'

'Oh, do you?'

Why should she change her habits to suit another person? Here he was, though, asking her to accompany him, to walk up the hill or down into the town. And here she was, agreeing to the request.

Why did everyone else – the parents who wanted to find in-laws for their children as like themselves as possible – why did they presume that she was more interested in *their* lives than in her own? Wasn't it high time to remember herself?

Years ago, a couple of tweedy sisters had been the Hydro's matchmakers.

Young Marjorie Connell regularly visited as a guest. The pair kept their beady eyes trained on her, and every so often they would swoop, one on either side of her, and try to wheedle out of her whatever it was they needed to know, about herself and those she mixed with. She knew what their game was, and she became adept at giving them less than they wanted. She also wondered why she didn't go along with it, like all the others. But, to do that, maybe she would have had to believe that marrying anyone was worth all this foreplanning.

No one proposed to her. She was bridesmaid at a friend's wedding, then at a second, but she declined the invitation to a third. She watched the scramble to find a husband, in those years when good men – of sound limb and mind – were at a premium. She felt quite detached from it all, the horse-trading. Chance, she knew, had a lot to do with the matter, who found whom. But chance can always be given a bit of assistance. She acquired a reputation among her contemporaries for perspicacity in this department: she had a knack of spotting any trouble that might be brewing for this or that couple, and she would be the first to detect some worth in those overlooked individuals so backward in coming forward.

Marriage was now ruled out for her. Mr Right hadn't come along, her mother explained to friends, sounding not too disappointed about her plight.

Marjorie Connell was aware she was being dragooned into spinsterhood.

She found a job, and some financial independence. But her social status depended on the fact that in a large crowded room she could pick out pairs of harmonious souls – even if *they* didn't know they were – at fifty yards' distance from each other.

Perhaps it was a gift, like second sight, like fortune-telling. She heard the jibes – 'If it's so easy for her, why is she single?' – and because there wasn't a proper answer she learned to put on a flinty demeanour, an invulnerable front. She spoke with a cynical twist in her voice, so that people might suppose it wasn't of the least concern to *her*, and that she was elevated above such pettiness.

Lawrence McFarlane had been a widower for ten years, since his late thirties.

The experience of his friends had shown him that they married too soon.

'It's a question of values,' Miss Connell said.

'But people also change. How you are at twenty and how you might be at fifty . . . '

She couldn't deny that. Values weren't everything.

What was he saying? That at their time of life, coming into the middle part of middle age, there was a lot less time left and so less scope for change?

Or was he saying, why not learn to surprise yourself?

Marjorie Connell didn't keep up with most of her protégées. She wasn't in the habit of mapping the progress of their romances. Why, then, should she have told anyone about her own?

Next Easter she was absent from the Hydro, for the first time that most of the staff could recall. In fact she was on her honeymoon, in the Lake District.

The end of June came round, the schools broke up, but no summer booking had been received in the familiar spiky script, on the usual grey headed notepaper. Room 509, up under the eaves, was occupied by a succession of other guests; some of them complained, about the confined space and the heat and the feeble water pressure.

She did appear, but only briefly, for one night. They got there at teatime. She wasn't immediately recognisable as Miss Connell: a wave in her hair instead of permed curls, a jersey two-piece in hyacinth blue, no gloves, a basket-weave summer handbag.

The eyes, so intensely violet, were the giveaway, never letting up for a second, scanning the public rooms and into every corner, as if she was still winkling out the wallflowers for their unsung virtues. Here and there were the parents (not to be confused with the casuals, the visitors to Carnbeg who came *without* ulterior motives); one generation repeated the ways of its predecessor, and hardly took time to draw breath.

She hurried through tea, urging her husband to take his entitlement from the cake-stand.

'We might as well,' she said, 'we've paid for it.'

And, in wider terms, she felt she had paid for this unexpected new footing in life she was still adjusting to, her contentment to be a married woman. She had paid for it with her fifteen years of application, not wholly selfless, measured out in studious narrow-eyed tilts of the head and little sage smiles, always pledged to other people's futures.

God willing, it was goodbye to all that. Now it was about give and take.

The two of them were still establishing their parameters, their limits.

It would take time, and some patience. But since time was in shorter supply, all the more need to be excusing.

There was some divine justice after all, she felt, in having others cast their furtive glances at *you*.

Sometimes it occurred to Marjorie McFarlane, as she now was, to ask her husband, did you know you would find me at the games room that day? Had you really lost your way?

But behind those questions would have been a more disturbing one.

Did you ever speak to a guest at the Palace called Annette Ralston? Rather, did she single *you* out to speak to?

But she didn't want to hear his answer. A 'yes' to one or both would have been too much for her; and would a 'no' ever ring quite true in her head whenever she played it back to herself?

That was Miss Connell's story, and how she met her match.

It was hard for anyone to say whose the victory was.

Was it Miss Ralston's? Had she achieved her finest triumph, by pairing off her erstwhile colleague/arch-rival?

Or did the last word belong to Miss Connell-as-was, because she had passed out of the state of singlehood into the condition of the blessed?

'What is it, Marjorie?'

'Marmalade, please.'

Her husband passed her the dish.

'It looks a bit jellyish,' she said.

'Is it different from what they used to have here?'

'Their marmalade used to have peel in it.'

'They've got a new chef over at the Palace,' he said. 'So I believe.'

'I've always found that place very gloomy. Those turrets.'

'I just wondered.'

Momentarily Marjorie Connell was diverted by two teenagers

crossing the dining-room in opposite directions, each unaware of the other.

'Wondered what?' she asked, spreading butter on her toast.

'It doesn't matter.'

She smiled first, and then he did.

'Spain,' she heard herself saying.

'Spain?' he repeated.

It must have been the thought of the Seville oranges.

'For next year.'

'If you like, Marjorie. Yes.'

'They say everyone'll be taking their holiday there soon. So we should go before it gets ruined.'

'That's fine by me.'

In the bright sunshine, Marjorie McFarlane felt, she would forget all about turrets and tackwork, and people would meet or miss one another entirely, turning into the next street as perfect strangers. Some would fall in love, because far from home it's the sort of thing they do, head over heels, without rhyme or reason, and that was where she suddenly wanted to be, putting up with the absence of Dundee marmalade if she could pick the smaller, sweeter eating oranges straight off the tree.

Mischief in Chinatown

Sheena's first experience of Mrs Anstruther was when her mother bought plants from a trestle table at the front gate of Alt-na-Crè. The long, low pink house was just visible in the background. They were served by the lady herself, who had courtly manners from another age. Her hands were caked with dried mud from the garden. In the car afterwards, her mother remarked, 'Fine long fingers. And did you see the diamonds on that ring?'

The ring *was* a beauty. A cluster of big diamonds, flanked by rubies. Not vulgar, when worn by someone who wouldn't have been out of place in a castle.

The box of annuals cost very little, and Mrs Anstruther seemed embarrassed to be taking money. Her handsome son had hove into view. He used to be a student, but wasn't one any more; an only child, he lived at home, helping his mother tend the garden.

As Sheena's mother was paying for her purchases, Mrs Begg stopped *her* car and got out. Mrs Begg would step in where others cared not to follow.

'We haven't seen your husband for a while, Mrs Anstruther.'

'No.' The lady attempted to smile. 'He isn't here. He's – '

' – out of the country,' Torquil cut in.

'Yes,' Mrs Anstruther said. 'That's right. He's out of the country.'

Mother and son looked at each other, and Mrs Begg knew at once – or so she claimed later – that Mr Anstruther was no such thing.

'Somewhere nice?' Mrs Begg asked.

Mrs Anstruther looked at her handsome and clever son, who had dropped out of university, although no one knew why.

'Dad's not supposed to talk about it,' Torquil said.

Funny to think of Mr Anstruther, with his military appearance, being called 'Dad'. Nobody had expected a dentist to have a military appearance.

Did dentists go abroad 'on business'? Wasn't Carnbeg good enough for him?

But he hadn't shown up at the surgery for the past eight months. Mrs Begg's appointments, like her friends', had been turned over to his partners. Rumours were still doing the rounds about his shaky hands and the smell of alcohol on his breath, which he tried to cover by swilling pink mouthwash.

Sheena's mother took the begonias and antirrhinums home and planted them in their own garden. They were quality plants, as you might have expected of anything brought on by Mrs Anstruther. She had rescued the garden of Alt-na-Crè from sorry oblivion, doing most of the hard graft by herself, and with help from Torquil when he came home from boarding school and university, until he became a drop-out, clever and very handsome though he was.

The begonias and the antirrhinums went from strength to strength, and Sheena watched them become knitted into the garden, and then have offshoots transplanted to other parts of the garden, colonising it. She felt the plants established a bond between here at Tummel Road and Alt-na-Crè over the hill, although her mother didn't see it that way, not replying when she put the thought to her one day.

It could have been that her mother was just being nosey on the two or three further occasions when she stopped off at the Anstruthers', wanting to examine that engagement ring again and wondering if there would be any clue as to whether Mr Anstruther was back home and in residence, or not. The whole town wondered. Recently the man had been spotted, two or three times, being driven by Torquil in a battered Ford Sierra. Changed days. But he had only himself to blame, having lost his licence when he spectacularly drove his own car through

Carnbeg's floral clock and ploughed into the Gartcarron roundabout.

Sheena's friend Gillian's mother remembered when the Anstruthers had first arrived in the town. They had been left Alt-na-Crè by Cecilia Anstruther's great-aunt, and maybe there was some money also, because the husband decided to transfer his dental practice from the New Town of Edinburgh to Carnbeg.

The garden in those days had been nothing like the garden it became, but it remained as it was until Torquil was sent away from home at seven or eight years old. (A boy with a name like that was *fated* for boarding-school life, Mrs Murdoch said, with a shake of her head.) It was only then, when she was in her late forties, that Mrs Anstruther discovered an interest, or more properly a vocation, and her fingers (so to speak) turned green. Mr Anstruther wasn't the type to lift a spade or a fork – he'd grown up in Borneo or Java or some such, with an amah and servants and gardeners, or so he liked to tell people – and it was his wife's inheritance, or what was left, which afforded them labour in the garden.

With Torquil away, the gardener, Mr Keddie, was informed out of the blue that his services were no longer required. Perhaps that meant the inheritance was used up? (A dentist's salary would have been stretched to maintain the upkeep on a house with six bedrooms, and fees at Torquil's school, and running that Daimler they used to drop Torquil off and to collect him, and the annual Jersey holiday which was a ritual they seemed disinclined to break with.)

Sheena was intrigued to hear about the Anstruthers, remembering her few visits to the front gate to view the trestle table of plants and the very superior ring on Mrs Anstruther's muddy left hand, so nonchalantly sparkling as she took the palmful of (very) small change from Sheena's mother in return for the flourishingly green and unnibbled bedding-out plants.

'Mrs Anstruther has worked wonders with that place, she

really has,' her mother told her friends, and Sheena in her more literal moments imagined a supernatural sequence of events, wonders performed and a wilderness transformed. 'Who'd ever have guessed it?' asked Gillian's mother, a Carnbeg native, speaking for them all.

Sheena continued to associate those spreading, healthy plants at Tummel Road with the mystery of Alt-na-Crè and the Anstruthers. Whenever she heard the term 'woman gardener', it was the figure of Cecilia Anstruther who came into her mind. She was remembering the fine long fingers, and the big diamond and ruby beauty on the fourth.

These days Mrs Anstruther was noticeably more stooped. (She had given birth to Torquil in middle life, when she was forty or so, and that must have taken a heavy physical toll.) Her gardening clothes were frugal and threadbare, and they were all people ever saw her wearing now, even though when she'd first come to live in Carnbeg she'd been known for her stylish outfits, bought in Edinburgh's best shops.

'I don't know what's at the bottom of this,' the outspoken Mrs Begg winked at Sheena's mother one day, as if she understood full well the 'why' of the situation at least (Mrs Anstruther's loneliness), if not the identity of the 'who' (some predatory man-catcher among Mr Anstruther's former patients).

Mrs Murdoch, Gillian's mum, was a district nurse. She received a call from Torquil Anstruther, asking if she would come and attend to a minor accident, a cut his mother had given herself.

The wound was a few days old. Mrs Anstruther said that she had done it while gardening, but Gillian's mum had her doubts: the cut was to her neck, under her jaw, and luckily had been kept clean.

During conversation with Mrs Anstruther and her son she discovered that they were looking for part-time help in the garden.

'Some of the manual work. Digging and forking and sweeping up, they said. And a little planting out, and this and that. A few hours a week is what I think it amounts to.' Mrs Murdoch told her circle, which she guessed was what the Anstruthers had meant her to do.

It was Sheena who suggested herself. Her mother didn't object, so Sheena wrote to Mrs Anstruther. She received a phone call from Torquil. In his well-spoken way he asked if she would like to come for a try-out: to see if she and they felt it might be a worthwhile arrangement, for both parties.

She proved herself on the day. She dug and forked. She did a little planting out, and this and that, and at the end she tidied up the debris. She was able to convince Mrs Anstruther and her son that she was stronger than she looked, and it was agreed she would come up to the house for no less than seven or eight hours a week.

Sheena, at that juncture, was the happiest girl in Carnbeg.

It would be hard work. The Anstruthers hadn't pretended otherwise. But Sheena was ready for the challenge.

Torquil showed her what to do. For someone thought so handsome and so clever, he was awkward with himself and ill at ease. He didn't seem used to teenage girls, and hadn't much small talk. He restricted himself to practicalities: the composition of rooting mixture, how to trim the base of cuttings with a sharp knife, the way to layer bulbs in a pot.

The garden had always been a flower garden. But the Anstruthers now grew vegetables as well, which were Torquil's responsibility. The Ford Sierra had been joined by an even older Transit van, with its original owner's name painted out. (It showed through notwithstanding, like a ghostly reminder: BIRNIE & SON FAMILY BUTCHERS.) He packed the crates and loaded them himself, and then drove off to the shops he supplied, twenty or thirty miles further north.

Mrs Anstruther fretted whenever he wasn't there. She kept looking at her wristwatch, and trained her eyes on the road every time she heard an engine or the phutt-phutt of exhaust;

she left a certain window open in the house, so that she would hear the phone from the garden if he rang.

And then he'd be back from his deliveries, and the strain immediately eased on his mother's face, she would be off inside to make him tea – that horrible smoky tea they'd offered Sheena the first day, served in a china cup, which Torquil was thoughtful enough to replace the next time by a tea-bag in her own mug. Sheena would look over and see them talking busily by the kitchen door, as if the absence had been weeks not hours, and (as usual) speaking too quietly for her to overhear them.

After tea Torquil would unload the empty crates, and stack them, and brush the root soil from the van's floor. Then he would hurry off to the vegetable beds: just like a man who had lost valuable time with the objects of his devotion, inspecting them as if they might have magically grown in the interim. To make up to them he would work on late, and long after Sheena had gone.

None of this quite seemed to fit with the cut-glass voice, and the terms of encouragement he gave her – 'Good show!' or 'Well done, you!' – and the fact of the long, supple fingers he'd inherited from his mother. It was a strange life for him, Sheena decided, for a thirty-year-old man, especially when not so long ago he had been famously handsome and clever; although his handsomeness was of the overbred sort, and his cleverness hadn't been the kind to thrive at university.

Sheena mostly kept her head down, quite literally, working to earn her wage. She felt that Mrs Anstruther wasn't comfortable having someone else on the premises like this: which must explain why, as often as not, she chose to keep to the opposite end of the garden from where she, Sheena, was.

From day to day Sheena didn't know if Mrs Anstruther was going to speak to her or not.

There were two Cecilia Anstruthers.

The courtly one was preferable.

She had a soft voice, which she never raised above the level of a confidential conversation. Her diction was very clear and deliberate. Sheena didn't have to ask for anything to be repeated; she was hooked on every word, since the words were so sparingly given.

Mrs Anstruther had learned a lot as a child, watching those she was sent away to stay with, in far-flung parts of the British Isles, where the conditions for gardening were quite different. She had picked up an impromptu directory of dos and don'ts from listening to old wives' tales, which always had more than a grain of truth to them.

When it had come to cultivating the Alt-na-Crè garden – for reasons which she didn't ever explain to Sheena – she had been schooled by trial and error, by putting right her own mistakes. Saddled with ignorance, you had to be modest and humble. When there's no one to tell you what's right and what's wrong, you have to discover for yourself. It may be there *is* no 'right' or 'wrong' way: rather there's a 'natural' way, which obeys the rules of nature itself.

There was another Mrs Anstruther, however.

This one didn't speak, and hardly even deigned to look at Sheena. Why should someone who wore a ring which (Sheena's mother said) must shine in the dark and (Mrs Begg said) would have drawn the eye of the greedy old Duchess of Windsor herself, why should such a person have any truck with a callow teenager from the town?

When Mrs Anstruther seemed not inclined to be sociable, Torquil was the go-between, passing on his mother's instructions about what was to be done.

This, Sheena supposed, was merely how people of Cecilia Anstruther's upbringing and vintage were, either choosing to be approachable or insisting on the distinctions between herself and others.

Really, Sheena decided, her time at Alt-na-Crè was an education in life, every bit as much as in gardening.

Afterwards 'they' would ask Sheena about her afternoons at the Anstruthers'. Her mother, Gillian, Gillian's mum, and of course Mrs Begg, who had no qualms about stopping Sheena in the street and interrogating her bluntly.

'What're they like to work for, then? Hard taskmasters, are they? Won't stand for any slacking, I'll bet. Time is money. Are they a bit tight with you?'

Sheena responded by telling them only what she wanted to tell them. She felt she needed one part of her life to be private, if not secret. She wasn't even sure that she understood the Anstruthers herself, so how could she try to explain them to others?

When 'they' spoke about the Anstruthers, it was also Mr Anstruther that they were meaning to talk about. He was never there, as far as Sheena was aware. She had nothing to tell them, but the sneaky enquiries persisted.

'Is there nothing else for them to discuss with you except the garden?'

'Nice for some, isn't it, getting the house all to themselves.'

'That old van must be an eyesore, when it's a big posh Daimler they've been used to.'

'Not much to uncork a bottle for now. Who's going to propose a toast to the first lettuces, or the new line in carrots?'

The house's previous owner, Miss Heron – Mrs Anstruther's great-aunt – had employed a gardener. He'd been a man well past his first flush, a one-time gardener's boy; now Mr Keddie was probably Carnbeg's oldest inhabitant, but his memory was clear. He recalled the condition of the garden at the time Miss Heron passed away, and he remembered very vividly the falling-out he'd had with Mr Anstruther, which had proved to be irreparable. He was able nevertheless to give Mrs Anstruther her due. By all accounts she had coped very well with the garden – it wasn't how *he* would have done things, but she had a perfect right. Even though he hadn't been back to Alt-na-Crè, he said he was interested to hear from Sheena how the garden fared, what had changed since his day and what hadn't.

Sometimes voices carried to Sheena from the house. While she went about her work, curtains would close or open in one room or another. A door might bang shut: blown by the wind, or perhaps not.

Mrs Anstruther didn't mention her husband, and Torquil never spoke about his father.

So Sheena felt it was left to her to ask.

'Is Mr Anstruther a gardener?'

'*We've* always been the gardeners here,' Torquil told her.

'Does he approve of what you do?'

'Approve?'

'Does he like the results?'

'We garden for ourselves,' Torquil said, taking the subject nowhere.

Sheena then tried with his mother, on one of her approachable days.

'Does Mr Anstruther wish he was a gardener?'

'We're all of us made rather differently.'

'He must be very pleased with what you've achieved?'

'A gardener is never satisfied, I think,' Mrs Anstruther said, referring to herself and Torquil. 'There's always something else needing to be done, you see.'

'But . . . the overall impression . . . to someone who doesn't garden . . . ' Sheena was floundering. 'That must be – impressive.' Wrong adjective. 'Rewarding. Isn't it?'

'Not in so many words, for us,' Torquil interrupted. 'Out in the wind and rain. *You* try getting your hands clean after a filthy wet day out of doors!'

He held out his long, fine-boned fingers. He smiled. Normally he was rather a serious kind of chap.

'It's bad enough just standing up straight afterwards,' he said.

'I think you need danger money,' Sheena told him, in a jokey voice.

'We wouldn't be doing any of this,' Mrs Anstruther announced simply, without levity, 'if we didn't think we could manage it.'

And thus the conversation was brought to its final full stop.

Splendid as the azaleas were, outstanding though the lilacs might be, it was the roses which Sheena felt were the crowning achievement of the garden.

Of the *gardeners*, rather, since the rose bushes had been unexceptional when the Anstruthers moved into the house. Old Mr Keddie told Sheena so. They were mostly shrub varieties – reds like Heidelberg and Kassel – and some floribundas, with colours from salmon to flame, like Elizabeth of Glamis and Highlight. But they hadn't seemed very happy with their lot in those days. Mr Keddie used to give them mulch, and he put down straw, and he dug tea leaves from the pot into the soil, but it wasn't enough for them. Somehow, though, Mrs Anstruther must have got the measure of them.

The questions when Sheena got back to Carnbeg didn't stop. About the Anstruthers, all three of them, and about the house as much as about the garden.

Sheena continued to be evasive. She felt that the Anstruthers should be allowed their privacy, just like her. They didn't ask her about Carnbeg, and she didn't see why she should collaborate in making them subjects of gossip and conjecture in the town.

Sheena had a sense some days that she was being watched, and not just by Mrs Anstruther and by Torquil. When she went into the scullery, to wash her hands in the deep sink, or into the plain and functional WC (which Torquil called 'the privy') she had a notion that someone was hovering in the vicinity.

Was it the woman of few words, Mrs Lafferty, who came to clean? (Strictly, she should have been on the other side of the baize door, having decided the back quarters where muddy wellington boots left their prints were beyond her remit.)

Or was the frisson caused by Mr Anstruther, choosing to make himself invisible?

The Daimler remained in the garage, with its front offside wing still missing. A couple of times a taxi picked up or dropped off, obscured from view by a wall or a hedge, and it must have been Mr Anstruther coming or going. Jazz blew up one day on the radiogram, and it was Torquil's task – after conferring with his mother – to go in and have it turned down. A storm passed through the kitchen one teatime, a metaphorical one, but plates got smashed in its wake. Some days Mrs Anstruther seemed especially tense, and she only relaxed – slowly – after two or three hours of work in the garden.

To Sheena it was a restorative place, putting her in mind of those secluded walled gardens in Shakespeare and old operas, where rough magic might happen: all you had to do was walk far enough away from the pink house, out of the long summer shadows thrown by the chimney stacks. An archway in a hedge led you out of sight and sound of Alt-na-Crè, and it was likeliest that she would find Mrs Anstruther there. Torquil would probably be on the other side of the house, where the glass-frames were, which – Sheena realised – had a clearer view of the driveway, and from there he might keep an eye on any comings and goings, unanticipated to-ings and fro-ings.

The following year Sheena wrote to Mrs Anstruther, setting to the task at Eastertime. She realised just how much she wanted to go back, to see the results of last year's labours and also to share whatever of their lives the Anstruthers might reveal to her.

A reply was three weeks in coming, but at last a letter did arrive.

> If you're willing to agree to our previous terms, we should be happy to continue the arrangement.
> I trust this finds you in good health.
> In haste,
>
> Torquil Anstruther

Why 'haste'? Possibly he was off to make another delivery, his harvest from the glass-frames?

Sheena wrote back at once, agreeing to the existing terms. (Her father would have told her she was in line for a pay rise.) She sent her best wishes to Mrs Anstruther as well as to himself. 'Yours sincerely, Sheena Grimble'.

With the first intimations of summer, in mid-May, Sheena was back in situ, and she was glad to be there.

More of the same, she supposed. And yet it wasn't quite.

This second year at Alt-na-Crè was the summer of the roses. They bloomed, Sheena told her friends, like crazy. The biggest, most fragrant roses she had ever seen or smelled: they almost cried out at you, they were so full of life.

That was the funny thing about gardening, she realised. With some plants, you simply couldn't predict from one season to the next.

It might be that the weather had something to do with it, but Sheena had her doubts. Other people's roses didn't look much different from how they usually were. Certainly they weren't bursting with vigour, like the Anstruthers'. Peculiar, too, that it should be in *this* garden, with faded Mrs Anstruther as the presiding genius, and with Torquil not yet firing on all cylinders. (He looked as if he had been under some strain – a winter illness? His mother would throw him some sharp glances, which seemed to be reprimanding him, memos to please buck himself up in front of this familiar stranger.)

The roses were Mrs Anstruther's province. She made it clear to Sheena that she wouldn't require any further assistance with them. Sheena wondered if she had inadvertently caused offence last year. If the bushes had been wilting, she might have thought so.

Torquil repeated the instruction, several times, so that she was left in no doubt. The rose beds were the responsibility of his mother; she had her own methods of doing things. Weeding there was *verboten*; even general all-purpose hoeing in the vicinity was out of the question.

He apologised for dwelling on the matter.

'It's important to Mother, you see,' he said.

'Oh. Right.'

It did occur to Sheena that Mrs Anstruther was maybe trying to keep her horticultural secrets and tips to herself. But Torquil, as if he were reading her mind, made a point of praising

Sheena's efforts elsewhere, and passing on to her some odds and ends of reading in gardening manuals since last summer, during what he called his 'hibernation'.

Torquil, she knew, would never let her or himself (or his mother) down by forgetting his manners.

The three of them were having tea one day. (Two Lapsangs, one Tetley.) Mrs Anstruther was ensconced in an old saggy canvas chair, Torquil was leaning (in heroic pose, Sheena thought) against the door jamb, while she was sitting on the doorstep.

Torquil was busy talking, about nothing very much. Then Sheena noticed that his mother's hand was shaking; it was shaking so badly that she'd left her cup in the saucer at her feet, with the cooling tea untasted.

Sheena happened to catch the glance exchanged between the two of them. It lasted no longer than a couple of seconds. It signalled the need to be stoical, both of them.

'I could get you some fresh tea, Mrs Anstruther,' Sheena volunteered.

At the next moment she realised she shouldn't have said it: she was giving herself away.

The woman smiled grandly at her, as if nothing was the matter. Leaning forward she took a sip from her cup, and said in a clear and steady voice that she really must do something about cutting back the verbascum.

She would have seen Mr Anstruther if he had been there, Sheena felt. If he'd been ill indoors, she would have had some inkling.

His wife and son didn't ever refer to him: not in any tense – present, future or past.

Mrs Begg thought he must have absconded. 'Done a runner. Bolted. He had that look about him.'

Gillian's mother said she didn't think he was that type at all. 'A bit of a killjoy, if you ask me. Too set in his ways. Likes to rule his own nest.'

Sheena caught glimpses of Torquil, combing his hair in front of a mirror nailed up to the wall. His hair was thinning, he had a widening bald patch, and on windy days when his hair wouldn't stay in place he wore a cap to stop anyone seeing.

He was also starting to lose his looks. But since he had been very handsome to begin with, not too much damage had been done – yet. Being out of doors so much had weathered his skin, just as it had roughened his mother's complexion, which Carnbeg remembered as fine and flawless when she first came. But life, with its turbulent passages, demands many sacrifices from us, and a reddened face may be among the least of them.

The orders were keeping Torquil busier than ever, driving the van.

He spoke now about 'clients'. One afternoon he had a new one to meet and went indoors to scrub the dirt off in the scullery sink.

He was loading the van afterwards when he realised he didn't have his watch on. Sheena offered to get it for him.

She found it in the scullery, on the window sill. It wasn't the watch she was used to seeing on his wrist. This one was gold, and quite worn. She picked it up. There were initials engraved on the back. C. W. E. A. They were familiar to her from the nameplate they used to have at the dentists' surgery. Charles W. E. Anstruther.

Sheena went back outside with the watch. Torquil thanked her, ever polite, and fastened it to his wrist. Wherever the military-looking Mr Anstruther had gone, he must have thought he wouldn't need his gold watch to tell the time by.

Another day it started to rain. Mrs Anstruther returned to the house, and reappeared wearing a sou'wester and a long green trench-coat. Protected against the downpour she made her way back to the mixed border.

Sheena got on with some potting where she could shelter. When the rain had eased, she went to ask Mrs Anstruther if she could be of any help. As they were talking, Mrs Anstruther dug her hands into the pocket of the coat for some twine. Sheena saw that the sleeve cuffs had been doubled back. Something about the coat . . . Then she noticed that the buttons did up the wrong way. Mrs Anstruther was wearing a man's double-breasted raincoat.

The leather on the buckles was a little scuffed from use, but clearly the garment had been looked after well. When Sheena got back home she asked her mother, who told her that she remembered Mr Anstruther – cock o' the walk in those days – stopping the Daimler where he shouldn't have and getting out and striding into this or that shop, his big green Burberry flapping.

'Lots of material in the skirt. That's how you can tell they're expensive.'

So, wherever Mr Anstruther had gone, it was to somewhere he wouldn't be needing a waterproof raincoat either. Which, Sheena felt, whittled down the possibilities very considerably.

'They *are* beautiful,' Sheena ventured, as she and Mrs Anstruther drank their tea.

'What's that?' Mrs Anstruther asked.

'The roses.'

Mrs Anstruther nodded, acknowledging that they were indeed beautiful.

'Which are your favourites, would you say?'

'Some of the hybrids, I think.' Mrs Anstruther pointed from her chair. 'But I like to mix the varieties. Tea roses with floribundas.'

'What are their names?' Sheena asked, eager to learn. 'Could you tell me, please?'

Mrs Anstruther fixed on the distant rose beds.

'Mischief is pink and orange. Sterling Silver is best for indoors. Eden Rose doesn't always want to oblige, but has a wonderful scent. Gold Crown is more dependable, it's an excellent grower.'

'They *have* grown so tall.'

'The Chinatown has. It's started to hide the Mischief, but it's in there somewhere.'

'You must be very proud of them.'

Mrs Anstruther shook her head. 'It isn't straightforward.'

'To grow them?'

Mrs Anstruther was about to say something else, but she stopped herself.

Sheena was puzzled. Why would any gardener not be proud of these roses? They would have graced any flower show in the land.

Sheena went to call on old Mr Keddie.

He asked after the roses at Alt-na-Crè.

'Tip-top,' Sheena said.

'Miss Heron wasn't a roses person.'

'You'd think it had always been a rose garden,' Sheena told him.

'Afterwards I got to know the secret,' Mr Keddie said.

'The secret?'

'Maybe I could have persuaded Miss Heron, who knows?'

'The secret of rose-growing?'

'Yes.'

'I'd love to know.'

'What's it worth to you, young lady?' Mr Keddie grinned at her.

'Well, if you tell me something which even Mrs Anstruther may not know . . . '

'I doubt that,' Mr Keddie said. 'I don't know anything about roses *she* doesn't.'

'What's the secret, then?'

'Dripping.'

'Dripping?' Sheena repeated.

'Fat. From the butcher. Buried under the plant.'

'Really?'

'The foxes, you've got to watch them, they'll dig it up.'

Sheena told him that Torquil had fenced off that part of the garden, so probably no foxes came.

'Must be dripping, then.' Mr Keddie smiled back at her. 'That accounts for the blooms.'

'I can't imagine Mrs Anstruther putting down dripping,' Sheena laughed.

'You'd be surprised the lengths any keen gardener'll go to.'

Since she wasn't allowed to hoe in the rose beds, Sheena thought, who was to say what went down, and what was done when she wasn't there in the garden to see?

The problem was keeping up standards. How could the roses be allowed to bloom any less exuberantly than they currently were?

She could see that this was causing Mrs Anstruther some worry. Why else did she toil and toil?

And because his mother was concerned, so was Torquil, narrowing his eyes to look as he loaded and unloaded his crates at the back of the van.

The rose had never been Sheena's favourite flower.

In the small back garden at home, they had a ferocious climber. It offered miserly blooms, even against a south-facing wall. Worse, if you went anywhere near, it would reach out to prick you, as if it were an animate thing. Its stems were heavy with thorns, turned in two directions; the branches were like open razors.

This was Sheena's experience of roses, which she had brought with her to Alt-na-Crè. Only now, of course, she wasn't authorised to work on the rose beds: the prohibition stood, even though she had tried to prove herself worthy. Maybe there is no jealousy, however, to compare with a fervid rose-grower's?

One evening Sheena got home and realised she didn't have her purse with her.

She meant to go out with Gillian. She might have borrowed some money from her mother, but her mother would probably have asked her what it was for, and Sheena intended to keep her outings with Gillian her business.

She decided to go back to Alt-na-Crè. Should she phone first? But when she imagined Mrs Anstruther or Torquil hearing the ringing from the garden and having to down tools, she thought it easier to show up in person.

When she reached the house, the back quarters, the door was standing open.

She announced herself from the step. 'Hello! It's Sheena.'
She did the same again, but more loudly.
She could hear a radio on, through in the kitchen.
She walked inside.

The classical music led her to expect Mrs Anstruther. But it was Torquil she saw, working at the table. A bloody cleaver lay on the chopping-board. He was standing tearing the legs from some extenuated dead field animal: a rabbit or a hare. The bones of the joint crunched, followed by the ripping of sinew.

He hadn't seen her watching, observing from the doorway.

His deft fingers moved to the next leg. More bones cracked, then another brisk rrr–pp as the leg was wrenched out of its socket.

A symphony was playing, Mozart or Haydn. Torquil blew out his cheeks and oompahed along to the easy melody. Sunshine, revelling peasants, a watermill perhaps, a maypole.

His hand slipped inside the carcase, and he grabbed some organs, yanked them from restraining cords, flung them across the room and into the tip-up refuse bin. Heart or lungs or stomach, they plopped heavily into the plastic carrier-bag used as a lining.

Sheena couldn't bear to watch any more and withdrew. Forget the purse, she could do without it.

What bothered her, running along the road to make up some of the lost time, was Torquil's casualness. He was used to doing what he was doing. Those long, fine fingers should have been wielding an artist's paintbrush, or playing a musical instrument, or tracing beautiful calligraphy. Instead they were shiny and slimey with blood, trailing those strings of intestines. And she didn't doubt they were very good at their job, just as they had a winning way with vegetables in the garden. He had lost out on a university education, but really – Sheena understood now – his talents lay elsewhere entirely.

'Do they pay you well, those folk?' Mrs Begg asked.

It was none of the woman's business, Sheena told herself, and she wanted Mrs Begg to know what she thought.

'I don't expect they do,' Mrs Begg went on. 'I'd let them know you've had other offers.'

'But that isn't true.'

'A wee white one. Because if they're taking advantage of you like this – '

'I didn't say they that.'

'So they are paying you well?'

'I didn't say that, either.'

'I'm confused, Sheena.'

(Whose fault was that?)

'Well, you get the going rate, then?'

'I don't know what that is,' Sheena replied.

'I could find out for you.'

'No, thanks.'

'No trouble to me, dear.'

'I said *no*!' Even Mrs Begg was pulled up by the abruptness of her reply. 'No, thanks.'

Mrs Begg stared brazenly back. The woman obviously believed she wasn't being open with her, she was holding something back. She was sniffing a secret, or so she thought.

Sheena hurried off, aware that Mrs Begg's eyes were boring two burning holes into the back of her head.

Sheena had started to consider a career in gardening. Why not?

She could put herself out for hire, or she could get a job at a garden centre, or even enrol for a proper course of study.

It was important to discover those pursuits in life you felt enthusiastic about, which you might have a passion for. Some people never discover, and life pretty much passes them by.

Live life, don't they say?

That was why she felt she would always be grateful to the Anstruthers, for giving her a chance to *make* something of herself.

Never mind the lilies of the field, etc. When Sheena arrived one day, she found Mrs Anstruther standing, awkwardly, rapt in the beauty of her roses.

Torquil was taking her to the doctor. (They were short-staffed at the surgery, and couldn't promise a house call, so would it be possible to come into town?)

It wasn't for a cut this time, but for a prolonged bout of breathlessness and a dizzy turn.

Torquil explained to Sheena that they would have asked her not to come today, but she had already left by the time they rang.

Here was Mrs Anstruther looking at the garden, as if she wasn't sure when she might next see it again.

Sheena said she would stay, if that was all right, she'd keep an eye on things in their absence. Mrs Anstruther spoke *sotto voce* to Torquil, and Torquil hummed and hawed, then said it would be best if they locked the house up behind them, just in case they weren't able to come back straight away. He would lock the connecting kitchen door from inside, which would let Sheena use the scullery and the privy.

'That's fine, no problem,' Sheena told them, not thinking that there was, but aware that Torquil was a little embarrassed.

She saw them off the premises. Mrs Anstruther was still unsteady on her feet, and must still be feeling woozy, otherwise – Sheena suspected – she would have had the presence of mind to tell her please just to go home, it really didn't matter about the garden for one day, did it?

The car had gone. The Anstruthers' time would be taken up for an hour or two, and so Sheena had the run of the place to herself.

She realised that it was now or never for the rose beds.

She tried to remember all the varieties and names. Stella, Mischief, Piccadilly, Chinatown, Felicia.

Sheena noticed the darker, richer colour of the earth in the rose beds, round about the plants. It had a reddish tint, as if there were some invigorating ore beneath the ground, giving the bushes an abundance of nutrition. (Mrs Anstruther had proved that so many types would grow even at this northerly latitude.)

She reached down and picked up some soil, and let it crumble between her fingers. Then she took up another handful. While she held it, it felt oddly heavy and dense, weighted with whatever source of goodness it carried.

Squatting down on her heels, Sheena sank her hands into the magical earth. Would she ever acquire all the ways and means to become a good gardener, one who learned first and was then able to depend on her instincts? It struck her at this moment, at this sacred moment of illumination, that she had a vocation, a calling: to try to understand what makes plants grow, grow healthy and strong – to tend them to their fullest bloom and then somehow to store their fading life, conserving enough of that once rampant energy to perfect the next year's shoots, like giving them a surge of rocket fuel.

Wasn't that what it was all about?

Briefly the future was clear to Sheena, and it was being lived out already, but far from these backwater three acres. Happily she rooted around in the soil with her spread fingers.

Beneath the top surface of soil, four or five inches down, her fingers touched something. She pulled it out, whatever it was.

A piece of bone.

A left-over from a fox's meal? But foxes didn't come into this part of the garden.

The bone was oversized for a chicken or a rabbit, too solid.

She didn't like touching it even, and she dropped it, on to the top soil.

Then she noticed on her wrists a few clinging strands of hair. Horsehair? It seemed longer and finer than that. One strand was grey; it had coiled itself round her watchstrap.

She yanked at the hair, and it broke at the clasp. She speedily undid the clasp and pulled out what was left of the strand, desperate to have no more contact with it.

She got to her feet, stood up too quickly and thought she was going to lose her balance. But she managed to keep upright, even though green and yellow trails were dropping in front of her eyes.

She started walking backwards. The bone gleamed whitely against the copper-coloured earth.

She didn't want to think any more about it. She wished she could blot the matter out of her mind.

Something was terribly wrong. The sunlight and the hope had suddenly been filtered out of the day. Life had shrunk right down. She was here by herself, walking backwards, with her eye fixed on the bone, on its obscene whiteness.

Dripping, Mr Keddie had said. Fat from the butcher. That old van, with the lettering not quite painted over. SOMETHING & SON FAMILY BUTCHER. Torquil ripping the carcase to pieces, as if home butchery was his forte.

Sheena looked down and saw her hands were rubbing her wrists. Her wrists were bright red – and, yes, sore.

It might all be just fancy, a bad dream. She'd had toasted cheese for lunch at home, the usual Scottish cheddar; why *today* it should have affected her, she couldn't tell, well, actually she could, but she was making a very determined effort – wasn't she? – not to think about what was lying just beneath the surface of the situation.

She turned round, looked behind her. But she was alone, because Mr Anstruther wasn't here, or not in so many words, he wouldn't be returning from the hypothetical place he might or might not have taken himself off to.

God, God, God, I'll make up a month of Sundays! If only . . .

She got to the gate and out on to the road before she had a sighting of the Sierra.

Sure enough, there it was at the foot of the hill, making its way back from Carnbeg. It must have been touching 50 mph on that incline. It contained only its driver. From behind a tree Sheena watched the car race past on the flat.

Torquil must have been sent back, on instructions from his mother: just to prove that Cecilia Anstruther was still quick-thinking, head clearing by the minute, her *mind* versus all-comers, the *flesh* and *blood* and *gristle* and (most obstinately) *bone* of the matter.

Sheena didn't sleep well that night.

She put her hands under the pillow, behind her head, so as not to scratch at her wrists. She lay smelling the soap she had scrubbed herself with, over and over.

She lay with her eyes open trying to remember Mr Anstruther, the sight and sound of him, and the colour (the precise hue of grey or silver) his hair used to be.

The late Mr Anstruther.

Next day Torquil was due to travel to Dundee, to try selling his wares to some new shops.

Sheena waited until he'd driven off in the Transit van before she reported for work.

She noticed at once that the bone had vanished from the surface of the rose-bed. Mrs Anstruther had never looked less like fainting. Thin and stooped she might be, but this afternoon she had the stamina of a man, of two men, and the craftiness of a savannah wildcat in how she never directed her eyes where she didn't want to be seen looking, to Sheena, to the person uppermost in her mind and already her marked quarry.

Sheena went away early, leaving a note for Mrs Anstruther.

> I've got a bad headache, and don't feel very well.
>   Shall we call this a half-day?
>   With apologies,
>   S

As soon as she got home and let herself into the house, Sheena could hear Mrs Begg's voice. The living-room door was ajar. Mrs Begg and her mother were talking.

Neither of them seemed to have noticed her coming in, or Mrs Begg might have lowered her voice.

Sheena heard the name 'Torquil', and she moved closer to the living-room door.

At one of the shops where he delivered, the owner's daughter was in the family way.

'They're saying it was Torquil. Why else is he back and forth, arranging things?'

'Arranging what?' Sheena's mother asked.

'How they're going to deal with' – pause – 'their embarrassment.'

Nods must have been exchanged in the living-room.

'The girl's parents are churchy. So she'll have to have it.'

'And then what?'

A sharp intake of breath from Mrs Begg. 'Then they'll get rid of the thing.'

Sheena couldn't stop thinking about the girl, and Torquil, and the baby that was such an embarrassment and shame and nearly ready to be born.

At the same time she felt that something stern, a weight, had settled on her shoulders. And, conversely, a kind of mistiness inside her head.

She had the sensation of not-quite-thought-out thoughts: notions that she was afraid to entertain.

Torquil – and the daughter of that churchy couple – and the baby, which nobody wanted.

The summer would soon be running down. Everything, Sheena realised, was change and alteration. Over the autumn and winter the garden would rest and replenish. Come spring, the rose bushes would be hungry again for life. Piccadilly, Gold Crown, Highlight, King's Ransom. The old soil wasn't quite enough, it didn't offer sufficient sustenance, even when it was manured and mulched.

If next summer the buds swelled and burst, it would be apparent that some extra attention had been paid, and the ground enriched.

Mischief would be burgeoning in the middle of Chinatown. Marie Antoinette fighting over space with Madame Gregoire Staechelin. Stella slugging it out with Lili Marlene.

But Sheena wouldn't be there to express her admiration, in a few carefully chosen words and with her voice sounding strangely tight in her throat.

Next year she would be away at college, or putting in her nine-to-five at a garden centre. Either way, she would – most definitely – be unavailable for hire at Alt-na-Crè.

Life was too short, Sheena felt. Yet never *too* short for the Anstruthers.

Even the life of a baby.

Sheena wished she could stop thinking about the pair up at the house.

Mrs Anstruther didn't try to get in touch. Nor did Torquil.

When she was out and about Sheena would look round every now and then, back along the road, half expecting to see a Transit van shadowing her.

The Anstruthers had discovered how to bring their repeat-flowering roses to glory. Out of personal misery and humiliation something spectacular had been retrieved.

But beauty is heartless, with a dark eye. This was the terrible knowledge Sheena had acquired, but as yet had only half-digested.

Beauty is never content, can't ever be beautiful enough.

It's a kind of oblivion, and the price of oblivion is to have no feelings at all. No emotions, no conscience.

One day Sheena will understand this fully. She will be reminded whenever she looks at a rose, every time she encounters a branch of thorns and then has to sidestep its sudden scissorhands slash.

The Man Who

(*After Pirandello*)

ONE

'You've forgotten your watch!' Margaret called after him impatiently, holding it up for him to see.

Jack Cumming stopped at the front gate. He returned up the grassy path and took the watch from his wife.

Margaret was standing on the front step, tight-lipped, in no mood to talk. He murmured something in the way of thanks, but she wouldn't have heard, for she turned on her heel and went back inside.

Before he was halfway down the path, the front door had closed. Wash-day, which meant long hours in the scullery. 'It's all right for some!' that curt closing of the door was meant to tell him.

He stepped out into the lane, leaving the gate flapping behind him. No time to put on his watch, with its fidgety buckle on the strap, so he dropped it into his jacket pocket to do the job later.

Every so often on his way uphill he pulled the watch out of his pocket to check the time. It would only take ten seconds to put down his suitcase and umbrella and fasten it to his wrist, but those ten seconds seemed crucial – if he was to knock the case over or if his umbrella started to unfurl, as he was used to it doing.

Later, of course, given the upshot of events, he would understand that that was precisely what he ought to have done. Those ten seconds were to affect the scenario of the future out of all measure.

As it was, he reached the station too late.

He was at the end of the platform, arm aloft, and saw the train steaming forward. Even if he'd sprinted, he couldn't have caught it.

How had it happened?

Because, it registered only now, because the engine hadn't sounded its whistle.

Unconsciously he always waited for it. But his thoughts had been in turmoil, like the clothes in Margaret's tub.

This day of all days.

That bastard train-driver.

The normal thing would have been to go home. But today wasn't normal. He never missed the train, and never failed to catch his connection south. He'd sensed that Margaret wanted to get on with her chores, and he was bound to get in her way; more than that, she'd seemed not displeased to have the house to herself for the next few days.

Which left him with another hour on his hands, an hour to kill, and then even longer in Edinburgh between trains.

What a bugger.

Here's the man who couldn't even get to the station on time.

There was nothing else for it but take himself off to the Laigh.

'What can I be getting you, Mr Cumming?'

'A pint, please.'

'Heavy?'

'No, pale.'

'Pale it is, sir.'

Cumming looked at his wrist as he picked up the glass, remembering he still hadn't put on his watch.

As he was heading for a table, he collided with someone. Their eyes were at the same level; the man was looking at him intently, but Cumming didn't recognise him. Tousled hair, an open-necked shirt, white cotton like his own but soiled and frayed. The man was still staring.

You'll know me next time, won't you? they said down in

Glasgow when you were eyeballed like this.

Why so much attention? Cumming wondered. Did the man think they were long-lost brothers or something?

Cumming realised he'd spilled drink on to the man's shoes. But they were down-at-heel and dusty, and the man didn't think to apologise for knocking into him.

Even so, Cumming offered to buy the fellow a drink.

'Right you are. I'm dry enough.'

The stranger joined him. He eyed the suitcase with an envying look.

'Off to see the world are you?' he asked in a broad Lowlands accent, and laughed.

'I'm off to York. Oh, it's a glamorous life.'

(Only my wife has an expression on her face sometimes which says – or this is what I read into it – that it's not a *real* man's job.)

But Cumming merely told the man that his wife would rather he was at home more often. If only because shelves won't put themselves up, and a drain might need unblocking; the whole place cried out for repapering, and the woodwork to be painted.

The clock in the corner clanked, chimed, it was half-past already. Cumming got to his feet. He realised he shouldn't have drunk a full pint, he didn't have a good head for alcohol in the middle of the day. He felt woozy, and supposed that the man – also standing there by his side – was steadying him.

He reached into his back pocket and pulled out a couple of ten-bob notes. 'Get yourself something to eat,' he told the man, and the man smiled so readily that his benefactor suspected he wouldn't. On a warm day like this all you wanted to do was slake your thirst.

So be it. Cumming felt he could afford to be indulgent. He watched from the doorway, nodding back at this stranger, about whom he knew not a jot more than when he had sat down. So be it.

He got to the station in time for the following train.

It was only when he'd found a carriage and sat down and the

train was in motion that he put his hand into his jacket pocket for his watch.

It wasn't there.

He checked in the other pocket.

Not there, either.

Nor in any of his trouser pockets. He even searched his coat pockets.

He tipped his cuff back, examined his wrist just in case.

No watch.

Where the hell was it? Christ, what had happened to his watch?

By the time the train reached Edinburgh Cumming felt he knew that it had been stolen. The collision in the Laigh, probably; or afterwards, when he'd got to his feet too hastily, and found the man's hand reaching out as if to help steady him. That crafty smile when Cumming had passed over the two ten-shilling notes, as if he was paying for the man's attention for the past while.

He would have to tell Margaret it had happened in Edinburgh – on the street, can you credit it, in full daylight – someone grabbing his wrist, there were a couple of them, and yanking the watch off, the leather strap must just have snapped, it had got a bit worn and thin anyway, didn't she remember? In cities they'll go to any lengths.

Or the deed could have been done in York, if that seemed more plausible than Edinburgh.

In any event, Cumming knew he'd been conned. He'd felt sorry for the man – the scruffy shoes, the uncut hair, the frayed shirt collar – and in return for his charity he'd had his pocket picked.

A good deed gets thrown back in your face.

And now, sod it, he was left with no bloody watch.

He was so used to looking down and seeing that particular face and those shapes of hands on the dial. Jesus wept!

He had to be careful about his blood pressure, but that was all very well for a doctor to say, not taking into account the next

big knock-back waiting for you round the next corner, or in the
public bar of your local.

Walking the concourse of Waverley Station, Cumming couldn't
think of anything else.

Soon after he was demobbed, his watch – old faithful, the
'Challenger Perpetual' – had stopped telling the correct time.
First it gained, then it lost, then it stopped going altogether. He
had joked about the peace coming as a shock to it.

He'd bought another, with money left to him by a great-aunt.
A proper Swiss wristwatch, with a fine movement, on an
ostrich-skin strap.

The same watch that was stolen from him this morning, this
fateful morning, in Carnbeg.

First stop was York.

Margaret wasn't pleased that he was having to do York *and*
London on this trip. She got irritated because he was seeing
different places, and she wasn't, never mind that most of his
time was taken up with humdrum work.

Last week things had reached a crisis point. Another quarrel,
about something trivial: a cup and saucer left unwashed in the
sink, or a wet towel deposited on the side of the bath.

'D'you think I've nothing better to do than go around tidying
up after *you*?'

If they'd had children, she would have had her days filled.
But nature hadn't blessed them: one miscarriage, then a still-
birth. They had considered adopting, until something put
Margaret off the notion and she started talking about 'other
people's cast-offs'.

Last week's to-do had brought them to a new nadir.

'I don't think,' Margaret had said as her parting shot before
going upstairs to bed, '*this* adds up to a life, do you?'

Something became clearer to him during his four days in
York. He realised Margaret might have had cause to think he'd
trapped her into marrying him.

She had first set eyes on him when he was wearing his air-force blues. He had come into her life trailing the glory of other men, those who had achieved greater feats of daring than himself. He hadn't lied to her, but he had allowed her – in those early days – to treat him with more awe than he knew he deserved.

During these last months in Carnbeg, the awe was all gone. She had seen through to the flesh-and-blood man. He came home one day to find that his uniform wasn't hanging at the back of the wardrobe; it had been packed away in an old cardboard box and taken up to the loft.

'Well, you won't be wearing *that* again, will you? It's just clutter.'

He had told her about his air-force buddies. For a few years he'd kept up with them. Christmas cards were sent off to those bespoke-sounding addresses in the South of England, but one by one the recipients stopped reciprocating.

Margaret didn't get a chance to meet them, but would she have been quite up to par with those new wives they had, with names like Rosemary and Penelope? In the middle of a war the amount of money in your pocket hadn't mattered so much, or even the details of your background. To those he flew with, his Scottishness was of the romantic kind: just as, to Cumming, their Englishness was different and therefore exotic.

In the new peace people had gradually reverted. It was unfortunate, but inevitable. You felt less charitable towards your neighbours. Every man was starting to relearn how to look after himself. It was a harder, colder world, not much disposed to forgive or to give time to understanding others.

Three nights in York.

Days spent passing round samples, discussing the new weights of paper, and the different finishes, shade-cards to distinguish between all the hues of white and cream.

A bit of spiel, a bit of talking up, a bit of downright invention.

Business as usual, in other words.

This time there was to be a brief diversion, to Derby (with an overnight), and then on to London. In York he always felt fresher, and he sometimes listened to himself sounding so enthusiastic and thought, even *I* might be convinced by what I'm hearing.

London by comparison was a long, wearisome slog. His reward was the prospect of escaping home on the train and spending the journey fast asleep in his corner seat.

He didn't usually communicate with Margaret while he was away. A phone call entailed going via a neighbour, and too little of note ever happened to justify a letter; two sides of top-of-the-range blank from his samples was too hard to cover, even with his most expansive handwriting. On this occasion, the truth was that he felt still less inclined. By the time he got home Margaret might be in a better mood, but he wasn't counting on it. She would ask him what was going on in London, and he would try to satisfy her curiosity – the actors' names lit up outside the West End theatres, the colours of this season's women's clothes – by skimming through the newspapers beforehand to discover. They would talk about her maybe accompanying him sometime.

Maybe.

He was sitting in the dismal little lounge of his commercial hotel in Clerkenwell, putting off valuable time as he watched for the rain to ease.

The greasy wallpaper, the stained antimacassars, the threadbare patches of cord on the carpet, the green linoleum surround.

He turned the page of his *Chronicle*. More news stories, and then his eyes were hooked, tugged out of their sockets by the sight of his name.

John Cumming, 36, a commercial salesman.

His body had been found in a weir near his home. The identity of the drowned man was confirmed by the watch he was wearing, engraved with his initials. Mrs Cumming was reported to be in a state of shock, and unable to speak to the press.

He sat staring and staring at the lines of print. He lost all track of time. His arms were aching when he put down the newspaper. The blood was cold in his veins. His head felt as if it was floating free of his body, a helium ball, a balloon held by a string. He imagined he was falling backwards, head over heels, tumbling through black space . . .

It was only half an hour, perhaps. But now he felt he was on the other, far side of everything that had previously been normal.

That man, John Cumming, was dead. Here was the evidence of it, in black and white newsprint, the truth to other people.

How could he convince them? Knocking on the front door of the house, turning the handle, walking in, pale faces, they're seeing a ghost . . .

Who are you?

Who I say I am.

No, no. No, you must be an impostor.

It's all as clear to him as if the scenes are actually taking place.

The lounge door was open. Cumming looked over at the telephone box in the corner of the hall.

What was stopping him going and ringing Carnbeg? He could give the number of a neighbour and someone would go to find Margaret. He could ring one of the Scottish newspapers, in Edinburgh or Glasgow, and tell them that the story was false, John Cumming (known as 'Jack') was alive and quite well.

But he kept on postponing.

It was as if a mighty hand was pushing down on him. It should have been the simplest thing, to go out into the hall and pick up the receiver and place that call north.

He walked up and down the lounge, crossing and recrossing the floor, wearing away more of the carpet. He saw an actor playing the part of himself: sweat beading his forehead, a hand being run through his hair, manic eyes.

That would have been the film version. In reality he felt heavy, ballasted; his mind juddered awkwardly from one unfocused thought to the next.

The telephone looked like an ugly black toad, crouching on its shelf.

And still nothing happened.

Cumming didn't go to where he was supposed to be going that afternoon. He stayed in his room.

This 'he', this putative being. A watery sun cast a human shadow on the flock wallpaper. Whose was it? Did he amount to anything more than a shadow, a trick of the light?

He pictured the funeral. The congregation in the church he never visited, those people who thought they knew him. And Margaret casting an eye over them all, counting the total, remembering who might have come but hadn't, calculating the slight done to her and to him.

And suddenly she was pitying him, as she's pitied herself for these last few days. This is what a life amounts to, to death, a slow preparation over years for the end. Does experience add up to nothing more? Fatal mathematics.

He saw Margaret weeping into a handkerchief, crying for the past and for all the finer feelings they'd both known and which she would now never get back.

Cumming didn't sleep that night. He was afraid he might not wake up again.

He got up at dawn, and stumbled across to the mirror. Someone was looking back, a man with a haggard, unslept face – ghostly white – and two fearful eyes.

Turn away, look round quickly – he was still there, staring over his shoulder.

Dead men didn't do a job of work. This wasn't his usual hotel, so they wouldn't know where to find him. He was invisible, and only that gaunt, eldritch face watching in the glass was privy to his whereabouts.

Curiouser and curiouser. He couldn't have foreseen the next stage of the process, this transformation he was undergoing.

When he did go outside, to get away from that dingy bedroom, a different sensation hit him.

He felt he'd sloughed off a skin.

Somehow he was lighter on the pavements now. He'd got an elasticity into his stride. The air – even here in London – tasted sweet, as fresh and invigorating as it used to when they first moved to Carnbeg.

He felt he'd had a revelation.

Everyone else was alive, and he was dead, but it seemed the other way about. He'd been reborn, while *they* were going through the motions of living, a living death! He'd been sluiced out inside, he felt cleansed and resolved, blessed by light.

What were they doing in Carnbeg? Mourning him? Let him be the first to tell them, *life goes on*. He didn't know about heaven and hell, but he certainly believed in the after-life.

He thought about the stranger who had stolen his watch, and inadvertently sold his soul – taking on *his* identity, and so permitting him his freedom.

It was ironic. Absurdist. A joke, but no one for him to share its cruel black humour with.

He wondered if Margaret *hadn't* truly believed that the body in the weir was his, and that was why he had experienced no sixth sense, no telepathic signals, no transmitted shock-waves of grief.

The watch, of course, was the crucial item of evidence. Somehow it had survived the force of the water, which must have already pummelled the man's head to pulp. On the back were the engraved initials: *J. M. C.*, incontrovertible proof.

If Margaret's love had been strong enough, it would have conquered all objections. When they got married they'd told each other their love would never die. But bit by bit life had worked on them, sapping them of their youth, dulling their bright confidence. Later on, at their worst moments, he wondered if Margaret had any love left for him at all.

He had married someone different from the woman he found he was living with years later, and yet the fault was more his than hers. He'd been insistent that Margaret shouldn't work, it was his role to support her; hence their move to

Carnbeg, where money went a little further than it did in
the city. He had only helped to wear Margaret down, though,
by landing one crummy, ill-paid rep's job after another, until
this last.

It had taken him until now to appreciate these things properly.
He regretted the failings in himself, and wished he could offer
amends, make up to Margaret for that lost time and the waste of
possibilities.

No wristwatch. Cumming had to use public clocks instead.
There was one on nearly every street corner. He hadn't been
aware that time was supplied in such generous quantities. He
had no excuse for not being where he should be; he only had to
raise his eyes and (so to speak) a pair of hands pointed the way.

He could have replaced the watch with a cheap substitute.
But it annoyed him to think he was reduced to wearing
something so humble. Anyway, now he was a free man, without
constraints.

Time didn't count; time was only an artifice designed to keep
us human beings in a state of subjugation. Without the false
concept of time, life lost its linear structure. You floated on the
surface of time rather than following a straight track. Future
and past were equally inconsequential.

From where I am, he considered, I have no responsibilities, no
owings.

What about Margaret? What was she going through?

Several times Cumming started a letter to his wife, his widow,
but he never got beyond the first sentence. He sat with the nib of
his pen picking over his commas and dots and dashes, but the
words wouldn't come.

How could he explain that he wasn't dead, even though he
was supposed to be? How did he account for the fact that he was
here in London, sitting at a table in a dreary hotel lounge, with a
piece of folded cardboard wedged under one of the table's legs,
and that he hadn't immediately made contact with her?

Should he pretend he knew nothing about the newspaper

story? But why, then, hadn't he shown up for any of his appointments, or filed a report for his employers?

He didn't want to shock her. She would have so many questions to ask *him*. Amnesia, he would claim. He'd need to have his excuses worked out, knowing how sharp Margaret could be – used to be – at tripping him up with his white lies, hoisting him with his own petard.

The top was put back on the pen, and the pen replaced in his suit jacket's breast pocket. The sheet of notepaper was torn in two, then – as he was about to toss the halves into the sputtering flames of the miserly little fire in the grate – he rid himself of the embarrassment by tearing the letter into tinier and tinier pieces and dropping them into the big brass jardinière that held the aspidistra in its cheap, chipped clay pot.

On a bill-board a British Railways' poster advertised the night-ferry service: Victoria–Dover–Calais–Paris.

A monochrome illustration: a ship berthed beside railway tracks, sleeper carriages newly unloaded, an air of dreamlike anticipation.

What was missing?

He was, that was clear.

They were waiting for him at the quayside.

The man who got wise, the man who got away.

Before leaving Carnbeg that last morning, he had put on his great-uncle's signet ring, something he rarely did. In London it gave him something to sell, along with the silver cigarette case given to him for his twenty-first birthday.

He had his expenses money, in cash as usual, but on this occasion more of it was left. The hotel's proprietor was away, and the stand-in at the desk misunderstood, thinking that he had privileged status and didn't need to pay until he handed in his room key on the final morning.

It wasn't much, but when you're light-headed with the possibility of freedom it was more than enough.

TWO

On the train south from Paris he started to feel the same exhilaration he'd felt during the war, the thrill of the night flights. Into the unknown, the blindness of clouds. Then – once you were above them – brilliant moonlight, the unsullied whiteness, a celestial eiderdown, the careless plenty of stars. Up there you might have travelled on for ever.

How many men had ever set eyes on such beauty, up there where the air was so cold and chaste and pure, where nothing lied to you?

When it got dark he borrowed a pack of cards from a fellow passenger who wanted to sleep, and put himself through his paces.

He had picked up his know-how in the mess rooms. Chemmy, black jack, vingt-et-un, seven-card poker. Sometimes they'd sit for hours, through the night, until they got the call. Underneath that solitary low-hanging lampshade, with the windows blacked out; there was something almost scholastic – no, *monastic* – about their application, their keen-eyed study of the rules and variations. Digg and Foxy would recall games they'd played together, or spins they'd had at roulette tables in clubs up in town. Just by associating with them, he used to feel, it was as if he was being honoured with admission to some closed order, a charmed masonry of daredevils.

He woke with sunshine streaming in through the carriage window on to his face. The playing-cards were scattered on the floor. He pulled himself up in the seat and screwed his eyes tight to look out at the view.

Blue sea, white cliffs, pine trees.

The Bay of Angels.

It seemed like too much beauty, he felt quite breathless with this prodigality of light.

In Nice Cumming told the garage-owner he knew about cars, and they gave him a job.

[265]

It was dirty work, but uncomplicated. He lay under the ramp with ratchets and spanners, or probed inside the engines.

Cars were just cars. Machines.

He needed a little money to get by, to feed himself, to give him a roof over his head (a ceiling so low, in the event, that he knocked his head against it a dozen times a day).

Only for a few weeks, he promised himself. And then . . .

The owners came to the garage with their cars and returned to drive them away again. He noticed how many troubled and careworn faces there were, as if those folk in their finery were heading for their own mechanical breakdowns.

'I don't think *this* adds up to a life, do you?'

The words would come back to him, and he revved the engines louder to cover over the sound of Margaret's voice. At lunchtime he walked fast enough not to hear, on the city's busiest streets. At the end of the day he stood among the noise at the zinc bar in the *tabac*. Back under the eaves he opened the window to let in the sounds from the street, he turned up the music on the radio.

From the open window of his attic room he looked down at the tides of movement. Cars, pedestrians, trams.

'I don't think *this* adds up to a life, do you?'

Sometimes his eyes fixed in a stare, drawn by the abstract composition of competing flows, and he leaned so far forward that another few seconds of inattention might have sent him pitching over the sill, somersaulting down there . . . .

The cars rolled up on to the ramp, or were left parked at the back of the repair bay, awaiting their call.

Cumming listened to the talk of the older mechanics. They remembered who had driven their cars in here in the past, comparing this new lot unfavourably. On the Riviera coast people appeared from nowhere, they acquired fortunes or titles, or pretended to, and they behaved as if they had always been rich or ennobled. Some found no luck here, though, and drifted off again. But they were lucky compared with the ones who lost their wealth, their reputations, their friends, even their sanity. The garage hands had seen it all, and turned the events into stories.

And still the cars presented themselves on the forecourt: the cars that brought the arrivals, that transported the stayers, that would carry off the losers at the Casino Ruhl if they could afford the petrol and (cue men's accompanying laughter, from the pit or from under the raised bonnet) if they could resist the temptation to go driving off the corniche on to boulders, into the sea.

Waking up in the morning, Cumming had to puzzle out where he was.

Someone's window shutters banging open. The cars down in the street, sounding not like British cars. A gull or two circling overhead.

But as the weeks started to pass, he found it easier to resist the pull of his memories. Or, rather, it was as if he was beginning to lose the memories – the sun was fading them, like photographs, like the pattern of a carpet. He stopped asking himself what Margaret might be doing now, or picturing what the house looked like, or any of those old corners of Carnbeg.

That life was over. It was buried under turf, beneath a headstone inscribed with some concluding biblical nicety. And that, thank God, was *that*.

Meanwhile, here in Nice, he was walking across the foreground of a painting, or an architectural engraving. He turned the corner of the street just as the gigantic page of a novel was being turned. He was an 'atmosphere person' in a location shoot.

The buildings on the seafront clung to the rocks, just as their inhabitants clung to the notion of reality.

Mannequins in a boutique window. A girl was dressing them with silk.

Cumming stood under the shop's canvas awning to watch her. She turned round and looked at him.

He smiled in at her.

After a couple of moments she smiled back.

Which only proved to him, he felt, that yes, he *did* exist.

Cumming continued to smile, meaning to express his heart-felt gratitude to the girl.

At any remotely personal question Yvette answered the Scotsman with a simple, complex 'Pass'.

When she tried to turn the tables on him, over another coffee or glass of campari, he found himself doing the same. 'Oh, it's a long story', or 'I forget'.

But he guessed that she wasn't very interested in knowing, not really. Which suited him quite well.

Anyway, she would much rather talk about the people she saw through the shop window, or the casino-set whenever she was sent along the coast in a taxi with an express delivery for a customer.

'What's so interesting about *them*?' he asked her, in his increasingly serviceable French.

'When they play the tables, they think they've got nothing to lose.'

'They'll probably lose their bets.'

'That's not what's in their minds. But the whole place is a fantasy, anyway.'

'Have you ever felt tempted?'

'Oh yes.'

'But you haven't played?'

'Only because I couldn't compete with real gamblers.'

'And if you did?'

'Then I wouldn't be here.'

'Talking with me, you mean?'

'Working in a shop window, I mean,' she smiled.

'You'd be living like one of the customers?'

'I can dream,' she laughed back at him.

Outside a pawn shop on a little street at the back of the town he found a dinner jacket and trousers hanging up for sale.

They allowed him to try them on. They were a standard fit, and he was a standard man.

He offered some money, plus his tie-pin to cover the difference.

He doesn't tell Yvette in advance.

He gets his hair cut, and trims his moustache. He takes his white business shirt to the laundry. He buys a tin of black shoe polish. He selects a black bow-tie in a gents' outfitters.

He washes off the day's labours in the sea, then he goes back to his room and gets ready. He feels self-conscious leaving the building in the dress-suit, and sitting on the train, but in the streets of Monte Carlo – the closer he gets to the casino – no one looks askance. If they do look, he feels, it's only because he's making an effort to hold himself straight, as if this is something he often does of an evening, as if he's quite au fait with gaming-rooms and the fumes of Cuban cigars insinuated with Chanel trails on the air.

At the tables the players are too intent to notice him.

There are tanned faces, and there are ashen white, which never see sunlight. Heads of every artificial tint of hair, and those bleached by yacht-deck sunshine. Lissom manicured hands, and others gnarled and knotted by meanness; the deft-fingered declare and throw down with a grand gesture, while the claws open just wide enough to grab their winnings.

He has beginner's luck at faro.

He stakes a week's wages on the order of the cards, and wins five times that.

Next time he doubles his total.

Then he loses a game, and he's back to a quarter of his winnings, but it's still more than he began with.

He takes Yvette out for dinner.

The evening doesn't feel quite real.

This is how he imagined his wartime colleagues living it up in the aftermath, in London nightspots or in Home Counties waterside inns.

He doesn't explain how he can afford the food, the champagne.

He walks Yvette back to the hostel where she lives. She drops her head on to his shoulder.

They look up at the moon. It's the same moon, he thinks, which lit their night forays above the clouds, which is shining now on a stretch of river in Carnbeg.

O silver moon, up in the boundless sky.

Yvette slips out of his arms, she steps – glides – into the hallway of the building with a chaste good-night, smiling her thanks. He stands on the street, waving up at her from the pavement when she briefly appears in a lit room. She waves back, and then the window blind is drawn.

He goes back, to the Casino des Princes.

This time he wins one game of baccarat.

The banker pays out.

But he loses the next two games.

He misses the last train, and hitches a lift back.

Already, though, he's planning ahead. He'll sell his suitcase – a garage mechanic has no need of a leather one – and he'll pawn or sell his cufflinks, he'll live on bread and cheese . . .

A steady nerve, his fellow card-players in the mess used to tell him, and they weren't talking about the night patrols.

Luck has to be seduced, just like a woman. Why else is she called *Lady* Luck?

On his third evening, at the chemin de fer table, he places a modest stake to begin with.

He wins.

He places his winnings on another game.

It's another win.

The third game.

What will he bid? Everything, he hears himself say, and he agrees to the raised odds.

Now he's throwing every impulse of caution to the wind. But what has he got to lose? He reminds himself he has no name, no history, no life to go back to.

A steady nerve.

He wins 200,000 francs.

He is scarcely aware.

He wants to continue, but a siren is ringing in his head, the cards are thrown down in the mess room and the game's left unfinished, running footsteps now, but they're high heels, Margaret's strappy shoes as she runs about the backstreets of the town, no, she's at the treadle on the sewing-machine, working it furiously for all she's worth, trying to stitch her life together again.

He staggers outside.

He tips a cigarette out of a packet, lights it.

Now he's whistling. A tune Teddy Morland was always whistling in the mess. *'The Man Who Broke the Bank at Monte Carlo'*.

He hasn't quite, but it feels as good as.

Suddenly he stops in his tracks when he sees Yvette sitting on a bench. She's been waiting for him.

'You should have told me,' she says.

'I just wanted to see what happened.'

'And . . . ?'

He senses that she knows.

He sits down beside her.

'Your hand's shaking,' she says.

'Hold it for me, please.'

She continues to hold it as they have dinner, another dinner to celebrate his success.

Later a woman passes the table, and stops behind Yvette. He wonders if she recognises him from the casino, but she's looking down at his companion.

'I recognise that dress' is all she says.

Yvette springs to her feet, addressing the woman by her name. She's her boss at the dress shop.

The woman tells her, in a chilly voice, that her services aren't required any more.

'The dress can be your first purchase,' she says to the man of the evening. 'I shall expect a cheque at your earliest convenience, m'sieur.'

Now Cumming, or the man he'd become, could sleep late and wake to a blue sky.

Yvette was asleep beside him, her face and her body criss-crossed by the jagged shadows of a palm tree outside the window.

He lay listening to the dignified swish of expensive cars being driven along the Promenade des Anglais outside, the yapping of lapdogs as they met, the tuneless whistling of the road-sweeper.

It amazed him how easily events had overtaken him like this. One thing leading to another, leading to another . . . He wondered who it was lying here in this bed, turning these thoughts over in his head.

When he got up, he always put off looking in the mirror until he had dressed and made coffee on the primus and taken it through to Yvette, to drink with her. He would go off again to shave, and it was only then that he allowed himself to look at the reflection in the glass.

He leaned forward and examined the face more closely, investigating the surface for sun damage, for freckles or fissures that might deepen into cracks. He undid one of Yvette's tubs and took some of the cream on his fingertip and applied it to a new trouble-spot, hoping that some care now might prepare him for the future.

What future?

But the sun was shining, warming up the day, and Yvette was in a very generous mood with him, and did it really need to matter, what was still to come? The *point* about the south, about the Riviera, was that you were alive to each moment as you lived it – and existence, mercifully, added up to no more than the sequence of each fresh pleasure.

Yvette didn't like the moustache, though. Definitely not.

He'd had one during the war, and he'd let it grow again a couple of years ago, about the time he started to lose his authority at home.

'It makes you look older.'

'More mature?'

'Hmph.'

'Experienced? Worldly?'

'Just older.'

She convinced him she was right, and he shaved it off, in no more than two or three minutes.

In return he won back some youth.

She told him, 'Ten years, I'd say.'

'That much?'

'Trust me.'

He wondered how much experience she'd had of men's moustaches, but decided it might be better – for the moment, while their luck was holding – not to ask.

The war had been the most unlikely part of all, the long nights, the card games under the low-hung lampshade, not knowing if you'd live to see the end of the next day, there but for the grace of God, so mightn't this be the last throw of the dice he'd get.

'Never mind,' Yvette told him if he woke up out of his night sleep.

If he started trying to explain, she put her fingers on his lips. 'Ssshh!'

She was right. Least said, soonest forgotten.

And yes, she was right, too, about that other matter.

He certainly did look younger whenever he saw himself in a mirror.

He stood straighter and taller. His eyes had a shine in them he wasn't used to. The clean-shaven upper lip.

He no longer needed to look like an ex-pilot. His war was at last over.

Which gave Cumming the confidence, ironically, to ask Yvette the question he had put off asking her.

'We don't talk about the past,' he said to her one day, at their café table.

She failed to reply.

'Neither of us does,' he said.

'D'you want to?'

'No. But isn't it strange?'

'I don't think so,' she said. 'Not at all.'

And for emphasis she shook her head.

He stirred his coffee slowly, with his eyes lowered.

'You don't need to know anything more,' she told him.

He laid the spoon in his saucer.

'And I don't either,' she added.

The sun felt as if it had been lying in this spot for hundreds of years. All those long ages were swept up into one continual, everlasting moment. Which might be either your consolation or your despair, he couldn't decide which.

He tried smiling back at her.

For this everlasting moment in the sunny square, he felt as if he was a perfect blank. The famous secret wrapped up inside an enigma.

Yvette smiled back at him, giving as little away of herself as he did. She was telling him with her smile not to worry. They were each what the other one saw, which was only the common currency of human transactions.

This was no more than their truth.

He took a sip from his coffee cup. He had stirred up some of the dregs from the bottom and the flavour was more bitter than he was expecting. He kept a straight face, however, recalling that coffee not many weeks back had been a weak, insipid, beige travesty of proper coffee.

Reality always tastes of its own strength.

In shops she looked out clothes for him to try on, and told him which ones she thought he should buy.

A blazer and white cotton yachting trousers. A Prince of Wales-checked grey suit. Suede shoes. A sailor's striped jerkin. A washed-pink silk shirt. Pale blue slacks. Rope-soled espadrilles.

Cumming had difficulty recognising the man in the mirror. The shop assistant's flattery also sounded strange, but he enjoyed its gentle warmth, as if he were being coddled in a bain-marie, the sort brought to their table in restaurants, in which the sauces and soufflés were kept at serving heat.

He was now wearing clothes one size larger than before.

For all she knows, Cumming thought, I could be a convict on the run. I could have any kind of evil intent. I could be a murderer, and it doesn't appear to bother her.

That was a relief. Yvette was giving him her trust. The last thing he had any right to do was question her.

With other people it was a different matter, and he and Yvette enjoyed making up stories to tell people about themselves. It was a rule that neither of them caught the other's eye, or that would have given the game away completely.

He was a crown equerry, or a tycoon, or a dance instructor, or a defrocked priest, or he was a police officer on holiday. 'The man who . . . ': anything you like.

She was his dancing partner, or his muse, or a m(asse)use, or a journalist, or a politician's mistress, or a runaway duchess.

They were heirs to their uncle's scar-iron fortune, or they were poodle-breeders, or . . .

The possibilities were endless.

'Like Scheherazade,' Yvette said.

Would it last as long as a thousand and one nights? Cumming wondered.

But no, he had to remind himself, the point is you *don't* plan. It's day to day, however many of them there turn out to be.

He wasn't really tempted to go back to the casino: just a little, but now an instinct for caution won.

They spoke about opening a little shop for Yvette somewhere else, out of temptation's way, in a town like Vichy.

'Sometime', they agreed, leaving the matter vague.

THREE

One month after another peels from a wall calendar, and the pages go flying, like a flurry of autumn leaves.

Christmas comes and goes. Spring arrives. It blossoms into summer.

Time passes, and to that ineluctable fact everything surrenders.

On one of the less fashionable streets of Monte Carlo a window display in a jeweller's window caught Cumming's eye as he passed.

There was a watch exactly like the one that had been stolen from him.

He went into the shop and enquired about the price. It was, of course, very affordable to him now. He was in a position to buy a grander watch, but he realised that the need was also psychological: to cancel out the shame of having allowed the original to be stolen from him.

He asked the shopowner, could his initials be engraved on the back? That would be no problem, monsieur. He requested a piece of paper, and sketched the style of script, and how the letters intertwined.

He walked out of the shop feeling he had done something which he had intentionally left off doing; he had re-established contact with the past, perhaps even made the first tentative attempt to rescue it.

He had started to miss the changes of weather he was used to in the course of a Scottish day.

Here, too, they had greyness, but it would last for that day only; the next would be clear, sunny, perhaps even hot.

In Carnbeg, when you left the house to go out you debated, a coat or an umbrella, or both, or shall I damn all and do without? (That was as risky as life got, back there.)

Margaret was never very far from his thoughts now, and he couldn't understand why she hadn't been in them more often before, unless he had been dreaming all this long while.

What must she have been suffering ever since they found the body?

Cumming realised he had been unfair to her, not seeing what it was that she'd had to put up with: losing the child and not being able to get pregnant again, and the slur it seemed to put on a wife living in a small town. He hadn't wanted her to work, having the same pride as his father, but he didn't earn enough to open the doors in Carnbeg that would have offered her distractions.

When he'd landed his windfall at the casino, it hadn't seemed like authentic money at all, not proper pounds, shillings and pence. While he was planning what to do with his jackpot, he should have been dressing Margaret, driving her somewhere in their new car, to a smart hotel. He should have been setting them both up in a new house, letting her choose the furniture. In different surroundings she would be a new woman, and her disposition, too, would be changed, to bright and optimistic. They would be easier with one another, and sex – being woken in the middle of the night by Margaret's fingers sleepily tugging the cord of his pyjama trousers – wouldn't be the chore for him it had become, and she would smile when he nuzzled her awake her in the morning.

Perhaps it could be done on willpower alone, without the need of money: because they wanted to make their marriage work, still, and because they wanted their lives to be fulfilled.

He watched the international pleasure-seekers, and felt now not fascinated but irritated, repelled. Inside himself he felt dark moral stirrings at the sight of them with their meticulous suntans and frivolous laughter. Everywhere except here men and women toiled: perhaps for the very purpose that this place could exist, with its idle rich and the peripheral impostors. He was conscious of his disapproval seeping out of him: just as, he thought, the stone walls of churches ooze musty coldness. And then he found that he was remembering the lowering red sandstone kirks of Carnbeg, with their off-key peal of bells.

'Jacques?'

He would hear Yvette's voice pulling him back from that other place in his mind. Only it wasn't *him*, of course, that she was trying to recover, but the man she thought she'd hitched herself to. He didn't blame her any more now than before: she was living on her wits, just like him, and God helps those who help themselves. But he thought she was a fool for having picked so badly. He saw now how desperate she must have been, and how amateurish, when he had supposed she was an old hand at this game.

Hadn't they actually deserved one another?

He scrutinised her whenever they went out.

Who she looked at.

Who looked at her.

How she was sitting, or standing.

Did her eyes follow the angle of her head when she turned it?

Had she really just been where she was telling him she'd been?

Why had she chosen this café/bistro/bar?

What had kept her in the Dames?

All those question marks.

The heatwave continued.

His eyes had begun to hurt from the relentless glare. The sun was there in the morning, already hot, and it kept them hostage until it dropped down the sky, until it reached the level of the sea, out over Africa. Heat slammed down for thirteen or fourteen hours a day, and the residue of it in the air kept him awake until the early hours. And out there, he knew, a new day was preparing itself, only awaiting the sun's arrival, a wheel of fire about to climb the sky.

The soreness in his eyes gave him headaches: not stabbing pains, rather a dull throbbing perpetual discomfort – anguish, even – which took away all the reason and the energy for doing things.

The money from his win had bought him new clothes, but – so he thought now – it had also tranquillised him and numbed feeling. Which was no win at all.

He was shedding weight. His new clothes hung loose. His face, whenever he surprised it in a mirror, had a lean wolfish cast.

He felt on the outside of everything. He was the eternally watchful and excluded wolf treading a wide circle round the magical, pitiable normality of things.

There was enough money still remaining to give to Yvette.

It didn't really belong to him, anyway.

His win had been fairytale stuff. He might have read it in a magazine story.

And now Yvette could have a happy ending, for a while.

For himself, he felt that he'd left too much unresolved in the past; there were too many loose ends.

He was the man who had found himself again.

Yvette would understand, he hoped. There wasn't enough cash for her to set up in her own shop, not just yet, but she could buy the materials she needed and hire a couple of seamstresses, and by her industry or whatever it took – by hook or by crook – she would get her wish one day. A small shop on an avenue, shaded by plane trees, somewhere more temperate, in a spa town. Customers with sensible tastes, who would walk off into the quiet dusty afternoon, satisfied with their purchases. While Yvette watched them from the window of her boutique, before turning her attention to the other pedestrians, those oh-so-casual browsers who might or might not be such accidental passers-by . . .

FOUR

The carriage emptied at the first stop after Perth.

Cumming watched himself in the carriage window as they sped through a forest.

Anyone would have had to look twice to recognise him as the same man who'd left Carnbeg. Tanned, in blazer and flannels, hair neatly trimmed, no moustache. A gold filling where he'd cracked his tooth on an olive stone.

He concentrated on the unfolding scenery. First, the green forest thinning. Followed by the crags rising almost sheer from the cladding of fir and pine. Then the contours of the land flattening, swathes of grazing-land reaching far on either side of the wide, shallow river, the sister of the silvery Tay. As the line crossed it, the water sparkled beneath, clear and weedless, running no-nonsense over stones in its path. It made its stately progress south while the train proceeded north, belching smoke and steam and with its whistle shrieking.

He knew what he was looking for next: an early glimpse of rooftops five or six miles away – red among the usual grey, and the fanciful spiked turrets of the big hotels, the spire of St Thomas's, the blue and white saltire flags flapping on their poles.

Here he was, at journey's end.

He stood on the platform watching the train leave, until it had turned the corner beneath the road bridge and was gone.

He smelled the sobering freshness of the air, as if chilled by glaciers, spirited off the sides of mountains and blown across the moors, bearing the unmistakable tang of pine and bracken.

He kept his eyes on the way ahead, following the dog-leg turns of the back lanes, so that he wouldn't have to meet any watching eyes.

He heard an English voice, a man putting a 'Vacancies' sign up by his front gate. He didn't remember either the man or that the house let rooms.

He walked back.

'Would there be any chance . . . ?'

'Step inside, will you?' the Englishman said, smiling, plainly unaware that this stranger had any local history at all.

What would he say to Margaret, what would his first words be?

She would be so shocked to see him. What he said wouldn't register for a while.

He would need to be patient and kind. He would calm her, soothe her.

'I'm so sorry, Margaret.'

He would tell her, there had been a terrible trail of misunderstandings, and perhaps one day he would be able to explain to her. Meantime, might she find it in herself to forgive him?

The time away from her, let him confess to her, it had been like a long dream; and only now was he waking up and coming to his senses.

He found his gravestone.

There was his name.

Other graves had cut flowers on them, but not his. His only had daisies and clover, because the grass was uncut.

This was the reality of being dead: being neglected and forgotten.

Bird droppings crusted the top of the stone.

He walked along the lane. He had a sixth sense for where the potholes were, the leaning gatepost still at a slant, the long shadows.

He hadn't been away for so long that those details had changed. And yet . . .

He was aware of the tanned skin on his face, his neck, his hands. It signalled that he was out of the ordinary run of experience.

Weight loss or not, his skin felt tight, a closer fit than when he'd left.

He had to readjust his eyes to the sparer light of the north. It was as if daylight had been sieved through some heavy muslin, to this thin and inconsequential slop.

The south had been awash with light, as generous and profligate as the north was close and hammer-fisted. For the past sixteen months he'd enjoyed a beneficence of the stuff.

This was a kind of half-light, rather, like black-and-white after full-colour, grainy matt with all the shiny gloss taken off it.

He felt the excitement of his heart, bumping away inside his chest; blood was pounding in his head.

He had his first glimpse of the house, fifty or sixty yards away.

A child he didn't recognise was playing in a garden.

'Is Mrs Cumming at home?' he asked, nodding in the direction of the house.

'Mrs Sweeney?'

'No. Mrs Cumming.'

'Along there?' The girl pointed towards their house.

'The end cottage, that's right. Mrs Cumming.'

'Mrs Sweeney.'

'You must be confusing her.'

'My aunt told me.'

'Told you what?'

'She got married again. She's Mrs Sweeney now.'

'What?' He stared at her. 'What's that?'

The girl carried on walking backwards, away from him. 'I've got to go now. Back inside.'

He turned away. His head was spinning.

Nothing had prepared him for this.

He started making his way back along the lane, the way he had just come, but completely inattentive to his surroundings. He steered himself instinctively, by touch – picket fences, walls – or by the smell of a hedge or a plant.

Whatever.

Che sarà.

Serendipity.

The man they'd all forgotten.

Slowly, inch by inch, the circle was being closed.

He waited until nightfall before he went back.

The sound of water guided him, and here and there the lights in cottage windows.

He made out the bulk of their home. No, it wasn't, not that, not his home, not now. The scullery window was lit, and upstairs – with its curtains drawn – the bedroom window. He didn't want to wait outside, in case he was spotted.

He walked on, looking back over his shoulder at the illuminated square of window under the eaves.

He only had to go back to the guesthouse and collect his bag, then sprint the distance left to the station. A train would take him to Edinburgh, and from there he could head south, and south again, to as many souths as he liked.

He would get by. He had survived a war, so he could make do for himself in a peace.

But for that he would have to put everything out of his mind, scrub it clean. And the effort, it seemed to him, was just too much for one man.

He was back in front of the house. Midnight had been and gone, rung from St Tommy's church tower.

They were asleep, both of them: Margaret and the man in his place, sleeping in *his* bed in *his* house.

He looked in through the windows. The kitchen window was the one he'd never got round to mending, which had a broken catch. He tried the frame, applied some upward pressure, and the bottom sash started to rise. Her new husband hadn't mended it, either.

It took some manoeuvring, getting himself up on to the sill and clearing the draining-board with its dishes (he always used to wash up and dry last thing at night), then he had to effect a 180-degrees backward turn and drop his legs over, find the floor.

He tried to remember which was the route to cross the floor silently, so that the boards didn't squeak.

From the hall he could see upstairs. The bedroom door was closed.

The living-room, examined by moonlight, was the same but

not the same. They had moved the furniture around, and the pictures were on different walls. A cigarette box he didn't recognise was on the mantelpiece. He opened it. The cigarettes were Turkish or Egyptian. He picked them out and threw them into the coal bucket. He was thinking about removing the box but put it back when he heard sounds from upstairs.

A squeal – Margaret's – and then a man's grunt, and then the rasping of the bed springs. More grunts. A yelp of encouragement.

How could she do this to him?

She was plunging a knife into a ghost, and imagined he had no feelings left. She couldn't be more wrong. All he was was this intense focus – fusion – of his past experiences, the distillation of all his pains.

The memory man, but in no one's recollection except his own.

Upstairs she grabbed at her pleasure. Snuffles, snorts, sniggers, and the mattress bellowed along in cahoots.

He didn't close the front door behind him, he left it wide open, so that the night air could get into the house, filling all its rooms and cleansing the place, purging it of these desecrations.

The gate rattled on its rickety post, as it always used to do, as it had done the day he left to catch the train for Edinburgh that he missed. Her new husband was content to let everything be, and for the moment she allowed him, but her patience was bound to pass. That was his only consolation walking away along the lane, that the day would come when Margaret accused this cuckoo in the nest of laziness and the long honeymoon was at an end.

Somewhere a dog barked. The dog was a new addition to the geography. A guard dog rattling its chain under the moon and growling at invisible presences.

Unleash all the hounds of hell!

He followed the swirling progress of the river, on the other side of the cottage gardens. He started to catch sight of it beyond the trees, gleaming black. Oily, sloe-black, liquorice-black.

The water was high, from early rain.

It pulsed through the night, the true life-force of the town which had grown up around it: Carnbeg's raison d'être. Sweet-flowing, seductive, inescapable.

Someone thought it was a sack swollen with water, which had floated downstream and got caught in the weir.

On closer inspection, from the branch of a tree, the sack took on a human form. A dead man, another corpse – the second in two years – with his head and hands mangled in the metal palings by the force of the current.

He couldn't have been looking where he was going.

The last gaslight wasn't working that night. It would have been hard to tell. Even for someone who had often walked that way, where the path led. The meadowsweet and thistles obscured the fact that the ground suddenly sloped and dropped away, and in the darkness all it would have taken was a couple of wrong steps.

Suddenly you were falling, and nothing to do but grab at stinging nettles and briars, with the soft earth crumbling beneath you, opening up under your feet . . . No cries would have been audible at that point, where the river, with a final surge at the bank, rushed towards the weir.

The police fished the body out of the water.

They found a watch on the victim's wrist. On the back it was engraved with initials which were familiar.

The assumption was that the drowned man was a thief, until the recently remarried widow admitted that she had sold her first husband's watch to a jeweller.

The death was a mystery.

The man's skin was tanned. An itinerant field worker? Possibly he had some gypsy component?

The fine Monte Carlo clothes couldn't hold the water, they split and shredded, and looked just like a poor man's. Only one tiny scrap of paper was found wedged into a corner of a pocket: it said ' . . . *des Princes*'. French. (Could the man have been an onion johnny? A matelot? It was all just guesswork.)

Some lives just turned out unlucky, a police officer confided to a reporter over a dram in the lounge bar of the Stag. That was the luck of the draw, how the dice rolled.

In Carnbeg and round about, for the little distance this local legend travelled, he was known as the man who died twice.

An Extra Place

Carnbeg is surrounded by grand houses. One of the grandest is Easterrig (pronounced 'Eas'rk'), out on the moors.

The house had belonged to the Dalrymples for most of its history. The last Carnbeg Dalrymple left living in it after the Second World War was Andrina, a spinster.

Nephews and nieces visited, and reported back to their parents on what it was they wanted to know, the property's state of repair or disrepair. Andrina shared ownership of the house. The rest of the far-flung family had busy existences, in Toronto and Phoenix and Johannesburg, and they left her to live the grand life of her forebears: perhaps as guilty recognition of the fact that she had cared for her parents while her three brothers pursued their careers.

It was a family custom that an extra place was laid at the long table in the dining-room. It dated back to the time of Andrina's grandparents, and no one had thought to alter it. If someone should roll up uninvited at a mealtime, a seat would be waiting.

Sometimes it happened that a member of the family or a friend who was in the locale *did* appear just before a meal was to be served; or the kirk minister might chance to call by, or the lawyer from Perth, or even Dr McKean. Perhaps knowledge of the extra place meant that it could be taken advantage of, but there was always food to go round, and as much drink as the Dalrymples – who had a strain of abstinence in their genes – judged suitable.

Outsiders might have found it hard to believe, but Andrina Dalrymple had no recollection of ever having eaten a meal in the house when there wasn't a complement of family or friends or favoured domestic staff at the table. Brothers and their wives,

[287]

their children, a cousin or two, whoever might be staying as a houseguest, or Nanny Michie or the factor, Mr Duff.

Plus one extra place laid, which on most occasions went unclaimed. It had been a token of her grandparents' Christian charity, a small act of generosity which her parents had been ready to take over, even though the atmosphere of the times after the Great War was less feudal and there were fewer funds with which to be generous.

It happened that in February 1971, company at Easterrig was unusually reduced. A couple of great-nephews were visiting from Canada, but there was no other family to hand. A number of Miss Dalrymple's friends were due to visit; the first appeared on the day when the great-nephews had to return south, setting off for Carnbeg station in the old Armstrong Siddeley, which groaned under the weight of whisky flagons and bales of tartan. (They had decided to set up shop when they got back to Alberta.)

In winter especially the house needed voices, and the movement of bodies, and the warmth they gave off. The friends stayed, then departed. The factor was absent: he'd taken a cold, and his wife followed suit. Miss Dalrymple had old Nanny Michie fetched from the other side of Kinreevie, and asked her to put up for a few days.

It felt strange, only the two of them for dinner: one on either side of the table, with a third place laid by Mrs Sproat, who came in to cook, or by Bella, who worked about the house.

Then Nanny Michie, ninety just before Christmas, took a tumble. Dr McKean decided that she should be removed to the cottage hospital for treatment.

'Best thing for everyone,' he assured Miss Dalrymple. 'Then there's no need for you to worry.'

But it wasn't Nanny Michie's condition she was most bothered about. For the first time in her life that she could recall, and not excluding the last war, she was being thrown back wholly on her own resources. The thought made her very uncomfortable.

It didn't normally occur to her to dwell on the size of the house, and its situation. The estate's factor was seldom away, but she had agreed that he and his wife should take themselves off to Cumbrae, to Mrs Duff's sister's hotel in Millport, for some sea air after their confinement indoors.

A cold snap settled on them. Snow and ice. Friends didn't want to travel.

Now there was no family, and no friends, to share dinner with her. Try as she might, Miss Dalrymple couldn't bring to mind any other time like this. It used to be that ten or a dozen would be at the table: parents, children, relatives, guests, maybe the tutor of the day. (No, a dozen was wrong; it had been a superstition of her grandfather's that a dozen was unlucky, being in fact 12+1, the extra setting. So, they would go looking for a thirteenth, in order to have fourteen places laid at the table.)

Now there was only herself and . . .

Dr McKean for one evening. Dr McKean's sister for the following night, although it meant making her risk an icy road over the moors. The next evening, she had no alternative but to ask Mrs Sproat to sit down with her, even though the cook clearly didn't feel it was appropriate and ended up saying next to nothing. When Mrs Sproat went home and found her husband feverish after falling into a frozen ditch, Miss Dalrymple reluctantly conceded that it must be her first duty to nurse him. Next night the girl Bella did the honours; her eyes were red from crying in the kitchen over her clumsy culinary labours.

'Sit down with me, Bella.'

'I couldn't do that.'

'You must. Please.'

Two places were laid.

'That should be three,' Miss Dalrymple directed.

'I'm sorry, Miss Dalrymple, I forgot.'

Bella's father came in the coal van to pick her up from the front gates. On the way home Bella told him about sitting down to dinner, and Mr McGrath took umbrage: he didn't approve of the old families lording it, and certainly didn't approve of his daughter being shown up, demeaned, for her ladyship's entertainment. He said it would do him no good with his Labour Club mates, and that enough was enough, and so Bella had to write a letter to say she wouldn't be returning, she would try to get a respectable job in a shop somewhere.

The letter was written, and posted, and arrived the day after the next, when it was too late.

For the evening between, Miss Dalrymple intended inviting the lodgekeeper and his daughter for dinner. The telephone in the lodge was faulty, and with Bella inexplicably absent she set out herself in flying snow to issue her invitation. But the snow drove her back. It would have meant a trek of half a mile there and back, and Andrina Dalrymple knew that – being within a shout of seventy-eight years old – she hadn't the strength for it.

She would eat in the kitchen. Or she wouldn't eat at all.

But, she realised, it wasn't as simple as that. When had the table not been set for dinner at Easterrig? In the silence she understood that her parents and their parents expected no less of her. Form and precedent, and standards to uphold. Which had always marked the Carnbeg Dalrymples as separate and apart.

She realised her hands were shaking as she set a place for herself, and an extra place. The room was cold, just as the entire house except the kitchen was cold. She banked up the fire, and watched until the flames started to grow. She held out her hands to the heat. They were still trembling.

She went over to the window. Snow and ice. She stood listening for the sound of a car, or even voices. But there was nothing. Only silence.

The telephone didn't ring, however hard she wished it to.

She was alone in the house. But no, she wasn't. Or at any rate she wouldn't be. That was the point.

Because there were two places set for dinner.

The empty chair was an invitation.

Who was going to call on an evening like this, though?

She could clear one of the settings away.

In that case she would be undoing the ritual of decades.

Or she could remove *both* settings.

And that way she would be admitting defeat, wouldn't she?

What if someone *did* manage to make their way through the snow, and for the first time she was unable to offer them that easy assumption of hospitality which made Easterrig synonymous with conviviality? It was always open house here, Liberty Hall: in a way which might have been ordained by the Bible itself, the Good Book being both a comfort and terror to her Dalrymple grandparents. Never mind that there was *no* guest: in refusing a welcome, she felt she would be going not only against instinct but against the tenets of her family's first faith.

Therefore she left the table set just as it was.

She went to the kitchen and looked about her. She wasn't hungry. The stove was warm, and she stationed herself beside it for a little while. She opened the square of door in the front and stooped to peer in at the bed of cinders.

It was as if she was waiting for something momentous to happen. The ring of the telephone. A knock on the oak front door.

Instead the house was noiseless.

The silence was as deep and eerie as an old well.

Miss Dalrymple couldn't even hear birds, or deer or foxes, or the fieldmice which had secret ways into the house.

It was a monumental stillness like nothing else she could remember, vast and directionless and leading her mind out into night and black outer space. Silence as apocalypse.

She couldn't go back into the dining-room. She didn't want to see the two place-settings, and then be obliged to sit down, facing the empty chair opposite.

If she wasn't feeling like eating, why do so? But she realised that being hungry or not wasn't really the moot matter.

She walked out of the kitchen and made her way back to the

big panelled hall. She started dragging herself upstairs. She had left several lights on about the house, to help keep up her spirits. Now she wasn't sure where she was going.

It was too early for bed, although she suddenly felt unutterably tired. Her limbs were like iron weights.

The doors stood a little ajar, as Bella knew to do. Miss Dalrymple went from one to the next to the next, remembering which bedroom had been whose. The door of the main guest room was closed; she automatically reached out to the door handle, and then thought better of it. Bella must have forgotten, or perhaps she had closed it herself yesterday, when she'd looked in and wondered who she might ask to come and occupy it for a few days.

And then she thought she did catch a sound. From downstairs. She listened, straining to hear. A sound just like the clapper ringing on a bell, the small silver hand-bell that always sat on the dining-table.

She stood rooted to the spot.

Had she heard the sound or not? The bell was a summons for the meal to be served. She must have imagined it. The house was empty, except for herself. Empty, and as quiet as the graves that held her parents and grandparents and all the sundry other clansmen who made up the Carnbeg Dalrymples.

All she could hear was her heart beating wildly. It didn't seem to belong to her any more. She felt she was being called wherever its jolts and lurchings meant to take her.

She turned to look back towards the gallery.

Blood was throbbing inside her head. Her temples felt ready to burst.

The upstairs walls came closer and then receded. The bell rang again. The figures in the paintings moved in and out of focus, and she couldn't remember who any of them were.

Then suddenly the floor gave way beneath her. In an instant she was being pulled down, into space, into darkness, and – somewhere – a door slammed shut once and for ever.

A nurse heard fragments of a story, whispered to her and told out of sequence. To the nurse and her colleagues at the hospital, they were the tiny elements of a mosaic which, patiently assembled, might come to make a picture.

It seemed a tall tale. But the patient was in a bad way, and too far gone now to distinguish between true and false, between fact and imagination.

Soon enough the story, like all stories, reached its final full stop. Poor maundering thing she ended up: God grant her soul rest in peace.